BEAUTIES

ALSO BY MARY TROY

Joe Baker is Dead
The Alibi Café
Cookie Lily

BEAUTIES

a novel

MARY TROY

BkMk Press
University of Missouri-Kansas City

Financial assistance for this project is provided
by the Missouri Arts Council, a state agency.

Cover art: Stephen C. Proski
Book interior design: Susan L. Schurman
Managing Editor: Ben Furnish
Editorial Assistant: Elizabeth Gromling
Advisory Editor: R.M. Kinder
Editorial Consultant: Karen I. Johnson
Thanks to Sarah Eyer, Karla Deel, Heather Inness,
Deirdre Mikolajcik, Noelle P. Jones

Printing by Walsworth Publishing Company, Marceline, Missouri

Library of Congress Cataloging-in-Publication Data
Troy, Mary
Beauties / Mary Troy.
p. cm.
Summary: "This novel is told from alternating viewpoints of two
cousins—a former model and a woman with a disability—who run a café in
south St. Louis, Mo., in the 1990s and face challenges with love, adoption,
the law, and urban life"—Provided by publisher.
ISBN 978-1-886157-74-3 (pbk. : alk. paper)
1. Cousins—Fiction. 2. Women with disabilities—Fiction. 3. City and
town life—Missouri—Fiction. 4. Domestic fiction. I. Title.
PS3570.R69B43 2010
813'.54--dc22

2010028782

This book is set in Thornburi, Arial Narrow, and Garamond Pro Typefaces.

For Pierre Davis—artist, editor, critic, and more

and for Mark, Anne and John Troy

BEAUTIES

SHELLY

Of course the lawsuit frightened me. Just because I'm beautiful, I'm not so bubbleheaded I wouldn't recognize a threat. But fear and hope are opposites, and of the two, hope is the essential one. It was Bev's lawsuit anyway, though that was really the worst part of it because she, poor thing, did not need more trouble. Not that I did. Just thirty-six and two divorces under my belt already, neither one my idea. And here I was, back in the neighborhood of my childhood, taking refuge, regrouping and recouping, in a fledgling café. I joked with myself that I should have a punch card with two holes already in it from my two divorces, and after just one more the next would be free. The St. Louis County Courts and Division of Family Law should look into such a promotion. In fact and in spite of my track record, I believed strongly in marriage as the tie that connects one being to another and so makes all of our lives not as crushing as they otherwise could be. Well, it was the love that did that, of course, but marriage, the official part of love that said to the world "we are better as a pair," was our gift to ourselves. Sure there were bad marriages, but there were bad dinners, too, and people didn't stop eating. I once bought a skirt that didn't fit, yet I still bought skirts. I would marry again

Why in the world had Bev put her café here? That was what Grandma would call the $64,000 question. More self-punishment, I thought, a further attempt at proving how out of step she was with the world. But I doubted I'd ever know for sure. We seldom questioned her thoroughly, usually acted content with whatever superficial answer she gave that explained nothing. She was handicapped, and that alone kept us from badgering her, but it also kept us smiling, our lips stiff and our chins up. *Us* meant my family, and that we were not Bev was often our solace.

And the question of what I wanted, where I was going, was unanswered, too, at least temporarily. I was an adventurer looking for a challenge, a pilgrim on a journey to someplace so sacred I couldn't even name it to myself. I tried to foster that sense of impending newness, knowing that if I were Bev I would call it emptiness instead. And no matter what abstraction it went by, no matter how I chose to think of it, it was just possibly not caused by my current lack of a man. Or not only my lack of a man. Lately I'd been spelling out success in my head, over and over. Success doing what? Maybe it was the café, I told myself on my first day there; maybe saving Bev and her café would fill me, become part of my path, a stop on my journey. Maybe.

We were informed about the lawsuit by a deputy to the sheriff of St. Louis County on my first day of work, and I felt a chill immediately because lawsuits always come from a deep-down meanness. Someone may as well have been shooting at Bev, at the very least, calling her names. The suit against her was for grievous harm, and in spite of my initial fears I told her not to worry about it, said it was just some minor irritation cooked up by stupid people, but we would survive it. "We'll do it with grace and humor, too," I said, and when Bev sneered at that, I smiled at her, choosing to believe it was possible.

The Alibi Café was in a brick building. All was brick down there on the south edge of the city, the color of singed tomatoes. The downstairs front had a black tile façade with a few missing tiles and quite a few more cracked. The whole building was only twenty-five feet across and sixty-seven feet deep with two doors side by side on the right front and a picture window completing the downstairs. My first look at it was in late January, 1999, near the beginning of what most incorrectly called the last year of the millennium. Bev showed off the café and building to me because I would soon be moving in. The living quarters were upstairs, and from Meramec Street where we first stood, I could see three front-facing windows. Above the fancy brick work at the top of the building, every other brick jutting out to create a geometrically intriguing cornice, the roof was flat and, no doubt, black. The gutters seemed sturdy, but two of the triple-track windows I could see were cracked. There were no windows on the sides, of course, for the neighboring buildings were separated only by gangways, egresses to the back yards of four or fewer feet. It wasn't much different from the building a few miles northwest I'd grown up in, where Mom and Dad still lived separate but equal lives in seeming peace, he up and she down.

So Bev and I were going to operate a café in this neighborhood that, as I told her that afternoon, seemed to whisper *loser* with the hiss of each passing bus. That was an old joke, first made by cousin Chuck on a wet, summer day of our adolescence as we sat on my parents' stoop, one of the many days we felt trapped on our humid block, not yet old enough to drive away. Bev didn't laugh at it now, but I did, deciding the setting was merely an obstacle that would make success all the more amazing. It wasn't only the cracks in the tile façade, the pawn shop across the street, or the two boarded-up two-families less than a block away, and it wasn't only the butter-scotch-colored man wearing jeans and a black T-shirt, no shoes or jacket, who leaned face front into the dumpster across the street as he sent a steaming flow of urine down the cobblestones, but it was the whole package, all of it together that would make my, our, triumph truer. Bev pointed with her bumps toward the sign hanging out over the uneven sidewalk like two giant Frisbees back to back with a light inside and *Alibi Café* printed on each side, red on white. There was a short somewhere and the sign blinked and popped, even sizzled. Bev said she had already called the electrician. Twice.

"If you like it, so much the better," she said in response to my vigorous smiling and nodding. "But I'm not really interested in your approval."

"I can work with it," I said.

"I mean," she said, "Take it or leave it. It's my home, my business, my money. You can live here if you want."

"Thanks," I said.

"And to earn your keep, you can cook anything you know how. Doesn't matter to me what."

Alibi Café was written across the front picture window, too, and Bev pointed to it.

"Nice stenciling," I said, and she frowned, started to open the door, then stopped, still looking at the window.

"We don't have our hours on it yet because I don't know when we'll be open. Are you a morning or an evening person?"

"We can't open at night," I said. "Not down here."

"I'm partial to mornings myself," she said. "Breakfasts are easy enough, and I can probably do simple lunches. But it's not dangerous down here," she said. "It's just, just..."

"Ugly," I said.

She narrowed her eyes at me. "I was going to say *poor*."

Once we were in, she gave me a long tour, pointing out each burner, each shelf in the walk-in refrigerator, each pot and griddle, the deep fryer. She counted the napkin dispensers and ketchup bottles for me, demonstrated the computerized thermostat. I ooohed and aaahed, said fine and good idea and nice until I was dizzy. Luckily, the upstairs, our living quarters, did not require so much attention.

"Living room, bedroom, bath, kitchen, bedroom..." Bev stood in the upstairs hall at the top of the front stairs and pointed east, south, west, and north. "You get the front bedroom. I have the back one. There's a tub, no shower. Washer and dryer are in the basement with a lot of my junk. You can park on the pad off the alley out back or on the street. Street cleaning is every second Tuesday on this side of the street, every first Tuesday on the other side."

I told her I'd move in in a few days, over the upcoming weekend. "I have lots of furniture. Is there room?"

"We'll squeeze it in," she said. "We can take some of this other crap and put it in the basement. My stuff's not so good anyway, and I don't get attached to things, not like I know you do."

That was a crack I did not deserve. After all, I'd been smiling and nodding, agreeing as hard as I could. "I can store it somewhere else."

"No. Bring it on. Let storing unwanted stuff be my problem. I'm used to being used."

"No one is forcing you to take me in," I said, and she narrowed her eyes at me again, smiled with her lips tightly closed the way you do with the feeble-minded or the drunk. It made me wonder. Maybe the family had twisted Bev's arm, conspired to save me from myself. I knew my mother worried that I kept one light on in each room when I started living by myself, ever since Richard left to be with Aurora. And I did need a place I could let go dark again. My eyes had tiny purple bags under them. "Thanks," I said.

Bev was seven months younger than I, had lived exactly a block away all during our childhoods, and was what Grandma Stillwell called, with a tinge of relief in her voice each time she said it, our main family tragedy. Grandma knew God never gave you more than you could handle, claimed she'd read that in the Bible or some other inspirational book she could no longer recall the name of, and she interpreted that to mean each family had an allotment of suffering and tragedy. Bev, she believed, was a big chunk of ours.

Bev's mother, my Aunt Josie, claimed to know the exact second she conceived. Family legend has it, she got up, stood beside the bed, spread her arms out, and told Uncle Al there were now three beings in the room. He is reported to have said "More than that, if you count what lives in the web hanging over the closet door." Aunt Josie said he could be forgiven for his irreverence. He was only a man, knew nothing of a sudden quickening in a womb. One night later, Aunt Josie dreamed of fish, big ones gobbling up tiny ones, and called it a bad omen. Something was wrong with her child. Then she threw up morning, noon, and night for three solid weeks, taking that as further proof. Finally Doc Redmond, her and Mom's gynecologist, tired of reminding her morning sickness was common and would not last forever, gave in and told her to take a new product, an over-the-counter morning sickness medicine called Mother's Help. Doc Redmond was not much of a drug pusher, usually seemed to believe his women were being wimpy, acting too delicate when they complained. But as he explained to Aunt Josie and Uncle Al and even to Mom, Aunt Josie's anxiety would do no one any good, and that included him. He did have other patients, after all.

Mother's Help got rid of the morning sickness, Aunt Josie's dreams went away, and Grandma said everyone relaxed until Bev was born. She had only one finger, the index finger on her right hand, and no thumbs. Eventually, she did grow bumps about one-tenth as long as her regular fingers and thumbs would have been, but as a newborn, her hands were smooth, soft, and almost digit-less. The bigger problem was her legs. She had only one full one and one that ended about mid-thigh. On her only foot, she did have all her toes, and everything else seemed to be where it should have been, at least at first. By the time she was one, it was clear she would also be virtually chinless, but so was Grandma's brother, Uncle Herbert, and we could not truthfully count that as a deformity. She also had light hair, nearly albino white, that hung limp like fringe no matter what Aunt Josie or later Bev herself did to it, and so thin, that even when she was a child, it barely covered her pink scalp. And maybe all her unattractive parts convinced her it was no use keeping up her figure, or maybe her lurching kind of walk was so tiring she chose not to go in for exercise, but for whatever reason, she let herself go, and by her thirties was not merely fat, but lumpy, like a down jacket that has been mangled in the dryer. She was bitchy, too, but that was what we never mentioned, not even to ourselves, what we forgave her for without acknowledgement. After all, she was deformed.

By the time Bev started grade school, the pharmaceutical company that made Mother's Help removed it from the market, but it took until she graduated from high school for connections to be made, for the lawsuits to start. Doc Redmond wrote to Aunt Josie from his retirement condo in Florida and said Bev deserved some compensation, and though Aunt Josie and Uncle Al were both the kind who would drink cold coffee in a restaurant rather than complain, Doc Redmond convinced them to hire a lawyer, make a claim. Sixteen years later, the lawyer took his $150,000 out and gave Bev a check for $700,000, and a year later she squandered fifty-two grand of it on the old building in South City and opened the Alibi Café.

Just a month before my first glimpse of it, she'd explained her choice of location to me. We were sitting at Aunt Josie's breakfast-room table, watching Cousin Chickie and her son skateboard around the obstacle course they'd constructed by arranging trash cans, portable grills, and concrete blocks on the driveway. Aunt Josie and Uncle Al had bought their ranch house in this far west suburb a few years earlier. Aunt Peg, Chickie and Chuck's mother, lived in a similar suburb across the river in Illinois. Bev and I and Chuck had all scattered to homes and apartments in the burbs, too, away from the old neighborhood. It was only my parents who still lived in the circumscribed sixty-one square miles called the City of St. Louis. But Bev was about to move back, and I was confused.

"I fit in there as well as anywhere." She was sipping one of her mother's specialties, a piña colada.

"It's full of derelicts. It's a mess. Not safe."

"Every place seems crappy to me," she said. "So the people down there don't wear expensive clothes or drive new cars. So what if they're on the bottom rung of the great symbolic ladder we're all supposed to be climbing."

"It's not a neighborhood anymore. Too many weirdos, thieves, transients."

"Could you see me opening a café in the Galleria? Some chic place in yuppieville? I don't understand garnishes."

"I'd help."

"I don't care what rich people eat." Just then Chickie and her son, Hilton, came in, both breathing heavily. Dad always thought it a good joke, Chickie naming her son after the hotel he was probably conceived in. In fact, she had named him after a fellow actor, not the father but, we surmised, the one she wished were the father. Chickie's last acting job was in a commercial to promote a detergent. In it she played a frazzled housewife whose husband tried to do the laundry with new and improved Tide. It ran during the daytime talk shows about incest and drunk drivers and hate crimes, and since I had lately been home all day in a well-lighted place with nothing to do, I saw it often. She hoped it would get her a job in a sitcom, had her fingers crossed she said.

"How's it going for you two St. Louisians?" she asked, then laughed. Chickie and Hilton lived most of the time in LA, and she seemed to enjoy rubbing it in, her being the one to get the farthest away. She wanted us to feel provincial, stuck. And I suppose we were, but neither of us had to be. With her money, Bev could have gone lots of places, could have bought a small house on a pretty lake surrounded by hills, could have put a down payment on a café on a beach somewhere. And I could have earned my living anywhere, too, in any of the cities or near the beaches I'd been flown to for shoots. I didn't know what stuck me to St. Louis. I was prettier than any of my pretty family, even Chickie. I had often been told I was another Natalie Wood, a reincarnation, and I could see the resemblance. I had more brains than most people I knew, and that was not boasting, just the truth. I had piled up fifteen hours of college credit by the time I graduated from Bishop DuBourg High School, and if I had not signed on with the Sue Spritz Modeling Agency and Academy, I would have gone to college. All my life I had known I was that rare mixture of brains and beauty, and I used to wait and see what wonderful thing I would do with my life.

I had turned my ex-husband Richard's family's siding and window replacement business from a low-end, modest-return company to a locally known moneymaker. We went from eight employees to thirty-two in the first three years. I suggested the name change from Belcher Corporation to This Side of Paradise, and I wrote the funny radio commercials about cracked windows, came up with the ideas for the specials, like "Tell them Shelly sent you and get an extra 10% off," or "Free installation with four windows." Even after he left, Richard and his whole family admitted I'd saved the business.

I could do the same anywhere. For any business. I knew I still had it.

But Richard's choosing Aurora, with her thick ankles and thin lips, over me sapped some of my strength. *Temporarily* Grandma and I said to each other, because when the first punch hit me in the gut and sent me sprawling, I worried briefly that it could be a permanent knockout, that what Grandma called my coping mechanisms were failing.

Richard was my second husband, but the first one hardly counted. He was an actuary for an insurance company by day and a bass guitarist in a rock band, the Blue Ducks, at night. We'd shared a love of single-malt scotch and reruns of *The Beverly Hillbillies*. We eloped two months after we met, and our marriage was a mere ten months old when he decided he didn't want to be married. "I have a low threshold for boredom," was how he put it. "I've been bored for months already." I cried a bit, but, as usual, I told myself to get over it, to stop the weep-weep-weep stuff that weakened my eye muscles and find someone better. The truth was I wasn't all that attached to husband number one. Less than a year later, I had a new blue-eyed and broad-shouldered husband who told me early on I could never bore him. And in the beginning, I felt Richard had been my destiny all along, my electrons fated to be pulled into his orbit. Nothing less than the laws of physics held us together.

A few months after the wedding he told me he didn't want children because they would take our attention from each other and he wanted all of mine. Though I'd always believed I was destined to have beautiful children, it was as if a stone had been removed from my chest when I understood I would not have to. I remember taking a deep breath. I know women are not supposed to admit that; the motherhood urge, need, virus, whatever it is, is supposed to go deep, as if all by itself it's a thick strand of protein on one of the X chromosomes. The thing was, I did fine guiding myself and finding ways to come out on top, but I considered that a full time job. Other people, even those I loved, were mysteries to me. I doubted I'd be able to guide a child. There were too many ways to fail with a child.

My mother kept her own un-maternal feelings to herself, confiding, of course, only in me.

"If you weren't here, I'd be dancing on a table in the moonlight in Portugal. I'd be making love under the stars on the top deck of an ocean liner. Maybe I'd be in a home for beautiful women who go insane for love," she said. I remember we were housecleaning for her parents' thirty-fifth wedding anniversary party. Mom was swatting the drapes with a feather duster, making me sneeze. "I stay because of you." She had told me this before.

"Thanks," I said.

"If it weren't for you, I sure wouldn't be here in the same neighborhood I was raised in with a man so lacking in imagination he won't even sing in the shower."

I did think that odd. I had been humming as I scoured the sink.

"But he's not what traps me." She shook the feather duster out the front window. "Tell me who it is."

"Me," I said. "You stay for me."

"Right. Good." She ended her speech with a caution, also one I'd heard before. "I can't say any of this out loud, though. It's unwomanly to wish for childlessness. You'll see. And if you tell anyone I said it, I'll say you are a liar." I laughed then at what I knew had not been a joke.

Anyway, Richard and I eventually got dogs, two shelties we named The Owl and The Pussycat. Though I tried to think of them as Richard did, more than furry eating machines, I was self-conscious, awkward, and foolish cuddling or talking baby-talk to them. Not Richard. "Where are my doggy dogs?" he would yell as soon as he entered the house, even if he had merely been an hour away at the grocery. And they would bound around him, sliding down the stairs, squealing and barking in a frenzy as they bounced almost to his shoulders. He would smile with delight at what his words wrought. I laughed along with him, but the truth I never admitted even to Richard was that, though I had named the animals, I couldn't tell The Owl from The Pussycat. They were identical shelties, sisters from the same litter, same coloring and pattern, same weight and height, same happy but slightly anxious looks in their eyes. Needless to say, they liked Richard better than they did me, but I had the business to run anyway, going in even on Saturdays to check the books and orders while Richard took The Owl and The Pussycat to a park.

Richard's leaving was why I kept my lights on. I was not really afraid that one day the earth would fail to complete its spin, never again turn back toward the sun and dark would win. Sure, that was what I told my mother. But the truth, at least a part of the truth, was I simply feared the boogeyman. The house settling in creaks and snaps, the wind rattling at the doors in the dark kept me jittery, and lights were a simple way of coping.

I moved in above the Alibi Café on a rainy Saturday in early February, tried to unpack a little Sunday, and by Monday morning at seven o'clock, Bev put me to work making what I said I knew how—sausage gravy. She did the biscuits.

She'd been operating the café for almost two weeks without me, but that wasn't enough time for anyone to know we were there. We had three customers my first morning, and one was an elderly man with skin like burlap, wearing an ill-fitting blue suit, shiny in the knees and seat, too tight across his back. He sat at the counter and ordered coffee, loaded it with sugar and cream. I refilled his cup three times. He followed Bev's movements as she lurched and stomped across the room, putting out the salt and pepper shakers, setting the tables. I had forgotten how often Bev was stared at, how impossible it was for her to blend in.

"You'll get robbed. Goes without saying," he said. "I mean, Christ Almighty, look where you are. Everything gets robbed down here, eventually."

"You exaggerate," I said.

"If it was me," he said, "I'd get some of that yellow police tape, wrap it around the front and back doors after you close, make the crims think you've already given. Know what I mean?" He looked into the kitchen and talked to Bev's back.

I was leaning against the counter, wondering if we should start small or go for the big-bucks TV ad right away. "Know what I mean?" he asked again, looking at me this time.

"Well, it's an idea," I said. "It certainly is an idea."

He nodded. "It is."

About an hour after the coffee drinker left, a young couple entered and tried out two tables. First they sat at the table right in the center of the window, but he detected a draft, so they moved to the deuce in the corner. She rolled her eyes, but then gave him such a fake smile, I could tell they were breaking up, but I couldn't be sure if either of them knew it yet.

"Our sausage gravy is our special today," I said when I went over to take their order. "And we serve it over high, flaky biscuits." That part was especially true. Bev's biscuits were amazingly light and flaky, made with real butter and lots of it.

"Too much fat," she said.

"Well, you only live once," I said, "and delicious food is one of life's few pleasures." I used the teasing tone I'd heard other waitresses use, familiar but not rude.

"Food like that can kill you," he said. "Give us some wheat toast."

"And?"

"Coffee," he said.

At noon, I spooned my gravy into a bowl and covered it with plastic, hoping it would keep for another day.

"Don't worry about it," Bev said when she saw what I was doing. "You can make more tomorrow. We can give that to the cats out back."

I said I guessed she was right, but knew such waste was no way to run a business, so I decided to push it for lunch. Bev had a computer in what she called the office, the alcove under the back stairs, and I used it to make a sign with curlicue borders and arrows that said we served breakfast all day long. In the corner I wrote: Special today, sausage gravy. I taped it on the door under the open sign, and it might have worked if we'd had any customers.

Finally at about two o'clock, just as Bev was saying we may as well close up and not even seeming sad or discouraged by the miserable day we'd had, a woman about my age entered. She was wearing a gold and navy, wool suit, the kind with a cropped jacket and a tight, short skirt, and one that fit her, too, not a Goodwill purchase. She sat at a table near the door, and she set her leather briefcase on the chair beside her. She ordered a glass of Merlot to start with.

"We don't have a liquor license," I said.

"You used to," she said, tucking her straight, blonde streaked hair behind an ear. Her skin was smooth and dark brown, a matte finish.

"Not us. Maybe it was someplace else around here."

"No. It was you," she said, then frowned and asked for iced tea instead. When I brought her tea, she ordered a twelve-ounce T-bone, medium rare, covered with onions, a baked potato with extra sour cream, and a fresh spinach salad. I didn't know where she got that. True, we didn't have menus yet, but we hardly looked like a steak place. What we had for lunch was egg salad, tuna salad, or ham salad on wheat bread or onion buns. We also had deli pastrami and ham, also on wheat or onion buns. We served all our sandwiches with chips, large wedges of Aunt Josie's home-made dills, and an ice-cream scoop of too-sour coleslaw Bev had been experimenting with. We also had apple and coconut-cream pies, made fresh by Bev that morning.

When I explained our fare, the woman told me we used to have steaks. Bev was leaning over the counter, listening, and I looked to her for help. It was possible, I thought, she had once made a steak or two. But she just shrugged. "Our sausage gravy has the protein of steak with more zip, and the gravy is so creamy it would put any sour cream to shame. It's thick and rich and filling."

I wanted to grab at least one customer my first day. Though I'd fished only twice, both times with Richard on some muddy bug-infested bank of the Missouri River, I pictured myself doing it now, reeling this one in carefully.

The woman shook her head. "Things change too quickly," she said. "As soon as you find something you like, it's gone." I noticed her eyeliner was a midnight blue, and her mascara seemed a gradu-ated mixture of the blue and black, blue at the eyelid, black at the tips—a professional job.

I offered to give her a free sample of the sausage gravy, assured her that if she liked it, we would make it always. It would never be gone.

She sighed but did accept the free sausage gravy, then ate all of it, scraping her plate with her fork to pick up loose biscuit crumbs. I told her the tea was on the house, too, just this once, so she had no bill. She smiled at me as she stood to leave, said thanks, said she would probably be back. Later I saw the two dollars she had left beside her plate.

Well, it was a kind of success.

After we turned the Open sign around to read Closed, I took stock, already interested in making a profit and the café a success in spite of Bev's lack of concern. I found out she bought the pastrami and the ham from a deli down on Broadway, paying retail for it. She bought her bread at the supermarket, her chicken and tuna, too. The sausage came from an expensive meat market downtown. She told me she charged $3 for the tuna salad on wheat, for example, because figuring two slices of wheat bread, a third of a can of tuna, about a dime's worth of mayo, forty cents worth of chips, and roughly forty cents of cole slaw per plate—the pickles were Aunt Josie's contribution—that was twice what it cost her. I reminded her she had to figure the equipment, the overhead, our labor, and the waste for a start. I told her we'd taken in $5.15 all day, and the heating cost alone for the downstairs was about $4.00 a day, not to mention all that leftover sausage gravy that was a 100 percent waste. I told her we would have to buy in bulk what we could, would have to buy wholesale, and that I would look into it, starting with Dad who was a retired meat cutter with connections. I said I was surprised Bev hadn't thought of Dad already. "Maybe you can handle the rush for a day or two without me this week."

"Ha!" she said.

As we were cleaning up, a deputy for the sheriff of St. Louis County knocked hard on the door to our living quarters, but Bev heard him and let him into the café. He was a jowly white man with a head of thick, black hair and what Grandpa used to call a government worker's gut hiding his belt buckle. He introduced himself, showed us his ID, and his smile was bashful, faint and apologetic. He handed Bev a sealed envelope of thick, creamy paper with an official notice inside. When Bev read the notice, she turned as white as the insides of her biscuits. "I despise humans," she hissed.

The deputy patted her on the arm, said these things happen every day, and left.

"I'm like prey," she said, then handed me the paper. She was being sued by Dr. and Mrs. Hilker who sought compensation for their pain and suffering brought on by Bev's harm to their minor child, Madison Hilker. Bev was to have her lawyer call the Hilker's lawyer and author of the notice, Donna Wicher. I heard the deputy pull away from the curb, squealing his tires as if eager to put this mess behind him. "Guess I'll call Howard," Bev said, referring to Howard Figg, the lawyer who had won her part of the Foxborough settlement. "Goddamned rich bastards. " She kicked the side of the stove hard.

"Well," I said, afraid she'd damage the only foot she had. "It may not be as bad as it seems. Obviously these Hilkers don't have a clue, calling what you said harmful! Why worry about stupid people?"

"Don't say a word. You know nothing about this." She kicked the stove once again, but stopped when I reached out and touched her shoulder. "And stupid people should be your biggest worry," she said as she turned toward me. "They can ruin your life." She did call Howard, and later, as she helped me unpack the rest of my stuff, she said Howard had laughed at the lawsuit, called it a nuisance, had said suing was not winning. She even chuckled about it herself. Hadn't I said the same general thing? I wanted to remind her of that, but instead said, "See? It's like a joke." Then I showed her photos of The Owl and The Pussycat I had with me— over the years we had taken so many pictures of them that there had been plenty for Richard and me to divide—and she said it was easy to tell them apart. One looked inquisitive and the other was depressed. I humored her, but knew neither one had been depressed. I may not have been as close to them as Richard was, but I knew that much.

We ate tuna salad on stale onion buns for dinner, and I asked her, why the café? "You have so much money, can do anything with it, why this?"

"I have to do something."

"I didn't know you liked to cook. In high school, you never even took Home Ec."

"I want to do something that doesn't take thought. No analysis and no discussion. The café idea just popped into my head after that teaching fiasco." What she called "that teaching fiasco" was what Mom and Aunt Josie called another of our family tragedies, not as serious as Bev's missing leg and fingers, but tragic nonetheless. And now the genesis of a lawsuit. Bev was the best educated of us with a master's degree in English and a teaching certificate. She'd had a good job at Agnus Dei High School, a school in west county for girls she called too rich to know how dumb they were. When she used to talk about it to us, she claimed teaching there was like being a missionary in foreign lands. "It's not just that they wear brand names on their clothes or drive box-like vehicles. Everyone does that. These are girls who have been to Paris so often they can say the musical performances in the Luxembourg Gardens aren't what they used to be, or that Montmarte is boring. For our senior trip we'll have to hike the Himalayas to find something they're not already bored with. That or go to East St. Louis." She snickered about it, but claimed to be making headway. She taught them Wilfred Owen and Siegfried Sassoon. Making them think, she called it. "Put away childhood," she said she told them. "Don't fall for advertising."

Richard used to say Bev lectured when she talked about her job, said she meant it for all of us, too, not just her rich students. I argued with him about it, though I knew he was right. Her reported talks with her students about vanity and the specious need to look good were aimed at me. I knew it, felt the sting of her words, but so strong was the habit of not criticizing Bev, I couldn't agree with Richard.

"Your dances and parties are meaningless," she said she told them. "Grow up."

When she told us what she'd told them, Richard nodded at me. "She's never had fun at a dance or party herself," he said. "She doesn't want anyone else to. See, there's a hard nugget of selfishness there."

What she said to some of the girls, an off-hand remark during a homeroom discussion on dating, was that they didn't have to tell their parents everything they did. She said the parents were often better off not knowing anyway, and the girls had to be their own bosses at least some of the time. Two of them told their parents who told other parents who told others, and soon the principal and the Parents' Association were involved. A few of the parents, the wealthiest ones (like the Hilkers, I guessed now) wanted Bev fired, said this kind of attitude was ruining our youth, creating the lax moral environment we were all forced to live in. The principal, however, much to his credit, went up against the money and said an apology was all that was needed. But Bev said, truth be told, she was not sorry for anything she'd said. Her money'd come through by then, so she could quit and did. "I leave education in the hands of the idiotic and the hysterical," she said on her last day. Aunt Josie claimed to have cried for a solid week at Bev ruining her life so completely, and then she had to meditate twice as often the following week to regain her equilibrium.

After dinner, we watched television for a few hours, Bev complaining and grumbling at the screen all the while.

When the detective offered to help a drug addict get treatment, Bev said, "Yeah. I imagine that really happens." When in another show the kind father had a talk with his oldest daughter before her first date, Bev said, "This is where the music swells to twist our little hearts until they are wrung dry." Later the canned laughter of a sitcom annoyed her so much she muted the television and added her own dialog.   I tried to tell her she was looking at television all wrong.

"It's not supposed to be real or even interesting, " I said. "It's like Valium, some kind of drug that allows your mind to wind down so you can sleep."

"But it's not calming. It's annoying."

"Then don't watch it," I said.

"Well, it's you who doesn't get it," she said, pointing her finger and a few bumps in my direction. "If we weren't watching television, we'd be talking. You'd tell me about ordering wholesale. You'd laugh and talk again about our very few customers. You'd want me to say we'll do better so you could agree, tell me the sun will rise brighter and higher, faster, tomorrow, or one of those lies you tell yourself. After that you'd bring up what you are dying to discuss, the Hilkers, who are not worth discussing, and the lawsuit I know nothing about anyway. Maybe out of lack of anything else to say, you'd tell me something about your marriage, perhaps about your divorce that, number one, I am not interested in and, number two, I have heard all about from your mother and mine, and, number three, was not nearly as surprising as you make out it was. See, people can't talk to one another that much without repeating themselves, and what they say is usually meaningless the first time."

"I'll try not to bore you in the future," I said.

"Oh, don't be so touchy. It's a general explanation. I just used you and what's his name, your ex, as an example."

I knew she knew Richard's name. "I'm going to bed," I said, and stood. "But I still don't know why you watch TV at all."

"I keep hoping I am not the only intelligent person on the planet. I keep expecting to see something worthwhile."

I left the room as she was talking because cynicism is a disease without a cure and highly contagious. "Don't worry about the lawsuit," I called back from my room.

"I'm not," she called back. "I'm worried about you and how well you rationalize. Would it kill you to admit TV sucks, the world is mostly stupid, and stupidity is dangerous?"

I closed the door behind me and lay down on the bed in the dark. Through the closed but cracked triple-track window and storm window, I listened to the sounds of the street—horns and radios blaring, brakes whining, tires squealing, buses wheezing. Above all that were mothers yelling at children to come in or else, girls calling one another whore, men and women calling one another baby and darling. Phrases like "make me," and "keep out of it" were propelled through the air.

"Honk if you want me," a woman called. Someone giggled insanely and that was answered by a belly laugh that seemed to come from the pawn shop across the street. The darkness, though, was what I craved, an old friend I'd lost contact with. It was warm and pure and safe in ways it had never been when I lived alone.

Eventually, I felt safe enough to undress, and I was enjoying the freedom of lying naked on top of my bed across the street from the belly laugher. And as I thought of my naked self, I knew two things. I knew without looking that my body was good and fine, better than most. Its skin was mainly smooth, its stomach was firm, its upper arms were solid, and its legs were well curved. I also knew it would perish, and I wished I could surround it with bubble wrap and put it away, save it for good like a pair of expensive shoes, a Sunday dress. Then I heard, underneath all the other sounds, the heavy chords of the wedding march. It was played on an organ in the pounding method used by church organists everywhere. I heard it played through twice before it changed to another song, this one a real church song, a spiritual maybe, but one I didn't know the name of. The pounding continued. Maybe the organist for St. Paul's lived behind us, or more likely, one of those foursquare-gospel, storefront churches this neighborhood was becoming so full of was next door. Either way, I told myself, when you were sleeping naked in the dark, there was nothing wrong with organ accompaniment.

But that one didn't work. I already recognized a familiar dread creeping into my mind, and knew it was from the wedding march and how wide Richard's smile was as I glided gracefully toward him more than fifteen years ago. So I pictured the woman who had cleaned her plate thoroughly, forced myself to hear her fork scraping across the thick china and pressing down on errant crumbs. Her shoes had been navy-blue leather, possibly Brazilian, they looked that soft, with two-inch heels and gold confetti-like flecks at the toe, just like a pair of Rhythm Steps Mom paid $200 for. Yet my, our, food had made her smile. I went to sleep thinking about her, and when I awoke the next morning, I thought maybe I had been smiling back at her, smiling in my sleep. It was a good sign. Bev would call that smiling in my sleep stuff as fake as her leg and knee, but I'd no intention of telling her anything. My dreams were mine.

BEV

For my fifth Christmas, I got my first knee. "To Bev from Santa" was printed in red on the card attached to the plastic wrapping. I'd been using a stump, the therapists' word for the solid piece of fiberglass and wood that attached to my own stump, just fine, but it was time for me to bend, to walk better, to be able to sit. We all hoped I'd be able to ride a bicycle, play kick the can, do a cartwheel, or at least a somersault. Four months later, I slammed a solid oak closet door on my only finger. On purpose. The only finger I had and I wanted to get rid of it.

"Are you insane?" Mom screamed at me. That picture stayed with me: Mom's face contorted in horror, the flush of blood in her cheeks and chin, the white ring around her mouth, her blue irises opening like an accordion. I cried that day, a few days shy of my sixth birthday, at the pain in my finger, and I watched her watch my finger swell and turn scarlet.

"You have enough against you," she said. "Don't make it worse by going crazy. I won't be able to stand it."

Her anger at me was rare. I had to work hard to get her to raise her voice at me, to so much as look cross. But that wasn't why I hurt my finger. I wanted to cut it off, snap it onto the closet floor. That finger, the index finger on my right hand, was whole and pudgy and marred the otherwise symmetry of my hands. It made them look stranger than they were. The leg could be covered, so it always was. I wore long pants summer and winter. And though I never succeeded at it, when I was nearly six I believed I would learn a graceful walk, would use my knee as if it were real. But the hands offended more than me. Even my cousins didn't want to touch them, would hesitate to hold hands with me in the neighborhood games of Red Rover where I was always the weak link.

Later, I learned to use what became three-eighth-inch bumps to perform wonders like typing, picking a single sheet of paper off a pile, turning the page in a book, tying my shoes. I could impress my family, my classmates, teachers, bosses, students, but my one finger never did fit in, continued to be an offense. And no matter how old I got and how so-called enlightened we all became, no one wanted to hold my hands. Even those who loved me held me by my wrists.

I told Shelly I chose a café as the place to waste my money because I wanted to do something simple. I told Mom what I guessed would appeal to the touchy-feely, let-me-locate-my-karma kind of person she'd become during my adulthood, that I wanted to create a refuge for the less than perfect. Of course, if I truly wanted to be around rejects, blend in with other losers, I would've tried to find the other 1,116 co-plaintiffs in the suit against Foxborough Chemical, makers of Mother's Help and other wonder drugs still on the market, including three hay fever remedies and two sleep aids. I had daydreams in which all of us co-defendants limped and lurched and wheeled and crawled into a hotel ballroom, embraced as well as possible with whatever appendages we had, compared our missing parts, cried on one another's shoulders, assuming we all had shoulders, and vowed to be pals forever. In real life, I tried to avoid the deformed.

Once she started at the café, Shelly gave the impression of working hard, ditzing around as if she had a purpose and a plan. But we still had no business to speak of, not after two weeks of her endless ideas. For one thing, neither of us could cook, though to Shelly those were fighting words. Who makes the best pies in town, she'd ask, the only answer she'd accept being me. I never gave her the answer she wanted. I made her supply it herself to see how long it would take her to grow tired of asking and stop. She claimed her barbecue sauce would win awards, and in fact, had won one once, but that was just in the giant-stick-and-brick house subdivision she'd lived in and the judges were middle-class trend followers who normally ate take-out or packaged and micro-waveable food. Once Shelly rediscovered her sauce, refined it with even more garlic, she added barbecued pork and beef sandwiches to our menu. She said our prices were good, our food wholesome and some of it tasty, so she was not being unreasonably optimistic to predict success. I was wiping down the counter one afternoon when she said we needed more advertising.

"Absolutely not. No advertising. We can't have more because we don't and won't have any at all. No, no, no." I despised commercials with the same unhealthy passion Grandpa had reserved for evangelists. How many minutes of our lives were ad free? My e-mail was clogged with offers; the credit card and time-share/resort-property people called all evening. I could ignore TV commercials, junk mail, billboards, storefronts, buses, AM radio, and even people who wore brand names on their T-shirts and bill caps, but I ground my teeth anyway, exhausted by so much ignoring. I was under siege by what I thought of as swarms of blood suckers, like mosquitoes, all wanting to feed on me. I would never advertise, and in fact, regretted the sign outside and the name in the window.

"People won't come here if they don't know we exist." She spoke clearly, pausing between her words as if giving each one that much more power, throwing them one by one into my brain like darts at bulls eyes. She thought she could make me understand. Hers was a simple fact of life, and I was an obtuse child.

"No," I said. "And if they don't come, they don't come. It makes little difference to me."

"Right. Who needs customers?" She spoke as if she had me there, a hint of laughter behind her fake question.

"I don't care about customers at all." I had reverted to childhood by then and she had, too, as we held fast to our non-points. I was proud of my absolute stance that made me impossible to argue against.

She threw her big yellow sponge across the kitchen, and it landed on the stove, the right front burner, with a barely audible plop. Not much of a statement, but when she spoke she no longer had laughter in her voice. "Don't you ever get tired of not caring?"

"I care," I said. "I care about the animal noises you make when I'm trying to sleep. Sounded like a tree frog massacre in your room last night."

"I mean about the café."

"Why does orgasm make your voice so high-pitched?"

"Who cares?" She turned her back on me, ran water full force into the sink.

"I do." I had always cared about orgasms. "And why do you choose the jokers you do? That was old, bald and stupid Roger from Auto World last night wasn't it?" I knew it had been. The first time I'd met him, Roger told me we should be open seven days a week. He had figures, even a chart, that proved we would make more than an additional one-sixth our weekly gross if we opened every day. And later, after he found out I'd been a teacher, he told me the school year should be a month longer than it was, quoted an article that documented greatly increased retention for students who spent more time in school. I'd yet to find a topic Roger wasn't expert in, didn't have articles or figures to prove his points.

"He's not bald. He shaves his head as a fashion statement," she said. "And I think this café could give our lives meaning. Those who feed others are valuable parts of society, any society. But you have to care." She waved her arms about as she talked. "All lives need passion."

"But you already have Roger. Roger the passionate."

That made her laugh, but she wouldn't be side-tracked.

"I'm not talking about some physical function. The café is our chance."

"For what?" I was going to tell her to give me a break from the motivational speeches, knowing if I did, she would throw something else—she was that predictable—and this time it would be something more breakable than a sponge, which I found myself wanting. The quick vision I had of us trashing the place was almost pleasant. Let's tear it to shreds, I would say. Let's ruin it now so we don't have to talk about chances of success. But just then I heard the beginning chords of "The Old Rugged Cross," and knew Mike was trying to cure himself again.

Shelly heard it, too. "What a place," she said. "Loonies as far as the eye can see."

Loony was a fairly apt word for Mike, and the other word, the one I attached to Mike as if it were part of a hyphenated word, pathetic, was appropriate, too. Pathetic-Mike.

I had met Mike as most folks in the neighborhood as well as the police and watch captains had, through his music. He rented an upstairs flat in a building that faced Compton Street and backed up to the juncture of our alley and the cross alley behind Compton. His place was sort of catty-corner from my back door. I could see his kitchen from my bedroom. He lived above a barber shop, and by default his flat came with a two-car garage the barber didn't use and the owner who lived somewhere in Texas didn't want to bother with renting. Of course, Mike didn't have a car. One look at him convinced you he had little besides the ratty looking clothes on his back, perhaps a few other T-shirts and a back-up pair of jeans, possibly a used recliner or a couch he'd beaten the junk man to. And even if he'd had a car, he never would've been allowed to drive. The only unexpected item in his short list of possessions was a pump organ, according to the story he told, left him by his recently dead mother, shipped to him from some little town a few hundred miles away, and now set up in the otherwise empty garage. When he was on the wagon, he would throw open the large doors to the alley and play church music all day and most of the night. When he was off the wagon, he played louder, his selections more mournful. A few weeks earlier the music had lured me to his side.

"Come on in," he'd said when he spotted me looking in that afternoon. "Don't be shy. All are welcome." He was playing "Amazing Grace," said it was his mama's favorite, and this was his mama's organ. Normally, I have nothing to do with grown men who say *mama*. "She played it at our church," he said, "'cept for those years we didn't have no church. Then she played it at home, and folks came to our place to worship."

I said it was a nice organ, even though I knew nothing about music or what made an organ nice.

"Even when we were so poor we couldn't eat she kept the organ. She lost a baby to starvation rather than sell this. She gave it to me so it'd save me. She knew I needed saving. It can save you, too."

"Save you from what?" I asked, though I had a good idea. He had the kind of face that is skinny and puffy at the same time, sort of gray complected with intricate webs of veins in reddish-purple across and around his nose and cheeks. His eyes were dull-looking and his lips were cracked. Though it was January, he was shirtless, and his chest was nearly concave. He had a red, short-stemmed Y with the scar tissue bubbled up around it on his right shoulder, and a smaller, white scar like a horseshoe on his chin.

"I'm a sinner. A drunk, a thief, a murderer, a liar, a fornicator. I'm not ashamed to say it out loud." A tear escaped the corner of one eye and dried on his cheek.

"Good," I said. I took a few steps back.

"I can tell you got a problem with your leg, but it's only symbolic of what's missing in your soul. Want me to pray over them fingers, the ones not there?"

I shook my head, took another step backwards.

"But God don't take things away without making up for them somehow."

"God gave you a rotten life," I said, surprised at saying what I had been thinking.

"Sister," he said. "All lives are rotten. It's God's plan. Mine's no worse than some. My mother was a saint, and I should've been better."

"I gotta get back," I said. "Thanks for the concert."

"I play every Sunday at the Harbor Light," he called after me. "Gonna let me preach soon."

Where was Grandpa when I needed him? I knew if he were still alive, I'd tell him about Mike and he'd laugh as he had laughed at all who saw God as a person, a giant person with lots of power who had to be convinced to help you. That God, Grandpa explained, was a being that kept making up tests. "Why aren't you supposed to take God's name in vain?" he would ask me. "Have you ever thought of that? Why would a god care? So what's the reason for that rule?"

I would shrug. "Don't wear it out?" I'd guess.

"Bull," Grandpa'd answer. "That God just wants to see how well we can follow rules. And He already knows the answer. Not very."

"It's just to be mean, then," I'd say, but Grandpa didn't approve of that answer either.

"Hard isn't the same as mean. Besides, I guess all the tests that big God gives us add interest to our lives and his. Story is he created us out of boredom. It's just that he goes so far overboard. Boom, you could be in hell for flunking. And what does *vain* mean anyway. If it gets something done, if you say 'Don't be such a God-damned idiot,' and the guy stops throwing rocks into your yard with his lawn mower, your words were not in vain. Still, you have to think it through. This God we've created is no simpleton."

Two evenings later, the one before Shelly moved in, Mike rang the doorbell I hadn't known worked. He was leaning against the green and white vestibule, his right eye closed. "Help a buddy," he said. He took a crumpled pack of Marlboros from his back jeans pocket. On his T-shirt was a faded picture of UFOs tying up to the Gateway Arch. He shook the crumpled pack in my face. "A smoke for a tall cold one? I'm busted."

"I don't smoke," I said, but then I told him to wait. I took a can of Budweiser out to him. "It's my last one," I lied. "You can have it, Mike."

Instead of going home, moving away from my café door as I had hoped, he sat on the single step I had just ten inches up from the sidewalk, a slab of concrete he treated as a stoop. "Don't call me Mike," he said. "It's the name of the guy my mama was screwing before I was born. I don't claim him as daddy and he don't claim me. Works out. Mama ran off to chase him after I came, left me with anyone who'd feed me every now and then. Or not. She didn't care."

"You can't sit out here," I said. "Not drunk. The cops'll get you. You'll give me a bad reputation."

"I go by Cockroach. It's a name I gave myself. Save others the trouble of making up an insult for me. I killed a guy once for calling me Roach. It's Cockroach, the whole thing."

"Go home." I went inside, locked and bolted the door, then through a crack in the blinds, watched until he finished the beer, heaved himself up, stumbled away. He kept talking to himself the whole time he was out there, and when he moved off, heading toward Grand Avenue and not his home, I realized what an easy target he was, zigzagging down Meramec Street.

"Roger says you should watch out for guys like him, ruined long ago. Roger says you can do better." Shelly said that to me one morning, maybe two weeks after our non-conversation about advertising, as I was rolling out my biscuit dough, half-asleep from listening most of the night to her animal screams.

I did not deign to answer. Roger was an ass. And I wasn't "doing" anything with Mike. I took him the café leftovers every now and then and listened to his concerts. Sometimes, when he needed one, I gave him a dollar for a ninety-four cent Busch tall boy he bought at the Mobil station up on Grand. And about doing better, I wondered how the comparisons were made. Who was qualified to make them? The older I got the less qualified I was to judge good or better. But beyond all that, I remembered my fifth Christmas. My first knee.

The physical therapists told me at Thanksgiving I was doing so well with the leg that did not bend that it was time for a knee. I was five. I was flattered to be told I was doing well. Only later did I learn that five is the normal age for legless children to get their knees. Because I got it a few days before Christmas, Mom said Santa brought it early, came by the doctor's office with his sack because I'd been such a good girl all year. I demonstrated it Christmas day at Grandma's. They said I was a marvel. I heard them: Uncle Jack, Shelly's father, said "She's a fast learner. She's got the hang of it already." Grandma said, "She's so brave, falls and gets right back up." Mom directed all present to "see how natural it looks." There was one main trick to using the knee. You locked it by stepping back on the heel of the fake foot, so I had to remember to finish each step with the missing leg straight and the heel on the foot I couldn't feel touching the floor first. The knee would bend only when the whole leg, my right one, was in front and I put the toe of my fake foot down. I did that by leaning forward, shifting my hip slightly. If I didn't complete the step by again hitting the heel to the floor, the knee wouldn't lock, and I'd topple. On Christmas day I'd already had three days of practice and one whole day in physical therapy, but still I fell on top of Grandma's coffee table, spilling cokes and scattering pretzels. We all laughed then, even me.

But you can know things without knowing you know them, and it was then, that Christmas day, I knew I would be an awkward, too-eager crippled girl, yearning to be on the inside but kept outside all my life. I didn't know I knew it then, but I tasted the knowledge, sour and metallic in my stomach, though I kept smiling, trying to be graceful, ignoring the fatigue in my own stump, the ache in the thigh of my whole leg, the swelling bump marking the spot my forehead had hit the table. "She'll be riding a bicycle in no time," Dad said, and when Cousin Chuck laughed at that, his mother, Aunt Peg, dragged him from the room. Roger's comment that I could do better took me back to that Christmas. No, it wasn't my leg finally, the whole one or the new one, and it wasn't the missing fingers either that enforced my loneliness. It was my eagerness to be normal combined with my fear that those brave predictions for my future were no more than hope. I quickly developed into an awkward girl.

It was the first Saturday in March, and Shelly spent most of the day fussing with her new menus. By then, she had added other items besides the barbecue sandwiches. We now offered a chef salad and a side order of macaroni salad with frozen peas and mayo she called the Alibi Pasta Salad. We also had side orders of french fries and onion rings. Our choices of breads now included sour dough and pumpernickel. Shelly had had the new menus laminated so the ketchup and coffee stains would wipe off. She was placing a few on each table, sticking them between the chrome napkin dispenser and the salt and pepper caddy, standing back to check, then turning the whole thing sideways. She was careful that the milk glass bud vases, each with a fresh mini-carnation bought at Sav-A-Sum the evening before, were visible. I could see her from the kitchen where I cut large rounds from the sheet of biscuit dough. Whenever she looked at me she would roll her eyes or frown. It was because of Mike. He sat at the counter, sipping and blowing on his third cup of free coffee so far that morning. He smelled like decaying fish. He was on the fourth stool from the register, as far away from any customers we may have had as possible. Shelly said he ruined the ambiance of the café. True, she admitted, there was not much to begin with, but it was, or could be, sort of a retro diner combined with neighborhood friendly. He made it seem like a homeless shelter, she said, and I did have to agree. Still, I wouldn't ask him to leave, not sure if my stubbornness was caused by pity for him or was merely a perverse reaction to Shelly's efforts.

So Mike, a.k.a. Cockroach—a name he denied when sober, claimed I was making it up to drive him crazy—was at the counter the day Toby first entered. Toby's expression as he approached the counter was pure disgust. His top lip curled up to his nose. He squinted as if the offense came in through his eyes as well as his nose. I laughed out loud, and that was when Mike and Shelly noticed him. Toby recovered his composure immediately, hoisted himself up on the stool farthest from Mike, and said he was selling candy for St. Hedwig's computer lab.

"Who was Saint Hedwig?" Mike asked. "Man or woman?"

Toby shrugged, refused to look in Mike's direction. He was short and so thin I could see his collar bones through his knit shirt. I guessed him as seven or eight, but he told us later he was ten. "Want some candy, Lady?"

From the beginning, Toby was special. His skin was eggplant black, and his ears were each normal sized, in the right places on the side of his squashed-in head. That was all you could say good about his looks. His forehead was covered by gray bumps, some sort of rash, and his eyes were large and distorted behind the extra-thick lenses he wore, and his eyeglasses were joined at the nose piece by masking tape. His nose seemed mashed into his face, and his mouth was crooked, his lips disappearing halfway across, running out before his mouth did. His cheeks and chin were covered by the same rash as was on his forehead. "I'm Toby, Lady," he said, reaching out to shake my hand. "I got to sell this stuff."

I reached across the counter to shake his hand, and he pulled his back.

"Yikes!" he said. "Who cut your fingers?"

"I was born like this," I said, holding my hands out for inspection.

"That one there is out of place." He pointed to my only finger.

"Yes," I said.

"Sounds like a made up name to me," Mike said.

Toby turned to him then, almost snarled. "It's real, Mister. It's from the Bible."

"No," Mike said. "I know the Bible upside down and backwards."

"Might make more sense to you right side up," Shelly called from across the café.

I opened the cash register, asked Toby how much his candy bars were. They were a dollar a piece, and I bought twenty, counting out the last two dollars in dimes and nickels to impress him. It worked. "Wow," he said over and over as I picked up one dime after another. Shelly came up and bought twenty also, went upstairs to get her own money rather than taking it from the cash register.

Toby unloaded the forty candy bars, most of the box, pocketed the money, and started to jump off the stool when I stopped him. "Hungry?" I asked. "It's on the house."

"The gravy is superb," Shelly said. "Lots of sausage."

Toby nodded his head, but Mike spoke up again. "It'd be like a Saint Footshoe."

"I gotta go," Toby said, and jumped down.

"I thought you wanted to eat."

He was at the door by then, but he turned and he nodded at Mike's back. "Stupid men are bad luck for me. I can't use no bad luck."

Mike swiveled on his stool, turned to face Toby, and pointed a finger at him. "It's a made-up name."

"For God's sake, Mike," I said when Toby was gone. "What nerve ending has finally snapped in your brain? Toby is a name."

"Hedwig. Saint Handring, Saint Buttpants."

Shelly shook her head at me over his shoulder. "Saint Bev," she said. "Refuge for the worthless."

That night, I was home alone. Mom had invited me over for dinner, but I declined that, said I was tired, which was partly true. Later, Shelly left to go dancing with Roger, and though both had invited me to join them, I declined that, too. "You don't have to dance," Shelly had said. "Just sit at the table with us. Make fun of the other dancers."

Mostly I wasn't sure why I wanted to stay home, but I did. I wasn't feeling sorry for myself, but after thirty-five years, was no longer needy or too eager. I more than accepted my solitude, and in fact believed nothing about humanity was worth chasing after. I decided to scrub the bathroom, polish the large mahogany breakfront, buffet, and mantelpiece Shelly had moved in. It'd been a long time since I'd had any interest in cleaning, and I decided to tackle as much as I could. It was midnight when I stopped, having waxed the kitchen floor, washed the woodwork with bleach, and dust mopped the entire flat. When I sank down into my bed, feeling the usual relief that comes from taking my prosthesis off, removing the sock from my stump, and allowing my skin to dry out, I heard Mike's rendition of "When The Saints Go Marching In." I laughed out loud, all alone in my bed, as I remembered his litany. I wondered if Saints Buttpants and Footshoe were in the group marching in. Just when you thought his brain was fried beyond salvation, he said something that showed he still made connections. "He's not a stupid man, Toby," I said. Just ruined.

I never walked with two legs. I hadn't lost most of my left one; it simply never developed, was never there at all. And that not developing happened eight months before I was born, not even old enough to be called a fetus. So why did I dream of running, dancing, kicking with two real legs? Why was it a continual surprise to wake with one leg? Why did I so often start to get up, stand, walk while half asleep as if the leg were newly missing?

I was having one of those dreams that began by my running along the rocky bluffs above the Mississippi River north of Alton. I ran through a cave with petroglyphs, probably from the extinct Mound Builders—red birds breathing fire. I left the cave and ran up the rocks, feeling the jagged edges under both feet. That was the miraculous part. My feet bent, moved in all directions as I adjusted my stance, gripped the slick face of the rocks and turned sideways in the crevices. Of course, in the real world my fake foot not only had no feeling, but did not bend or flex except for what the rubbery bottom and the two-inch split between the second and third toe would allow. I had to watch where I walked always, knowing my foot would not adjust to uneven ground, and as little as a larger- than-usual piece of gravel could become an obstacle and send me plummeting. But in my dream, I climbed to the top of the bluff. I jumped over a chasm in the rocks, took a running start and was airborne for almost thirty seconds. I remember watching the second hand on a silver watch as I flew. I landed with a good thud, keeping both knees bent to cushion the shock. I scrambled down the rocks, and came to a pool, deep and green and mossy. I jumped in with a splash, tasted the limestone in the spring water as I let myself sink, then swam back and forth for hours, never tiring. I did the crawl, the butterfly, the breast stroke, and the backstroke, my legs kicking and paddling and pushing the water back as efficiently as if I were an Olympic swimmer.

I was letting the water run off my strong limbs, enjoying the sharpness of the minerals in it that trickled into my mouth, when I heard Shelly and Roger stumble up the front stairs. Even half asleep, I could tell they were wasted, lucky to have made it home in one piece. I tried to call out to them, to say I knew how to run after all, but when they didn't respond, I gave up and dove back into the bottomless pool.

I awoke next in the blue light before true dawn, heard the grackles haranguing one another outside my window. I started to get up, but before I could hang my legs over the side of the bed, I saw my prosthesis across the foot of my bed where I kept it, and had to shake my head at what a slow learner I was. I wasn't an amputee after all, shouldn't have missed a leg I never had. As I used my finger bumps to buckle the leg strap around my hips, I thought it odd I never dreamed I had fingers.

After coffee and toast, I decided to go to St. Paul's, which had always been our family's parish church. It was a large gothic structure with pastel scenes of the life of Christ painted high overhead on the plaster arches and vaults. All the faces had creamy, pink complexions and their eyes were blue like Mom's and nothing like those of the Middle-Eastern folks they were supposed to be. The pastor was deaf, and he told stories about World War II chaplains in his homilies; the organist played and sang off key; at least half the parishioners who straggled in were eighty-something-year-old women who prayed their rosaries during Mass, and the others were young women with three or four children who cried and wrestled with one another all during the service. Sunday Mass was seldom a spiritual experience at St. Paul's, nor was it even interesting. But what the hell. The early Mass was fast, and I was up and already depressed that my dream had been one, so I decided to go. But when I tried to open the outside door, I realized I was stuck.

The door from the street to our flat had a lock attached to the doorknob, and a deadbolt added by a previous owner. We used both locks, but relied more on the deadbolt. Screwed into the doorjamb was a chain that was meant to fit into a track high up on the door. We had never used that, knowing that if the deadbolt failed, what chance would a chain have. But either Shelly or Roger had hooked the chain behind them the night before. Whichever one had done it, had done it wrong; the knob on the chain had been jammed in sideways, so not only wouldn't it slide, but it would not come out. It was wedged tight. I pulled and yanked and twisted the chain end as much as possible with my bumps, tried it with the door opened and closed, but nothing worked. My hands were red, my bumps tender.

If I had fingers I could do this, I told myself. If I had a roommate who didn't stay out all night drinking, I wouldn't need to do it. If I had fingers, I reminded myself, I wouldn't be living with my drunken cousin who brought odd men into our home at all hours of the night. Even without fingers, I could be the one bringing men in if I were willing to stoop as low as Roger and other know-it-alls, and if I put my mind to it, I could probably get one or two who were better than Roger. And it was not technically our home; it was mine. I bought it. Who had said she could bring men into it, especially a man like Roger she knew I disdained? And sticking the chain end in sideways reeked so of idiocy, Roger was probably the one who'd done it. I had an urge to stomp up there and shake them both awake, but I could picture them rolling their bloodshot eyes at each other, understanding how out of control Shelly's deformed cousin truly was.

I could've gone to church out the back way, or I could've gone out through the café, then later on forced one of them to jiggle and pull on the chain until it came loose. But I decided the chain had to come off right then, should've been off already. I got out my set of small household-use screwdrivers and first tried to take the chain off the door jamb, but the top screw was stripped, spun uselessly but did not release its grip. Next, I tried to remove the slide from the door itself, but it seemed to be connected by small brads hammered into the wood. I didn't have anything to pry it off with. In frustration, I called a locksmith, the goal no longer getting to church or getting out of my own home, but getting the damned front door opened, disabling the offending chain lock once and for all.

Of course it was expensive. A Sunday morning emergency call, and all he did was tell me to open the door a crack, then he slipped his wire cutters in and snipped the chain. Seventy-five dollars. When I saw what he did I realized I could've gone around and done that, the sort of jealous anger I thought I'd outgrown freezing my brain as it always had. The early Mass was already over, and I was out of the church mood anyway, so I stomped back upstairs, knocked hard on the door to Shelly's room, then opened it, threw the bill in, and watched it flutter down on top of Roger's sweaty back. Shelly opened one eye in my direction.

"Have a nice day," I said, then slammed the door, making Roger say "Shit."

By that evening they were apologetic, slinking around the upstairs like whipped puppies. Finally they went down and built a fire in the kettle, grilled ribs and tossed a salad. I said the barbecue sauce made me belch. I played with the salad for a while, then went back into the living room and turned on the television. As usual, there was nothing on.

Shelly was still trying to kiss up on Monday, even going so far as saying the sauce probably did have too much garlic in it, not enough molasses. She made three new versions of it, asked me to taste each one and give her my opinion. She said nothing improved her cooking like honest criticism, that failure was just a step on the road to success, so I should feel free to say what I really thought. Toby came in about three o'clock on his way home from school and that cheered me up some. He was taking orders for pizzas for St. Hedwig's band uniforms, and I ordered ten. Shelly ordered twelve, trying to prove to me she was good and not the airhead I had called her. I finally told her her last batch of sauce was passable, though I thought it tasted like all the others, and its quality and taste made no difference to me at all. She took it as forgiveness, and started talking to me again about ways we should try to improve our business. She thought we should mail out coupons, buy one get one at half price, stuff like that.

"No," I said. "No mailings."

After Toby left, she mentioned Roger. "I hope his being around doesn't bother you. He's not a keeper, though I admit I like the way he likes me so. Still, we both may be killing time."

"An optimist like you wants to kill time?"

"Just with men, just for now. I'm planning something great otherwise, plan not to waste a minute. And even you have to admit, Roger's better than TV," she said.

"You know you'll get married again. You don't have enough imagination not to."

She shrugged. "I must have had an extra-bad hangover all day yesterday. My temples throbbed."

"I mean, the third time may be a charm."

"One can only hope," she said. "But my head feels just as bad today. Did you notice I haven't eaten much?"

"I know you starve yourself to be able to zip those size six jeans. And they're too tight anyway."

"I wouldn't marry Roger."

"Let's close up," I said. It was four o'clock, and I had lost track of the conversation. Besides, no one had eaten in our café since a couple of sewer workers and one gas company guy left at one o'clock, that was not counting Toby who had finished off two pieces of my chocolate cream pie.

We went up the back stairs, and as we got to the upstairs kitchen that was seldom used, the phone rang. It was Howard with news about the lawsuit, the first I'd heard in a few weeks. He said Madison Hilker was pregnant. He said that made the charges more serious. He said I shouldn't worry, but he wanted me to come in to see him as soon as I could. He used the word *strategy*, talked about getting the story right.

Maddie Hilker had pink hair and a silver ball pierced through her tongue last time I saw her, but underneath the trappings of her times, she was a young woman on the verge of great growth. She was lively and witty, curious enough about the world not to live in herself alone. Like all my students, she and her classmates had wanted to know about my leg and my fingers. After I told them the familiar story, she asked what no one else ever had: "Have you forgiven your mother?"

"For what?" I asked, but knew well what she meant. "No one knew the drug was dangerous," I said, but the question, though one I would never answer, was a good one. I'd cursed my luck for a long time, asked God night after night why he let Mom take that medicine. Wasn't he supposed to have our best interests at heart? And what was a little puking compared to my forever life? Once connections between the drug and birth defects started to surface, I summed it up for Mom, relieved to have someone to blame for my misery so far. "If you weren't such a wimp," I said, "you wouldn't have ruined my life. And it's the only life I'll ever have." I stood before her as she sat at the kitchen table. "Look," I said. "I'll never have two legs."

"Don't let it get you down," she said. "My goodness. You do so well with what you have, better than many who have all their limbs. But," she said. "I do hope you can forgive me." Later I decided the real problem was not my forgiveness but that Mom hadn't forgiven herself. I was seventeen by the time there was conclusive proof Mother's Help was to blame, and I believed each time Mom looked at me during what should have been my beauty-contest-winning years, she was ashamed of herself for not suffering in silence. I thought I hurt her conscience.

"But she could have borne it all for a few more weeks, suffered a little bit so you would be whole," Maddie said.

"She thinks so," I said. "She agrees with you."

"Poor thing," Maddie said. She also asked what many others had, if it hurt and how I learned to use my bumps so well—I didn't know how—and if I slept with my leg. "Does it have a name?" Maddie asked once in homeroom, making all the other girls laugh.

I laughed, too. "I used to name them, called one Pinkie for its obnoxious dye job. This one I've had for eight years and haven't named."

"Hortense," Maddie said, and they all laughed again. It stuck. "Good-bye Hortense," they'd say as they left the building on Fridays. Or if I went to one of their volleyball games, one would call out as I entered the gym. "Look, it's Ms. Burke and Hortense."

I knew Maddie was too bright to be corrupted by me or by anyone. Nevertheless, when I told Shelly about Maddie's pregnancy, we both grew sad. "She's so young," I said.

"It is a nuisance suit," Shelly said. "Suing for that. Might as well sue God for giving her a uterus." I told her Howard was not being so blasé about it. "I just don't get it," she said more than once. And I kept thinking about Maddie's age, roughly half mine. We ate leftover barbecue beef in silence. Later, we sat in the living room, the TV off. We were slumped down on opposite ends of that ugly orange couch of hers, like a giant pumpkin, and my anger at Maddie's stupidity—her not-yet-lived life was ruined, or at the best, postponed, and postponed was often the same as ruined—seemed matched by Shelly's confusion over what she couldn't reconcile or understand enough to put a good face on. The doorbell made both of us jump, and as I tried to push myself up to a full sitting position, she went down the front stairs. As soon as she opened the door, Toby rushed in and up, tripping over a few steps in his rush, no doubt banging his knees or some other body parts. By the time I was standing, he was at the top of the steps, gripping the side piece of his glasses, breathing heavily.

"You ladies got to let me hide out here," he said. He wheezed and coughed. As Shelly asked him all the responsible questions—who, what, why—and got no answers, I fixed a bed on the sofa. It was the best we could do for him. Shelly said we should call the police, but I argued that could result in sending him back into a bad situation, that we should know more before we acted. Mainly, though, I liked the looks of him in my home. He was ugly enough to fit in with me. No, I was not a harbor or sanctuary or anything so dramatic, and I had no desire to be. Those of us no one wanted did not have to want each other. I wasn't a savior. But at least Toby wasn't poster-child material, would never be foster child of the week.

"I hope this isn't considered grievous harm, too," I said to Shelly, before I bent down to tuck Toby in. "You'll be like Peter Pumpkin Eater's wife," I said to him. "Kept in this giant and ugly pumpkin shell."

He took his glasses off and blinked up at me. "Man, that was a close call," he said as I leaned over, and I got a whiff of his breath—like chicken skin left in the sun for a day—and decided to find him a toothbrush before whatever I would do, send him off or call someone, in the morning.   And because Shelly was frowning and looking serious like one of those responsible do-gooders the world was full enough of, especially since none of them seemed to do any real good, and I knew she still wanted to call the police or some other civic authority, I told her if she didn't relax, she'd have permanent frown furrows in her forehead, would no longer be considered one of the Stillwell beauties. That would be too bad, I said. Just when she'd finally gotten rid of the bags under her eyes.

SHELLY

The Stillwell beauties, were the trio of Stillwells that Chickie and I were added to to make five. Bev was usually included by Aunt Josie or Mom because of what they called her "inner beauty," though she'd told her own mother that being patronizing was one step lower than being contemptuous. And Cousin Chuck's wife was sometimes added to the list to make seven beauties, mainly out of politeness. Nevertheless, we were five beauties, not seven, and we knew who we were—Marie, Peg, Josie, Chickie, and me, Shelly. Five beauties, only three ever named Stillwell. According to Grandma Stillwell—not a beauty herself, too German-looking she used to say, bulbous nose, protruding brow—giving the world three beauties was her reason for existing. Once she tempered her German genes (a bit of French in there, too, but thank God, she said, recessive) with the aristocratic Anglo look of George Stillwell who had a Spanish grandfather, the mix was unbeatable. Grandma Stillwell would've and did put her beauties up against any others. My mother, Marie, was Miss Dutchtown St. Louis two years in a row, an unheard-of honor, and Bev's mother, Josie, was Miss St. Louis, Miss Missouri, and Miss Midwest Dairy, all in the same year. All three were homecoming queens, the Stillwell reign at Bishop DuBourg High lasting three years in a row. Aunt Peg held the queen record because she was also May Queen for St. Paul's parish when she was sixteen, seventeen, and again when she was eighteen.

The three Stillwell girls had an innocent, natural beauty, and they worked hard at enhancing it. Charm school, dance lessons, speech and recitation classes, sessions of hair and face care, exercise and diet regimes. Grandma Stillwell saw that they stayed on their diets—never allowing seconds of anything, not even salad—that they didn't slump or slouch, that they crossed their legs in one fluid motion without a bounce. She also screened the boys who flocked around the Stillwell house, a three story on Grand Avenue next to, in those days, Ambrose's Italian restaurant. "Housecleaning ruins your looks," she told her daughters. "It ruined mine." When Grandpa would object, out of guilt Grandma said, she would be quick to reassure him. "But that's okay. Looks were not my blessing to begin with. It's my girls who should stay beautiful as long as possible." She wanted to find boys for them who would grow into men with enough money for household help. "Never get down on your knees to scrub anything," she told Mom on the night before her wedding. "Each time you do, you add a year or more onto your looks. You'll look fifty before you're forty if you're not strict about it."

Aloyishus Burke was approved of for Josie. Connections of his, and not too distant ones, owned two confectioneries in town, and his uncle was an executive in a life insurance company. Al was a good bet. Ralph Owens was a good catch for Peg because he was going to college, majoring in business and finance, and his father was part owner of a dry cleaners. And Dad, Jack Sturgis, had been a member of the meat-cutter's union for three years before he proposed, ever since he was eighteen, and so had enough promise to be approved for Mom. Grandma knew meat would never go out of style.

Even after they were Marie Sturgis, Josie Burke, and Peg Owens, they were known in South St. Louis as the Stillwell beauties. Chickie and I joined their ranks almost as soon as we arrived in the world, certainly by our third birthdays, and we eventually continued the tradition of being Bishop DuBourg High's homecoming queens—me in '81 and Chickie in '82. I was Miss Convention Center in '82, and Miss Dutchtown St. Louis in '83. Chickie was also a few Miss This and Miss Thats. Whenever the five of us, the original three and me and Chickie, went out to lunch, people stared. Heads turned. Waiters flirted with us, even when the original three were closing in on sixty. Salespeople helped us before others. Not one of us ever got a speeding ticket.

Aunts Josie's and Peg's beauty was an English garden variety—peaches-and-cream skin, honey-colored hair, breasts like fat crème puffs, boyish hips. Mom, the oldest child, had a little of what Grandpa Stillwell called the Spanish mud thrown into her coloring, giving her olive skin, dark eyes, and mink brown hair. She had the same full breasts but a bit more hip than the others had. All three had long, gracefully curved legs, long fingers, too. Chickie and I both looked more like Mom, but my nose was the smallest, my eyes the darkest, and my lashes the longest.

All of us Stillwell beauties were proud of our looks, and not ashamed of our pride. As Grandma said, it was not vanity to be proud of what God gave you. And all that hogwash about pride going before a fall was meaningless because there would always be a fall no matter what went before, and so humility also went before a fall. Modesty, too. "Now," she said more than once, "it would be a crime, a sin, for me to be proud of my own beauty because I don't have much. It's different for my girls."

So I was proud of my beauty, and if not for Bev who so clearly was not and was missing a few body parts besides, we would all have admitted it more, luxuriated in our blessing. And not that I needed to, but as the original Stillwell girls had, I worked hard at making the most of my beauty, spending extra time at night on moisturizing my skin, extra time in the morning blending lipstick colors. The Sue Spritz Modeling Agency and Academy had had makeup artists who could make my eyes look larger and my dimples more symmetrical just by variations of shading, and I continued to use their tricks. I left modeling in my prime, having been in a Lord & Taylor and a Saks catalog the same month, because modeling is a young woman's game. I knew then that my beauty would not last forever but for quite a few more years, though increased upkeep would be required. Already I applied a gel made of mint leaves and vitamin E to my neck twice a day to keep it smooth, and I hoped I wouldn't need my neck done until I was well past Mom's age. Once you started the process, neck skin had to be re-stretched every few years.

About a month before Richard left, Mom'd had hers done for the first time, and I volunteered to spend the night with her in case the pain killers confused her. I was sitting in her living room at dusk, looking through the front window at the suddenly peaceful street and wondering how much longer before my body needed repairs that required stitches, thinking of how exasperated Richard sounded each time I made him tell me about my looks. As I tried to explain to him, none of us know what we look like totally because we can't take in our whole selves; even in full-length mirrors, we don't see our faces and feet together. As I was thinking how right I'd been and how deliberate it was of Richard to remain annoyed, Mom stumbled into the room, moaning and bandaged like a ghoul, bumping into an end table and then crying at the bruise she had created on her shin. "You never have taken proper care of me," she said when she saw the place on her shin turn red and head toward purple immediately. "You should have warned me about the table. You should have helped me walk."

"You're supposed to be in bed. Why didn't you call if you needed something?"

"Thank God I hardly ever need you," she said.

Unlike Mom's beauty, mine had a purpose. It was now paying off for the café business. Many of the men who came in flirted with me, and a few hung around an extra fifteen or twenty minutes, long enough to have a slice of pie, a scoop of ice cream, because I smiled at them.

My main method of helping the café business, though, was by trying to make the food better, to create something that would set us apart. My barbecue sauce was a contender. Even Bev called it okay, a grand compliment coming from her, and Grandma said

I could bottle it and sell it, keep a supply at the cash register. I thought I would do that, too, but for the time being I was making minor adjustments. I went to Soulard Market early one Saturday and bought a bushel of tomatoes, came back and boiled them down. After they boiled, I ran the whole pot through a sieve, then mashed and pounded the solid stuff left behind. The result was pure, fresh tomato sauce. It took a long time to make, though, and I decided the barbecue sauce made with canned tomatoes as a base was better, the slight metallic taste a plus. One morning I made a mushroom quiche to add to our breakfast menu, but the only customer who was even halfway interested in quiche was the new custodian at St. Paul's, and he was allergic to mushrooms. Bev and I ate the quiche for dinner that evening, and as she rubbed in the fact no one had wanted it, I shrugged, humble enough to laugh at my failures, able to put up with her jokes. I relished this good-ness in myself. She said, "Thank God there's some left," and "This quiche sure tastes like a best-seller."

Though I had never wanted to be in the restaurant business, I was taking what came, making of it what I could. I knew that was better than wallowing in pity. And our business was growing bit by bit. We often had three or four customers in at the same time, and the crossing guard for the public grade school a block down Meramec told me that my sausage gravy was as good or better than his mother's, may she rest in peace.

We had three deuces across the front window, three four-seat-ers in the middle of the room, two more deuces on the far wall, one four seater along the wall by the door, and four stools at the front counter. I daydreamed about all twenty-eight seats being filled, wondered how the two of us would manage. I also daydreamed that one of our customers was the *St. Louis Post–Dispatch* restau-rant critic who would write a rave review of my gravy and Bev's biscuits and pies, would maybe mention my barbecue sauce. I wondered if the picture of me on the bottles of sauce should be in color or just pen and ink. I wondered if Bev would ever admit my ideas were a part of our success. I wondered, too, if Bev would be angry when I finally told Mike the Cockroach to beat it, some-thing I was on the verge of doing no matter how she took it. Mike could not be around when the restaurant critic came in.

I wondered about other things, too. I wondered what I could use for the headaches I was getting lately. And I wondered, as I had been doing for nearly a year, why Richard had left so suddenly to be with someone less beautiful than I, especially since we hadn't been fighting, and when I pressed for it, he couldn't come up with even one concrete reason for choosing Aurora, our vet's receptionist, over me. I knew it had to have been because of a fault in me, and though I wondered, I didn't truly want to uncover that fault, feared it ran deep and wide.

I wondered, too, about how the Hilkers got up the nerve their ilk always seemed to have stockpiled. Suing Bev over their little tootsie's own fertility and the potency of her young man's sperm! "Oh," the little tootsie would simper, "Ms. Burke told me to get pregnant." And the supposedly intelligent grown-ups around her would pretend to believe her.

April fifteenth was in the wrong month. It belonged in July or August. By seven in the morning when we opened, it was already eighty degrees, and the humidity that should have needed three more months to build up was higher than the temperature. The weather reports had said something about a line of high pressure, a stalled storm to the west. I cut up three chickens, put them in a pot of salted water. I knew chicken barley soup was not the best special for this kind of day, but Mom had come by the night before with three chickens from her basement deep freezer, already thawing. I had to cook them. The kitchen was sweltering by eight. This was the first real test of the new AC Bev had had installed for the downstairs when she bought the place, and it was failing. We positioned three fans around the café to circulate what was only slightly cooled air. The laminated menus were being blown off the tables, I had a constant whirr in my head, and my nose itched. Yet, still I sweated.

After I boned the chickens, I cooked their muscles, fat, tendons, and skin down to a swirl of gray meat. I removed the pot from the stove and set it aside as I chopped carrots and celery. We had a foursome from the water company in for breakfast, so I had to take orders, spoon gravy on top of biscuits, refill coffee cups, and even scramble a few eggs. Bev was busy all the while making up bowls of tuna and egg salad for lunch, then beating up frothy meringue for the lemon pies she had just made. Roger walked by the front window on his way to Auto World, but I was too busy to return his wave. It was odd the way even a few customers jammed us up that morning, made it seem we were working underwater, furiously but ineffectually, getting nowhere. I blamed it on the heat. It took the water workers forever to pay their bill. I stood at the register while they argued and discussed who should pay for what, who had change for a ten, who would owe whom.

After they left, I finished my chopping quickly, dumped the vegetables into the chicken pot, and returned it to the heat. An hour later, I added barley and by eleven o'clock it was ready. I kept it warm on the back of the stove as I printed up a sign announcing the soup of the day. I wondered how it would go over chilled, and even played around, and made an alternate sign advertising "Pottage de Poulet Froid."

We sold two pastramis and one corned beef on rye, one tuna salad, three egg salads, and five slices of pie that afternoon, . That was all. Not only did we sell no soup, but no one wanted barbecue, either. We did our briskest business in ice water. Bev shook her head at the large pot of hot soup but didn't say a thing. I knew I should've made chicken salad with Mom's gift and wondered why I'd thought of it too late. Bev could've thought of it, too, though, could have told me, given me a little help.

Toby came in at 3:30 on his way home from school. He was taking orders for crocks of Wisconsin cheese, said the money would go toward a St. Hedwig's science lab. Bev bought ten crocks at four-fifty apiece, and I was going to pass, say with what Bev had purchased we had all the cheese we needed for a while, but when I looked at him, I relented and took five more. It was because he was such an ugly child—that flattened-down nose, the large glazed-looking myopic eyes. And someone could have shown him a toothbrush, explained what to do with it. Even worse, he was the kind of ugly child you just knew would become a truly ugly adult when he didn't have youth to make him endearing. Still, I couldn't resist a jab. "What are you studying at that school anyway, salesmanship?" He ignored me.

"Is your leg glued on?" he asked Bev. "Do you use crazy glue?"

She shook her head. "I have a strap from the top of it that goes around my hips. But it mainly stays put from the pressure of my weight on it. My stump fits into it pretty tight."

"How fast can you take it off?"

"Less than a minute if I have to. Why?"

"Could you beat someone with it, someone who was coming up behind you?"

"No. Think about it for a moment," she said. "If I took it off, I'd fall down."

He laughed. "But you could be sitting down, like hiding around a corner, then hit the person coming around, get him in the knees, make him fall, too."

"Who would it be, this person coming around the corner?" I asked, and both of them looked at me sideways as if surprised I was listening. Well after all, it was a small café and there was nothing else going on. How could I not listen? Anyway, I asked, as Bev should have known, to get at the truth about Toby. He had spent the night on our sofa, my sofa actually, about three weeks earlier, and had never said why, whom he was hiding from. We had not heard of anyone looking for him, no neighborhood rumors, no parish news that would have traveled from St. Hedwig's to St. Paul's. Bev had asked him if his family had been worried that night, and he'd said he didn't know. Nothing more. He was vague about where he lived—"stayed" as kids like him said—just pointing toward the south when we asked. He once mentioned someone named Shirley, and when we asked who she was, he grew vague again. "She's the one who feeds me oatmeal," he said.

Bev, I thought, could have been described as the one who fed him pie, and I wondered if Shirley owned another café nearby. That afternoon, Bev fed him two slices of lemon meringue pie and two glasses of milk.

Toby told us the cheese would be in in two weeks, and we'd have to have our money ready then. So far, we'd bought candy bars, pizzas, and entertainment coupon books for various St. Hedwig projects, Girl Scout cookies he said he was selling for a friend, boxes of all-occasion greeting cards he said were for the Knights of Columbus, and a stack of twenty-five cardboard coasters to raise money for the missions. Now he had sold us cheese crocks.

While he was sitting on the swivel stool, twisting first one way, then the other, Bev quizzed him about what he was learning in school. "Have you done state capitols yet?"

"Nope," he said as he spun. "We ain't even done all the states."

"Don't say *ain't*, Toby. People will think you're ignorant." She touched his shoulders to make him stop spinning.

"Okay." He rolled his head about, his ears grazing his shoulders, to prove to us how dizzy he was. "We know the states. I'm just pulling your leg," he said, then giggled.

"Ha ha," Bev said.

Meanwhile, I poured my soup into two large mason jars, one for Mom and one for Dad. Howard Figg, Bev's lawyer, called for her while I was filling the jars, and that left Toby all alone at the counter, staring across at me. I wondered if he thought he was putting something over on us, all that selling. I wondered if it was the big time for him to be manipulating two grown-up women, and suddenly I was remembering how big I'd felt when I was crowned Miss Dutchtown St. Louis. Grandpa Stillwell told me I was at the peak of my life, and I nodded, smiled then, too dazed and happy to do less, but thought it better not be true. How do you recognize the peak? What would you do if you knew the highlight of your life was passed? So far, the best day of my life had been the day I married Richard, but I believed something more was coming, something to top that.

"Want some?" I raised the soup pot in Toby's direction. He shrugged. He didn't take food from me as readily as he did from Bev, but, except for his first visit, he'd never turned down a bite either. I ladled a little into a bowl and set it before him.

"Who made this, Lady?" He wrinkled his flattened nose, making his eyes move closer together. "It stinks."

"Beggars can't be choosers," I said.

"I ain't no beggar." He slid off the stool. "I mean, I am not a beggar. Tell the other lady I left because I was insulted."

"Good riddance, then," I said. "It's no problem for me if you pass up free food." Someone should have wanted my soup, at least for free.

"It's rotten," he called from the door, and just then, I took a deep breath of the steam rising above his bowl and knew he was right. The chicken had turned, maybe from the heat, maybe it had been in Mom's freezer too long. Maybe I had created a deadly poison. No matter how, it almost made me gag now as I stood at the hot counter, a fan blowing the stench up my nostrils. There was too much to send down the garbage disposal, so I poured the mason jars back into the pot, covered it, and set it aside. I'd find a container, maybe one of the plastic jars our ketchup came in, and throw it out early in the morning for the trash collectors. Thank God I hadn't taken it to Mom's or to Dad's. Well, Mom may not have eaten it anyway, was probably on the no carb diet, or the all carb one, maybe the no fat. Besides, it was her chicken to begin with, mine only through an uncharacteristic fit of generosity brought on by her yearly freezer clean-out. Dad, on the other hand, ate everything Mom sent up, whatever I brought over. Though he lived in the upstairs, converted into a complete flat with a working kitchen, he never cooked. Part of their deal when they divorced and he moved upstairs was that Mom would still cook for him. He'd convinced her he'd starve to death otherwise, and she said she didn't want to kill him. In fact, she was the worst cook in the family.

When the split occurred, I was thirteen, in the eighth grade. I was already registered at Bishop DuBourg High School for the fall, and while still at St. Paul's, I was a patrol girl complete with a sash and a badge, editor of the school newspaper, and the star of our eighth grade play, *Snow White Meets Frankenstein*, written by my Cousin Chuck.

It was April, a breezy blue day. I walked home from school alone that day, laughing out loud at the way large, fluffy white clouds would suddenly appear between red brick buildings, would seem to squeeze the buildings apart. I skipped some of the way. It was a day that made me itch on the inside, a day of blooming forsythias and new love. Bill Budding had just asked me to ride with him to DuBourg's freshman picnic which would be at a park on the banks of the Meramec River in four weeks, just after our eighth grade graduation. His mother would drive. It would be our first date. Bill and I both knew we'd be an item at DuBourg. I had a thought as I walked home from school that day, walked past the women's hat shop full of pink silk gardenias on straw, past the opened door of Meineke's tavern and the cool mustiness inside, and past Grandma and Grandpa Stillwell's house and what was by then a Mexican restaurant. I thought "this is fun." I remember it. "This is fun." I laughed at myself even then for thinking it, happy I had said it only inside my head.

My girlfriends and I often passed around profundities that year. Five or six of us would be out walking or sitting on someone's front stoop, and one of us would speak of what we called the meaning of life. "I think mean people are really just jealous," one of us would say. We'd all agree, throw in examples of our own to prove it. "Boys don't cry as often as girls do because they don't worry about being liked," another would say. We'd nod. We'd give one another problems to solve. "If you accidentally killed someone, should you have to go to jail?" We'd complicate it. "What if the person you killed was Hitler?" "Would you make love to someone you didn't like to save his life? To save yours?"

But trite as my thought was, as corny, as silly as it seemed, and as much as the other girls would ridicule it, it was true, too. It was all fun then. A block later, when I turned onto Bingham Street, I saw the contractors' truck in front of my home, and three shirtless men in jeans sprawled on the set of eight concrete steps leading up from the sidewalk.

"Will you be in the top or bottom, girlie?" the ugliest one asked me as I stepped over them all and into what just that morning had been our foyer. The linoleum had been ripped up to expose a black tarry mess, and two-by-fours were already in place, floor to ceiling, indicating where new walls would be. I could tell our home was being converted to a two-family. My stomach lurched when I realized we'd be taking in renters. I could already hear the other kids' jokes about the butcher needing fresh meat. It would be some oddball old man living alone and talking to himself, or a family of creeps, the ones my age wanting to hang around me all the time. I hoped we'd at least move upstairs where my bedroom and the screened porch all across the back was. I stood in the former foyer and said a quick prayer. Good St. Paul, make the renters normal, better yet, invisible. Don't make this as bad as it seems. Of course, it was worse. Mom was in the living room, sitting on the couch but twisted around so her back was to me and she faced the window. She knew I was there, though, and when I stepped in from the former foyer, she spoke without turning around. "We're staying down here. Dad's den will make a good bedroom for you."

"But my bed's upstairs."

"He's going upstairs." She turned toward me then, and I couldn't tell if she was trying to smile or trying not to. "You can go upstairs with him if you want. Or better yet, you can probably have a room in both places." She had a glass of wine in her hand, and she looked into it, sloshed the red around the sides. "I suppose you want to ask me something."

I swallowed. "Why are you drinking wine now?" It was not the question I intended, but the wine was unusual. Mom had a glass with Christmas dinner, sometimes on Thanksgiving. That was it as far as I knew.

"I think this is a momentous day, don't you?"

"Can I have a sip?"

She passed me the glass and watched as I took a mouthful, held it in as long as I could, letting it trickle down my throat one drop at a time.

"Who gets Mrs. Shrenk?" She was the older woman in our parish who cleaned once a week for Mom, Aunt Josie, and Aunt Peg.

"We'll share her."

I nodded.

"Are those all your questions?"

"Why?" I asked.

"Because I want to. As simple as that." She took the glass back. "How was the wine?"

"Warm."

"Every now and then you really can do what you want," she said.

It was the first of many times the world turned upside down and didn't take me with it. Grandma and Aunt Josie both said about the same thing when I asked: "Oh Honey, it's been coming for years. Should have happened long ago." Cousin Chickie said her mother said it was doomed long before the *I dos*. When I cried to Aunt Josie that now we were no longer a family, that family was what everybody needed, she told me some families were worse than having none at all, that it was better to be without than to be part of a strange one. Then she assured me she was speaking broadly only, didn't mean to say my family had been so bad I was better off without it. So I was confused and angry at the whole passel of grown-ups who were not able to give me one solid reason for the split. Another thing I was was embarrassed. How many people got divorced and continued to live in the same house? When my friends asked about it—"Is it true that Butcher and his wife still live together?"—even laughed about it, I told them it made perfect sense. I had cast around for an explanation and come up with a good one, one that made some of the girls cry, one even the boys and the snotty kids who laughed at me could accept. I said, "They both want to be close to me," and though I knew they loved me, I knew that wasn't it. They weren't normal for divorced parents, and I would've been better off with creepy renters.

For as long as I continued to live at home, for six more years, I lived downstairs and carried Dad's breakfast and dinner trays up to him. He told me to tell Mom the stew was good, or she made a nice omelet. Sometimes he wasn't so complimentary. "Tell her the meat loaf was too dry," he'd say. "Ask her why she's so heavy-handed with the salt." And his meat-cutter expertise would come to the fore. "Bottom round is as tasty as top round," he'd say. "Remind your mother not to waste so much money." Or "Tell her never to dry-cook brisket. She should know better." His phone number was on the top of the pad by our phone, though I don't think we ever called him. After I moved out, Mom took the meals up herself, seldom talking to him about anything except his appetite and what he may want for dinner.

Neither of them dated again, as far as I could tell. "What would be the point?" Mom said when I asked her why. "I know

I'm still beautiful, so I don't need some man to tell me, to make me feel desirable. Anyway, Catholics can't re-marry. As if I would want that again." It was my personal mystery, my puzzle to solve, finding out why they divorced, what went wrong, whose idea it had been. Had he grown tired of her primping? Her high pitched laugh? Had she been sickened by the dried blood on his work aprons? Did he squeeze the toothpaste from the wrong end? Later, I had two divorces of my own to figure out.

I was writing POISON on a piece of cardboard I'd torn off a box of crackers when Bev came back down. "This soup may be lethal," I said.

"Deposition's been postponed for six or eight weeks," Bev said. She sat on the stool nearest the cash register, and twirled like Toby had. "The Hilkers are on an African safari. When they get back, Howard's going to Provence, then the Hilkers'll be in Alaska."

"Maybe we should go somewhere," I said.

"Poor Maddie. They say I encouraged reckless behavior. Howard believes we will have a real fight on our hands."

"Shit," I said. "The suit is bogus." My cousin, probably a virgin at thirty-five, was called a promoter of sexual intercourse among the young, and not just intercourse, but unprotected, dangerous intercourse. She now had to fight back, prove she was not a wicked, deformed older woman who got her jollies by ruining the lives of fertile, young cuties. That Howard was not laughing was beyond me. Bev looked at my sign.

"Is that for me, or did your famous barbecue sauce take a wrong turn?"

"It's the soup," I said. "But what are you and Howard going to do?"

"Prove I'm a nice lady," she said. "Try to. I'm not sure I care enough." She flattened her thin lips back in an evil-looking smile, tilted her head so her fringe-like hair covered a side of her face. "Maybe I should just go ahead and be bad."

"It could be good for business," I said. "Come and eat food cooked by a degenerate, a corrupter of youth. Take a chance."

"The Hilkers could end up with the business. It will be the Maddie and Child Café. If you ever learn to cook, can stop creating poison, they may hire you."

I knew she was teasing, but I couldn't let it lie. I had to defend my cooking. "No one can make good soup from bad chicken."

She sighed again, spun herself all the way around. "No one wanted it anyway."

A customer entered, then, a young woman in her early twenties with stringy, black hair that grazed her shoulders. She was dressed like a nun who thinks she looks like a lay person—a brown polyester A-line skirt, a reddish-orange sleeveless blouse with a Peter Pan collar, and navy blue Keds at the ends of her skinny bare white legs. "You still serving?"

"No," Bev said, but I said "Yes" at the same time.

"Okay," Bev said. "Want some soup?"

"Yuck," the woman said. "Don't you have sandwiches?"

She took the stool next to Bev's and ordered an egg salad with extra chips and a large iced tea. She swiveled back and forth, too, but the two of them were so out of sync, I gave myself a headache watching them. When I closed my eyes, I saw bright splotches of color—oranges and greens and purples—on the inside of my lids.

"Do you do much business?" the woman asked Bev.

"Tons," Bev said. "Gobs. Bunches."

"Are many of your customers children?"

"Scads," Bev said. "We have children coming out of our ears."

"I'm checking up on the boy I told you about before."

"What boy?" I asked as I set the plate down before the woman.

"She's been snooping around in here before," Bev said to me. "When you were at the market or somewhere."

"African-American," the woman said. "Sort of ugly. Big glasses."

"This is Miss Something or Other," Bev said to me. "From some agency or another. I've forgotten."

"Lemp," the woman said. "Jeannie Lemp."

"She's a sneak," Bev said. "She spends her time spying on children, writing things up about them. I think she loves her work."

"I'm a social worker," the woman said to me. She reached across the counter for my hand. "And I do love my work."

I took her hand. It was dry, felt like the parched earth of an August ball field. I wanted to rub vitamin E into it, wondered how she let it get so bad. "What do you want to know?"

"Does someone like that boy ever come in here?"

"Yes," Bev said. "Someone like him does come in."

"Well then," Jeannie the social worker said, "That's all I needed to know. How often?"

"Someone like him comes in every day," Bev said. "Sometimes there are two like him at once."

"I have a right to ask questions," Jeannie the social worker said. "It is my job."

"I don't have to answer," Bev said. "I don't have a job."

"I need to turn in reports. There's no need to be difficult."

"Au contraire," Bev said. "There is always need to be difficult."

I thought of Toby as Bev's in some sense, not mine at all, so I knew I had to let Bev handle Jeannie the social worker, hoped she'd eventually explain all. Jeannie the social worker ate in silence then, and ate fast, too, as Bev sat beside her and glared. After Jeannie left, Bev told me it was a trick she had mastered while teaching. "If a student is likely to give you grief, you know, one of those you've had it up to here with, you look at her and think, 'you are a worthless white worm. Every word out of your mouth is foul.' You can even smile while you think it. Eventually, she'll slither away."

"Back to the Maddie business," I said.

"My corrupting ways?" She slid off the stool, carried Jeannie the social worker's plate to the dishwasher.

"Yes," I said. I wiped the counter as I talked. She re-arranged what was in the dishwasher, never happy with the way I loaded it. "Doesn't this seem like one of those silly dreams?"

"My dreams are better than this."

"How do you know what to do when what is real doesn't make sense?"

"Weep, weep," she said before she turned on the dishwasher. "Like Blake's poor little chimney sweep. My students used to cry along with him. I laughed. If we're happy, God makes us miserable."

But I barely listened to her answer. Of course, I knew the poor-little-me routine, the self-derision taught to all of us by our mothers to keep our self pity at bay.

"You want sense," Bev said. "Logic. May as well want peace on earth, happily ever after." She opened the back door. "Here comes Mike."

He sort of slid in, slinking around, leaning on the stove and the chopping block at once as if he were liquid. "How dee do, How dee do?" he said. "What can I take off your hands today?"

"Have some soup," I said, and as Bev walked by on the way to the refrigerator, she took a short detour, stepped on my toes with her fake foot. She ignored my yelp.

"Could you take a few sandwiches?" she asked.

"I guess I could find room for them."

I said it along with Mike, having heard it nearly every day, at least his sober days, then I hummed loudly as I cut in front of Bev to go upstairs. I hummed the song she had told me not to last time, "Hallelujah, I'm a bum." Sometimes I did "La Cucaracha."

By the time I had climbed the steep, uneven back steps, I was back on that Maddie Hilker business. I decided if we got some good reviews, we could become trendy, camp, maybe get our names mentioned in the local gossip columns. If so, we'd be well known, and well known was harder to knock down, trample on, especially by the Hilkers who, I now knew, liked being thought of as trendy. An African safari. Alaska. They were that easy to type. I had already sent three e-mails to the *Post-Dispatch* suggesting a review but had not even received the courtesy of a reply. It was time to make a phone call, which I did. I pressed all the right buttons at each menu and finally was allowed to leave a message for the food and entertainment writers. I said our barbecue sauce was outstanding, one of our claims to fame. I said we were helping to revitalize the city, said we attracted a mix of professionals (Jeannie the social worker) and locals.

After that, I took two aspirins for my headache, then stretched out on my bed, appreciating the power of my new window unit at full blast. I remembered I was supposed to do something with Roger that evening. I reminded myself that Roger was perfectly nice, and could hear Dad say nice just didn't cut it. Nice was not a substitute for fun, for passion, not a reason to be alive. Dad used to yell about it when Mom said he was (or was not) nice. That was Dad's way, ranting, carrying on, at least in those years we were together before the up and down division. And before he got so odd, Dad *was* nice. He was willing to please if able, driving me and my friends around when we were younger, teaching us to play poker on rainy Saturdays. Well, Roger is nice, too, I told myself, talking to Bev in my head. She answered that his so-called facts and studies were usually bogus or only a small part of the story and so should offend my mind. I agreed, but told her I found his confidence in his facts endearing. I didn't tell her, not in our imaginary conversation or in reality, that after I told him about the Hilker's lawsuit, calling it that tootsie case, he told me about one he knew of, a man who sued his former babysitter for sitting around in her underwear. She took the sitter part of the word literally, Roger joked. The guy claimed she had made it difficult for him to have any kind of normal or healthy sexual relations once he was grown. The guy sued his parents, too, for hiring the sitter, and, according to Roger, he won both suits.

I wanted to rest, but couldn't, and it wasn't thoughts of Roger that kept me up. It was the review. I couldn't stop thinking about the newspaper write-up. Was there anything not to like about us? Sometimes the critic visited twice, and I was glad we had enough variety to our menu for that. Often the owner was written up as well as the place. In this case only one owner but two of us running it, and we could get equal billing. Maybe photos. The critic may be tempted to refer to my beauty, and if so, I would have to tell him not to write anything that would leave Bev out, make her feel ugly. I'd steer his attention back to my barbecue sauce, her pies with the meringues three inches high. "The food is the star," I was saying to the reviewer, not truly asleep but more like daydreaming ,when Bev pounded harder than she had to on my door.

"Arise, look alive," she said. "The answer man is here."

BEV

I felt needles of heat prick my shoulders, arms, cheekbones, pierce my joints, tendons, cartilage. Every capillary expanded. The rough, pebbled cement I sat on poked me through my knit pants, but I wouldn't feel it for long: my ass was already growing numb. Sitting still, I was as inconspicuous as possible, just another fat and ugly woman taking a load off. It was a hotter June than most, and those tiny lawns in my neighborhood had turned brown, were overtaken by a creeping weed we called hog grass; dust was carried from stoop to stoop by the hot, morning winds and washed into the street by the evening thunderstorms. In between, the afternoons were still, rarely a leaf moving.

A week earlier as I'd stood in the entrance of Mike's garage and listened to a mournful rendition of "Please Check Your Book Again." Mike had interrupted himself. "Step all the way in," he'd said. "Come into the cool shade. You sweat a lot for a woman." I remembered that as I sat on the cement wall catty-corner from St. Hedwig's schoolyard, watching Toby and feeling the tributaries flow down from my scalp.

I knew Toby'd seen me, had almost waved to me when he'd stood beneath the basket for his free throw. If he'd followed through, I would've waved back. This was a day camp he'd said he had been signed up for, typically not saying who signed him up. I knew from Jeannie Lemp his was a foster-care situation, but between the two of them, I had no real information. And that wasn't why I watched him. I wasn't like that insipidly dull social worker who convinced herself she was meddling for his own good when it was really for hers, to make herself feel righteous and valuable, or to earn a meager paycheck, or maybe both. No one had a right to dissect and examine the troubles of any other human being without offering her own life to be dissected and regulated in turn. I knew it had to be tit for tat. But I was not examining Toby's troubles. I wanted merely to watch. I wondered how he played.

My maternal yearnings were zero. What so many other women called a need, pissed and moaned about, bought the eggs and sperm of outsiders for, took drugs to promote, accepted Papal blessings and made novenas for, eluded me. Chickie had a theory that our mothers, the original Stillwell beauties, had all made motherhood seem such a hardship, none of us wanted it. She said Chuck claimed Aunt Peg often told him straight out how surprised she was he had reproduced, thinking him too smart to have children. And Chickie said her own son, Hilton, was not only a mistake, but one Aunt Peg seemed still discouraged by. "Of course, we all love Hilton," Aunt Peg had said to Chickie as recently as Hilton's thirteenth birthday, "but you cannot deny he's an example of how long and heavily some people have to pay for their mistakes. I mean, he's been a burden to you for all these years and will be one for a good while longer."

Shelly laughed when Chickie told us that, as if laughter could make Aunt Peg's attitude harmless, reduce it to eccentric and misunderstood speech, but then Shelly herself admitted her childlessness seemed programmed into her. She did think it a bit sad, though, there would be no third generation of Stillwell beauties. Well, I knew I'd always been a burden, knew they all tried hard to pretend I was no such thing.

Besides that, I knew overpopulation was a problem, and I told myself that even if a man would ever love me enough to make me his present and his future, I wouldn't add a child to the mix. I'd been disappointed often at girlfriends who claimed social consciences, but after they married, sooner or later had burrowed so deeply into domestic bliss that the outside world ceased to exist, who began procreating like bunnies who see the warren as the whole world.

So I didn't want to be anyone's mother, and especially not Toby's. But was there a name for the part I wanted in his life? Whatever it was—friend or counselor or protector or lover—I was caught. He had reached in with his small grubby hands and sunk his fingers into my heart muscle, knotted them around the valves and through the chambers.

Well, he may have been the ugliest child ever. And he was small and frail but also tough and wiry. He had probably been discarded but eventually had been found again, was being cared for after a fashion. What was his hold on me? I wondered, not really caring if I found the answer or not.

It was a Wednesday afternoon. There'd been the usual lunch crowd, maybe eight all told. When I left, I told Shelly I was taking a walk, needed a break from the hot stove, and she protested a bit, reminded me we often had a late afternoon rush. I shook my head at that and she laughed.

A rush? She meant we sometimes had two or three city/water company/gas company workers take their afternoon break with us, sipping coffee and wishing they were someplace more exciting. I told her she could smile and flirt and handle the rush by herself. Or not. She could close up if she felt like it. The café was not a hit but rather a losing endeavor that grew duller by the day.

My sitting on a three-foot-high cement wall around the retirement apartments catty-corner from St. Hedwig's school yard would've confused Shelly. I doubted she'd sensed my connection to Toby any more than she'd sensed Richard's growing unhappiness and distance, the look he wore in the last year they were together of something left unasked and therefore unanswered. She claimed his leaving shocked her, and she said she'd been shocked when her parents divorced, too, but the rest of us saw both of those coming. On the other hand, if I told her about the pull Toby had on me, she'd be all agog with hope and plans, would think Toby could become my meaning, give me reasons to smile.

After watching Toby for twenty minutes or so, picking out the quiet laugh of his that came just a fraction of a second after the other laughs, that lasted a touch too long, I thought his lot not a bad one. His laugh, though slow, was genuine. A few of the other children spoke to him; one boy grabbed him by the arm in a kind of running game, and another whispered in his ear. One boy on the opposite team in some game involving a kick ball, tried to trip him but Toby zigged out of the way, looking almost graceful. They were treating him like a normal kid. He was not chosen last. When he made his free throw earlier, someone shouted "lucky shot." No, there was nothing pathetic about him being in this place and time.

As I watched and listened, a young woman joined me, sat down beside me on my wall, and started talking. "Hot, huh?" she said.

I looked at her and agreed it was indeed hot. She was skinny. A limp, dishwater-blonde ponytail clung to her back, and thick orangish makeup almost covered the pimples on her chin. Her shorts were tiny and pink, and her legs were as thin and supple as new spring sycamore shoots. "Heat makes me puke," she said. "Don't know why."

I nodded, then looked away.

"Which one is yours?" she asked. "Mine's the squirt on the trampoline."

I turned back, looked closer at her then, trying to see a line, a set of her lips, a hint of bone structure under what though thin was still a baby face, smooth as putty. The child she claimed was at least eight, and I decided she must have been younger even than Maddie when she conceived. I wondered who had been her bad influence.

"None are mine," I said. "I'm watching one, though. That slightly built black boy by the fence." I pointed with my finger.

She laughed. "You sound like one of those weirdos TV tells us to watch out for. A strange woman spying on a little boy she likes. You're not, are you? A weirdo?"

"No," I said. "Course, I'd say no if I was one, too."

"Right." She laughed again, this time nervously.

I caused grievous harm. Was a very bad influence. A tear in our moral fabric. I heard the whistle then, knew this was the part Toby'd told me about. All the day campers were called together for a short talk on sportsmanship and working together, followed by a few group songs.

"They'll do 'Johnny Appleseed'," my wall companion said. "Jeffrey says the kids laugh all during 'Johnny Appleseed.' I mean, that one was corny when I was a camper."

"I think they're supposed to be corny," I told her. "What else do you want at camp?" I knew the great clump of children would break apart suddenly and soon. I didn't know if Toby would acknowledge me or not, and I didn't care, knew I'd see him at the café in a half hour. Just in case he wanted to walk with me, though, I decided to stand. I had to make sure both feet that dangled just above the sidewalk were lined up and facing forward. Then I had to scoot forward until I could launch myself off the wall, land on my feet. It wasn't hard, just took some checking, lining up of parts.

"What's happening?" the young mother said just as I was scooting into position. I thought she meant me, but when I looked up, I saw the mass of bodies surge closer, then break apart, then surge in again, pulsing like one organism. Soon a piece broke off, grew larger as it moved across the schoolyard toward us. It was Toby. He was running, stumbling into the street, crying. He ran right to me, buried his face in my lap.

"They say I stole Scott's lunch," he said, his words strangely clear even though he spoke into my thighs. "He gave it to me. That's the truth. Just because I said it was good, he changed his mind. I couldn't give it back. I ate it."

Without thinking, I stroked his head, caressed the hollow space behind his ear with my sole finger.

"They say I can't come back until I apologize. But I didn't do anything wrong."

I felt the coldness of a familiar anger, not white hot but like a steel bar, stiff and lifeless. I'd been here before. Everyone wanted apologies. Apologies were in vogue. I pushed Toby away just enough so I could again point my feet right and drop off the wall, then, still holding him by a wrist, I pulled him across the street, up the sidewalk alongside the cyclone fence, and into the school yard. We went directly up to the leader, a chubby redhead in baggy denim shorts and a red T-shirt, sweat-stained and untucked. Except for his mustache, half red and half gray, he looked like a larger version of the other kids. I stood directly in front of him, touched his arm to get his attention. "Have you any reason not to believe this boy here?"

He looked from me to Toby and back to me, wrinkling his brow. "Have I any reason to discuss this with you? Who are you?"

"A friend."

He rolled his eyes.

"More than a friend," I said. "A sort of guardian, kind of a counselor."

"I know his guardian," the old camper said. "I know some of his counselors. You aren't any of them and never would be. They're trying to get rid of this cross-cultural stuff."

"Toby does not steal." At least I hoped he did not. "Why would you assume the worst?"

"Look," the overgrown kid said. He sighed, rubbed his hand over his mustache. "It's none of your business, but just to get rid of you, I'll explain it. This is the third time he's been accused by one of the other campers. We're a poor school, a poor parish, but if he needs a lunch, and clearly he does, he has to ask. I'd give him my sandwich if he'd only ask for it."

"Is that all? Lunch?" I was relieved. This was an easy problem to solve. Lunch was what I did. I could feed the whole day camp if I had to. I'd see that Toby got fed. I'd deliver it myself every day, throw in a pie or two for all the campers. I said as much to the leader, but he shook his head, unmoved.

"He has to apologize. We're in the character-building business. You can bring lunch if you want to, but Toby has to learn to ask for what he needs, to say he's sorry for his mistakes."

"No," Toby said. He had been quiet so far, standing limply beside me, but now he pulled on my arm. "Let's go. I'm not sorry because I didn't do anything."

"Someone should have built you a character," I said to the leader as Toby nearly pulled me off my good foot.

"Same for you," he said, but seemed to remember he was Christian, and added he would pray for all of us. I turned before he finished speaking, then stomped the three blocks to the café, pulling Toby behind me all the way. When we passed the young woman still sitting on the wall, her son beside her as if they were watching a play, she spoke. "No one ever believes it when you say you're innocent. Just makes everyone pick on him more."

We kept going, the two of us, knowing she was right, but pretending we hadn't heard.

When we got back to the café, I gave Toby a barbecued beef sandwich and two slices of coconut cream pie, as much milk as he wanted. "Scott's lunch was not good," he said between gulps of milk. "I just said that."

Shelly was in the kitchen, leaning against the stove. Her eyes were wide opened and her lips pursed, and I knew she was dying to solve a problem, maybe had gone all day without one, so I told her the story, glossing over why I had been there in the first place.

"Good for you," Shelly said to Toby when I got to the part about his refusing to apologize. "None of us stand up for ourselves enough."

"I wanted to make him see what he'd lost," Toby said.

"Who?" Shelly asked.

"What's with all this apology stuff anyway?" I asked. "It's like making someone cry uncle."

"Scott," Toby said to Shelly. "He laughed because I wanted his stinking tuna sandwich. It smelled rotten. So I said it was good, yum, yum. Good stuff." He rolled his eyes behind his thick lenses, then giggled. Shelly laughed, too.

"I'm afraid to go home," Toby said when he stopped laughing. "Think I'll stay here." And he did. Well, of course, I didn't say yes, okay, good idea. I knew a ten-year-old couldn't decide where to stay, and Shelly was all for calling the cops, reporting him to someone who should've been worried, maybe finding Jeannie Lemp in the phone book and calling her at home. I told her, though, we would just wait and see. Not only did I want to keep that busy-body social worker from getting all worked up in our lives, but Toby's *I'm afraid* worried me. I didn't know how seriously to take it. Mike came by for leftovers just after closing as he usually did when he was sober, and this time he seemed more than merely sober—logical and able to think of something besides his own misery. When he heard the story, he said kids needed someone to stand up for them, said Toby would remember this always, said wherever Toby lived, chances were he wasn't believed and would be punished again for stealing a lunch when one time was enough for a tuna sandwich, even if he had done it. And the tuna had been spoiled besides.

A half hour later, all four of us were lined up on the orange couch, watching the five o'clock news closely for mention of a search for a lost boy, of a family frantic and suspecting foul play. Nothing. But when the phone rang, I jumped, imagining the camp leader had described me, had tracked us down. It was only Roger for Shelly.

When I overheard her tell Roger what was going on, I thought at least we weren't hiding him, and if someone really wanted to track him down, his whereabouts would be easy to discover, blabbed all over the airwaves as they were. And if no one wanted him, it was just as well he stayed with us. When Shelly got off the phone and said Roger said I should go over the fat leader's head to the pastor or to the Archdiocesan summer school and camp office or whatever it was called, and I should be the one to get an apology, I agreed, but knew I would not. The words were easy, and people gave advice out as if it were air or water, essential but nearly free. Predictably, most of it was worthless. As far as science had discovered, humans were the only beings capable of rational thought, of using reason, and that was precisely what was wrong with humanity. Our thoughts were inane, our solutions just so much wind, what we called reason little more than platitudes or excuses.

After the five o'clock news, Mike stood, stretched his arms up toward the ceiling so his dirty, black jeans slid further down his missing hips, and exhaled loudly. "I'll go, leave, as Mama always said, before anyone wants me to." He had set the box of leftovers from the café on the kitchen table, was planning to go out that way and down the back steps, but when I didn't follow him out, see him to the door as usual, he stood still. He shifted his weight, standing on one foot, then the other, shuffling. He coughed. "There's one more thing," he said. "I may want a beer to wash this down with. Ease the pains in my legs and help me sleep, too."

"Water works for that," Shelly said, and I gave her what I hoped was a shut-up look.

I hated hearing someone like Mike, so clearly on the bottom of the pile, beg, explain, ask, and lie. I pushed myself up, led Mike into the kitchen. "Here," I said. I opened the top drawer of the tin cabinet closest to the sink where I kept my cash. I handed him a five, thinking I was either being good and generous with him by giving him more than he expected, or I was contributing to his illness, hastening his death by giving him enough to get sick on. Of course, he wasn't a child, and it wasn't my place to control him. He was not my mission.

After he left and I plopped back down on the scratchy, orange sofa, Shelly remembered to tell me Mom had been by when I was out sitting on the cement wall. Mom had run into a sale at Dillard's, so had bought me a half dozen knit summer shirts, some boat neck, some crew, all washable and good for wearing in the café. Shelly had told Mom the shirts were nice, but we were planning on wearing the same thing when we worked, the two of us, a color scheme she had not decided on yet, but maybe khaki pants and black T-shirts. Nevertheless, she'd told Mom one could never have too many summer tops.

I nodded. I knew Mom knew better than to pay much attention to her niece Shelly and her plans of a unified look in the café. I knew we'd both just wear whatever we wanted, anytime. After all, the café was an imitation of freedom.

Toby and I were watching a rerun of a sitcom he had seen before about a wealthy Black family with a know-it-all father when Shelly left an hour later.

I told Toby I didn't cook except in the café but would order a pizza for us, a super supreme deluxe from Mama Parenti's, which I did. While we were waiting for our pizza, I sorted through the Dillard's bag, holding up one shirt after the other, asking Toby what color he liked best. "I like green best," he said. "The color of money."

I held the green one up against him, and though it was much too large, it looked good on him, the sort of willow green making him look more trustworthy than the faded purple Batman T-shirt he was wearing.

"You know," he said. "Those won't help. Won't do you no good at all."

"No?" I said. "What do you mean? Good for what?"

"You'll still look like you. It needs more than a pretty color to make you pretty."

"You're right." Of course he was, but it hurt. "You know that was rude, don't you? No matter if it is true."

He shrugged. "You know I stole that sandwich."

I wasn't sure I had known, but I was not surprised. What I was surprised at though was his wounding me that way, his trying to. Surprised, confused, deflated: I was all of those. And angry. Mostly and surprisingly angry. If this were a game, I would play it, too, and better than he could even imagine. "Let me put it this way," I said. "I'll let you sleep here tonight. I'll feed you pizza, give you breakfast. You don't seem to have lots of choices. Not too many others, I notice, are standing in line to be nice to you." I looked at him, slouched in a corner of the sofa. He was studying the N stitched on the sides of his shoes. "But I want you to tell me you're sorry. You did not mean to say that to me."

He wiggled his feet, knocked his high-top court shoes one against the other. "You'll never be pretty. Not in a million years."

"One-hundred percent beside the point," I said. "I'm not asking you to say I'm pretty. I want you to say you're sorry for bringing it up in the first place."

The doorbell rang. I looked out and down, saw the delivery car double-parked on Meramec. "I can pay him, tell him to keep the pizza and eat it himself. I will, too."

The doorbell rang again. "It's very good pizza." I said. "Too bad."

"Okay," he said, looking up at the gold-framed mirror Shelly had hung between the windows and not at me. "I'm sorry I was rude."

So I had won round one with a ten-year old. I'd gotten from him what he'd refused to give at camp and what I'd refused to give at Agnus Dei. I had made him say something he didn't mean.

When I set the pizza out on the kitchen table, I realized the anger I was already ashamed of was still alive even if unwanted. I was determined to be merely fair, no more. So I ate as fast as he did to keep up, piece to piece. I took the pieces with the biggest pepperoni slices, the most cheese. Aggressive eating, defensive eating, whatever it was called, showed me a side of myself I'd looked away from most of my life.

Toby and I barely spoke the rest of the evening. I told him he should thank me for the pizza, so he mumbled "thanks" as he left the table. We watched TV—cop dramas and game shows—for a few hours, and I tried not to think about me at all. We watched the ten o'clock news, but still no reports of a missing child. I believed Toby wanted to be looked for, wished someone missed him, and I knew he was a needy child and I was a petty adult and it was a blessing I'd never had children—God knew what he was doing when he made me ugly—or siblings for that matter. I was that much of a bitch.

Toby's comments about my lack of beauty should have rolled off, no sting. After all, I was the one ugly duckling in a family of beauties. The genetic dice had come up snake-eyes for me and there was Mother's Help besides. Shelly wondered—not to me of course, but out loud to her mother, to Chickie, to Aunt Peg, and it came back to me—why I didn't take my money and have plastic surgery. I could create a new face, new body, could make myself a close approximation of a Stillwell beauty. A bit off the nose, a bit off the brow, a greater distance between the eyes, a delicate chin, a shapely neck, small and straight shoulders, a lot of fat sucked out of everywhere, a weave or a hair transplant, tanning beds for a healthy glow—I could afford all that. None of it was impossible.

But I had built my life on a phrase I'd convinced myself had merit: "Looks don't count." I'd said it to myself each morning of my life from as far back as my eighth or ninth year, maybe earlier. In high school I wrote it in a notebook ten times each morning, a ritual I practiced so the idea would spread throughout the world, and I wouldn't be the only one who accepted its truth. By my twenties I did believe it, and by my thirties I no longer cared. I was the looker now, not the thing looked at. I was the subject, not the object. I had no interest in what others saw when they looked at me. If I was ugly, well, tough view for them. I saw out. I judged the lot of them, came to a few conclusions myself. Mean women, for example, grew into their personality, developed jowls that gave them the bulldog look to go along with the fighting spirit they'd been born with. Men without convictions slumped as they aged, their lack of backbones finally revealing their true natures. And no matter the sting in words spoken by a child, ugly himself for that matter, ugliness was my lot, long ago accepted.

Toby fell asleep on the sofa, the television still on, late night folks with miseries yelling at one another on stage. I was restless. I left the living room, sat at the kitchen table and watched the play of lights in the alley caused by passing traffic. When the doorbell sounded, I was happy for a break, even though I expected the police. It was Mike.

"Here's what you should know," he said.

I let him in, something I had vowed to myself never to do when he was, as he said, drunk-dog crazy. But I was eager for a diversion, and he was at least that. I helped him up the stairs, led him back to the kitchen, and as soon as he plopped down in a kitchen chair, his legs tangled with the table leg, he put his head back, and let the tears flow. "I have no excuse for being alive," he said. "Why should someone as worthless as me be here or anywhere?"

"I know the feeling," I said. "To what good is this consciousness connected to this body to make this being? What's the big idea?"

"You don't know," he said. "You're a fine person. I'm a bum."

"Should people be judged by whether or not they earn a living? Surely you contribute to the world as much as someone who works, as much as a stockbroker, a cook, a musician. I mean, you have a place, right? If any of us do." I wasn't drunk, but still wanted to play about with what masqueraded as big questions. I could safely talk all that garbage with Mike. He wouldn't listen, and even if he did, wouldn't remember.

"People should be judged by how many times they've killed," he said.

"Well, they are. Some of them are put to death themselves, locked up."

"People are bastards."

"Is that what you came to tell me?" I was hoping he'd say something funny.

"It's true," he said.

"None of us have fathers?"

"I've killed people. I've killed animals. I killed Mama."

"You are despicable," I said, thinking I may mean it.

"I'm worthless."

"You already said that."

"I'm evil."

"The very definition."

"Shoot me," he said. "Please. Go ahead. You really should do it, do something for the world."

"My pleasure. Where's the gun?"

"I'm worthless," he said. "Worthless."

"Don't repeat yourself," I said.

"What do you think I am? What am I? I want you to tell me."

"Worthless," I said.

"That's it. You got it. I am worthless. How did you know?"

He sat at my table for at least an hour, unable to pass out. I gave him all three beers I had, then a glass of chardonnay, then another. I had two glasses myself, and the bottle was almost empty. He was unconscious, but his body didn't know it. Once I left the table, decided to let him talk to himself, but he eventually realized I was gone, tried to follow me into the living room, but tripped himself up on the table leg, fell face down on the kitchen floor. I helped him up, almost ending up down there with him in the process, and still he kept going. When I righted him, he went through the list one more time of how many people and animals he had killed. He said he knew he'd go straight to hell, and that was fine, what he deserved. Said he was looking forward to it.

"Give me the flames," he yelled, and I was afraid he'd wake Toby, so I sat down beside him, asked him to go over it all again, to tell me whom he'd killed. I'd known him for a few months, that was all, but did not believe he had killed any of those he listed—the high school football coach, the two bums under the bridge, the woman who ran off with his father, his sister's cat, his half-brother, someone named Wolf—but I believed the desire could be enough, that what with his short-circuited brain, *want to* could change to *did*. And the truth was if he had killed them all, what was it to me. I wished he had done more, told myself he wouldn't have been so monotonous if his list were longer.

After listing his victims for about the fifth time, he leaned back in the chair and, almost in mid-name, started to snore. I poured myself the quarter inch of chardonnay left in the bottle and sat across from him, listening to the breath that got trapped behind his nose try to escape. He was ruined, true. But the torture he lived with was not much greater than what those around him suffered. He was getting back at the world, in a sense, by inflicting himself on others. I supposed we non-ruined could take it, pretend it was a bad dream, or no worse than a root canal. But then I thought we were all ruined, one kind of ruination not substantially worse than others.

When Shelly and Roger came home a bit after midnight, I was still sitting across from Mike, and Mike was still gasping and choking in what passed for sleep. Roger half carried and half dragged him into the living room, Mike talking to us then, saying "We can't forget the bastards, okay? Don't forget the bastards." Roger let Mike collapse, drop like a duffel bag, onto the carpet a few feet from the orange sofa Toby slept on. I looked at Toby's eyes moving like jumping beans behind his lids and, satisfied he was sound asleep, went to my bed for a pillow for Mike. I lifted Mike's head to position the pillow underneath, and his eyes shot open, then closed quickly. "Thanks," he said.

"When did this become the Sunshine Mission?" Shelly asked, and giggled. "When you took me in, your sad and lonely cousin, did it go so well you decided to expand?"

Roger laughed with her, and she wrapped an arm around his waist. Still sort of bending over Mike, I looked up at them, the ceiling light making his bald head shine, and knew I could say she seemed to be opening a branch of the Sunshine Mission herself, giving losers like Roger a place to stay. But instead, I said I had not chosen either of the two sleeping in the living room, had not invited either to stay over. I had been chosen.

The following morning, Shelly and I were halfway through the breakfast business when we heard Roger and Mike clump down the back steps together. Mike moaned loudly all the way across the alley to his place, and moments later a dirge-like version of "Jesus Wants Me for a Sunbeam" filled the neighborhood. Toby came down and into the kitchen a little after ten, and I took him to St. Hedwig's day camp. Neither of us mentioned the night before, or had much to say at all on the ride over. I told him I'd bring lunch, and he said okay. When we arrived, the campers were already working on a craft project involving weaving strips of leather for what I guessed were belts, and Toby went right up to the leader and apologized for stealing and lying. "I don't know what comes over me," he said. "I will try to be better." The leader embraced Toby, and led him over to the craft tables. Toby didn't turn toward me, but the leader looked back over his shoulder and scowled. I left then, but when I got to the café, I loaded up my car with roast beef sandwiches and Bavarian cream pies, got it all there in plenty of time for lunch.

That afternoon, Howard Figg called and told me the Hilker's attorney, Donna Wicher, would take depositions in her office in two days. He'd call and schedule a time, then pick me up and take me there. He would be with me the whole time, he assured me, as if I would trip myself up, get tricked into admitting my harmful ways without his interference. Because this idiocy was progressing at all, because adult and relatively sane people like Howard and Donna Wicher were not laughing so hard their sides hurt, I was beginning to think I had harmed Maddie and was just so out of step I would never recognize that harm. But when he told me about Agnus Dei, I remembered the kinds of people Maddie came from and changed my mind. The school, he said, had been sued, too, separately, for employing me, and had settled out of court. They were afraid of bad publicity, Howard explained, and I knew they had found some wealthy parents of a low intellect girl, parents who under other circumstances would have built a gym rather than donate the fines to pay off the Hilkers. Probably the Pattersons, I guessed, or maybe the Gilliams, parents of twins who each stared vacantly into their opened textbooks, squinting occasionally at the big words. Shelly told me that Jeannie Lemp had been back in while I was on the phone, but she had merely ordered coffee and a slice of pie—Thank God I hadn't taken all the slices to St. Hedwig's camp, Shelly said—eaten it, and left. She had not asked about me or Toby.

At 2:30, four gas company workers came in to take their breaks, to drink coffee and flirt with Shelly, and a young couple came in soon after. The man was just barely thirty I guessed, sandy hair, full but slicked down to give him a gangster look. His jeans and chambray shirt looked new, and his sandals were the expensive leather kind with padded backs and thick brass buckles you saw in catalogs. She had blonde hair, probably highlighted, and wore dusty rose colored capri pants and a white silk shell. She had tiny gold hoops in her ears, and he wore one gold ball in his left ear. They were not our usual crowd. The woman carried a notebook, took notes even before they ordered.

Shelly was sure they were food critics, but I told her we were not the kind of place that would be reviewed, and besides the food critic for the Post was an older guy with a meaty face.

"Well," she said in her usual way of coming up with an explanation for anything she wanted to be true, "they probably didn't send their main critic to us, we're so new and small. They probably sent the new kids just trying to break into food criticism."

As usual, she convinced herself she was right, and took special pains with their glasses of water—putting lemon slices in the water which we didn't always do—and their flatware—checking for spots left by the dishwasher, wiping a knife on her slacks before taking it out to them. I think she had the nerve to ask what they were writing, hoping they'd confess, but from what I could tell by the exchange, they told her, politely of course, it was private. Nevertheless, when the woman ordered the barbecue beef sandwich and the man asked for the special, another of her quiches, this one spinach, she was even more convinced they were what she hoped. She told me to smile more, to talk nice to the gas company workers so we would come across as a friendly, relaxed place. One of the gas company workers ordered a slice of pie with his coffee, and I gave it to him, but Shelly was nearly hysterical when she realized it. "They will order pie. It's one of our specialties. They have to try it." She whispered so as not to make a scene, but that only made her hiss. The young couple looked up at us, as did the gas company worker, his slice of pie half eaten. "You took so many to Toby's camp, that we gave the last piece to that gas guy. Now what will we do? We can't say we're out, not to a critic."

"You don't know they are critics," I said. "Besides, won't it make us seem popular to be out of something?"

I could tell she was tempted to argue with me, to point out the flaws in my statement, by the way her mouth opened, and her eyes brightened. She was searching for the words when she changed her mind, said never mind, and ran out the back door and continued to run around to the front. Seconds later, I heard her car screech away from the front curb. I guessed, too, where she was going, and sure enough, in less than twelve minutes, she returned with a cream pie from the bakery a block up. It was banana, not Bavarian cream, and not as good as mine, she said. But then she shook her head and smiled. "No matter. This'll do the trick. I have no doubt."

Sure enough, the couple each ordered a slice, and they smiled as they took their first bites.

We closed up a few minutes after they left, and Shelly sat in their seats, looked around to see what they could have noticed that would've been negative. "What went wrong?" she asked. She said there were no cobwebs, no cracks in the plaster, no chips on the table top. All seemed in good order.

"Nothing went wrong," I said. She went into the kitchen and tasted her sauce again. "I know they liked that," she said. "How could they not? Are the buns fresh?"

"Yes," I said, but she took one out of the bread bag and poked it herself anyway. "When do you think they'll run it?"

I didn't know, and was tempted to ask her what difference it could possibly make. How could success or failure of the Alibi Café matter? But then she would ask why I ran the café in the first place, and we would have the same old discussion during which she would say something worth doing is worth doing well or something equally slogan worthy.

She finally went upstairs, but I hung around the downstairs a bit longer, looking through the door with the "closed" sign on it. This was the first time all summer Toby had not stopped by after camp, and I missed seeing his lopsided face and his under-nourished body perched on the end stool. I expected his report on how the lunch went over, how the other kids treated him after his apology. More than that, I was ready to apologize to him myself. I knew he recognized power struggles. I knew he knew I had played the bully.

But by five that evening, we were upstairs, just the two of us this time, and I worried harder about Toby. Was he in trouble with his foster parents for being AWOL the night before? Was he being punished, or was he making me suffer? What was he running from?

Shelly said the pie had cost $9.50 and since she'd used her own money, she'd reimburse herself from the cash drawer, not to be stingy, but to keep us straight. "I'd like an accurate profit and loss report for once," she said. "I don't care about the money, as you know. I buy all the stuff Toby sells with my own money."

Suit yourself, I told her, or something like that, knowing she was babbling so from the excitement of the possible review, or from some other forced hope she was dwelling in.

I was in the living room, but I heard her sudden and sharp intake of breath, like a backwards whistle, followed by silence, so I pushed myself up from the sofa and, because my foot had fallen asleep, wobbled into the kitchen. She was standing as if frozen, staring down into the opened drawer.

"Nothing," she said. "Not even one dollar." She turned to me and shook her head. "Son of a blind bitch," she said, hissing as she had earlier in the café. "One of your lost causes has cleaned you out."

SHELLY

Muggy days were the worst for my headaches. My temples throbbed so much I must've seemed to be nodding, maybe keeping time to a song playing inside my head. I wasn't worried, didn't seriously think tumor or hemorrhage, but I wanted the pains to stop. Number one on my daily to-do list was "Stop Headaches." Extra-strength pain killers were not extra enough.

"Think about something else, Shelly," I told myself. "Learn to live with it. Pain is part of life."

I knew I could conquer the pains by thinking about other things like how to increase our business, but I wanted a permanent and final cure. What had all the doctors and researchers been doing for all these centuries if they still could not cure a headache? Though I knew medicine was part voodoo and part luck and only a bit science, therefore the connections were often surprising discoveries, accidental.

For example, Candy Swendle, one of the Sue Spritz models who was best at runway work, for months had a sore on her chest, a tiny sore she first thought was a pimple until she decided it must be skin cancer because it wouldn't heal all the way. Her dermatologist had a bad feeling about it—he said he didn't know why—and he referred her to a specialist, and after many tests, it was discovered she had come in contact with a rare bacteria that was eating her flesh. Her life was saved, just barely to hear her tell it, all because of her doctor's unexplained bad feeling. The steroids and other injections caused Candy to swell like a crème puff, though, and within a month of her initial check-up, her modeling career was finished.

And Mom once had a childhood pal who lived with a brain tumor for more than twelve years before it was discovered and removed. Once his surgery was over, the young man in question had perfect vision, his nearsightedness caused all along by the tumor. I knew more stories like those. There was the case of our grade school bus driver whose mouth blisters had been caused by a dye in her shampoo that reacted poorly with her denture grip. Sure, the body was a puzzle, but I wasn't seeking the cause of my headaches, just their end.

The sad truth, though, my headaches aside, was that the rest of my body was no longer a source of delight either. One of Richard's tricks had been licking a line from behind my ear to the very nape of my neck, and that sent such tremors through me, I'd want to ride him down to the ground, straddle him, pump him, taste every inch of him. Roger, though, was a grabber. He started with my breasts, moved down to the source of my heat immediately, stroking and poking at my vagina. I'd told Bev Roger was a time filler, a time killer, and once or twice I'd been as annoyed as she by his know-it-all attitude. I would fall in love again. I knew that as well as I knew my heart would keep pumping and my blood would be forced through my veins for many more years. Roger was not my love object but was a step towards it. A bottom rung, a first step, a boost toward my destiny. But for the past week, I'd been repelled by any of his touches; the barest contact irritated and burned. There were no juices, and I'd told him not to spit on me to make me wet. I knew he had to go.

"I don't want to see you anymore," I said one sunny afternoon when he was the only customer. Not a kind or even interesting line. He was sitting on the center stool, kicking the counter, half finished with a slice of key lime pie, and talking about whether the city should go ahead and ante up the money for a new stadium for the Cardinals. He had figures of increased revenue and taxes that proved it would be a healthy investment, one of those things that made money in the long run no matter the initial outlay. "An extra one million in business revenue the first year alone," he said.

I wanted to tell him my German grandmother's belief that you never saved money by spending it, no matter what the bargain, and I wanted to ask him how a clerk at Auto World had come by all the budget figures, had grown into a financial genius. That last fake question that came suddenly to mind made me know I was dumping him not a moment too soon.

And I was envious, too, of his kicking. I used to kick my foot as I talked, could remember sitting at the dining table and kicking, swinging hard and wide when I got going, in the midst of an exciting story about my day in school or about one of my friends. The table shook with my exuberance, and every now and then I'd land a blow on Dad's shin, or Mom's. "Don't do that," they said. "Can't you eat like a civilized person?" they said. "It's just nervous energy. Channel it elsewhere." So I did. I guess I did. I stopped kicking, though I don't know where all that energy went. They were right, of course. Kicks in the shin are not to be taken lightly, and having gravy wiggle, then slosh over the sides of the bowl is not part of fine dining. And of course Roger was making marks on the counter even as he sat there. Yet I wondered. Hadn't I been more interesting then? Hadn't my mind and body, my thoughts and feelings, all worked in better harmony when I kicked? Where had that energy gone?

When Roger paused in his analyses of city budgets, I took a deep breath and told him we were through. I felt mean, hard, cold, all the things I knew deep down I was not.

"Why?" he asked.

A brave question, one few of us ever wanted the answer to. I shrugged. "Who can understand the workings of the heart?" I hid behind the truth, knowing I didn't understand the heart, and knowing, too, Roger had little to do with mine.

"I can change," he said. "Maybe we should talk more."

I shook my head.

"Are you sure?"

"I'm sure," I said.

"Well," he said as if deciding to be brave and get it over with, too, "I'll miss the pie." He stood up, leaned across the counter. "And much more. But I won't lie to you. I'm not heart-broken. You're not the love of my life." He sighed. "This is awkward. I'll probably be sadder as the day goes on."

"Me, too" I said. "And we'll still have pie."

He walked across the café, then turned at the door and gave me a two fingered salute. "You're probably the prettiest woman I'll ever have."

I knew that went without saying.

"You can always get a free slice of pie here." I watched the door for a while after it closed behind him.

I had thought we were alone, Roger and I, but when I turned around, Bev was in the kitchen. I didn't know how long she'd been there, and she gave no indication of having heard anything. She was packing a wicker basket. She had half of the key lime pie wrapped in foil already and was cutting thick slices of pastrami, laying them out on pumpernickel, then wrapping the whole thing in waxed paper. I looked in the basket and saw a bottle of sparkling grape juice, two of my good wine glasses from upstairs, and the red and white checked tablecloth Chickie had given her last Christmas. I had one, too, but mine was blue and white. I knew she was going on one of the picnics she'd been having with Mike lately. For the last three weeks, they'd been heading out to Carondolet Park a few evenings a week after we closed up. I cleaned up while she dined alfresco. She said it was friendlier than merely giving him some leftovers he would carry back home and eat all alone, though she still gave him leftovers on the evenings she didn't load her car and honk for him at the door of his garage. She said she would've invited me on the picnics, but I had such a hard time being polite to Mike, so this way was more fun for all three of us. Well, I'd known she had a soft spot, maybe even a preference, for the troubled and out of touch, but Mike was a step or two below troubled.

Besides, though I suspected Toby more, Mike may have been the one who took her money. Bev had refused to ask either of them, and had continued to take lunch to Toby's day camp, to feed him pie on those days he dropped in on his way home. She even bought some of the giant Tootsie Rolls he sold, telling us the money was for St. Hedwig's youth program. And even if Mike weren't the thief, he was a taker, taking food and comfort from Bev with no reciprocation at all, unless you could count irritation as something worth giving.

Bev smiled as she packed the basket, hummed one of those catchy tunes I knew had come from a forties musical, one that never would find its way out of my brain once it got in. After knowing her for thirty-five years, I never would have called Bev a smiler or a hummer, and I knew I should be happy for her and what Mike must have been adding to her life. But would I have been happy to watch a hungry woman eat half of a cheeseburger from a dumpster?

This afternoon, Bev wore her favorite red knit shirt, the one with three-quarter length sleeves and the ballet neck that broke up the line, the slope that went from her ears to her arms like a distant hillside. She wore white slacks, too, which she seldom did because no matter how many socks and wrappings she used, where her real leg joined her fake leg was always visible under white, and of course so was the hip belt and buckle. I almost commented on the white when I saw what she wore, but decided no matter what she looked like, Mike would be funnier looking—black jeans that floated around his hip bones, a T-shirt clinging to his sunken chest.

Well, so she had a friend, and merely the anticipation of meeting him made her hum. What could be wrong with that? And I did understand Mike's attraction. He would not run off, would not judge her appearance, his own being so depleted, his circumstances so paltry. And I knew she was lonely, had been for so long it must have seemed a permanent characteristic, and horny went without saying, but still I cringed when I thought of sex with

Mike, wondered if any of his parts still worked. It would be like going to the auto-parts graveyard a few blocks up and finding a Chrysler K-car with a working transmission. It could happen, I guessed.

Before Bev left, she reminded me to wipe off the oven hood when I cleaned up.

"You're going out, so I get stuck cleaning up," I said. "It's really not fair."

"What's the not-fair part?" she asked, as always missing my jokes. I was beginning to take it hard, her thinking me incapable of humor, judging me too pretty or too undereducated or both to be more than literal. She set her basket down on the edge of the stove, and faced me, hands on her hips. "Is it not fair that I have paid and do pay for everything? Is it not fair that even on days I clean up, you mess it all up again with your so-called creations? Or is it not fair that I let you live in my apartment for free, even let you bring your men in?"

"Roger's history," I said.

"I'd have to be deaf not to know that," she said, then picked up her basket again. "Quit whining about being poor little Cinderella." She opened the back screen door, but leaned back in, the door propped on her elbow. "What's today's culinary delight?"

"Meatballs, "I said. "Milanese style."

"Yuck," she said. "You can get those at The Dinner Bell Cafeteria in the mall."

"You'll eat those words," I said as she continued out the door, let it slam. I knew the meatballs would be good. I was using veal, pork, and aged beef. I had two pounds of each—a slab of veal roast, a round of pork loin, and a piece of boneless chuck.

Odder than Bev going out was that I was staying home, and even odder, I was happy to be home alone. I had a project. I discovered I liked cooking, probably because it was hard but possible, because it required my full attention for short periods, because there was praise in it if I did it right. The meats were waiting, and I could hardly wait for Bev to leave so I could screw the meat grinder onto the counter's edge and start grinding and mixing. I was using the old hand-crank meat grinder I'd found on Dad's side of the basement. He was the one who told me meat was better ground in one of them than in a food processor because the hand grinders wove the fat into the muscle, distributed the various textures evenly, and a food processor tore too much, made the meat tougher. Dad told me to add a bit of lubricant to the meat as I cranked, so I rubbed each piece with olive oil, and while I was at it, stuck a few garlic cloves in the red muscles. I did the chuck first, thinking it would be a tougher grind and I would be less tired when I had to push and strain. It went easy, though, and I did the pork next, then the veal, and finally had a bowl of ground up meat I could stick my hands in, mix, and play with. It was great. I picked rosemary, oregano, and thyme from the little herb garden I'd put in next to the back door, added a few basil leaves, chopped a fennel bulb as fine as possible, and worked it all in together. I divided the mixture and covered half, placing it in the walk-in refrigerator. I was experimenting with whether the balls would be better placed in the sauce and cooked just before being served, letting the flavors blend in the refrigerated mix, or whether they would be better cooked the night before and the fat skimmed off after they cooled.

I used two different sauces, too, a thick ragu I had frozen from three weeks earlier, and a meat broth and red wine concoction I made up on the spot. Soon I had two pots on, golf-ball sized hunks of meat simmering and bouncing in them. No one knew it yet, but I had recently decided to study cooking, and was hoping to go somewhere far away. The schools in California and Arizona didn't appeal to me as I'd never been a fan of Southwest food, and California was where Chickie and lots of others like her lived. I had seen an ad in *The Restaurateur Magazine* for l'École de Cuisine Internationale in Montreal, and was planning on applying there, taking the eighteen month program leading to *le grand diplôme*. Montreal was far enough away. The Alibi Café was a logical springboard to this next phase of my life, but I was not ready to tell anyone else about it, not yet, because plans had a way of evaporating, of becoming less urgent, once they became public, meaning family, property.

The meatballs in the broth and wine cooked faster than the others, were done in ten minutes, and I laid them out on brown paper to dry. By then, the balls in the ragu were ready, but those I let cool in the sauce, then covered the whole pot and put it in the refrigerator. Finally, I wrapped the dry balls in a foil pouch and refrigerated them, too. I dumped the broth and wine mix, wiped up the kitchen, turned on the dishwasher, and went upstairs. It was after eight and starting to get dark, and I was pleased with my efforts, wished there was someone I could tell who would care. Maybe Dad, I thought. At least he would want to know how the grinder worked.

The answering machine said we had four messages, unusual for us, especially since most of the people who called us knew we were in the café all day. I played them back and found the first three were hang-ups, one after a while of what must have been in-decision, some heavy breathing and a throat clearing. The fourth message was from Howard Figg. He said the Hilkers had chosen to ask for a trial by jury, and Bev should call him soon. He added that all things considered, a jury was not a bad thing because Bev would almost certainly gain their sympathy when they saw her.

By 8:30, I decided to visit Dad rather than call. The warm and loud night gave me energy, and I wanted a long walk through the neighborhood that, though changing, I still knew like my child-hood bedroom or like I knew the home Richard and I had just disposed of.

I took the long way, heading east down Meramec instead of west toward Dad's, past the hat shop and what used to be a used furniture shop and was now nothing. I jaywalked to the south side of the street so I could walk by St. Paul's, run my hand along the cement blocks on top of the short brick wall around the front yard, close my eyes as I did it, and think I was back in grade school. Each groove in the cement was familiar, worn and touched by fingers for the seventy years the wall had been in place. Just as I passed the post office but before I got to the funeral home, an old woman and a dog blocked my path. The woman was nut colored with white frizzy hair, and the dog was one of those big ones that pull sleds in Alaska and must be 100 percent miserable in St. Louis summers. The woman pulled on a rope knotted around the dog's neck, and used a stick, a small branch from a Bradford Pear tree maybe, on its hindquarters to get it to move. She pulled twice, then reached behind and tapped the dog twice with the stick, then pulled twice again. She was quiet, gave no commands, and the dog didn't seem hurt or bothered by the tugging or tapping, but every now and then would give in and take a few steps before stopping. I guessed the two of them would take the whole evening to go two blocks. I jaywalked again—the sidewalk would not hold all three of us—and walked past a few of the old homes with three stories and pointed roofs and small covered front porches, black metal fleur-de-lis stuck in the bricks between the first and second floors. Window air conditioners hung from many windows. Some people were on the porches. I heard them laughing as I passed by.

I wondered if the Asian azuki bean would work on a bed of linguine, mixed in with the meatballs. I thought it would be worth a try. The application to l'École de Cuisine Internationale asked if I had ever created a dish by joining the tastes of two regions or cultures, and I was trying to do one so I could say yes.

I passed a small park with a green and white bandstand, its roof sagging, and wondered whether Bev had ever been abandoned by someone she loved. I had assumed she chose messes like Mike to avoid being hurt but knew such avoidance was usually the result of first-hand hurt, not merely caution. I had found out about their picnics just a few weeks earlier. "Do you think you can save him from himself?" I asked.

"Are you saying he needs saving? What gives you the right to say so?" She was stomping through the café kitchen, putting the dishes up, throwing leftovers away.

I was wiping up the stove, but mainly watching her as she jammed an entire container of old tuna salad down the garbage disposal.

"Well," I said. "I suppose he doesn't need saving, that is if you overlook his stealing, his confusion, his leeching off us, his lying. Most of what he is is either against the law or against decency." I was surprised when that word, *decency*, popped out, and I hoped it was not one more side effect of closing in on middle age. I hoped it was not a sign that I would someday support the war on drugs or music video censorship.

Bev laughed at the word. "Oh, so sorry. I'll try not to fraternize with those who offend you."

"Knock it off," I said. "You know what I meant."

She leaned on the counter across from me, shook her head so her thin hair fanned out from her face like a halo. Her tiny eyes held mine in triumph. She enjoyed my discomfort. "Is he an abomination?" she asked. "That's it, isn't it? You think he's an abomination." She laughed harder.

"OK. Never mind. But you know he's beneath you."

"I'm taking up your ways," she said. "I'm slumming. So sue me."

I said I'd have to stand in line to sue her, another of my jokes she decided not to get.

When I got to Broadway, I turned south for one block to Gustine, then headed west toward Dad's. Some of the households I passed on my way back toward Grand were sites of high drama, lives being ruined, adjusted, confirmed on high volume. A few souls were being ordered out, some told to fuck off. The screamers mostly wanted to be left alone, claimed they did. It was the last year of a tired and worn out millennium, and for years some had been calling it our limit. Mankind, the world, would cease to exist on January 1. If that were true, I imagined some of my neighbors would be told to fuck off at the very end. It would be their last order. And some would go still wanting to be alone.

After crossing Grand, I made a right, then a left, and was at Mom's and Dad's two-family. Lights were on up and down, but I chose up. Dad appreciated meat. He'd just finished the chicken and dumplings Mom sent up and said it was too bad he hadn't known I was coming by. He would have saved me some.

"Your mother doesn't eat that stuff, of course," he said. "She's gone almost entirely vegetarian and tells me not to take it personally. Still, it's nice of her to cook the old foods for me, though I do wish she would learn not to boil the chicken so fast. Makes it tough."

"I made meatballs this evening," I said and told him about it, the grinding, the mixing by hand, the stickiness of the meat in my palms as I shaped the balls. I said I liked the idea of dead muscle sticking to live muscle, or was it fat to fat. He rolled his eyes, said not to get too carried away, but added he was pleased I was not a vegetarian like Mom.

"Maybe I should be," I said, partly but not entirely joking. "Vegetarians live longer, keep their looks longer."

"Why would you want to keep your looks? What will you do with them? What good are they? Your mother's sixty-one. Why not look like sixty-one? It's not a shameful thing to be."

"Maybe she can't help looking good. It's who she is."

"It is," he said. "Vain is who she is."

I was more interested in meatballs. "I cooked two sets of meatballs," I said. "Put some up uncooked. Do you think those will be better?"

"So you're really interested in meatballs? You used to care so much about siding, right? Well, well. I'm surprised you found something to care about so soon after your divorce."

"It's been almost a year." Was he saying I had not loved Richard enough? "How long is it supposed to take to get back to living?"

"Spoken like a Stillwell," he said. "Things happen, So what? Just go on. Onward and upward, as long as you look good doing it."

"You shouldn't be here," I said. I had said the same for years. "Why are you here?"

"To quote my daughter, 'How long is it supposed to take?' It hasn't taken with me yet, not after twenty-four years."

"Maybe you need help. Some counseling." I had suggested this to him before, too, even before I met and married Richard. His not being able to move on had always frightened me. "I mean, you should be able to move away, fall in love again. Do you even remember why you loved her after all these years?"

"Love," he said. "Not loved. We're still together, just in a different way."

I knew it wasn't real love, but some odd waste of time I didn't want to hear about. At least Richard and I had been able to keep living, to remain full human beings. I told Dad it was a nice night for a walk, said I guessed I would be leaving.

"Don't think everyone has to act a certain way. Don't ever believe the word normal has any value whatsoever."

"I'd like to try it," I said. "Normal. In my next life I'll be normal."

"Do you know why we split?"

"Lots of reasons, I guess." My hand was on the knob. I was ready to run. Why was he talking about this now? Had I started it? All I wanted to discuss was meatballs. Besides, they'd both given me lots of explanations over the years. Mom's main line was, "Love died. It will do that." Dad had said she was confused, depressed, mentally ill, crying out for love. Now he said it different. "She did not want to be touched. Could not stand it. Not even an accidental brushing of her arm, a gentle peck on her cheek. It wasn't just with me. Think about it. Was she ever a hugger, a kisser?"

I shook my head. He knew she hadn't been. I thought of myself, of how Roger's touch had burned by the end. "Bye," I said. "I'll save you a few meatballs."

"Aren't you going to visit your mother?"

I shook my head again. I opened his door and ran down the steps. I wanted to walk, and like many of the others in my neighborhood, I wanted to be alone. What was the point in breaking up with Roger if I couldn't get at least one night to myself out of it? And I could close my eyes and feel the warmth of Richard's lips, the gentle give of his warm stomach. But Richard was history, and what if I was growing into my mother, becoming her? That may have been everyone's greatest sorrow in growing up—seeing ourselves turn into what we had struggled against all our lives. But then I thought maybe it was physical, not psychological, and maybe we both had a nerve condition that made touch painful, but we, Mom and I, could take pills or use creams for it. Her coldness that I hoped was not mine, knew it was not yet anyway, was probably a symptom of a little known condition or even a syndrome, but some researcher was already working on it. At best, it could be merely nutritional, cured by more beta-carotene maybe. And that hopeful thought led me again to the azuki beans, to wonder how they could possibly hold their own in my spicy and thick ragu.

While crossing Grand at Gustine, I saw him, the one I still

thought of as a restaurant critic even though we'd not yet been reviewed. His thick, reddish brown hair was slicked back as it had been before, but his clothes were looser and lighter to accommodate the evening's heat—a white sleeveless T-shirt and a pair of shiny green athletic shorts. He was tall and tanned and had the thick thighs and exaggerated calf muscles of a soccer player. I had wondered about him so many times since he came in to review us a month ago, I almost waved as if he were a friend, but stopped myself in the act, pretended to scratch my head in case he was watching. So I was surprised when I passed him that he moved into step beside me down Gustine. "How's the café?" he asked, and before I could answer, he said, "Maybe you don't remember me. I ate there once. Had a marvelous quiche. I guess I'm a fan."

I laughed, told him I did remember him and the woman he had been with, but he didn't take the bait and tell me who she was or had been to him.

"I like to see new restaurants thrive down here," he said. "It's hopeful. Is that other woman who works there a friend of yours?"

"Bev," I said. "She's a cousin. She's the owner." I decided to get at the truth. "Are you a critic?"

He placed a hot hand on my arm, and we stopped walking. We were almost at Michigan, still a few blocks from the café. "I can't tell you what I do for a living," he said. "Not yet."

Intrigued by the word *yet*, I told him I could be patient, adding, "Some things don't have to be spelled out."

He talked then about his favorite cuisine—Northern Italian because they mix dairy products and meat right in with the sauce as it cooks—and we made our way to the Alibi Café. I almost invited him up, but instead told him to come by the café sometime and taste my experiments with meatballs. At the door to our upstairs apartment, he reached for my hand, looked down at it as he held it briefly, then gave it a quick squeeze. No one, he told me, was more important to humanity than those who cooked.

Let's run away to Milan. I imagined saying that to him as I went up the front stairs, realizing then that I didn't know his name. Let's butter ourselves all over. The hand he had squeezed still tingled, and I took that as a good sign. Not a burn, but a tingle. I was not like Mom. My problems with touch had been Roger's lack of finesse, skill.

It was after ten, and I guessed Bev was at Mike's garage, listening to "The Battle Hymn of the Republic" that came in through the back windows. I sat in the kitchen to listen for a while, and decided Mike's music did add something to the old neighborhood. How many other neighborhoods had musical accompaniment? As I sat at the kitchen table, I thought I should tell Bev that her friend at least could play, give credit where it was due. I realized I had been full of nothing but criticism lately, telling Roger he wasn't good enough, telling Bev Mike was not worth it, telling Dad he should get counseling. At least I could admit to Bev that Mike was not a complete washout. I laughed at myself, thinking I would say he played a "decent organ," see if she'd get that joke. I also decided azuki beans wouldn't work and I should think of something to mix with ragu that would not be overpowered, knew I would. I would create something so extraordinary, a mixture of not only cultures but also opposite tastes—sweet yet salty, bitter yet soothing—and when it was perfected, would call the *St. Louis Post-Dispatch* again, talk to my restaurant critic whose name I'd know by then, demand a review. I knew I was lucky it hadn't happened yet. My dishes were getting tastier daily.

I poured myself a glass of chardonnay and decided to move into the living room, opting for comfort over hymns. No matter how good Mike was, all music becomes redundant, especially hymns. Just as I sat, pulled my feet up under me, leaned back into the cushions and closed my eyes so I could listen to the cicadas and tree frogs better, I heard the crack. It was loud enough to stop my breathing. I dropped my glass, knowing without knowing how or what that I was in danger.

I ran into the center hall and back toward the kitchen, away from the sound, from what I knew to be at least two men rushing up the stairs. "Where's he at? Where's he at?" one or both of them shouted. I thought I saw one rush into Bev's room and one into mine as I reached the door that led down to the café and outside. I yanked it open, rushed down and out imagining them thundering behind me, then all the way across the alley to Mike's garage. I said *stop* and *help* and *goddamn* and *help* a few more times, added a few *my Gods*, not knowing if I was saying any of it out loud. My breath hurt as if caught on the jagged edges of my chest as it finally rushed out, but I finally managed to say there were two grown up men in our apartment. I said they had kicked down the door. I was shaking. I repeated the *my Gods*, said again there were men in our apartment and knew then, the knowledge producing a painful chill, that I could have been killed. I said if we were going to live around motherfuckers and lowlifes who break down doors of innocent people, why didn't we have guns or some weapons, and then I remembered Toby's suggestion that Bev's leg could be used as a weapon, and I wondered why we didn't at least keep the spare one out for emergencies because I'd had absolutely nothing to defend myself with, and then I thought about Toby and I knew. "They were looking for Toby," I said. "They still are."

Bev turned paler than normal, and in a voice so raw it cracked, told Mike to go in and call the police. I closed my eyes to remember exactly how many and what they looked like, though not much came to me. Two men, one black, one white, not kids. Jeans, T-shirts, athletic shoes, ball caps, the white one was stocky.

"I can't call from here," Mike said. "Then they'll have my number."

"They're the police," Bev said. "They already have your number."

I opened my eyes and looked across and up at our apartment. No shadows at the two windows I could see; all seemed calm.

"I'll go back and call." I heard myself say that brave thing, and knew it could not be me talking. My heart was thumping in my ears. I wished my head would go ahead and explode.

"We'll all go," Mike said. So we did.

The deadbolt on the front door had held, but the old wood that was the door facing had been torn from the wall, ripped cleanly out of the brick and plaster. We saw it first, having decided to go in the front door because it was more visible. Little upstairs was damaged. A table had been overturned in the living room, books that had been on it scattered, its lamp broken. Our closets had been ransacked, hangers pushed to the side, shirts and slacks strewn across the beds and floors, the vacuum cleaner now out in the hall, a few old hats and purses and bras kicked into corners. Our bedclothes were on the floors, and the paper sacks and plastic bottles we kept on the floor of the pantry had been thrown out into the middle of the kitchen. Nothing seemed missing. Even my purse, the one I used and kept hanging on the back of my bedroom door, was untouched, money and credit cards and keys all still there. Eventually, two policemen showed up. One dusted for fingerprints, even on the front drapes. "We never catch anyone this way," he said. "It's just one of the things we can do after a break-in. Beats standing around."

"We think they were after a boy who visits us sometimes," Bev said.

" 'Where's he at,' they screamed. The boy is the *he*," I said.

They both nodded, acting as if break-ins and boys being chased by men and whatever else they encountered in the 'hood were merely part of their normal routine. The one not taking fingerprints asked the boy's name.

"Toby," Bev said. "Toby Cheng."

I was surprised she knew his last name. It was the first I'd heard of it, and I must have looked surprised. "The camp counselor told me. It is how he's registered at St. Hedwig's. It's the name on his birth certificate," Bev said. "He stays with a foster family, but I don't know who."

Well, that last part we had already guessed. It was only the Cheng that surprised me. "Address?" the policeman said.

"I don't know," she said. "His social worker is Jeannie Lemp."

The policeman scowled at Mike, looked him up and down, then told us to fill out a report of what was missing, said if we thought of something later, we could call and have it added to the report.

"Nothing is missing," Bev said. "Besides, we don't care. I'm worried about Toby. Find him."

I saw how she leaned into Mike as she spoke, allowed his arm that was around her shoulder to brace her, accepted his squeeze. The policeman gave us the report number, said he'd keep his ears open for news of a Chinese kid in trouble.

"He's not Chinese. He's black, big glasses, skinny," she said.

"Ugly," I said. "I mean ugly in a cute way." Both policemen nodded.

"Anyway," Bev said, "can't you do more than keep your ears open? Surely you can find out where he lives, call social services, check the foster care registers." Her voice was a high pitched whine.

"That's what we intend to do, it's what I meant. Keeping my ears open is just an expression."

"A poor one," she said. After they left, Bev called Jeannie Lemp who wasn't in. Bev left a message on her machine: "Toby Cheng's in trouble. Some mean people are looking for him. Call me. Call the police."

The next day, Bev didn't bother to open the café, explaining she wasn't up to making biscuits or pies, and I understood. We spent the morning with a locksmith, the same one who had snipped the chain when Roger jammed it in upside down last March. The locksmith remembered Bev, and started to tease her about being locked in, but she was all business. "Make this door impenetrable. The whole place solid and 100 percent secure," she said. "Do what you must."

He said new facing and a six inch deadbolt, steel front and back doors on both the apartment and the café, and bars on the basement and first floor windows would make it harder to get in. Nothing could make it impenetrable, though, and he would never imply otherwise. He could get a team over to fix the facing, put in new doors and deadbolts that afternoon, but the bars would have to wait a week, be custom-made so they fit. Bev agreed to it all, surprising me by allowing the bars. She used to agree with Mom and Dad and others in the family who said they would never live behind bars, not in their own homes.

After Bev left to call on Jeannie Lemp and the state social services office, I opened the café without her. It was nearly lunch time by then, and I knew we'd do a nice business from those who wanted to get in on our tragedy. The curious had been walking by all morning, staring at the locksmith and the hole where the door used to be, and I was certain most of them had looked from their windows at the police evidence van last night.

I was right. We had more customers than I could handle alone, and some left complaining about the service, the water I never got around to delivering, the haphazard table setting. Even the four young men the locksmith had sent over, what he called the team, wanted sandwiches carried out to them as they worked on the back doors. We had a break at three o'clock or so, and I started to close up early. I was tired, but more than that, I'd felt close to tears all day. I knew about traumas and shocks, so I knew what I was going through, but that was no comfort. Toby was a child, and he was up against people who were at least chronologically men.

All day I had expected one or both of them to walk into the café. I wondered if I'd recognize them, wondered if I was safe even in broad daylight and with locksmiths close by. I could not understand how a person who would break into the home of another, how a person who would run into someone's home screaming and tearing the place apart, how a person like that could ever be talked to. Men like that seemed a different species. I realized that if one of them walked in, no one else would see danger. They probably looked like one of us, but were not. I wanted them to be a rarity, but knew better. Things like that happened all the time, so there must have been many of the monsters around passing for normal, and I may have served some already, asked them if everything was all right, fawning and eager for their approval. I was taking the money from my last customer, a middle-aged blonde with a poor dye job who worked part-time for the psychic down the street— she had told me when I took her order she knew how I felt—when the restaurant critic walked in. He sat on a stool, and asked if I was all right and had anything been taken. Before I could respond, he apologized for being so forward.

"I'm Ted Younger," he said, and reached again for my hand. "Nice to meet you. I often forget the preliminaries."

I told him Bev and I were both fine, unharmed, though I knew that was a lie. Ted was interested in the details. Did the ball cap have a logo on it? Did the men have an odor? Were their athletic shoes new or worn? Were they armed? My answers were

I'm not sure; not that I recall; new; and I assumed so. He seemed more interested in Toby and the other details than the cops had been, and he leaned over the counter toward me, and his hair was so thick and his eyes such a deep brown, I thought again about suggesting we run away together. I did tell him his concern made me feel safer—a lie—and he said perhaps we could see more of each other, and asked if I liked line dancing. I wasn't sure what line dancing was—country of some kind I decided—but said sure I liked it because I knew I would with his arms about me. I was still smiling at him, knowing I could charm this critic into a rave review, when a young girl walked in.   She looked like a twelve year old trying to look twenty. She had dyed black hair that stood up in spikes and her left eyebrow was pierced with a gold M on a hoop.

"Welcome to the Alibi Café," I said so Ted would write us up as a friendly place.

"I'm looking for a job," she said.

"We're not in the market for help."

"I'm pregnant," she said. "I need enough to feed my baby."

"We really don't need help. Not yet. We're very new."

"But I know the owner. Is Ms. Burke here?"

"You must be Maddie," I said. It was an easy guess. No one called Bev Ms. Burke except her students, and this one was pregnant.

"I like being pregnant," she said in response to a question I hadn't asked and never would have. "I need something to care for. It'll do me good. We all need to care for someone else."

And just like that, as soon as she said it, I did not want to care for anyone or anything, not even the café and not my parents and not Richard and not myself and not Ted the coy critic, and surely not this teen-aged slut in front of me, acting as if her so-rich and proper and greedy family would not feed her bastard, so I said "We have no jobs. We are almost closed. This is a dangerous place in a dangerous world full of people with no regard for you or your life. Ms. Burke is not here. I don't like either of you." I turned to Ted and back to her. "My head is about to explode."

She backed up, moved slowly to the door. "I can feel it kick every now and then," she said, her hand on her barely protruding stomach.

"Congratulations," I said. "At least you know it has one leg." As soon as I said it, even before I saw her face twist up as if she'd been slapped, I was more than sorry. I was ashamed. I was doing worse than turning into my mother. I was someone I didn't want to be around but didn't know how to get rid of. I was a piece of gum stuck to my own shoe. Even Bev wouldn't have said something so harsh.

"Wait," I said. "You must be hungry. Right? Pregnant women are always hungry, right? I mean you can eat anything, can't you? Anytime?" I had come out from behind the counter, and as I talked, I took her by the elbow, guided her to the center four-person table, and set her down. "Stay here and you'll get a treat," I told her, and I motioned Ted over, too. "Both of you. I do like you. A free meal."

"Take it easy," Ted said to me as he sat at the table with Maddie. "It's post-traumatic shock. I've seen it before." Maddie did sit, but on the edge of the chair, ready to bolt at any minute.

"You can't help worrying about the boy," Ted said, and I nodded because he was right, but I didn't tell him the boy was only part of it. I was already worrying about all meanness, and worrying wasn't the right word, either. More like living through, seeing, being overcome by. I put a pot on to boil for linguine, took the meatballs that had been cooked in the sauce out of the refrigerator, set them in the oven on medium heat, and said I'd get Bev. I knew if I left the kitchen, though, Maddie would bolt, so I used the phone and called upstairs. No answer. I looked outside and didn't see her car, thought she must be at the police station by then, or maybe just cruising the neighborhood.

We hadn't seen Toby for two or three days. Bring Toby back, I prayed to whomever could possibly be listening. I heard Ted tell Maddie to forgive me because I had been shaken down to my bones, and the nerves in my brain were working overtime. Then he told her they were both lucky because the off-menu specials were always worth an extra wait. I busied myself in the kitchen, mak-

ing garlic butter for the Italian bread and slicing red onion for the
salad I would serve with the linguine, and I talked the whole time
to keep Maddie there. I told her about our break-in and the new
doors and the locks we were having installed, and Ted joined in,
told as much as I did, filling in the details as if he'd been there. I
asked if she was still dating the father of her child, but she didn't
answer. I told her I'd been married twice, and that my parents had
divorced years ago but lived in the same house anyway, that Mom
fed Dad every evening, and that Dad seemed to spend most of his
time sitting alone in silence. Perhaps he was nurturing his hope.
I told her I was not going with anyone, was free as a bird for the
time being. I told her I had been Homecoming Queen and Miss
Dutchtown South. I said beauty was as much a curse as a blessing because it could scare good men off. That last one was merely
something I'd heard others models say. Through all this, Maddie
said little, only once interrupting me to ask when Ms. Burke would
be home. By the time her meal was ready, I'd asked her about the
lawsuit, and she had shrugged, called it another annoying stunt of
her parents.

Ted asked her about the lawsuit then, but she gave him no
more.

"Just shit," she said. "I think they practice being obnoxious." I
carried two plates to their table, set them down, and stepped back
to watch. She took a bite, a large forkful that included both linguine and meatball, and swallowed. She smiled, then ate rapidly.
Ted ate his slowly, twirling his linguine around his fork for each
bite. I saw him slip a small notebook out of his shirt pocket, write
maybe a line or two. He blushed when he saw me watching.

Maddie slumped down in her chair a bit, kicked off one of her
sandals, and talked as she finished off her plate. She said the father
of her child was a poet, a prophet of sorts, and she was in love with
him, that they may eventually marry, but not yet. He had written
a poem to the unborn child and she would send a copy of it to Ms.
Burke. She said her mother told her not to eat too much because
weight after childbirth was difficult to lose, and she should not
ruin her figure before she went away to college, but I was right,
she was hungry all the time. She told me the girls in Ms. Burke's

homeroom had named the leg Hortense. She scraped her plate with her fork, almost licked the dish.

"This is the best food I've ever had," she said.

"What did I tell you?" Ted said. I told both of them I was working on something new, creating a food that would be light and thick at the same time, smooth and crunchy, comforting and exciting, restful and uplifting. I laughed at my words, and so did they, but I knew I could and would do something spectacular. I was determined to find a new taste. When I offered seconds, they both accepted, and though my hands still trembled and my temples throbbed, I awaited my recovery, looked forward to being steady Shelly once again, the beauty who could do amazing things. So intent was I on that vision, I didn't know I was crying until Ted had to come around the counter and lead me to a chair.

BEV

We had red-painted steel doors, front and back; our window bars were also red. We had three-inch-long deadbolts and new door facings all put in by the same locksmiths I'd called in my irrational anger about the chain lock. I had an alarm system installed, and my code was a series of numbers I kept forgetting. We were well trapped. Days passed, each the same as the one before. My biscuits lacked baking powder, were too watery, and came out slick and tough. Weeks passed. I cleaned the stove, wiped tabletops, and mopped the floor. I turned thirty-six and blew out the candles at Mom and Dad's. I listened to Mike's daily organ recitals, to his nighttime litany of crimes and failings. I watched Toby eat while he kept an eye on the door, listened to his lies, heard the fear underneath each "I'm not scared, no way."

I heard his spelling words, checked his math homework, practiced many Venn diagrams with him: "This circle represents all humans missing legs," I said, drawing on a piece of butcher paper. "This smaller one is those born without a leg, and this tiny one is

those born without a leg who live behind bars." He laughed at my
sets and subsets. I began to wish, to hope. I worried more, talked
nicer to Jeannie Lemp, double checked the door locks each night,
wedged a café chair under the front and back door knobs, locked
all the windows, even those upstairs, made sure the alarm was set.
I kept the outside lights on all night. I jumped at my own reflec-
tion in the windows, and I wished and hoped even harder.

I was a bundle of yearnings, a tangle of desires. I had dreams
of struggling up a hill, trying to run but never reaching the top, my
legs—both legs—aching, the shinbone I had and the one I did not
pulsing with pain. I would awake in emptiness, knowing I wanted
too much. I wanted Toby. And I wanted Mike. What did I want
with either, I asked myself in rare lucid moments. I was asked it by
others, too, about Toby. No one knew I wanted Mike.

"You are not the mother type," Cousin Chickie called from
LA to tell me. "You don't have a clue what it's like. Hilton's a good
kid, but he drives me crazy."

"He'll break your heart," Aunt Marie said. "Your children do
that."

"Ha!" Shelly said when I told her about her mother's call. "As
if she has one."

"Don't be so rash," Mom said. "You're always rash. Quitting
your job, moving down to that neighborhood where you have to
surround yourself with bars. Now this."

"You can give him money, send him to school," Dad said.
"But you don't have to make it official."

"Genes are important," Grandma said.

"He's too old to be saved," Shelly said.

Even Cousin Chuck, Chickie's brother who normally stayed
out of what he called domestic matters, sent me an e-mail. "Are
you completely crazy?" he wanted to know.

How much was completely? Probably not I decided but did
not say.

My family. This was the group, the tribe, that bent over backwards to make me feel smart and right about most things, at least
until lately. My missing leg and fingers had always curbed their
expressions of disapproval. Bev was frank and incisive, not crabby

and bitchy. Bev was a no-frills-kind-of girl, not a fat and ugly one with no fashion sense. Bev was her own person, "marched to a different drummer," not too stupid and hard-headed and arrogant to listen to sound advice. I had known the party line since I was a child, since before I got my knee.

Because I was unfortunate Bev, I had to be turned into an enviable figure so they could live without pathos. I was one of the Stillwell beauties. They seemed to believe in what they created, and for a while in my youth, I tried to fall for it, too. Their pretense wore thin when I quit my job—Agnus Dei, a prestigious place—and moved down here. The rumblings, though, were minor until I said I wanted Toby.

And I did try to be reasonable. I knew he could break my heart. I told myself this was not for flowers on mothers' day, a day that would more likely be spent with me visiting him in prison, talking to him through glass. I told myself, only halfway joking, to save money, put a little away for bail. I imagined things going so wrong that the only time he'd call would be if he were on the run—"Help me, Ma," he'd say. "I need a hideout." His first few years, few months, even prenatal months, had shaped him already. And there were genes to add to the equation. I knew he was a liar, a con man, a user, and a thief already. The road ahead, adolescence, could only be worse. It wasn't need. I refused to think of it like that. Why would he need me? Why would I need him? It was want. He was on the road to trouble, but he was bright and not ruined yet. We liked each other, even without trust. Nothing could have been clearer. Sure, we would cause each other heartache and pain, worry and anger. How could we not?

Twenty-three days after the break-in, and my biscuits were like Styrofoam, though my pie crusts were still flaky. But I had lost interest in them, too. I used canned peaches in the peach pies, pudding mix in the banana cream. Shelly rescued the café from my culinary incompetence—I know because she told me she was doing it, reported later that she had done it—by adding more exciting and better dishes to the menu. We offered a chilled blueberry soup for dessert when she could get blueberries, sometimes a blackberry sorbet. She made a flan with caramel chocolate sauce one afternoon, and she assured me I shouldn't worry about losing my touch with pies; her creations made us stand out more than pie ever had. As for the biscuit problem, she said she'd take over all the breakfast cooking, may as well do the biscuits as she already did the gravy, and besides, she had added a chard and cheddar omelet for Fridays only, and cheese blintzes on Saturdays, so we did not need as many biscuits as we used to.

She looked pretty when she described the dishes she made and was planning on, and though I'd never denied she was one of the most attractive of all the Stillwell beauties, she was even more so lately. She glowed. She shone. The few gray strands in her dark hair added highlights. The chiropractor who had his office in an old Victorian on Grand and Dewey started opening later, giving himself time in the mornings to savor Shelly's omelets and blintzes.

Well, I couldn't begrudge her the success, and had I cared, I would've appreciated her efforts. But after more than six months, I knew I would never care whether or not the Alibi Café succeeded, though I did like hanging around down there, and knew even dishwashing and table wiping could help put a lid on my intense yearnings which were strongest when I was alone. It was an afternoon in early August, somewhere between 1:30 and 2:00, and I was wiping the deuce in the center of the window, still our most popular table even with the bars, when Maddie came in. Her short sleeked-back hair was ink-black instead of pink, but otherwise she looked the same as when I'd taught her. "Hi, Mama," I said, and she waved shyly, then sat at the counter. Shelly had said she'd been in a few weeks earlier, but I'd not seen her.

"I was here when these reinforcements were going up," she said, pointing at the bars. "Are you that frightened?"

"Even more," I said. "Sometimes I sleep fully dressed, my leg still attached."

She took a stool at the counter. "You never seemed the type. Can I have a glass of milk?"

"Seemed means nothing," I said as I gave her the milk. I had never seemed the type to me either. I was the kind of prisoner I used to make fun of back in the old days, just three or so weeks ago, when I was brave and fearless. I would always live without bars, let what mayhem would come, come. I knew that about myself. I said so. If you're so afraid, I used to say to those others who barred themselves in in my neighborhood, move out. Leave the city to the tough. I said that in my mind only, said it to the dwellers in fortified houses. I laughed sadly at what I imagined were little old ladies who would likely die from their own fears, the bars making escape impossible during fire, the many locks keeping the paramedics out. And those fears were all out of proportion, fueled by the sensational local news reporters who knew only drama would get them ratings. All that was before my door was kicked in. And I was not even home to register the first shock, though I felt it daily ever since.

I thought at first I'd just sell the building, close the café, move out as so many down here did. Run to the suburbs. I would have, too, if not for Toby.

And yes, I had to admit, Mike the Cockroach. Maybe one desire fed another. Maternal led to sexual, though logically it should have been the other way around. I could only guess what caused what. I was like a cat in heat. I wanted to rub up against door jambs. My hormones could've been responding to survival of the species instincts—find a man to protect the child?— that should've been long since exorcised. Or maybe thirty-six years without was too long. Enough was enough. Gibson was his last name. Like with all people I knew, I knew what they chose to tell me, parts of a life that happened to come up in conversation while some of the more valuable details were skipped or forgotten. Had he ever been married? Did he have children? How much schooling had he had? Where did he get the meager amount of money he needed to live in the style he had so obviously become accustomed to by now? I didn't know any of that. He had told me a few things as we sat at a picnic table overlooking the fishing pond in Carondolet Park. He had been a bank teller for a while—how long he wasn't clear about—but quit because the bank was one of those large ones downtown, all marble and brass and the customers lined up quietly behind velvet ropes and waited their turns, hands folded in front of them, looking down mainly. "Too Roman Catholic for me," he'd said. "Body of Christ, Blood of Christ, Money Market Account of Christ."

As Maddie downed her milk in two gulps, Shelly came into the kitchen from the back. "Well," she said. "A meeting of the future mothers' club."

"Ms. Burke," Maddie said. "You're pregnant?" The high pitch of her voice together with her raised eyebrows, the M pierced through the arc of her brow moving slower than the brow itself, saying who would have done it with you? How drunk was he?

"I've decided to adopt. My family thinks it's a joke. Shelly's trying to be funny."

"And Ms. Burke is ignoring everything the least bit sensible or real." Shelly turned to me. "You don't truly believe how bad it will be. You're not afraid enough."

"I am afraid," I said. I meant of people who kicked in doors. Toby was easy compared to that. I knew Shelly was as afraid as I. On nights she was alone, the light in her room stayed on till dawn, just as I heard they'd all stayed on in the house she fled from to me.

"If you could see into the future, you wouldn't do it," Shelly said.

"Like my knee," I said. "If I had seen myself lying face down on floors, sprawled across coffee tables, in the aisle of St. Paul's on the way to communion, on the cobblestones by the garage door, if I had seen the future, I would never have been brave enough to take a step. Oh, I knew the dangers, but did not see them fully until I was face down."

"What could be so bad about it?" Maddie asked. "Ms. Burke will be a great mom, will raise up a smart kid."

"Thanks," I said, but Shelly sighed so loudly, I doubted Maddie heard me.

"He's already a smart kid," Shelly said. "I have to give him that. Smart in a stupid way. Want to try a slice of my cheesecake tart with mango topping? I made it last night, but it's not soggy."

Maddie said she did.

I'd already told Jeannie Lemp I wanted Toby. It was right after she told me he was safe, at least momentarily. Toby had been around to visit after the break-in, too, started coming around after day camp again, and since then and between the two of them, I'd pieced together a story that may have had at least a grain of truth to it. Toby's foster mother had three other foster children. By Jeannie's estimation, she was a good, kind, very religious woman named Lana who had raised two children of her own two decades ago, but was still young and strong enough to care for another batch. The problem was Lana's husband had had a massive heart attack, his third, a month ago. Lana's mother, meanwhile, was in a home for others like her with Alzheimer's, but she had blackened one too many eyes, was too belligerent for the home to keep. Lana had been called upon to remove her mother ASAP, but she was also sitting around in the ICU, waiting for her allowed ten-minute visit to come around every two hours. So Lana's attention left Toby and the others long enough for him to get by with staying out all night two or three times, long enough for him to get involved in a burglary ring two houses down.

He said he'd spied on the activities there for months, and soon figured out the woman of the house, a large white woman with frizzy red hair that the neighborhood children named Poodle Baby, sold stolen electronic items from her garage. Toby had seen some merchandise deliveries made in the early mornings. Once he realized what was going on, he got the bright idea of telling Poodle Baby what he knew, confronting her and saying she could buy his silence. The woman and her band of thieves decided they would rather frighten him into silence, and the attack on our apartment was the largest part of that fright. Toby, naturally, claimed it had failed, that he was not a bit afraid, and I thought Jeannie Lemp was a bit too calm about it, too. The burglary ring had been broken up, she told me, to which I answered "Hah!" Well, she conceded, if not yet, it would soon be. The police were on to them, and anyway, the burglars had no more reason to frighten Toby because he had no more reason to blackmail them.

The jig was up. Even more important, Jeannie explained, was that Lana had hired a well-qualified baby-sitter, another neighbor, who would stay with the children whenever Lana was called to the hospital or the nursing home, or elsewhere. "Lana's life just went crazy," is what Jeannie said. "It was a mistake in judgment on her part. She should have called us immediately, but it's okay now."

"A massive mistake," I said. "I wonder if she would've been so forgetful about her own kids. I wouldn't have been so cavalier about children entrusted to me. And what religion is she anyway?"

"Baptist," Jeannie said, and then shrugged to show me she wouldn't swallow more bait, would neither rise to Lana's defense nor lower herself to my level and trash the good woman. Besides, it was a matter for social services, for professionals like her.

"Can I adopt Toby?" I asked. "What do I have to do to get him?"

That got her attention, but after the sudden small jerk of her head, she regained her calm. She looked me over for almost a full minute, wrinkling her brow at what she saw. She was considering, and I knew she thought me a poor choice and would not put in a word for me. Still, she had been trained to be fair, prided herself on it probably, wanted to give me the benefit of the doubt, though she had many doubts. She explained it was a bit more complicated. Of course, final placement, permanence, adoption, was the desired result for all children, but Toby was not yet free to be adopted. He was called fatherless—his father had never been named, was unknown to all except maybe his mother. He did have a mother, though, Angela Cheng, and she'd been arrested a few years ago for assault. She'd beaten her postman with a Louisville slugger, breaking one of his elbows and a rib for delivering an eviction notice by registered mail. Her sentence was three years, but with good behavior she'd served fewer than nineteen months, and had been out for two months so far. She was in a halfway house and would be there for four more months. In that time, she had to prove she could be a good parent. She had to be made to understand that Toby should not spend nights and sometimes weeks by himself. She had to learn that his knowing how to use a microwave didn't mean he could feed himself. Jeannie thought it unlikely Angela would be deemed a fit parent because there was an addiction problem as there often was in what Jeannie called "such cases." And this assault conviction was Angela's second. Moreover, Angela was already displaying anti-social behavior in the halfway house, had been written up twice for fighting, and had cursed out her own social worker. But if Angela weren't approved of, Toby's foster mother was the preferred adoptive parent because bonds were already there. Lana had recently adopted one of her other foster children, and so would probably apply for Toby, too.

"But there are bonds here, too," I said.

"I suppose," she said. "But DFS prefers same-race adoptions."

"You mean same color," I said. "His name is Cheng. His race can't be clear."

"He is black," Jeannie said. "So is Lana."

"His mother sounds Asian."

"But to the world he is black."

"Does Lana want him?"

"She hasn't said. It's not an option yet until the mother either is declared unfit or makes it clear she doesn't want Toby. So far neither has happened. And we don't want to jump the gun. Miracles can happen."

"Can I at least put my name on the list, be a third choice?"

"Maybe," she answered. "We have to be sure you are OK, acceptable."

"Start checking," I said. "My life is an open book." I would rather have been a closed book, one sealed shut. How much of my life was relevant to my being a mother? None of it was my answer. I had never before wanted to be a mother. Sadly, the book of my life was too open. I'd been fired. I was being sued. I'd been a bad influence on a minor. I was a threat to children. I lived behind bars.

Was I fit? I was too frightened, too distracted, to remember the baking powder in my biscuits, and children were more complicated than that. In my favor, though, I had seldom wanted to kill anyone, not for long anyway, not even a member of my family, not even the Hilkers.

By the time Maddie finished her cheesecake, a matter of seconds really for she ate it in two breaths, I had seated a couple at a corner deuce. I had barely gotten their water and flatware, when in came four women in denim skirts or jumpers and carrying shopping bags.

Next were two men from the crew laying the fiber optic cable, and they were followed by the chiropractor, a deacon from St. Paul's, and a skinny young guy who came from the pawn shop across the street with his freshly retrieved guitar. The skinny guy took the stool at the far end of the counter, two away from Maddie, but the other two singles each took a deuce. It was a Thursday afternoon, a few hours past lunch time and even by senior citizen standards, not dinner time yet, so I was confused by the business.

Still, Shelly was prepared. Though it was early August, a dip in the jet stream had given us a break from the heat, and we did a great business on our barbecued beef and pork sandwiches, and on another of Shelly's new dishes, bell peppers stuffed with wild mushrooms. It looked like we'd be eating the tuna salad for dinner and sending a lot of it across the alley to Mike.

I'd never wanted to wear myself down, break out in a sweat just to give overfed people something to put in their guts. But the two of us rushed about, carrying plates and water and utensils, menus tucked under our arms, getting short of breath. And even as I resented the activity, I watched Shelly as she flirted back at the fiber optic guys and the chiropractor. How did she do it? She smiled, yes, but so did most of our customers.

We were a friendly lot. My smiles never made the recipients want to touch me. And she listened, too, at least pretended to, nodding once or twice, laughing at weak jokes and limp witticisms. But hadn't I tried that all my life, at least up through high school, the too eager gambit failing so totally I had had to take Cousin Chuck to my senior prom? Okay, I was not dense. I knew as well as anyone that smiling and nodding, laughing and tossing the hair from your shoulders worked for pretty women, and did not work for ones like me.

In the midst of our mini-rush—eight customers at once—Ted Younger came in. He was Shelly's new man, and he'd been eating in the café, tasting her latest creations, nearly every day. He consistently asked me about teaching, about advice I'd given my former students. He'd say, "Okay, Bev, let's say I'm a sixteen-year-old girl and my parents are divorcing and I start to get bad grades, and I pile up enough demerits to get a week's worth of detention.

Would you be able to help me?"

Well, that was the thing about teaching. You never knew if you'd taught, if they'd learned, and the same went for helping them with their adolescent problems. Nevertheless, I tried to help in just such circumstances, offered long talks, smiles, reassurances, poems that may put their lives in perspective, and once or twice could almost convince myself I had helped.

But I was not going to play these games with Shelly's new man. "I'd offer you congratulations on learning so early and fast about the misery we take from the mistakes of others, and about how much life sucks." Shelly said he was a food critic, but I didn't believe it, and my doubts required no insight or intuition. It was simply that we had not been reviewed, not after his hanging around for more than three weeks.

For Shelly this caused not doubt but frustration.

"Just do it. Do it. Do it," I heard her shout at him from her bedroom a week or so earlier, and had thought it a response to overly-long foreplay, that she was that eager and frustrated. She laughed the next afternoon when I said what I'd overheard, and set me straight. "The review. It's all about the review. When will he do it? I know it'll be a smash."

This afternoon, Ted sat beside Maddie at the counter, and said something I couldn't hear to make her laugh. Shelly was taking barbecue plates to the couple at the corner deuce, but she waved to him from across the café. The skinny guy with the guitar finished his stuffed peppers, and, as I was taking his money, Toby came in on his way home from day camp. He climbed up on the newly vacated stool at the far end of the counter, twirled on it so he was at an angle. I knew he wanted to keep his back to the wall so he could watch the door. I gave him a slice of the peach pie few others wanted, and a glass of milk. I set a coke down in front of Ted and refilled Maddie's milk. Then I introduced Maddie to Toby.

"Are you missing some parts, too?" Toby asked Maddie.

She shook her head. "This is the one you want?" she asked me.

"Want for what?" Ted asked, but I ignored him.

"Just checking," Toby said to Maddie, then looked at me.

"That lady I stay with told me not to come here anymore."

My stomach jumped. "Why?"

"I'm not afraid of nuthin'" he said. "Not of those guys."

"The ones who broke in?" Maddie asked.

"Thought they was so smart. I wasn't even here."

"The ones who scared you?" Maddie asked me.

I shrugged.

"We think there's a connection."

"You know there's a connection," Ted said.

"Well, I'm not afraid," Toby said.

"You should be," Ted said to him as he had many times in the past few weeks.

"Why can't you come by?" I asked, deciding I may as well hear it all now. Jealousy was what I thought, but that would not be the reason Toby knew.

"They shoulda just paid me," Toby said. "Wouldn't be all this trouble."

"Why?" I asked again. "What does your foster mother have against the café?"

His smile was wide, and his eyes sparkled behind their thick glass coverings. I wanted to hug him. He asked for more pie and kept quiet until I put the other piece in front of him. "Blah, blah, blah," he said. "Says it's dangerous since those guys know I hang here. Says I should stay closer to home. Says she gives me all the food I want. Blah, blah, blah."

"She wants to protect you," I said.

"I won't do what she says. She's not my mother. The man who used to be yelling at us all the time's in the hospital. I'm not afraid of him either."

Good, I thought, knowing I was already being a bad mother, more concerned with what I wanted than his safety. And Lana, whom I had to call incompetent no matter what Jeannie said, was probably right about this. The Alibi Café had become too dangerous for Toby, for me and for Shelly, too. But Lana was not being high minded, not necessarily. She had no doubt been told I wanted Toby, and she wanted to keep him from me. Nevertheless, I was about to give him some well-needed guidance, was ready to be big about it all and tell Toby that Lana was right, and he should stay away from the café, when Maddie spoke up.

"This café is not dangerous," she said. "It's already been broken into. No one, no matter how stupid, would try the same place twice. The cops would know who it was."

I nodded. She was a good, smart girl.

"But criminals usually return. Statistically speaking, that is," Ted said.

"But this has been reinforced. It may be the safest place in town," Maddie told Ted.

"But the lady I stay with says it's bad for me."

"Well," I said, disapproving of what I was about to say, "she doesn't understand. And maybe she doesn't have to know." I was ashamed for saying that out loud, but Maddie was probably right about the café being safe. I'd long known statistics were tricks. Lana was being either too irrational or too selfish. Besides, Toby would be in the café only in the daytime. Jeannie had already said he'd be accounted for at nights, and violence of the kind that had happened already was a nighttime activity.

Maddie winked at me. "Telling him to lie, Ms. Burke?"

"It's my way, isn't it?"

"Is it?" Ted asked.

"I won't tell her anything," Toby said. "It's not lying if you don't say nothing."

"Anything."

"But I could use some money," Toby said. "Just a few dollars to buy things like the other kids have. Pencils, paper, some snacks." He smiled, his mouth opened wide.

"Oh, I get it," Maddie said. "Blackmail."

Toby pushed his glasses back up the bridge of his nose and looked right at me. "If you don't got the money, that's okay."

"He's the one you want?" Maddie teased the question out the second time, rolled her eyes.

"For what?" Ted asked.

"I have lots of pencils," I said to Toby. "Paper, too. And apples."

He shrugged. "It's not blackmail," he said to Maddie. "She's just a nice lady. My friend." He slid off the tool. "Give me that stuff some other time." He turned at the door. "If you want to." He glared at Maddie when he said this last part. "Right now, I got places to go."

"Be careful," I said.

Maddie left soon after Toby, but not before telling me her parents' lawyer had told her to practice crying and looking sad. The lawyer, "Witchy Wicher," Maddie called her, said she had a few more months to prepare as the trial was not until the first week of October, and so, luckily, she would be bigger and more awkward by then.

"It'll be a battle of the pathetics," I said. "My lawyer thinks I will draw sympathy by just being there. I don't even have to cry."

"Boo hoo," Maddie said. "Boo hoo hoo hoo hoo," she said all the way out the door.

Shelly put a plate of her stuffed peppers down in front of Ted, and he took a large bite, pronounced it superb. I'd noticed he used one of two terms, superb or marvelous, for all her dishes. Not that there was anything suspicious about a limited vocabulary.

As we cleaned up that evening, Shelly told me she had an idea. She wanted me to think it through before saying no, and to consider how much fun it would be, no matter the work. She smiled, almost danced about the kitchen.

"Yes," I said. "To whatever it is. Do it. I don't care. Am I the kind that says no, that dampens plans and hopes? I'm funny looking, not mean." I told her not to tell me the idea, just to proceed with whatever it was, tell me later. I told her if it was fun, I, of course, was all for it. I said I may have been a cripple who took pains to corrupt children and who was seen as so needy she could be blackmailed by a ten-year-old kid, but I was not against fun.

"Don't get upset," Shelly said.

"I'm not." I'm ruined, I almost said. I have started to want again. Help me. "I'm sad."

"Sad? Well, we can work on that. It's a trick of perception."

I wanted to slap her, but "A Mighty Fortress Is Our God" was wafting across the alley, had been for a while I realized, so I told her I would smile through whatever she had in mind. I would, by God, stop being sad.

I wondered how drunk Mike would have to be to crawl into my bed, and how bold I'd have to be to give him the desire. I knew he was sober when I crossed the alley. I could tell by his playing, but I went over there anyway, even knowing he may be a harder sell sober.

"Sounds good," I said when he looked up and saw me standing in the doorway.

"God is our only strength," he said. "If I have talent, it comes from above."

"Want some tuna salad?"

"Don't mind if I do," he said. "Whatever you've got."

"Want something else?"

"I'll take it all, sister. The Lord gives. I'm a lily of the field."

"Want a one-legged woman?"

He stopped playing.

"Tonight. In her own bed," I said, unable to raise my eyes from my own penny loafers.

"A lily of the field," he said again. "Jesus loves me."

I turned and walked back across the alley, stumbling and nearly falling on one cobblestone that was higher than most others and one that I usually avoided. So it was that easy. When I entered the kitchen I quickly made two thick tuna salad sandwiches, bagged them up, remembering to include a few of Mom's homemade pickles. I crossed the alley one more time, set the bag on top of the organ without a word, not looking at him in case he would change his mind, and left before he could even finish whatever he was playing. I did not recognize it.

As I thought again about what he'd said, I hoped his answer had meant yes. I wondered if I should remove my leg before he showed up or if he would want to help me with it. Could unbuckling my harness be called foreplay?

Of course, I was a virgin, but not from any sense of propriety, morality. At Shelly's first wedding, I remember, there was a drummer I wanted to want me. He was fat with a bumpy and bloated face, and I set my sights on him thinking he wouldn't have many other offers.

During his break, I took him a beer, and stood outside on the steps of the fireman's hall as he drank it. He laughed about how funny some of the high school kids were dancing in there, and he put his hand on my shoulder, said my lavender chiffon dress was not as tacky as most bridesmaid dresses he'd seen. He said he didn't believe in marriage himself, and told me a joke about a man trying to keep three wives happy. I smiled at him, laughed at the joke, downed my own beer as fast as he did his, and thought this was how to get a man. During his next break, he danced with Cousin Chickie, throwing his head back and laughing at whatever she said.

Well, the drummer had been my best chance, I always told myself, though I knew he wasn't a chance at all, and twenty years later, I remembered the gold tooth that glistened when his head was thrown back and his mouth was open in a laugh I could not hear. And if he hadn't forgotten me, it would be because he still told his buddies, "I knew a girl with one leg once. Met her at a wedding. Think she was flirting with me." As if he could tell. I never was brave enough for a post office box and a lonely hearts ad, called personals now. I used to imagine the ad—"Bright woman with lots of love to give seeks man who judges by what's inside. Dreams of rock climbing, has spare parts."

Agnus Dei once hired a blind music teacher, and I had hopes for him until I learned his wife drove him to school each day. He lasted only one year anyway, and when he quit to work for a large public school district in the county, he made a speech. He said we had never been friendly enough to him. He said none of us had been able to get past his handicap and treat him as a person. I wanted to beat him with his own white cane for that remark.

Because I took Mike's lily of the field remark as a yes, I went in the back door and up to our apartment, grabbed my purse and went back down and out the front way so I could avoid answering any questions Shelly may have. I went directly to the dress shop just over a block away and bought a long black skirt, a sort of elegance I never affected. Though it was a jersey knit so my lumpy hips and thighs were accentuated in it, I decided it would be easier, certainly more graceful, to take off than pants. Maybe, I thought, its removal could be romantic. I could lift it slowly and ask Mike to unbuckle my harness, then remove the leg, and if I were already stretched out in bed, the effect of one leg would not be so sudden, my asymmetry not so noticeable. I wore a white silk shirt over the skirt, let it remain untucked to hide the tops of my hips. I pushed my ultra-fine and limp hair into a band at the back of my neck, but it wouldn't stay. I put blush on my cheeks to highlight them and to take the attention away from my missing chin. I used eyeliner around the edges of my eyes on the side away from my nose and did not use any at all near my nose to make my eyes seem wider spaced and larger at once. I looked foolish. I had to admit it as I looked at myself in the full-length mirror in Shelly's bedroom. But I supposed no more foolish than usual.

Shelly came home to find me sitting demurely on the couch. I didn't know if Mike would show up before he ate the tuna or much later, maybe not until after at least six tallboys. We hadn't named a particular time. Shelly didn't seem to notice the new look I wore but sat down beside me and began talking about herself, as usual. She had been at her parents' flats, and then had called my parents from her mother's.

Her big surprise was that we were hosting Thanksgiving dinner in the café, and Shelly herself was going to make the ultimate Thanksgiving dinner, one we would be more than merely thankful for, one we would talk about for years to come. Aunt Peg, Cousin Chuck and his wife and children, Cousin Chickie and Hilton, and Grandma had not yet been invited, but my parents and hers were pleased with the idea.

Thanksgiving was more than three months away, so I said fine. I didn't understand her need to show off and to shine before our family. Beauty should've been enough.

"How do I look?" I asked.

She stood up, backed away to, as she said, take me all in. She placed her hand on her chin, nodded, hmm'ed a few times, and said "Like a vamp. What do you have planned?"

I laughed at that. I knew I was as far from vampish as one could get, but for once I wasn't offended by being so patronized.

I did want advice. Oh, I knew I wouldn't become a beauty by combing my hair another way or by wearing a necklace, but improvement was improvement.

"You could add a bit of shadow around your eyes to make them look larger, especially on the outside edges. I would use a mauve since your skin is so pale, needs some pink to it anyway. Want some?"

"Sure," I said, and started to follow her into her bedroom. The position I was in, though, made my getting up a chore, and I realized it had been a mistake to stretch out like that. I started to move, and knew she could see me strain, watch my muscles twitch long before I managed to swing my prosthesis down to the floor and place my hips firmly on the couch cushion, facing forward. She reached down to help pull me up, but stopped in mid-reach, suddenly seeming to catch on.

"Mike," she said. "Damn. You are planning to seduce Mike."

"I would not call my feeble efforts a plan," I said.

"It's none of my business," she said. "But you know he won't notice what you look like anyway. I mean, if he noticed looks, he'd have to start with his own wouldn't he?"

"It is none of your business, but I'm throwing myself on your mercy. How do I go about getting him in bed? How does that work?"

"Considering you may be the only offer he's had in years and years, I doubt you have to say more than 'Come and get it.'"

I tried to laugh at that line, too. Mike was this decade's version of the fat drummer, the blind teacher. I hoped Shelly would have enough sense not to press further, would understand my needs and choice intuitively.

"Why Mike anyway?" she asked. "I've been wondering. What's the least bit valuable about him?"

She was true to form. This was the woman who hadn't known her marriage to Richard was about to topple about her ears, and the rest of us had seen it coming at least a year before it happened. She'd been so wrapped up in that siding business, in being businesswoman of the year, she'd missed his obvious longing. Mom used to say he had the loneliest look in his eyes, like someone lost in a blizzard and sure whichever way he turned would lead to his doom. Shelly never noticed it. The veterinarian's receptionist did, though, and all Shelly noticed about that was that her ankles were thick, her arms too freckled, her lips too thin. "Just give me the eye shadow," I said. When she finally pulled me up and into her room, set me down in her vanity chair, I was both impressed and disgusted with the array of products strewn about her tabletop. I was sure they didn't work, sure she didn't need them anyway, and knew she must've been a fool to fall for their advertisements. I was also impressed. How had she even known about all of them? I watched TV more than she did, and I hadn't known there were so many moisturizers, shades of blush. Was there an underground network that passed along beauty hints and names of products? Her fingers rubbing the shadow into the skin around my eyes were gentle and delicate, swirling like tiny streams of water. I hoped Mike's fingers would feel this good wherever they landed on me. And while the eye shadow didn't make me a vision of loveliness, it did help separate my beady little eyes, give me a look that didn't shout *village idiot* with quite the normal volume. Shelly had learned well in modeling school.

I positioned myself on the couch once again, but this time facing the other way so my whole leg was on the outside edge, close to the floor, giving me leverage. I unbuttoned the top three buttons of my silk blouse, wondering if I looked sexier that way, knowing the comparative adjective was wrong. I was not sexy; certainly, I had no cleavage worth accentuating. Shelly went down to the café's kitchen armed with her notebook and a few cooking magazines. I knew she could stay down there until the early hours of the morning, and unless Ted showed up, would certainly do so tonight. She must've been planning to creep up to her bed only when all was quiet and we were both snoring. I wondered then if Mike would stay all night, would sleep in my bed. I wondered if I wanted him to stay. I thought then of condoms and hoped he would bring some, but knew if he didn't, I could find some in Shelly's room. When would he show up? Had he understood me after all? We had not been as clear as we should have been, but wasn't sex supposed to begin with innuendoes and suggestions, not diagrams and written out invitations with RSVPs?

By ten o'clock, muscle cramps had forced me to give up my seductress pose, and I had started pacing the apartment to get the blood moving, even sluggishly, through my foot, to get the knot out of my spine. Each time I got to my bedroom end of the apartment, I glanced out the back window to see his place. No lights were on, but I knew he could be in one of the front rooms, hidden from me. I realized I didn't know what arrangements he had in there, which room was his bedroom, how many rooms the flat had, and if he used them all. Did he have a bedroom suite? It seemed unlikely. Would he be sitting in the dark? It was possible. He seemed to get along with the dark. He could have been passed out, could have fallen down and hurt himself, could've had an emergency phone call, could have stomach flu, could be deciding what to wear, could've forgotten all about me and our appointed tryst, could be disgusted by the idea.

By eleven, I convinced myself he was as frightened as I was. More frightened, in fact, for I was ready to go through with it no matter how late it got, no matter how drunk he was, no matter how bad at it I would prove or how foolish I would look and seem and be.

At midnight I thumped down the back stairs and checked that the new bolt was fixed to the new steel back door, leaving the chair I normally wedged under the door knob alone since Shelly had to come back in. I couldn't see next door, of course, but I heard her loud singing and imagined she whisked up something frothy. I went back upstairs, took my clothes off, but kept my leg on, still hoping Mike would show up before morning, wanting to be ready to get the front door. I didn't wash the eyeliner and shadow and blush off my face, and I wished I had a silk or at least a silky nylon nightgown, one with a bit of lace, a black one with spaghetti straps and a frilly hemline that would make me seem to glide and float above the floor. All my life, though, I'd slept in an old T-shirt or one of those flannel sacks with pink unidentifiable flowers all over it that Mom bought me. Tonight it was a royal blue T-shirt with "Agnus Dei Angels," the basketball team, scribbled in white across the front. It had a tear under one arm, and it hung just above where my leg fit on so the socket was exposed. But so what, I told myself. As if anything would happen.

It was 2 AM when the doorbell rang, and though I wasn't sleeping, I nearly jerked myself out of bed, and had I two legs, I may have done so. I had to lift my prosthesis up with my hands to get it over the side of the bed, but still was quicker getting up than if I had had to attach it. I fumbled with my robe as I lurched down the stairs, guessing by the light under the door that Shelly was in her room and alone. I looked out the front window but could see nothing, not even a shadow, and I wished Shelly would at least open her door as I went down the front stairs. What if it wasn't Mike? But it was, and by the time I unlatched the door and punched off the alarm, he was sitting on the stone threshold as if it were a stoop, his head resting on the bricks. His eyes were closed. "Come in," I said.

"Why should I?" he asked.

"Somebody will shoot you here."

"I'm already dying. What's the difference?"

"I can't stand here in the street and talk to you."

"Sit down." He patted the stone beside him.

"I can't. You won't be able to help me up."

"Suit yourself," he said. "But I can do it. I can always do it."

"Why are you here now? Where have you been?"

"I've been to the moon," he said. "I've seen it all. I know what it is."

I closed the door, but stood on the other side of it, wondering what I was going to do. Could I go back upstairs to bed and leave him there? How long would he stay? Did I care? Would he ring the bell again? I opened the door, stood above him. "Why did you ring the doorbell?" I asked.

"I didn't think you'd hear a knock."

"What do you want?"

"Death," he said. "After you've been to the moon, all you want is death. You've seen it all, and can die happily."

"Come in," I begged. "We can talk inside."

He didn't even look up at me. "A man called me today. Said 'here's the news. Your father is dead.' Just like that."

"Your father is dead? I didn't know you had a father."

He spat. "Don't have. That's the thing."

"Come in," I said. I was tired of leaning over him. I was cold.

"See he said Von Reid. The name written on my birth certificate is Reid. No Von."

"Your name is Gibson," I said. "It was a mistake."

"How could he call me like that? Hey buddy, your father is dead. Daddy is dead, Pops has popped off. Not a Von, I said. Wrong man, I said. Who the hell are you? I said."

"Who was he?"

"Didn't say. Somebody. Somebody looking for a Von, somebody obsessed with a Von. Somebody who was wrong."

"Stop it," I said, louder than I intended. I knew Shelly heard me even with her window unit humming. Her room was right above us. One car passed by, turned around, drove by us again. "Stop babbling. It was a mistake. Come in."

"Shit," he said. "That's what it all is. A mistake. Yes. I been to the moon. No Vons there either."

I reached down and pulled on his arm. "Get up."

"Stop," he said. "What makes you so bossy? Leave me alone."

"I'm going in, and I won't open this door again. This is your last chance."

He looked up at me then, squinting one eye, maybe trying to bring me into focus. "Maybe you already knew there were no Vons on the moon. Maybe you already knew they were all dead. Everyone knew but me, I guess. 'Your father's dead,' he said. Big news. Hey buddy, I have bigger news."

"Good night, Mike," I said, and closed the door again. This time I meant it, and as I pulled myself up the stairs, using the railing as if it was a climber's rope, I heard him yell. "I ain't no Von. No Von." He was not my concern. If Shelly called the cops on him, I wouldn't blame her. If he were a dog, he'd have been shot, but at least where he was he'd keep the monsters away for one night. I was exhausted, nearly seeing double as I headed toward my bed. It was all shit, Mike, all a mistake. Mike Gibson? Mike Von Reid? Or Mike Reid, no von? They all sounded fake. You made the whole thing up, Mike. Your brain is dying off in large chunks, whole sections already decomposing.

I swam all night long, but it was not exhausting, not a hard strenuous swim. I nearly floated, so buoyant was I, almost as buoyant as my fake leg. I think I sang as I swam, mermaid-like, sweetly.

Bacon woke me up. Bacon and coffee and I liked it. I wondered why Shelly was cooking upstairs when the best stoves and all the ingredients were downstairs. It was Sunday morning, and I heard the bells of St. Paul's, twelve gongs calling the late-sleeping faithful to noon Mass. Crazy Mike guarding the door had given me my first good night's sleep in weeks. When I noticed my leg was still attached, the details of my attempts at seduction, or whatever you call it, my attempts at overcoming my virginity, and how dismally they had failed came back to me. Shelly was fixing breakfast because she'd heard it all last night and felt such great pity for me only bacon would do. I heaved myself out of bed then, determined to put up with her pity as gracefully as possible, hoping to divert her with talk about the treats she had been concocting downstairs last night.

But Shelly sat at the kitchen table, sipping from a cup of steaming coffee. Mike was making pancakes at the stove. "Mama used to call this a bacon sandwich," he said. "Four buttermilk cakes with four slices of bacon in the middle, syrup drowning the whole mess."

"Mama Reid?"

He turned and looked at me. "Boy, do you snore."

"So," I said as I sat, pulling my robe closer around me, "you're alive. A testament to the peaceful city."

He carried two plates of bacon sandwiches over and set them before us, then returned for his own. After he had covered his plate with syrup, he took a bite, and turned to me. "Why did you let me stay out there all night? If it'd been you, I would've brought you in."

I poured syrup over my plate and looked down at the soggy cakes.

"I guess I went out to get away from the snoring," he said, "But I don't think I wanted to stay there all night."

"Bev's a sound sleeper," Shelly said. "So am I. I never hear anything that happens out on the street."

"Well, thank God you let me in this morning. Or what would you do for breakfast?" He refilled our coffee cups, then sat down across from me, grinning, even blushing a bit. "You're a hard woman, Bev Burke. Use a man up like that then let him sleep on the street." He smiled wider. "A hard, hard woman."

SHELLY

You have no excuse not to be seen at The ALIBI CAFÉ!

These two lines were on top of the flyer I made on Bev's computer. Underneath I listed our daily specials without prices to give them even more class. Red and green bell peppers stuffed with wild mushrooms and rice on Mondays, Tuesdays, and Saturdays only; cheddar and chard omelet on Friday till noon; cheese blintzes on Saturdays; linguine topped with Milanese meatballs Wednesdays and Thursdays noon to 4 PM. I included a line, also in bold type but only 14 point, "more specials added often." Then I listed our everyday features with prices to show how affordable we were. High, flaky buttermilk biscuits with sausage gravy—$2.00 all day long; spinach quiche—$3.00 all day long; sliced beef or pulled pork simmered in award-winning barbecue sauce and served open-faced on an onion bun with homemade dill slices and onion rings or fries—$3.95, lunch only; tuna salad, egg salad, ham, or pastrami on choice of bread and homemade dill slices and chips—$3.25, lunch only; chef or pasta salad—$2.75; homemade pies with extra-flaky crusts—$2.25 a slice. I added our address and hours, 7 AM to 4 PM Monday through Saturday, across the bottom.

I was defying Bev, so I didn't include coupons or special offers, didn't want customers to mention the flyer or my name. But what would she do if she found out I'd advertised? Nothing more than bitch. It was all she could do, maybe throw in a pout or a few sulks, a sneer here and there.

I could handle that all right, and besides, she already bitched constantly, sneered more each day. "What's Ted doing here all the time? Why is he so nosy anyway? It's bad enough having him as a third roommate at night, let alone a regular freeloader." I answered only the last part, telling her he was not a freeloader. He paid his bill mostly, and the rare times he did not, the times I offered him my specials to taste, I put my own money in the register for him. Her cases were the true freeloaders. My arguing back like that did as much good as arguing back ever does—zero.

Bev's bitchiness was natural to her, but it had grown worse now that she was fighting an undeclared war with the adoption bureaucrats. She had already filled out some papers, been interviewed by Jeannie Lemp's supervisor and two counselors, and been told they'd be in touch. This was all part of her officially putting in to adopt Toby, who was not exactly up for adoption yet. His mother would be given all the time allowed—one social worker Bev was interviewed by said this could be nearly a year— to prove she was able, and his foster mother, Lana, had yet to say if she wanted him. Still, Bev thought she'd get her request in early. No one in social services had been encouraging, let alone friendly. Bev said one counselor seemed to think she wanted Toby as an unpaid home health worker, saying, "I'm sure you see him as a great help in your day to day activities," and such until Bev finally emptied her coin purse on his desk and sorted the dimes and pennies with her hand bumps to prove how capable she was. The counselor had not seemed as wowed as Bev expected, though, and when Bev got back from that meeting, she banged pots and slammed cabinet doors all afternoon.

Her blossoming libido and the uselessness of Mike the Cockroach for any relief in that area was another of her troubles, and I bit the inside of my mouth more than once to keep from telling her how to find someone not merely better but possible. She hated advice with the same vehemence she reserved for advertising, but I knew a few things about men and was determined to give her some tips in such a way that they didn't seem like tips. Men were human beings, after all, and like the rest of us, liked to talk about themselves, to be admired for their fascinating lives and sought out for their expertise—real or imagined. Sure, looks were important, but sometimes a man would see himself reflected in a woman and she would become not exactly lovely but good enough.

So anyway, the flyer was in defiance of Bev's insane rule against advertising, but we all have a duty to defy insane rules, and besides, there I was, creating delicious dishes, planning and concocting and working harder than I ever had selling siding, and it would all be for naught if no one knew we existed. And though I knew I could handle her wrath, I decided to avoid it. On the evenings she spent watching TV or hanging out in Mike's garage listening to what the rest of the neighborhood wanted to cry uncle over—we all wished he knew at least one other instrument—I walked around and placed flyers in mailboxes or stuck them in the metal curlicues fastened across the middles of the front screen doors. Within a week, I had covered a square mile. I also dropped them at Reuben Meats, the wholesale butcher Dad had referred me to months ago, gave some to the vendors down on Produce Row, and put a few in the free newspaper racks in nearby grocery stores. I gave Aunt Josie and Aunt Peg a stack each and asked them to spread the word in their far-out suburbs, but I warned them not to tell Bev. "She'll be crabby about it," I told Aunt Josie, who corrected me.

"Bev never gets crabby," Aunt Josie said. "She is amazingly even tempered in spite of what she puts up with."

Ted helped me distribute the flyers on three of my evening outings, and afterwards we went to a club he knew out in South County, Spurs 'n' Saddles. Line dancing turned out to be good exercise, and exercise was more important than ever since I was creating and of necessity tasting new dishes. And those new dishes and my flyers created a slight increase in business. During the first three Saturdays in August, we had fifteen, fourteen, and fifteen lunch customers respectively, an increase from our usual twelve of July. Our weekday lunches also were busier by one or two diners. We weren't exactly packed yet, but I expected further increases.

By noon on the last Saturday in August, the tar was bubbling out of the cracks in Meramec Street; the faded red petunias in the planter in front of the pawn shop across the street hung their heads to the sidewalk, begging to be put out of their misery. Our downstairs central air unit, repaired twice already, was clanking and clanging but, so far, keeping the café cool. Ted and Mike sat next to each other at the counter, sipping iced tea.

"I remember one summer," Mike said, "it was so hot, the tar on these flats roofs around here would smoke. This was twelve, fifteen years ago. The fire department would go up and down the streets, spraying the roofs."

Ted nodded. "I remember one summer, back when I was in high school, when I was taking algebra in summer school, and I left my book out on the back porch for a few hours. It was so hot that the sun caused the ink to run and stuck the pages together. Not just a few pages, either. The book was unreadable. I had to drop the class."

Mike nodded. "Once I got second degree burns on the soles of my feet just by walking barefoot across a wooden porch to get the mail." He sipped his tea. "I don't believe those guys that walk on hot coals. Not after that porch experience."

"Remember the year it went from 103 actual temperature to forty-something in about four hours?"

Mike said he did not.

"Remember," I asked as I leaned across the counter to refill their tea, "when people had more interesting things than the weather to lie about?"

Ted laughed.

"No," Mike said. "No I do not. I wish I could remember a time like that."

Ted laughed at that, too. "Did you hear that, Bev?"

Bev was in the kitchen, spreading meringue across three lemon pies. "I don't eavesdrop," she called back, and tilted her head up in my direction and brought her upper lip up almost to her nose in a Bev sneer. I'd never seen anyone else match the perfect little tent made by her lip when she sneered. I knew it was about Ted.

"Why does he bring me into everything?" she'd asked me more than once.

I usually said he must like her, but I knew she took it for pity.

"Bev doesn't eavesdrop," Ted said to Mike. "She has so many good qualities. I wonder if she has any bad ones."

"I can't talk about anyone else's," Mike said. "I have too many."

They sipped their teas in silence for a while, and I left them to take the check to a foursome and to refill water and tea for the deuce closest to the door. It was just past noon, early for a Saturday, and we had six paying lunch customers. We'd had four in earlier for biscuits and gravy. I called it progress.

Aunt Josie and Uncle Al came in about one o'clock. They'd been to Bev's restaurant maybe a half dozen times so far, and had brought Mom and Aunt Peg twice, but never Dad who ate only at home. This time they had Grandma Stillwell for what she called an excursion from her assisted living home.

As she aged, Grandma's most distinctive features grew more pronounced. Though her face had shrunk, her brow protruded even more than ever, so her eyes were in perpetual shade. It must have been like peering out from a cave. Between those small and always shaded eyes was a gnarly bulb of a nose, looking like it could produce one of those huge leafy plants called elephant ears. Because her white hair was so thin, her ears were more visible, and seemed to bend out from her head more than ever. She was at least two inches shorter than Aunt Josie, who, I'd lately noticed, was about half an inch shorter than I was. A few years ago, Josie and I had been the same height.

I put them at the fourseater in the middle of the room, and before I'd had a chance to say much more than welcome and to tell Bev they were there, Ted took the fourth chair. "I'm a friend of your daughter's," he said as he shook hands with Uncle Al. I suppose I sniffed or coughed or made some noise because that designation did not seem the right one, and he smiled up at me. "And Shelly's, too, of course."

Grandma took command in her usual way and asked Ted what he did for a living, but before he could answer, Aunt Josie told him not to. "People are not what they do," she said. "Knowledge of a person's occupation only misleads. You may say you're a teacher, and I could immediately consider you to be patient, hard working, at least minimally intelligent, and very likely kind. But you could instead be a cynical, hate-filled government sloth. Or you could be decidedly, almost deliberately, unintelligent, but a nurturing baby-sitter type. We ask for occupation because it seems too rude, at least too much of a short cut, to ask for qualities, to say, 'what adjectives describe you?' So don't tell us. Just let us get to know you on our own."

"Your take on all of it is refreshing," Ted said. "Like with Bev, since you brought up teaching. If we knew she was a teacher who quit rather than apologize, we'd come up with a wide range of traits for her. Anywhere from firm and high minded to superior and stubborn."

"Bev was the best teacher ever," I heard Uncle Al say as I went to the kitchen to parboil the peppers. I had the wild mushroom/wild rice stuffing already made up and in a pan of water in a warm oven so it wouldn't get gummy or dry out. Once the peppers were ready, I had only to arrange them on plates, fill each with the stuffing mix, crumble feta cheese across the peppers and the plate, and drizzle a bit of chili sauce across the plate, too. I tried to make an S with it for Shelly. Bev had finished her pies and so had pulled a chair up between her parents, and as I arranged the pepper plates, Mike remained at the counter, talking either to my back or to no one.

"I measure time by how much has changed within boundaries," he said. "I make bets with myself. What will have changed by the time I finish my coffee? By the time the next bus passes? In between one wake and another at Schmitts funeral home? Usually nothing has, so I say if nothing's changed, time has not passed. It's still exactly the same no matter what a clock says. Clocks and calendars are made up anyway. Just like buses and wakes."

I knew I had heard him, but I turned to look at him anyway as if I had to see his lips move. The air conditioner blower was clanking so much that, though I could hear, I felt I had to tilt my head, incline it, to understand. I looked at him before I crumbled the cheese, but he was looking down into his tea glass. Maybe he had been talking to himself. "But," he continued, "it's always changing. Our bodies change completely from the inside out every year. I am not the same man I was a year ago. The exhaust from the trucks has eaten more into the cement cornices and sills. The acid in my coffee has worn away a bit more of my stomach lining."

I had the plates ready and picked up two. As I turned, he did look at me. "Things cannot change and stay the same. It must be our words that are wrong." I nodded, and walked out into the dining room with my plates. When I returned for the other two, he said, "It only seems the same. The redundancy is nauseating."

He ran his large hands through his very thin, black hair, making it stand up in devil's peaks on the sides, and if I hadn't been in a hurry, I would've taken advantage of him right then. What is your real last name? I would've asked. Gibson, Reid, or Von Reid? Who are you? He'd told Bev he was forty-six, but he looked closer to sixty, so I doubted he told the truth about that or any of the rest. But because I was busy, I passed him by, merely smiling at his inane talk.

While the four ate my peppers and Bev sat with them, answering questions about the lawsuit, I took the money from the deuce, cleared the table, washed more peppers, and refilled those salt and pepper shakers that needed it. I'd heard the deposition story already; it went fine; a jury trial was now scheduled for October; Howard was optimistic. I knew Aunt Josie and Uncle Al had heard the same version more than once, too, and weren't likely to get more. I refilled Mike's tea again, then took the refilled shakers into the dining room, overhearing snatches of conversation as I passed their table. Aunt Josie said something was "just like Marie," but when I drew closer to the table, she was talking about the heat. Back in the kitchen, I looked around, wanting to be ready for more customers. Our busiest time was around 2PM on Saturdays. Mike just stared into his glass again, studying rather than drinking his tea. When I looked back into the dining room, I saw that all but Grandma had finished their peppers, so I went to collect their plates, ask if anyone wanted more. Uncle Al said he was nearly as stuffed as the peppers but could be tempted. When I said I could give him half a pepper, Aunt Josie and Uncle Al both said that was a good idea. "Just a bite more," Aunt Josie said.

"No seconds for Josie," Grandma said. "Think of your figure," she said to Josie.

Aunt Josie nodded then, said her skirts were a bit tight at the waist. She was dressed in a long blue and green flowered rayon skirt that flowed straight down from her tiny hips, swirled about her calves. It was probably a size six. She wore a white silk shell, sleeveless, and even at her age, her upper arms were compact, not saggy. Uncle Al said he would pass on the half, too, just finish Grandma's. Bev did convince Grandma to try a slice of lemon meringue pie, and Ted ordered one, too. While they all sipped tea and the two carried on about the pie—"marvelous," Ted said— we got busier. We had five more orders of peppers to prepare, two barbecued pork plates, one beef, two egg salads, and two orders of coffee and pie. We were so busy that I merely waved good-bye from the kitchen when Aunt Josie and Uncle Al helped Grandma up and left. Ted hung around for a while, half sitting, half leaning on the counter, but because neither Bev nor I had time to converse, he left soon after the others. Eventually Bev gave Mike a slice of pie and he finished it, then stood to leave. Before he did, she opened the cash register and gave him two ones.

After all the diners left, I counted their tickets and found we had served eighteen paying customers in one afternoon. It was a record for us. The six in earlier for breakfast gave us twenty-four paying for the day, and the five free ones made twenty-nine we had served, thirty-one counting Toby and the girl he dragged in after everyone had gone.

The girl was taller than he but about his age. She was pinkish-white with dusty brown hair so oddly curled it could only have been a home permanent growing out. She was stick-figure skinny like many prepubescent girls, and barefoot, her toes as dusty as her hair. "Stop pulling," she said in a cracking, hoarse voice. "I told you I'd come in when I was ready."

"You're too scared to ever be ready," Toby said. He dragged the girl right up to Bev at the cash register, and said, "Here's a friend of mine. She wants to see your hands."

"I won't look," the girl shouted, struggling to free herself.

"Brats," I said.

"Don't be so uncivilized," Bev said, maybe to me. "Looking at them is nothing compared to living with them." She placed her hands, palms down, on either side of the register.

"Yuck," the girl said, but she did look.

Bev did her coin trick, scooping change from the cash drawer into one palm, and using the no finger hand to count and sort it, stack it in piles.

"Shit," the girl said, and Toby released his grip.

"I told you," he said.

Bev gave them both lemon pie. Toby told us his friend was Peaches. She was in his grade at St. Hedwig's where she was called Pat even though it wasn't her name.

"It's really Peaches," she said. "It's on my birth certificate. I was baptized Pat cause I had to be."

I knew how that went. At St. Paul's, they'd insisted on calling Chickie her baptismal name of Rosemary.

"I live with both my real parents," Peaches said. "I should get some credit for that."

"Show her your leg," Toby said to Bev. She moved from behind the counter and lifted her pant leg.

"Go ahead," she told Peaches. "You can feel it."

But Peaches just shook her head. "I don't touch body parts of folks I hardly know."

"This lady's no stranger," Toby said. "She's the one who gave us lunch at camp."

Peaches looked away, saying nothing.

"She's the one I stay with sometimes."

Peaches shrugged, still not looking at the leg.

"She's the one who wants me if Mom don't act better."

Peaches sighed, then ran her hand along Bev's artificial shin.

I noticed Bev had paled a bit at Toby's description, and she asked him, "Do you miss your mom?" It was as if she'd just thought of Toby's mother as a real person and of what it meant for Toby to be without her.

"No," he said. "She's not much to me."

"My mom says just cause you know how to get pregnant, doesn't mean you know how to be a mother." Peaches looked at Bev and Toby and even me as if daring us to disagree. "Want to know what my dad says?"

"Not really," Bev said.

"No," I said.

"He says the trick is in knowing how not to get pregnant."

Toby nodded his head at Bev. "But this one knows all that, how to and not to and everything. She wants to adopt me."

"Sometimes Toby stays at our house," Peaches told us. "We know him like he was part of our family."

I wondered how often Toby slept at his foster home.

Bev told Peaches she must have a nice family, and Toby reminded us how special it was. "She lives with her real parents. Both of them." If I had been born a quarter of a century later, I joked with myself, my parents living together may have been a source of pride, not embarrassment.

"Nobody did this to her," Toby explained to Peaches. "It's how she came."

"We gotta go," Peaches said to Toby. "We eat early on Saturdays, and we have to be there. All of us. I have three more kids in my family," she said to Bev and me. "Two boys and one other girl."

"So what," Toby said. "We got a few kids where I stay, too."

"Next time," Peaches said to Toby on their way out, "I want to see her fake toes."

"Where's my dollar?" Toby asked her.

We cleaned up the kitchen, and I made up two plates of the stuffed peppers we would take up and microwave later, and we finally went upstairs. It was almost six o'clock, and my coiled and dimpled brain seemed to be swelling, perhaps from the heat, pushing against my skull. I threw back four Tylenol headache pills and pulled my shade down to just above my window unit to keep the evening sun out, then lay down and tried to rest. The throbbing inside my head shook the bed as much as if it was one of those coin-operated vibrating ones. I was seeing a new doctor in a week, still not caring what was causing the pounding, just wanting it to end. Pills, exercises, food—I'd go along with whatever worked. Eventually I fell asleep, and when I awoke a few hours later, it was time to get ready for line dancing. Maybe, I teased myself as I swallowed two more virtually worthless headache pills, my brain cells had just gotten a jump on the evening's entertainment by practicing the Buckaroo Stomp with my nerve endings.

Spurs 'n' Saddles was packed on this Saturday night, and as usual, I had on the best looking outfit, not much of a challenge in a place where some of the women wore sequined American flags on their chests or dressed as a cross between Annie Oakley and a drum majorette, complete with white boots with gold trim. My jeans were deep blue with tight legs and a low waist, and my sleeveless T-shirt was sueded tan with one inch white fringe around the neck. I was supposed to look like a cowgirl, simple hearted and true-blue as the lyrics of most of the songs praised, and all I needed was a tattoo of a heart or a butterfly or a sad teddy bear on my shoulder, above a breast, or on my ankle. Ted and I came for the dances themselves. We rarely sat a number out, we seldom talked to other patrons, and we never made out in the shadows as some did. Even before the first intermission, we did the Cheyenne Swing, the Rock Island Turnaround, the Hot City Stomp, and three others, all alike, too—a few steps, a turn, a few more steps, and a spin. I tried to remember the names of the dances so I could tell Bev to make her sneer or, in very rare cases, smile. Ted and I were still stepping and turning with gusto by the last song of the evening, "Brown Gravy Boogie," and were breathless and dripping wet when we passed through Spurs 'n' Saddles front door into a fog of humidity. We nearly dog paddled to the car, laughing at our discomfort even though my brain cells were still boogying.

Once at home, I took two more pills and turned the dial on my window unit all the way around to the darkest blue there was. I knew we were about to work up another sweat.

Ted undressed and stretched out on my double bed, Richard's and my marriage bed, and when I saw him there, I pulled hard on the cord of the shade so the shade flew up and spun around its rod. I let the street lights in the room, liking the way they lit up Ted's flesh as if he were a glow-in-the dark toy.

When I flopped down beside him, he reached over and ran his hand along my side, touching lightly with only his fingertips until I had goose bumps. I did the same to him, then sat up and leaned over him so I could kiss him. His face had a bluish tint, and with his eyes half-closed and his neck arched a bit he didn't look like himself, and I had to remind myself this was Ted, a man I liked. His touch eventually became forceful, but never so rough I didn't want more. His tongue tasted more like wood and mud than like the pork rinds we'd had at Spurs 'n' Saddles, and though I'd known him for six weeks and had fucked him maybe a dozen times, I was suddenly aware that he was a person with smell and taste and texture never to be duplicated. Even when he was in me and we were as close as two could come to being one, the tab A in slot B stuff providing a secure fit, I was conscious of him as a separate entity, and felt privileged like an explorer.

After we both came, me twice, I think, and we lay in the stillness and peace that always follows, Ted reached again for me and held my hand. "I'm a P.I.," he said.

I heard him, but my mind was slow and lazy then. Those were letters, and they stood for something, and it was something he thought I'd know, and I was still caught up in the sex, so I thought at first the P was for penis, then prostitute, and I went through paralyzed and Protestant (maybe thinking that what we had done was against some belief) and pork (I guess from the rinds) and finally private. I knew then, almost laughing. Why hadn't he just said detective? Did he want to sound like one of those TV stars?

"A gumshoe," I said, and did laugh, but then it hit me. "So you're not reviewing the café?"

"No."

"All those dishes I tried out on you?"

"Marvelous," he said. "Superb. Thank you."

I rolled up to a sitting position and looked down at him. "You lied."

"Not technically," he said. "But I have more to confess." He reached up and traced my right nipple with a finger. "I'm on a case."

"Now? I'm the case?" I thought of Aurora immediately, but that made no sense.

"Bev. I've been hired by Donna Wicher to dig up some dirt she can use to impugn Bev's character."

I leapt up, took my robe from the closet and put it on, then turned on the light. It was too much of a betrayal for nakedness and darkness.

"Close the shade," he said, "if you want me to get dressed, too."

I did and he did, all the while telling me he was sorry, and he had nothing on her anyway. She was smart and, even if not pleasant, certainly not evil. One reason he'd confessed was that he had nothing at all to give Donna Wicher that would help the Hilkers' case.

He was sitting on the side of my bed, and I sat beside him, rested my head on his shoulder. "Never mind," I said and meant it. It was not betrayal, not a serious one. I said that to myself, but wondered if I were lying, trying to put a good face on his spying on us so I could keep him. Not only was he separate from me, I realized, he was not even what my need had turned him into. "I'll get reviewed one way or another," I said. I truly was not worried about Bev at all. Hadn't Ted said he had nothing? And no wonder. What could he possibly say except she was crabby, and that was further proof of how absurd the whole lawsuit was, how desperate the Hilkers were.

Their daughter fucked a boy she liked because her English teacher was a bitch! We undressed and lay back on the bed, I fully expecting we'd do it all again, but Ted fell fast asleep, confession evidently a soporific. As I lay there and listened to his ragged but faint breathing, I knew I would not tell Bev.

In the light of day, Ted's confession was 100 percent insignificant. I probably was falling in love with him and so should cut him some slack. Moreover, Ted could not hurt Bev because there was no dirt, and no one could be sued successfully for being bitchy. I knew I would get a review eventually. I would just have to try harder.

I'd have to try harder to create the dish I could use for my application to l'École de Cuisine Internationale, too, and I had one in mind already. By the time Ted left late Sunday morning, I was ready to try it, but first I needed a few ingredients from Sav-A-Sum. Because walking just the few blocks in late August heat would have made me light-headed enough to forget what I wanted, I decided to drive, and so I saw the disaster on Sunday, saw it before Bev did.

Can you call something so easy to fix a disaster? Probably not, but the sadness of it was increased by how often it occurred and how matter-of-factly the victims handled it. The passenger-side front window of Bev's car—a white five-year-old Civic parked behind my old car, also white—had been smashed in. Glass was on the seat and on the grass and curb along Meramec. A tire iron, a metal pipe, a ball bat—any of those could've been used. Some said kids, meaning teenagers, were responsible; some said age didn't matter. Mean people wielded the bats. Most of us pictured men or boys, and I don't know why we assigned gender to the meanies. This was the first time I'd been the one to discover the crime, but then I'd been back in the neighborhood a mere six months. Dad'd had his windows smashed a few times, sometimes a head or taillight, too. It was a hazard of street parking, and the kind of car made no difference. I'd fooled myself into believing my nine-year-old Toyota Tercel was safe, and Bev claimed her Civic was, too. It was one reason she said she kept the car, called it a city car, one not likely to attract vandals or thieves. Both of us must have tried hard not to notice the other cars in the neighborhood, the Neons and Escorts and those ten-or-twelve-year-old Oldsmobiles and Plymouths that had at least one plastic bag for a window. For that was the easy method of repair: a cleaners' or grocery bag duct taped around the window. For some like us it was a temporary solution, but for those without comprehensive insurance, it became permanent, a way of ensuring that particular window would not be broken again.

I used a thick plastic that had once been wrapped around thirty pounds of sausage to repair Bev's window. By the time it was securely taped and the glass swept and vacuumed up, I was drenched with sweat again. Before breaking the news to her, I told myself I'd ask what she was trying to prove by settling in here among mean people. I had asked her that often, and had yet to hear a good answer. Sure, not all were mean down in that area people called the near South side, but Aunt Josie and Uncle Al, in their far west suburb, had never had their car windows smashed. It was the heat making me crabby, I decided, making it harder than usual to smile over this minor problem. It's only a window, I told myself as I drove to Sav-A-Sum. After all, it's only a window, I said as I stood in the check out line. *It's only a window*, I repeated as I reparked my car in front of her damaged one. *It's only a window*, I said one more time before getting down to the job at hand, creating a new dish.

Dad often complained that pork cutlets had a bad reputation, low-class and fatty, fit only for boring old dinners when covered by gravy the color and texture of paste. Well, he'd say, he had to admit the cutlet worked well that way and the fashion of turning one's nose up at good food just because it was artery clogging and simple was one that couldn't pass soon enough. But, Dad said, the cutlet was also good for so much more. It was good quality pork, not like sausages at all. It was tender and, like, good chicken breast, would take on exotic flavors well. With Dad's words in mind, I decided to experiment with the cutlet. Because I was asked on my application to join cultural culinary traditions and the pork cutlet, as well as being the southside housewife's fare, was also in the fake version of Wiener schnitzel, I decided to add a Mexican touch to the German and dust the cutlet with cumin. Rather than gravy, I would make a sauce of orange and lemon juice and garlic to give it even more bite. Instead of the mashed potato/green bean/apple-sauce/sauerkraut accompaniment, I chose to serve the pork over greens marinated in an Asian sauce that would pick up the citrus flavors of the cutlet sauce. I made that Asian sauce first by mixing peanut oil, lime juice, a shallot, a chili, fish sauce, and sugar. Then I sautéed some mustard greens, bok choy, and some of the basil from my backyard garden, then tossed it all with the sauce and let it sit as I started on the cutlets.

Sure, I knew our clientele were not gourmets, but delicious was delicious, and no one, I thought, should be put off by any odd combination if it resulted in a good taste. I was proud of our menu as it was, but I knew even good food could get boring, and more specials would mean more business.

I also knew Bev didn't care. Nor, for that matter, did many others. As I mixed the juices for the pork sauce, I told myself that had often been the lot of cooks, maybe since the dawn of time. We prepared food for people who didn't care if what they filled their stomachs with was interesting or even good. Well, OK, most of our clientele cared that my food was edible, but that was all. Even if it wasn't especially tasty, they added enough salt and ketchup and cleaned up their plates anyway.

But as I dredged the cutlets in a cumin/flour mixture, I reminded myself that what I did was mix animal and vegetable matter that got cooked and went into mouths and was forced down tubes, mixed with acids, broken down to its elements, and absorbed into the blood. It was rather the essential cycle of life, and I was a valuable part of the cycle. More than that, some few would care. Ted, for example, already did. No, I was not feeding the starving or curing disease, not helping refugees or saving immortal souls, but I was making a few select lives better by adding taste and variety.

As I laid the cutlets in the melted, bubbly butter, I smiled at how valuable my creations would prove to be, even if there was no acclaim just yet. But the butter was already too hot, and when I left the cutlets alone for a mere few minutes to give the greens an extra toss and stir the pork sauce, the butter started to burn. When I smelled the burning butter, I knew the whole dish was ruined. Just like that. I should've used olive oil. I turned the heat down, turned the cutlets over, but the burn taste and smell was still in the butter, and the overpowering taste, no matter the other ingredients, was now carbon.

I finished the dish anyway and made up two plates, Asian vegetables underneath the cutlets as planned, citrus sauce over all. I carried the plates upstairs because Bev was waiting to try my cre-ation, and would sneer some more or bitch if I went up with just a barbecue plate after all this time.

"It's interesting," she said after her first bite. We sat across from each other at the Formica kitchen table, a small electric fan whirring under the table to help the large window unit in the kitchen by cooling our feet.

"Eat more of the vegetables," I said. "I think they're the best part." "Never cared for mustard greens," she said, and took another bite of pork. "Is there orange juice in here?"

I nodded.

She looked thoughtful as she chewed. "Too bad you burned it."

"The pork isn't really burned," I said. "Just the flour coating. Butter burns." I told myself I would be quiet from then on. Why did I want to defend my mistake?

"Whatever," she said. "I hope you don't intend to serve burned food downstairs."

As if you'd care was what I wanted to say.

She faked a laugh. "I mean, first poison soup, then burned pork. I'm beginning to understand what you meant by getting us a reputation."

I smiled. "I know the burned butter tastes bad. I'll try to do better." Bring it on, I told her in our imaginary conversation. I'm big enough to take it. But I continued talking to her in my mind. Don't forget the peppers. Don't forget the quiche, the barbecue sauce. Go ahead and pound on me if you must because you have one leg and no fingers. I'll smile. I can take it. No, I didn't feel humble, but rather thick-skinned, the kind that passes for vir-tuous. I remembered being eleven and confirmed in my Catholic faith, filled with the Holy Spirit and made strong and tough, good because I was thick-skinned enough to turn the other cheek. Bev would never know how much business I'd brought in already. I could be my own cheerleader for a time, do it for both of us if I had to, for me and the ungrateful bitch.

"Speaking of mistakes," I said, "the bastards got your car window. Maybe we should both park on the back pad from now on, overnight." That took some wind out of her sails. She sighed, looked down at her plate.

"Sorry," she said, as if it had been my car.

"It's only a window, " I said.

She looked up at me. "I'm tired of working so hard. I don't know why you talked me into being open six days a week."

"Most successful places are."

"Well, I'm going to hire Maddie to help out. Give her the job she wants. Don't know why, but some days, I just want to stay in bed."

By Tuesday, Bev did stay in bed all day, and Maddie was handling the cash register, filling water glasses, bussing tables. Those at least were her duties, but we had a grand total of four customers on Tuesday. All day. Rollie, one of the gas company guys, ordered biscuits and gravy mid-morning but barely touched it. He told me one short story about his defective satellite dish and his plan to get his money back, but that was it. Quite unusual for a guy who talked so much about himself that I knew the names of his dentist and his auto mechanic. The chiropractor had only coffee. He rested an elbow on the table and propped his head up with a hand as he sipped it. The two women from the thrift shop came in for lunch, ordered egg salad, and though they sat directly under the AC vent, they fanned themselves with our laminated menus.

Maddie leaned against the counter beside the cash register and rubbed her belly, burping often.

Out of boredom, I told the thrift shop women about Bev's car window, and they said it was too bad such things went on. Each of them had had windows smashed, and one had had the air let out of a tire. Kids, they said, and shrugged. I told them I was tired of living among mean people, kids or adults. I said I guessed some people were too poor to move out and had to live with it. Maybe those people had to get a bit mean themselves, so it was easy to see why poor people were meaner than most others. Of course, nice people also lived down in this area, I said. Take them as an example. They perked up at that—amazing how a small innocuous compliment can revive the wilted—and told me about their lives.

They were married to twins and lived near each other in a more expensive and farther west section of the city. One husband was a high school principal and the other an accountant. The women said they operated the thrift shop not as a profit making venture but as a community service.

"How did you end up with twins? Did you know each other before?"

"We had each gone to a bar, McNulty's on Bates and something, Eichelberger maybe," one said.

"The same night. A Friday in January. We didn't know each other then. I went in with a few girlfriends. She went in to talk her father into going home," the other one said.

"We saw these gorgeous, red-headed twins sitting at the bar. They had curly hair and blue eyes and they were doing a Bob and Ray radio routine for the few patrons.

"We both gravitated toward the twins. We stayed for hours. My girlfriends left, and all four of us went to dinner. She never found her father."

"It was twelve years ago," the first one said. "Twelve years of heaven."

"I understand," I told them, and because I thought we were sharing truths, I continued. "I had fifteen years of heaven before my husband left me."

"Oh," the first one said.

"He fell in love with someone else, and I didn't have a clue until he told me. I thought we were happy," I said.

"Well, well," the other one said.

"I was happy," I said.

They each placed a hand on my arm, shook their heads.

"I'm OK," I said. "Really." I meant it, but I had deflated their spirits with my honesty. Both refused dessert, then paid their check and left without even finishing their iced teas.

On Thursday, August 30, the wind came down from the north and blew fluffy clouds across a dark blue sky. The petunias across the street raised their heads, Maddie stopped burping, and I started thinking up other dishes. The gas company guy started talking again; the thrift shop women married to twin redheads smiled; our other customers returned and mostly cleaned up their plates.

BEV

Way back in mid-July, I was deposed in Howard Figg's office by both Howard and the opposing counsel, Donna Wicher. The questions and answers were taken down by a court reporter I felt sorry for because he had to work fast, and what he was writing was boring even to those of us involved, so I wished I could have thought of details to add that would have been funny or shocking or at least not so dull as the reality—a teacher who had tried to get a bunch of giggly girls to grow up. I was asked how long I'd taught at Agnus Dei—ten years—what I taught—English—how many students I normally had charge of—twenty in homeroom—if I considered myself successful as a teacher. I lied about the successful teacher question, said yes with no qualifications. I was asked the purpose of homeroom period, specifically the purpose of a general discussion period in homeroom. I told the court reporter that those general discussions had been instigated by the administration at the suggestion of the parents' association as a way of reinforcing values, and they called it character education. I laughed when I said it, just slightly less than I had when I first heard it from the principal. The court reporter kept a straight face. Howard asked me directly if I'd told the girls they did not have to tell their parents everything, and I said yes. Donna Wicher asked me if that statement was official policy aimed at character education.

The court reporter did not laugh at that either, and I nearly gave up on his sense of humor. I said my so-contested statement was solely my own, emphasizing the words *solely* and *my own* to let her know how stupid I thought her question. Howard asked if I'd ever made similar statements, and even though he shook his head at my answer, I said probably. I told all three of them I thought my girls should be growing into adulthood, able at least some of the time to make their own decisions. Donna Wicher asked if I truly thought of them as my girls, and Howard shook his head again. I just kept quiet, rolled my eyes at the court reporter who, of course, was not looking. Donna Wicher asked me if I thought making their own decisions precluded telling their parents about those decisions, and I said no, knowing I could do nothing about the court reporter's boredom and should quit trying. I said I had not said "don't tell." Howard asked if I had meant to advise secrecy in matters of dating and sex, and I said not necessarily. Donna Wicher asked if I wanted to correct my mistake now. Howard coughed and said, "Now wait a minute," but I was smart enough to see it as a trick, and merely said I did not think my statement had been a mistake, all the while wondering if the court reporter had recorded the cough, and if so, how. That was about it. The court reporter left without a word. Howard and Donna discussed their respective golf games, and after she left Howard told me to set up an appointment with his office manager for sometime in August to plan strategy.

But after the Hilkers opted for a jury trial, Howard called and said we would still meet in August, but we could relax a bit, had more time to play with. The trial was scheduled for October.

The Hilkers were asking for a few hundred thousand, not nearly enough according to them to feed and clothe the future child, but enough to make me sorry for my corrupting ways. Their pretense, of course, was that they wanted to spare others the sorrow that came from being around me. Howard said the amount was laughable, and even if they won it would be reduced. If the jury saw me as culpable, he said, it wouldn't be to the extent that Maddie herself and the child's father were culpable.

All that happened July 17th, and nearly two months later my parents and Shelly and even Ted were still full of questions I couldn't answer.

What amount would Howard consider not laughable? Dad asked. Was I sure it was too late to change my statement and say I hadn't meant any of it? Mom asked in various ways a few times a week. Shelly wondered why Howard had not asked questions to highlight the good and smart things I'd said. And though I knew she meant well, I gave her no credit for intent and asked her whose side she was on. What I'd said had been smart, and I told her to take a flying leap. She refused to be insulted, merely sighed. Whenever I recreated the non-drama of the deposition for any of them, they listened so hard their lips flattened out and their eyes narrowed and their noses wrinkled up and they nodded and frowned to indicate deep pondering, as if by exercising their facial muscles enough, they would find an angle Howard had missed.

Maddie's deposition was discussed, too. She said she'd admitted to liking me so much she considered my advice better than her mother's, but she also said she hadn't been paying attention and so hadn't heard me the first time, but had heard the offending remark many times later when it became an issue at school. All the girls from all the homerooms heard it then, and they all thought it cool. But no, she wasn't thinking of it when she had unprotected intercourse with Jason, the lover/prophet/poet/father I had yet to meet. Why hadn't she asked her mother's advice before said intercourse was another of Donna Wicher's questions. Well, duh, Maddie answered.

What Howard and I had made to Donna Wicher and the Hilkers in the beginning was a demurrer, not an answer. This meant we admitted the fact—my statement—but denied it was a cause for action. By July we'd also filed a cross-complaint seeking affirmative relief from the stupid lawsuit. Howard and I met in

August to begin planning my defense, one that would rely heavily on the jury pitying a deformed woman. He told me then that he wanted to be prepared for anything, no surprises was how he put it, and so he asked me to make a list of all the negative things that could be said about me. It was a big job.

I'd used Howard for my lawyer on the Foxborough Settlement because he was a fellow southsider from a family of southsiders, and Dad knew of him from another source, too. Dad was midwest district manager for Prudential Life then, and one of Prudential's lawyers had a brother in St. Louis who chased ambulances, specializing in personal injury. That was Howard. Though all of us damaged by Mother's Help had different lawyers, we all got the standard settlement of so much for each limb or digit or other missing parts, and, as far as I could tell, Howard's job had been merely to fill in the forms correctly, date and document my condition, little else. Still, because I won, I called him my lawyer and used him for the Hilker business, hoped to use him for Toby's adoption. But our conferring on facts and details, on plans and what he called strategy, hadn't created many stronger connections between us. He had no interest in literature, in teaching, in running a café. Well, come to think of it, neither did I, at least not any longer. But I thought golf an idiotic pastime, and worse. The waste of land and the chemical treatments used to make the greens smooth and the fairways attractive were damaging the soil, killing the worms and grubs, and hurting our water supply. Besides that, I was constitutionally unable to bond with those who sat behind super-sized cherry-wood desks with brass lamps.

One very minor connection we had was Sally Figg, Howard's daughter. The afternoon in August I met with him, I ran into Sally first. I was in the waiting room because another of Howard's clients was taking longer than the allotted half-hour, and Sally dropped in, hoping her father would be free for lunch. He wasn't, but she smiled when she saw me and gave me the kind of awkward hug that a standing person gives to a sitting one, exclaiming loudly and almost squealing how happy she was to see me. Her hair was so heavily hennaed it was the color of aged, raw sirloin. She had a long face with oval cheeks like iron-on elbow patches, and her lipstick matched her hair. I knew she wasn't the kind of beauty I'd lived among, but she would've been called striking, and, in her low-slung jeans and tight T-shirt, probably hip.

Sally was in my class at Bishop DuBourg High, but by the time we graduated, her father had made partner, and she was sent off to some Eastern US college, Howard no doubt hoping to distance her from the aura of Bishop DuBourg High. We in St. Louis called others down in the South Side hoosiers, and it had nothing to do with folks from Indiana. Hoosiers said *yous*, and often added *guys* behind it. Hoosier women screamed obscenities at their children, wore clothes that let all the cellulite show, and read movie magazines. Hoosier men spat on the sidewalks, and hoosier teenagers all smoked cigarettes. Hoosiers were TV- talk-show-watching mouth breathers who were too out of it to know they were hoosiers. Naturally, Howard wanted to shake the hoosier dust from him and his family, so Sally went east. Our paths seldom crossed, but by the time Howard was working on my case, he provided periodic news bulletins—Sally was living with a painter; Sally was pregnant. Sally and I hadn't been pals in high school, so I hadn't felt with her the desperation of being pushed farther and farther from the center as I had with those of my own circle who removed themselves with each milestone. So I could feign interest, and I almost liked her.

"I hear you have a café now," Sally said. "Sounds like fun."

I laughed, said fun was probably an overrated reason for doing things anyway.

"We should have lunch sometime, that is, if you won't see it as a busman's holiday."

"I'd like that," I said as she sat in the leather-covered wing chair beside mine. Maybe I would like it, I told myself. At least I believed her about lunch.

She was an architect, registered, certified, and licensed—whatever they did to architects. She was the unmarried mother of a preteen girl who would soon be sent to one of the more liberal versions of Agnus Dei for wealthy humanists. She lived in Compton Heights, an old section of the city that was surrounded on all sides by decaying and notoriously dangerous neighborhoods. Compton

Heights, though, was a gated community of mansion-like houses set on large lots and surrounded by hundred-year-old oaks and sycamores. The houses there needed upkeep, expensive upkeep at that, but not true rehabilitation. They'd been built for the wealthy in the first place, so weren't like the homes of former blue-collar workers now being yuppied up in a few other areas of St. Louis. Like most of the residents of Compton Heights, Sally sent her daughter to a private junior high school in the west suburbs. These were people who prided themselves on their commitment to the city but would never send their children to city schools or even to the local parish school. They relied on their gates, their neighborhood patrols, their motion-sensor lights and alarms, and their own sense of goodness to protect them, to enable them to declare to one and all they were not afraid of city living.

Sure, I saw it as hypocritical but was no more than normally offended. I wasn't naïve. I accepted, even partook of, hypocrisy, believing it a human condition we couldn't avoid, as much a part of us as envy and gluttony, as hard to notice in ourselves as cancer or bad breath. And I gave Sally the benefit of the doubt, too, created reasons for her hypocrisy. I decided she was following her heart, no matter the accommodations she had to make. Beauty, I guessed, was nearly all to Sally, and not the kind of beauty the Stillwell girls trusted in, but a more lasting, architectural beauty. Maybe beautiful women like the Stillwells had lived in the house Sally now lived in when it was new. If so, they were not merely dead, but their flesh was long gone from their bones, their beauty barely a memory captured on already fading photographs. Yet their house survived. I imagined Sally's heart quickening at the turret and the wide, sweeping porch, the bay window and the stained glass, the front and back oak doors, the three-foot thick outside walls, and the red tile roof. Hers had a marble entry hall, molded plaster cornices, oak window sills and baseboards, a ballroom, a butlers' pantry, three fireplaces, and a fruit cellar. I'd driven by the house, and knew the rest from Howard. Sally's house was one hundred and thirty years old, and I believed Sally lived there, as many of her neighbors did, as a protector of the beauty, protection being a part of love, and beauty always needing protection. I made her motivations up, of course. We'd never confided in each other.

"I hear you're involved in a nuisance suit," Sally said. "Even Dad's amazed at what people will sue for now, how their minds work."

"I'm not worried," I said. "Maybe I should be."

"Ha!" she said. "Just the opposite. No one ever should worry."

She leaned closer. "Speaking of worry," she said, "I hear you're back in the old neighborhood. Can you stand it? What's it like?"

"It's ugly. It's a mess. It's where I fit in." Those three sentences together, all true, left me unaccountably angry at Sally, and this immediately after I'd dismissed her hypocrisy. "What's it like? What do you mean what's it like? It's only two miles from your city on the hill. It's not Katmandu."

"I mean, so many of the good, solid families like yours have moved out. That's all. The people who have moved in are different."

"Yeah. The two-headed ones are the worst." It was the same old question in St. Louis—How's the neighborhood?—and it meant race, sure, but much more. It meant wealth and background and class, family roots versus transience. I wasn't down there out of a sense of duty but because nowhere else had been home. During my ten years at Agnus Dei, I'd lived in various apartments in western St. Louis County, sometimes alone but most often with fellow teachers or other girlfriends who ended up moving in with men, what I had thought of as our home life only a temporary situation to them. I'd been in places with pools and balconies and walk-in closets and had learned to see them as temporary, too, almost as movie sets. And I'd worked at Agnus Dei, surrounded by parents and their children who were used to getting their ways. I said as much to Sally. "You know it was not just that those wealthy folk at Agnus Dei who considered themselves high up on the food chain, like you maybe, wanted me to apologize. That alone wasn't what drove me from my job. It was that the parents there treated us teachers as if we were subordinates, merely providing a service.

If they approved, they rewarded us well with Waterford vases at Christmas as they did their nannies, their laundresses, their landscapers. But where I live now, the neighborhood you seem to have an anthropological interest in, the neighborhood that is so far removed from your kind, people not only accept disappointment and failure, they expect it. Well, sure it makes them the opposite of nice, but unlike those who hide out behind gates, they are not themselves props in their own lives."

Just then Howard's receptionist told me I could go back to his office, and as I stood, Sally did, too. "Don't be angry at me just because I live in a nice home."

I shrugged as I walked away, but wasn't ashamed of my outburst. And it wasn't about her nice home. I could buy one of those mansions if I wanted to. People like Sally were seldom contradicted, were smiled at often, given in to. Maybe I'd done a good thing by telling her off, for her own character, I meant. On the other hand, I knew Sally's innocent question—how is it down there?—shouldn't have set me off. I was not a preacher, and I truly did not give a shit about any of it anyway. I guessed Sally and I would not have that lunch after all.

By the very last days of August, I wanted to stay in bed all day, so I did. I knew in my bones that the entire Division of Family Services had met in secret and decided to string me along, maybe as a way to relieve their own boredom, but on no account would they give me Toby, not even if no one else wanted him. I'd accumulated enough black marks somehow to be dead in the water. And even a burnt-out drunk didn't want my body, not even for casual sex, and I understood him. I didn't want it either, but I still had to drag it about with me day in and day out. My car window was smashed, which further proved my poor choice of location. I was living behind bars, and what was worse than all of it, I was only halfway through my thirties. I could have fifty or more years of what was already a downhill run. That was unless the doomsayers were right and the world would come crashing down on January first. I was certain I would not be part of the rapture, and I knew I would rather take my chances with the damned.

At least I didn't need lights on all the time as comfort. Except for those nights Ted stayed over, Shelly had kept at least one light on in her room above the café since the break in. Yet she'd claim to be the opposite of a defeatist. A doer, she would say, much more than a survivor, a positive soul. She'd never give in. She ran from defeat as it nipped at her heels. Yes, I told her as I lay in bed and stared up at my cracked ceiling. You're a positive soul, and I'm a ballerina.

After four days of self-pity, I got up because even my dreams were depressing and my back was stiff and my teeth slimy. The heavy feeling of something pressing down on me and the vague feeling of wanting to flee but not going was still there, but Toby had been in looking for me at least once already. My maternal yearnings, sudden and surprising, didn't make me more accepting of other humans, either. I knew we humans were the cause of all sorrow, but Toby, the one I wanted to mother, had already been rejected, hurt, maybe ruined. All I was doing was cleaning up a bit of the human mess about me.

The morning I went back to the café, I started early, had two sheets of biscuits ready for the oven by 6:30 AM. I forced this energy by lecturing myself continually—don't let down, keep moving, smile. I sounded like Shelly on her worst days. It was a Friday, the end of Toby's third week back at St. Hedwig's, and to keep myself upright, I imagined his interest in algebra and world history, new subjects in the fifth grade, he'd told me, his quick mind already latching onto particles of knowledge that would tell him how the world worked.

Maddie was in and so-called working for us, but it was clear she wasn't cut out for a service job. She didn't chat with the customers and clearly resented pouring more water or refilling napkin dispensers. I couldn't fault her for that. She pouted when Shelly told her she would get tips if she smiled a bit, and I understood that whether Maddie liked it or not, she would become her mother, was already growing into the role, born to have help, not be help. So I vowed to say no if she asked off early.

Mike didn't come by that Friday until much later but instead went through what I guessed was his entire repertoire three or more times, never giving the organ a rest or us a break. We heard him above our air conditioner that seemed to be clanking a warning—"Take cover. I'm going to blow."

Shelly's blueberry soup was a hit for some reason, so she skipped about and kept herself busy by printing up little cards she folded as tents and placed on the tables, asking for comments. She was sure they would be glowing.

Toby came in at 3:15 and climbed up on his usual stool. "Want a sailboat?" he asked me.

"No," I said. "I have enough trouble standing on dry land."

"Afraid you'd fall overboard?"

"I would fall overboard. I'm sure of it."

"Can't you swim?"

"My fake leg makes swimming impossible, but," and here I paused before the part I knew he'd like, "it floats. I can't drown."

He gave me exactly what I'd hoped. He said "Wow," and I continued.

"Other kids used to hang on it in the deep water. Five could use it as a float at a time. Six counting me."

He looked at me with admiration, even envy. "Wow," he said again. "Wish we'd gone swimming this summer."

"Maybe next summer," I said, pleased with the phrase. Next summer extended our contact. "What's with the sailboat?"

"It's a raffle for our fall carnival. A dollar a ticket."

I took ten tickets and gave him a slice of apple pie. As he ate, I asked him what literature he read in the fifth grade. Any novels? He wasn't sure but thought he was supposed to read a book about a sled dog. When he turned his head so his thick lenses briefly did not reflect the kitchen fluorescent light, I noticed an extra sparkle in his eyes.

"Can I work it?" he asked.

"What?"

"Your leg. Can I put it on you?"

I hesitated. It was an intimate procedure, one I hadn't even envisioned with Mike. But then, perhaps still thinking of next summer, I thought of my bathing suit, thick and impenetrable spandex, and decided it wouldn't be improper to let Toby buckle my straps over my suit. Just as a demonstration. Maybe he'd grow up to be an engineer. Not one person had ever asked to put my leg on. Not one. "Sure. We'll try it tomorrow."

Shelly, who as usual had been listening, said, "I told you Jeannie Lemp was in yesterday, didn't I?"

I nodded. She'd made a point of telling me how good her cover for my absence had been. If she'd said I was at the market or on some other errand, Jeannie would've expected to see me later, so Shelly had told her I was at a small business seminar. Shelly'd said she couldn't remember the sponsor of the seminar—making it hard for Jeannie to check. It made me seem responsible, Shelly said. Concerned with success.

"Well, she said she'd be back tomorrow." Shelly gave me what could only be called a meaningful look—her eyebrows forming high arches and her mouth set in a straight line.

"She won't come in on Saturday. Government workers take the weekends off, you know, because of all that stress."

"Some do have a lot of stress," Ted said.

I didn't even look at him. He hung out at the counter so often he was like a piece of equipment we'd ordered but forgotten why we wanted it—an espresso machine, a video game station.

"Ms. Burke was being sarcastic," Maddie said, shaking her head at Ted. "I mean everybody knew that."

"Ted knew that, too," Shelly said. "His remark was a contradiction."

"Whatever," Maddie said.

Toby sold raffle tickets to Ted, Shelly, Maddie, and Rollie the gas company guy before he left at four. Maddie did a half-assed floor sweeping and table wiping, then left, too, without a word. Ted sat like a growth on his stool at the counter, twirling lazily and watching Shelly load the dishwasher. I was re-wiping the tables Maddie'd only made worse when Mike came in through the back door for leftovers. To keep myself from going back to bed, I suggested one of our picnics in Carondolet Park instead.

"Summer's dying," I said to convince him. "It will be months before we sweat again." I knew if I confided in Mike about my excitement at Toby wanting to strap my leg on, he wouldn't shake his head or wag his finger at me. Not that he was broadminded, but, because it had nothing to do with him and couldn't reflect back on his life or refer somehow to his own misery, he could talk about Toby and me and my straps, maybe even do it with interest. Being with Mike was a break in that way. He wasn't trying to protect me or keep me from making a mistake.

We chose a table on the terrace above the boat house lake. We ate Shelly's pulled pork sandwiches in silence, savoring the award-winning sauce, and I made one of those revelations that isn't new, that is made, the thing realized often. Eating with someone else, both of you biting and chewing and swallowing and tasting, creates a union that needs no words. But then I let myself be sad remembering my enforced independence. By the time I got my knee at age five, even Mom wouldn't strap my leg on. I had to do it myself, they all believed. They wanted me to think it no more of an ordeal than putting on my own shorts, tying my own shoes. A slight breeze blew our napkins off the table and all the way into the lake, so we were forced to lick the sauce off our fingers. I was going to tell Mike I should've been handled more, my straps worked more by others, but he spoke first.

"Going to preach finally," he said. "They're having a pancake breakfast on Sunday. Free food. It's for the homeless, really. They're going out in vans to round 'em up, bring 'em in."

"I would say the homeless have enough of a burden. Can't they eat without a sermon? Pretend they're at IHOP? Talk to one another or eat in silence?"

"The Salvation Army's first name is salvation," he said.

"Too bad."

"I know what you're thinking. A real sermon would be one thing, but what does this guy have to say? He's just a step up from homeless himself. That's it, isn't it?"

"No. I just don't like preaching."

"My title is 'How Can God Love Me?' It's a question. Want the answer?"

I didn't, but I nodded anyway.

"It's full of metaphors. He loves me the way a baker loves the cake that falls. He loves me the way a painter loves the painting no one wants, the one that comes out only halfway as planned."

"I think you're on the wrong track," I said. I watched a young girl being mobbed by Canada geese and almost pushed into the lake. She'd been trying to feed them from a bag of popcorn, offering one kernel at a time.

"God loves me," Mike continued, "the way a builder loves the house with unlevel floors, a sagging roof. Or like the dressmaker loves the dress with the upside down zipper. In other words, like a creator loves his mistakes. Not at all."

"Mike," I said, "I think you've missed the point of a sermon."

"God doesn't love his mistakes."

"The god you're talking about, the one these Salvation Army people claim to know, doesn't make mistakes."

"Lots of evidence to the contrary," he said. "There are two examples at this table."

I didn't argue. I saw the girl throw the whole bag down beside her in the grass and flee up the terrace toward us.

On Saturday, I was ready for Toby. I wore my black spandex suit that squeezed my excess body out at the leg holes under my slacks and the arm openings under my smock-like blouse, but he didn't show up. Neither did Jeannie Lemp, as I'd predicted. I wore my suit Monday, too, but no Toby. I didn't jump with both feet to the conclusion that he was in trouble just because he hadn't shown up when he said he would—it was his way, after all—but then again, he could have been and I would have no way of knowing. When Jeannie Lemp came in on Tuesday, I suggested she check up on Toby, giving as my reason Lana's track record of not watching him carefully. She took that not only as sour-grapes criticism of Lana—"Don't criticize unless you've been in her shoes," she said in her Minnie Mouse voice—but also as my telling her, the professional social worker, how to do her job.

She even said as much. "You don't have to do my job for me. I am a professional." What she wanted to talk to me about was the lawsuit. Was this the first time I'd been sued for harming someone else's life? I knew I'd get further by being polite, by pretending not to see the trick and her bias, but instead I referred her to Howard, said surely she knew enough, as a professional social worker that is, to go through proper channels.

"It was just a friendly question," she said.

"And it was not answered," I said. "And it was not a friendly non-answer."

Shelly and Ted both shook their heads at me, and as Jeannie Lemp walked out the door, I felt a sudden lack of oxygen. Why were Shelly and Ted always listening? Even worse, why was my life measured by unattainable desires? I'd lately fallen back on "Star light, star bright," started picking up pennies found on the floor or counters only if they were heads up for good luck, playing computer solitaire and seeing it as a good omen if I won the first game I played. I'd not known I was superstitious, but, though I had long since trained myself away from wanting, I couldn't get past my wants, my wishes now. I wanted Toby. I wanted to keep him safe, to raise him, to sacrifice for him. I wanted Shelly and Ted to mind their own business, and I wanted someone to say I was good enough to get my wish, at least good enough to befriend without needing advice. I was not a project. After Jeannie Lemp left, the air in the café was suddenly thin, and I had to get out, too. I stood on the gum-splotched sidewalk and took a few deep breaths as I watched Jeannie walk away. Then I closed my eyes and pretended the air I gulped was clean, and I was in a warm field of wheat.

When I got back in, Maddie asked me if she could take off early. We had only two customers, the thrift shop women, but it was not quite noon, and we would get more. I told her no, said I'd have to work too hard if she left, and I was the boss so I shouldn't have to work. She said she guessed she'd quit then; the job hadn't really worked out for her anyway. "I need more of a challenge," she said. "Something harder." I was proud of myself for not laughing.

All she did to quit was remove her apron. She continued leaning against the counter as always, kept staring into space as she had done since I'd hired her. "I think I'll have a glass of milk," she said after a time, moving from her post to a deuce by the wall. "Whole milk, not that two percent."

When we ignored her, she said, "If I have to get it myself, no one gets a tip." When we continued to ignore her, she got up, went back to the kitchen, and poured herself a glass. "That was a joke, you know, about the tip."

I did laugh then, remembering she wasn't far enough from high school. No matter that she looked like a grown up woman, even said grown up things at times, she was still on the verge, teetering between childhood and adulthood, leaning over, but not there yet.

"Mom is taking it, you know, " she said once she was seated at the deuce again.

"What?" Shelly said.

"What?" one of the thrift shop women asked at the same time.

"The child. It's a boy. She said she will raise it. Doesn't matter what anyone, not even Jason, says. Says she always wanted a boy. Says I can be like its big sister, come home from college and play with it. At least until I'm ready for it, if ever. She's quitting the hospital auxiliary."

I should've been happy that the kid wouldn't be fostered out or abandoned or raised in poverty and squalor as so many with teenage mothers were, but I wasn't. Maddie's mother was self-centered and supercilious and always got her way. Being the kid's caregiver (I knew that was how she would say it) would give her more cachet at the country club and, with all the nannies and home helpers, little of the work. If this kid turned out fine—and by that she would mean financially successful—she'd take the credit for selflessly giving up her life to raise him, and if he was a disappointment—anything other than financially successful—she'd blame it on Maddie's mistake, on Jason's genes.

"She wants to be home for Randolph James. She's already named him after her father. She's had a designer in to turn the guest room into a nursery. Randolph James is on the waiting list for Gatesworth Academy pre-school already."

We had our usual fifteen or so late lunch customers, and I pretended to be so exhausted by the rush that I had to go to bed as soon as we closed, even before we cleaned up. I got upstairs, just barely lay down—my leg still attached—when the phone rang. It was Sally Figg asking if Thursday would be a good day for lunch, and I decided I could put up with her for an hour or so, perhaps even remain civil. We agreed to meet at a place in a central west suburb.

"And just so you know," she said, "my younger brother lives in the old neighborhood. His daughter knows you, too. Calls you the one-fingered pie lady. Her name is Peaches." I thought then that maybe I could like Sally in the same way she liked the city, with very narrow vision, picking some good to focus on and ignoring the rest.

Just as I hung up, the door bell sounded, and I lurched down the stairs to find Mike leaning against the front of the building. He had come in the back, but Shelly had said I was upstairs, so he had walked around to ring the doorbell. "Couldn't she have just given you some of the leftovers?" I asked.

"She did." He held up a plastic bag. "This is about something else."

I invited him up, and he started talking before we gained the landing. "Want to know how it went yesterday? Good," he said, "Real good."

We were in the living room by then, and we sat together on the couch. "I was a hit."

"The God's mistake sermon was a hit?"

"I chickened out. Said what you said, God doesn't make mistakes. I said it just seems to us like he does because we are not en-lightened enough. I said it's all part of a plan and God's plan will always work."

"The same old stuff," I said.

"Exactly," he said. "One guy came up later and said, 'Thanks, Buddy. Thanks for telling the same old lie. Makes us feel better.'"

I laughed.

"That's when it hit me. I was a success. Success was easy, a question of telling the same lies I've heard. Not much thinking involved. If I had said what I thought, they wouldn't have liked it, would've booed or cried at the truth. So I've made a decision. I'm going to divinity school. I can do it as well as all those others. I'll graduate and get a congregation. I'll get a house."

I tried to control myself but laughed anyway.

"My flock'll invite me to dinner. I'll get to know them all, help most of them. And all I have to do is tell the same old lies, stop thinking. I can do it," he said. "I can do it like that." He snapped his fingers and smiled. "I've found my calling. Call me Reverend Mike."

The next day, Toby did come by after school, and I took him up the back way and into my bedroom, then closed the door. As he sat on my bed, I took off my shoes and pants and blouse, and so stood before him in my black spandex, my socket and straps visible. "Wow," he said. He stood up but didn't touch me.

"It works like this," I said and guided his hands along the leather straps, one front and one back, that ran from the top of my prosthesis to the bend in my skin at the leg hole of my suit. The front and back straps were connected there by brad and eyes to a belt I wore at an angle, buckling up across and above the opposite hip. Toby said "Wow," again as we both sat on my bed and I unbuckled the belt, then pulled the leg off, and even removed the sock from the end of my stump.

I was patient with him as he replaced the sock, then moved his hands up the top of my thighs to pull the straps up—always the hard part as I had to remain sitting for it—and then reached around me and fastened the hip belt at the second hole. I'd had this leg for nearly nine years, and had moved from the fourth to the second hole as my hips thickened.

He beamed when he finished, insisting I stand and walk for him, his crooked smile taking up most of his ugly little face. He ran his hands along the straps once more before I put my pants back on. I had never been happier.

SHELLY

On one of the last days of September, I saw something sad in the Alibi Café. Well, it may not have been sadder than many things that go on in homes and offices and other restaurants across the world. As Ted told me later, it wasn't nearly as sad as the killings and starvations and misery caused by dictators and foreign-run governments and CIA-bungled coups and assassinations. But I know it was sad.

Before this sad thing, though, I went to a new doctor, hoping to find one who could stop my headaches, which for a few weeks had come more often and with blurred vision. This one was an MD/homeopath/osteopath Aunt Josie had recommended because of my oft-made complaint that none of the other doctors had had a clue how to help. Bev said they were all quacks anyway, and I should face up to the truth, which was my head would hurt for the rest of my life, and lots of other things would hurt, too, as I aged. I nodded at her, but went to Aunt Josie's doctor anyway. Her name was Jamie Newburg, and even as I made the appointment her name made me decide I should do a Newburg sauce for shrimp or crab sometime, see how it went over.

Jamie Newburg believed in natural remedies as much as she believed in blasting away with extra-strength chemicals. She laughed, one of those shrill, animal-in-the-wild laughs that seem forced, and said she went both ways.

"Whatever works," she said. Her front teeth were so bucked, she pronounced "works" as "wux." She admired my posture, my clear skin, and my low blood pressure before she asked me to describe my headaches.

"Like an army of red ants and an army of black ants are engaged in guerrilla warfare inside my skull, using the convolutions in my brain as their trenches and tunnels. The casualties are high, but new recruits keep coming." I told her aspirin did not work, nor did acetaminophen or ibuprofen, no matter how extra-strength.

"What does?"

"Nothing."

"When does your head not hurt?"

Never, I thought, but knew that couldn't be true. Maybe it hurt less when I cooked, I told her, and especially if the dish turned out as the cumin-encrusted pork cutlets had on my second try.

"That's all?" she asked. "What about sex? How is your sex life?"

It seemed a rude or at least inappropriate question. A doctor is not a confessor after all.

"OK," I said.

"Full? Rewarding? Active? What does OK mean?"

I knew if she had been a he I would've felt violated by the questions, such is our hang-up with gender, but because she was a she, I elaborated. I told her I'd had two men since my ex-husband took a powder nine months earlier, and the second one, the current one, was the better of the two. I told her of course the headaches disappeared during sex, but neither partner had proved a lasting cure. She smiled, stroked my hand as she leaned closer to the examining table I perched on. Because she didn't write anything down, I felt betrayed, tricked into feeding her prurient appetite. I prepared myself for outrage if she asked for names.

"It's not welevant then," she said after what seemed a full minute. "Oftentimes it is. I have to check all angles."

Eventually, she asked me a series of questions that I considered more appropriate—pain or swelling elsewhere, history of
headaches, known allergies—all of which seemed dead ends. She
pressed down on my shoulders, back, and legs, poked my stomach,
closed her eyes and felt all over my face. When she finished, she
called Mercy Hospital and scheduled me for electromagnetic tests
she did not expect to reveal anything. She guessed my headaches
were an alwelgic reaction to a group of welated foods, and asked
me to explain my diet to her in as much detail as possible.

I could do better than that. I got off the examining table, the
paper gown I wore sliding off my shoulders as I moved, and retrieved my purse from the chair in the corner. I took out one of
the flyers I always carried and gave it to her. I'd intended to give
her one and drop the rest off in the waiting room anyway.

"Oh," she said, shaking her head as she read. "This will be
much more complicated than I thought. Almost everything you
have listed is a known al-wel-gen."

I told her I didn't eat much of any of it. Especially with the
real fattening items, I'd take only a spoonful to taste. I kept a
strict count, confined my calories to 1,300 a day in order to sustain
my weight. In fact, I'd never eaten a whole biscuit covered with
gravy, and I tasted my barbecue sauce by the quarter teaspoonful.
I knew she was on the wrong track. I expected the electromagnetic
scans to reveal something more serious, and I decided it would be
easier for me if I anticipated the worst possible news before the
results were in. I just hoped my hair would grow back as thick after
whatever surgery was deemed necessary. Bev said later that I had
wanted a tumor, but why would I? My insides were jelly at the possibility, but over the years I had learned expectation was a key. If I
expected the worst, I reacted better, no matter the news.

Doc Newburg gave me a schedule designed to narrow down
the food group that caused me trouble. Starting the next day, I
was to have rice, wheat flour, oats, corn meal, and any kind of
fresh vegetable except asparagus and leafy greens. The only spice I
could have was salt, and no animal meat, fat, fruits or their juices,

or dairy products. After three days, I could add dried legumes and a few Mediterranean herbs, and within a week I could add all fruits but citrus. It went on like that for eight weeks. I was to keep track of the frequency, intensity, and duration of my headaches, and note any other aches and pains. Before I left, Doc Newburg admired my fingernails, each one an individually painted abstract mix of brown, orange, and gold for the autumnal equinox. From one of the Sue Spritz Modeling Agency makeup specialists, I'd learned a valuable trick. Once my nails were dry, I rubbed a tiny bit of petroleum jelly over each one. It kept the lacquer from chipping or fading and it made the nails appear still wet. When I told Doc Newburg about my nail trick, she got out a prescription pad and wrote it down—the first time she had taken a note during our time together.

She said she needed something because her hobby was raising orchids, and the best way to determine the health of the plant, whether it needed repotting or feeding, was by poking a finger into the pot, gently rubbing and brushing against the roots on top of the soil, and she often chipped her nails this way. She said her husband thought the orchid house with its precise humidity and climate controls an extravagance, especially since the misting system cost as much as an in-ground pool would have, and she'd yet to place in the top three in any show. But, she continued, he did like the erotic possibilities of the orchid house, and admitted making love in it was more stimulating than doing it in a pool ever had been. It was the fwagwant humidity, she guessed, that and the danger to the orchids, taking a chance of killing a few with loud noises and heavy breathing. Often they killed one or two, at least sent them into shock.

I nodded, the polite response to such a show-off confession, and even joked with myself that she should've chosen to raise something she could pronounce; she had said awe-kid. But as I dressed, I wondered what kind of doctor was willing to kill something she cared about, something beautiful, for her own pleasure. And by the time I left her office, I knew I should've told her I found her attitude disgusting and that no lovemaking was worth killing a living thing. My search for a doctor was not yet over.

I'd always been a rule follower, but even before I drove out of the medical building parking lot, I knew I wouldn't keep to the food allergy detection schedule. How could I if I tasted my creations, and how could I create without tasting, and how could I get through one week, much less eight, without creating? Besides, I could almost feel the tumor. I located it in the top front left sector of my head, and not because that was where the pain was—the pain was everywhere—but something felt solid and thick up there, more so than normal. I pictured the tumor settled in, quietly, and I hoped slowly, gaining strength. My tests were scheduled for the following week, anyway, so the eight week schedule was moot. I would go for the tests, because I knew early detection was essential. I counted on surviving, no matter the odds. At the first stoplight, I took the allergen detection schedule from my purse, folded it many times into a tiny square, then pushed it way down into the litter bag hanging from my blower motor knob.

Later that night, I found myself telling Ted about my fears. "It's a punishment," I said. "It's a payback. I have always been in love with myself." Even as I talked I wondered how I could say such true things, even in the dark, even after making love. But I continued. "In love with my looks in particular. My best friend was always my mirror. Still is. I thought I was beautiful by myself, but if I was out with friends or dates and caught us all in a shop window, a restaurant mirror, I could be impressed by how breathtakingly beautiful I was compared to them. I was ashamed of that knowledge immediately, each time. Get over it, I'd say. Stop it. Who gave you the right to compare? But it goes beyond my face, my figure, my hair. My walk is graceful. My skin virtually blemish free, my eyes clear, my bones strong. My nails don't crack or break off. I guessed that inside I was better than average, too, my genes good, my cell walls strong but permeable. I've seldom been sick. But here I am, thirty-six. For some it's the verge of grown-up life, yet I'm in trouble. I have killer headaches and blurred vision, likely caused by a tumor. I'm falling apart early because I love me so much."

He lay beside me with an arm under my neck and around my shoulders. When I finished talking, he squeezed me. "You're not falling apart, Sweetie."

I laughed at *Sweetie*. Endearments often followed love-making, and though I did like Richard's calling me Honey, I had found it rude when Roger said it, even worse when he once called me Darling. Sweetie, though, was just plain funny.

"OK. Maybe you're not sweet after all," he said in response to my laughter. His voice was low and soothing, gentle. "But I am. Would you think so? I've been a security guard, a complaints representative, now a P.I. Not sweet jobs, any of them, but none of those are me. There's a lot unsettled. You know," he continued, even as he took his arm from around me, waved it in the air over our heads to restore the circulation, "children are often punished unfairly for what they didn't do, yet they get away with many other offenses. I'm like that. I was fired from my security job because of a boss's incompetence. He failed to check on an alarm light blinking for one of the offices in Boyd Business Park, and it wasn't a cat or careless employee that time, but a real break-in.

"Computers were stolen. I was blamed because it was an evening I normally would've been working, but I was taking a few days' vacation. And my boss knew it, too, was working in my place. After the break-in, though, he found the form requesting my vacation time signed by me, but not by him. Because he hadn't signed it, he claimed he hadn't authorized my time off and used that to fire me. I knew he never signed those things, and then I knew why. But okay, that was the wrongly accused thing." He turned onto his side, rested his arm across my stomach. "On the other side is Dillard's where I worked complaints. It just killed me.

"Women would bring in panty hose with runs, claim the product was defective, but the foot part would be filthy. They'd have worn the hose many times, not even giving me the courtesy of washing them out before I'd have to handle them. One woman brought in a child's playsuit heavily stained, looking like it'd been laundered hundreds of times, just used up and worn out. She claimed it was a gift and didn't fit so she wanted store credit. Each of them, the ones who argued enough, got what she wanted, but the sadness was in the lies. They told it all straight-faced, not even blushing. In return, I acted a bit sympathetic but skeptical, playing my role. We all knew I despised them and their greed, and they saw me as the enemy. I hated that job so much I called in sick, played hooky, at the least excuse—too dark out when the alarm went off, raining too much, too sunny a day to work, I had a stubbed toe, I didn't have a clean shirt. I called in sick so much I should've been fired, but that was one I got away with. The whole department once chipped in and sent me a get-well fruit basket, another time, a vase of flowers.

"But this isn't only about balance. Now I work for myself. I am in control, but this is not really me, this P.I. gig. I'm about to begin a journey. I don't know if it only involves my occupation or if there's more to it. But a sweetness in me will be revealed. I am sweet. That's really who I am."

When he finished, I turned toward him and we kissed. He was a champion kisser. His lips were like warm, buttered muffins and his tongue tasted of brown sugar. Nevertheless, as I kissed Ted, I thought about Richard. Seldom in the sixteen years we'd been married had he given as long a speech as Ted's. Maybe never. I couldn't recall his connecting parts of his life to other parts to make a point, at least not out loud for me. Richard used to smile knowingly, nod, wink, shrug, laugh, and hum, but he rarely put more than three sentences together. We used to spend large blocks of time in silence. We knew each other that well, or at least so I thought. Oh, I hadn't known he was restless, as Bev said, nor had I known he talked to Aurora. "I find myself talking to her for hours," he'd said once in some absurd attempt at explaining his leaving, to make me see he had to go.

"I know they'll find a tumor," I told Ted when we were both worn out from kissing. "I just hope it's operable. It might cause facial paralysis, ruin my looks for good."

"Shhhh," he said and turned his back to me. "It's just sinuses." He turned away from me and within minutes was snoring gently, like a motorcycle off in the distance. Sweet, I thought. Just sinuses, I repeated, and closed my eyes.

I awoke at 3:22 AM, the red numerals on my clock radio glaring at me. My neck was stiff and I knew my sleep had been fitful as I remembered parts of dreams about doors closing and my teeth falling out. As I lay there, trying to relax, I felt the heaviness of

Ted beside me, so I left the bed, went to the window and raised the shade, letting the streetlight on the corner shine in on him. He was uncovered, and he lay on his back, solid and heavy as a root vegetable, a tuber. His chest moved almost imperceptibly. His arms were at his side, close in, and his legs were straight, his feet touching. He seemed taller than his six-two stretched out like that. Denser, too, his shape roughly tapering from his shoulders to his toes. Like a parsnip. I watched him for a minute or two, then pulled the shade back down and stretched out beside him. I took one of his hands in mine, squeezed it, and closed my eyes. A giant, sweet parsnip. Very sweet.

The cumin-encrusted pork cutlets that finally turned out were offered as a special for three afternoons in late September, but I sold only two orders of them all together. That was not the sadness, though, not even close. By then I was used to wasting my specials on the unenlightened, and knew I'd have failures as well as hits. Ted and Mike and Maddie all got free samples, and Ted and Maddie called the dish superb and marvelous and unusual, carrying on so much that their comments were meaningless. Mike ate his in silence, but when I removed his plate, he looked at me and said, "Thanks." Then, apropos of nothing, he said, "I am a sentimental man, even though I don't feel much. I cried at Mama's death more from being in love with sentiment than from loving her."

Ted chuckled at that. Lately, Ted responded to all Mike said with a chuckle, as if Mike were being funny and only Ted understood the underlying humor. I didn't get it, and for lack of any possible response, said, "Oh."

Bev said Mike had explained the confusion over his last name. He told her Reid was the name of the last man his mother married, the name, as he put it, she died with. His last name was Gibson. Mike Gibson. When Bev told me, I asked what had happened to the Cockroach part, and she said he never mentioned it after that one time.

But about the cutlets, I wanted honest criticism, so I turned to Bev. And to my surprise, she said the cutlets were just fine, delicious even, but said I seemed to have the Alibi Café confused with some imaginary restaurant.

"You mean these hoosiers don't have sophisticated tastes?"

"No, Stupid," she said. "I mean we're a breakfast and lunch place. Think sandwiches. Or do you now think I should open for dinner?"

I ignored the "stupid" as you do for someone you're related to, someone you have been a child with. Besides, I saw at once that she was right. I had gotten off track. One of the two who ordered and paid for the cumin-encrusted cutlets was a stranger, an elderly skeleton of a woman using a walker and accompanied by a chubby younger woman who I guessed was a health-care worker. I had never seen either one before. The other who ordered and paid for it was Rollie, and he said it was good but would have been a bit better with gravy. He was Rollie the gas company guy to us. He had a head like a beach ball and a smile that was aggressively cheerful, showed both rows of his teeth. We never knew his last name, but we did know that his sister and her four children lived in Pomona, Missouri; we knew he had worked for the gas company for twenty years and could retire in another five, even before he turned 50; we knew his barber was named Dave and had a shop on Gravois near Bevo Mill. We knew Rollie lived near the Bevo, too, and could've walked to his barber, would have if he hadn't had to pass so many yards with rottweilers in them, a breed with no excuse for being; we knew Rollie's auto mechanic was a guy named Lloyd at a garage near River Des Peres, and Rollie's mother had some kind of heart trouble, and he himself had a gut that wasn't one hundred percent; we knew he'd never been married, and did not care for women who smoked, never had, not even back when it was normal for respectable people from good homes to do it; we knew he was not a churchgoer, but he did believe in a god of some sort and thought atheists were the biggest fools of all; we knew Rollie was a Democrat because his father had been one, though Rollie himself hadn't voted in at least ten years.

Rollie liked most of my specials, tried them all, rubbed his stomach afterwards, and usually threw in a belch, always excusing himself after. I knew if I wanted to be more of a hit at the Alibi Café on Meramec Street in South St. Louis, I should cook with him in mind, use Rollie as the diner I aimed my culinary arrow at.

But there was no joy in that. Creating something to elicit a belly rub and a belch from Rollie wasn't the challenge I was searching for. Like Ted, I had a sense of myself starting a journey, and Rollie would be not only the wrong ending, but also a false start.

Bev had hit upon the solution when she asked if we should open at night, and I realized immediately one night a week, a Friday perhaps, would be the ticket to getting a reviewer in. We could have what we called gourmet night, a different entrée each week, and I could distribute more flyers—Bev's never having found out about the first batch making me bold—listing the entrées for a month at a time. If we took reservations, Bev would know there'd been some advertising, so I would just have to guess at the crowd and make a little more. This would be a way for me to practice, too, until I got that surefire winner that would make me a star pupil and teacher's pet even before I matriculated at l'École de Cuisine. I wanted to do something with lamb soon, and veal medallions were always enticing, simply sounded tasty and expensive, and I wanted to use the meat grinder again, too. But Doc Newburg had put me on another path, and I knew seafood would be a big draw. It always was in cities like this, hundreds of miles from any sea. I thought of a Newburg sauce for crab, real king crab legs, not that pink-tinted, rolled-up junk fish often spelled *krab* that so many people, even those like Dad who was supposed to know food, claimed was good in salads and spreads.

I was still thinking about a crab night on an upcoming Friday as I cleaned up and wrapped the cutlets for the freezer, packing the Asian vegetables to go upstairs for my simple low-calorie dinner. It was a cloudless and dry Wednesday in September, one day past the official start of fall, but the earth was emitting one last, hot breath to make us know what we would miss. I envied Bev and Mike, their dinner in the park, and nearly invited myself, but decided I wasn't that desperate, hoped I'd never be that lonely. Bev loaded herself and the picnic basket into her car, pulled up twenty feet into the alley, and honked for Mike. As she was outside honking, Aunt Josie called, and I offered to run out and get Bev, but it was me she wanted.

Aunt Josie said she hoped I was free to come by later on, after dinner. She'd make a few pitchers of her famous piña coladas, and all the Stillwell sisters would be there. They needed my help, she said, and by the way, could I pick up my mother? That was how I ended up as a trainer for Aunt Peg, a contestant in the Senior Ms. America pageant. Round one, the crowning of Senior Ms. St. Louis Metropolitan Area, would be held at a county community center three days before Christmas, so we had to start working immediately. I picked Mom up a little after seven o'clock and headed west on Highway 40 to Aunt Josie's. Mom seldom spoke to me when no one else was around, so, as I drove, I had time to think about what I'd said to Ted the night before and how lacking in embarrassment I'd been, still was.

And I did understand that what I'd said was not the whole truth, merely a part of the picture. I was not in love with myself or my looks. In love was too strong a term. And I knew my looks were not myself, that my body and I would both change but in different ways, part company as it were with aging. I'd get better and my body would get worse. That made me think about my few gray hairs that were not yet visible enough to make my hair look dull, but eventually I'd have to color. And yes, coloring was always obvious, especially on brunettes, but why worry about being natural-looking. Look at Maddie whose hair had gone from pink to coal black in a few months, the obviousness of the dye job most of the point.

Because I was thinking too much about dye jobs and not enough about my driving, I didn't get into the right lane soon enough and not one of the type-A-for-asshole, road-rage drivers would let me in, so I missed the Baxter turnoff, had to go all the way to Boone's Crossing and double back. Mom snorted, but said nothing. Of course, I knew deep concentration about my hair color put the lie to what I'd just comforted myself with. Maybe not in love with, but certainly obsessed by. It was one more personality flaw to overcome.

Aunt Peg was already at Aunt Josie's, and soon all four of us were reclining on the chaise lounges that decorated the cavern-like living room. Aunt Josie had recently had her chakras explored, fine-tuned, and it seemed she was at her best when she kept her feet up, her energy level more evenly distributed which resulted in more focus. Her head, though, was supposed to remain above all. Uncle Al was so devoted to his bride—he still called her that— that he merely sighed and smiled when she donated the wing and club chairs to Goodwill and had Costigan's Fine Furnishings deliver five chaises. So there we were, four of the five Stillwell beauties, sipping piña coladas, lounging on leather or rayon (mine, a simulated leopard skin), none of us heavy enough to sink down. Now that there was an audience, Mom did most of the talking, telling me things she could have said in the car.

"Peg is a contestant for Senior Ms. America because Ralph has been dead so long she needs affirmation of her beauty and charm. Besides, she singed her eyebrows off at her own wedding, hasn't ever recovered."

I shrugged, waiting for someone to take the floor and make more sense, though I understood the affirmation part. We were all alike: Give me a spotlight. Applaud me.

"I have too recovered," Aunt Peg said. "Don't listen to your mother."

I sighed. There was nothing to do but ask for the story. Mom insisted I'd heard it many times, likely hadn't been paying attention. "I'm not surprised," she said. "You often don't pay attention. Your mind gets stuck on a track and so much of the world doesn't register. Like with poor Richard."

"What?"

"Oh, don't get huffy," Mom said. "Peg was actually a lot like you. Flitting from one thing to another."

"I flit?"

"Oh, you know," Aunt Josie joined in. "Modeling, then siding, then cooking. Not even a logical pattern. Willy nilly."

I was speechless. I'm still searching, I thought, but did not say, wounded by that "poor Richard" comment.

"I catered my own wedding reception," Aunt Peg said. "And don't listen to these harpies. My passions never lasted as long as yours, not long enough to give me the kind of headaches you claim. A month or two was my limit for anything. When Ralph and I got engaged, I was planning to design and make my own wedding dress, but I gave that up when I realized everyone else was doing it."

"Not until you had ten yards of French peau de soie delivered," Mom said.

"Dad was furious," Peg said and laughed. "Whatever happened to all that fabric?"

"Mom gave it away," Aunt Josie said, then continued the saga. "But after the dressmaking plan, Peg turned to cooking. She thought it would be the most unusual wedding ever, catered by the bride, so she cancelled the hall, and she told Mom and Dad she was having it at home."

"Dad was furious again," Mom said.

"As soon as we got back from church, I took the wedding dress off and put on a pair of scarlet hostess pajamas. Quilted," Aunt Peg said. "They had cost me as much as the wedding dress, and I hoped they would cause a sensation."

"But something caught fire," Mom said.

"Pigs in blankets," Aunt Peg said. "The broiler really. Old crusted stuff and grease. I opened it to check the piggies and flames shot up, singed my bangs and took off both eyebrows."

They all stopped smiling. "It was horrible," Mom said. "Truly horrible."

"We have no pictures of the reception, not one of the pajamas. I drew eyebrows on, but it was no good. I couldn't bear to be seen like that," Peg said. "I stayed up on the third floor, listening to the fun as it made its way up the stairs. Ralph came up every now and then but wouldn't stay with me. He was having fun at his own wedding."

"So that's why she wants to be Senior Ms. America," Aunt Josie said.

"I don't see the connection," I said, careful not to smile at what they all considered a sad story.

"My God," Mom said. "It's so obvious."

"It's why she had two children," Aunt Josie said. "She tried to make it up to Ralph."

"He understands this contest, too," Aunt Peg said. She looked up at the cathedral ceiling. "He'll be up there rooting for me. That is, unless the world ends in January," she said, then giggled.

Of course I agreed to be Aunt Peg's trainer, to give her tips I'd picked up from modeling, and try to be an objective observer of her walk, her smile, her overall grace and poise. Even Aunt Peg, the Stillwell beauty with the most crowns to her name, knew objective help was essential. We all understood competition. Chickie would have been involved, too, but she was part of a repertory dinner theatre company in L.A., and had two auditions for TV shows coming up, and a new agent who she believed would get her more and better work.

The four of us discussed Peg's talent at length. She had a pretty good voice, having undertaken voice training on two separate occasions, but Mom objected to singing. "No one really likes opera," she said. "It has a cachet for being highbrow but is not entertaining at all. Other songs need choreography, something for the arms and hands to do, and end up looking like storytelling for the deaf."

Aunt Josie suggested the flute, an instrument Aunt Peg played well at special church services.

"The flute is gentle, simple, pure," Aunt Josie said. "But again, is it entertaining?"

"What about the violin?" I asked. I knew Aunt Peg had had years of violin lessons, remembered Grandpa's moaning about the cost of all Peg's lessons.

"It does show talent," Mom said.

"And it shows my chin wrinkles. Besides, practicing creates more chin wrinkles," Aunt Peg said. "It's out."

"You can tap dance," Aunt Josie said.

Mom stood up and slapped her thighs to emphasize her objection to that. "It's the worst ever," she said. "Your thighs wiggle when you dance. Not yours specifically, Peg, but everyone's. Young and toned girls don't have much wiggle, and maybe you don't either, but if you do, it's the kiss of death. Remember, the contestants are supposed to be over fifty-five, but they have to look like thirty to win. Wiggling thighs won't do."

Aunt Peg jumped up then, too, and did a quick soft-shoe on the gleaming oak floor, her thighs remaining firm the whole time. She wore white nylon running shorts and a black halter top, could indeed have passed for thirty. Mom answered with her own dance, a more strenuous one that ended with a series of high kicks. Her thighs were also rock solid. "Big deal," she said when she finished, not even winded.

"The piano," I said quickly, afraid that if Aunt Josie joined the impromptu dance competition, I'd be up next. "I've known lots of girls to win contests with the piano. I did once."

To my surprise, they all agreed. Peg said she wanted to do a ragtime number instead of classical because things that were funny or upbeat usually got higher points. Mom and Aunt Josie agreed that her outfit for the talent part would have to be a jazzy, flapper-type dress with fringe and balls and spangles. "It will work great," Mom said. "The dress won't be formfitting, just sort of sack-like, so you won't show off your killer figure. But that's the good part. Your shape will be obvious in the playwear and the evening gown categories and only hinted at in the talent. Remember, the judges are not always in good shape and sometimes a green-eyed fellow sneaks in and votes, too. You can't show off so much you make the judges dislike you."

Aunt Josie said Mom was crazy. The ragtime dress would be the loveliest of all, and Peg would never wear anything that would make her shape ordinary. Besides, the judges were not that petty.

"It's subconscious," Mom said. "And beading and fringe can hide many a figure flaw. Even, well, even someone chubby or really fat would look cute in such a getup. You know, someone not real pretty."

Whether or not she intended it, Mom made us all think about Bev then. We seldom thought of beauty without its opposite, never thought of our own beauty without thinking of Bev. Aunt Josie tried to change the unspoken subject by asking Peg for the competition schedule, how many pageants led up to the Senior Ms. Missouri one, and when the final one was. Bev was still with us, though, and instead of answering, Aunt Peg brought up the trial. "It's the most absurd thing I've ever heard of. Insane."

"She's in more trouble than she knows," Aunt Josie said. "If the jury is made up of middle-class parents who know firsthand the pitfalls of raising a good child, or even if they only know secondhand from TV exposés, they'll bend over backwards to root out all corrupt influences. They'll be against Bev all the way."

The other beauties, including me, nodded.

"She's just not likeable enough," Aunt Josie said. "They'll get her."

"She's not serious about getting that little black boy, is she?" Aunt Peg asked Aunt Josie.

"She wants to be a mother," Aunt Josie said. "It's not a bad thing to want. She'd be a good one, maybe better than the rest of us."

The three of them looked at me. It was my cue to say they were all good mothers, especially mine. I looked down at the leopard skin I rested on.

"But still, "Mom said, unable I knew to understand the nurturing impulse, unable as I was. "She could get an infant, have a chance at least of turning it into one who won't rip her heart out."

"She wants this one," I said. "She loves him."

The beauties looked at me with lovely but blank faces. Love was not a foreign concept to them, at least not to all of them, so I knew their blankness was at my use of the word. What did I know of love, they could have been thinking. I'd been married twice, the loser each time. It was how I would've looked at The Owl and The Pussycat if they'd recited "Old Mother Hubbard." It was enough to make me say I had to get going, my second pina colada virtually untouched.

Mom did talk to me on the ride home. She told me how annoyed she was at leaving so early, and said it was hell to have such night blindness that you were beholden to those who did not care about your needs.

"What makes you think I can see well?" I answered. "Do you think I make this blurred vision stuff up?" In fact, my eyes were fine, the blurred vision a missing symptom for a few days now.

She said to leave her out of the whole ragtime piano thing, choosing music and rehearsals, all of it. Lately music had started to annoy her. It was just noise, no matter what anyone said. It made her jumpy. Laughter was the same. She had made Grandma leave Truffles the other afternoon because the women at the table behind her were laughing so loud it nauseated her. "Like hyenas," she said. "And in a place like that. It was either leave or slap them each, one by one," she said.

"You took Grandma to Truffles" I asked. "The Alibi Café is closer."

She turned away and looked out her window the rest of the way home. When I pulled up in front of her and Dad's two-family, she said "Your nails are nice, by the way," and got out without looking at me.

When I got home I called Ted and said since it was early, why not go for a few sets at Spurs 'n' Saddles. I told him my head would pound just as much lying on my own pillow as it would on the dance floor. He picked me up fifteen minutes later, and we were doing the Bighorn Shuffle by 10:30. When we took a break, he told me I was moving like a professional.

The next day, I told Bev we should try a Friday night dish-of-the-week experiment, and she said okay right away, barely paying attention. "Not this Friday," I said, meaning not the next day. "Next week. Give me enough time to plan."

"Whatever," she said.

I meant enough time to get flyers out. Bev was still in the dark about my advertising, and I guessed she thought we got new customers just from people driving or walking by, deciding to stop in. She must have thought that was how we'd get our Friday night crowd, too. They'd just see lights.

I decided to begin the gourmet series with my inspiration, Crab Newburg. For an appetizer I'd serve pigs in a blanket in honor of Aunt Peg (I wondered if Bev knew that story), then the Newburg over white rice with roasted zucchini strips alongside and a sourdough baguette. To cleanse the palette, a salad of kohlrabi, beets, hearts of palm, and blue cheese, then a sampling of hard cheeses, followed by coffee and my famous blueberry soup or a slice of one of Bev's pies. I'd offer a sautéed chicken breast in case one or two diners couldn't eat shellfish, but there would be no other substitutions. I was aiming for Friday, October second. I hoped for at least ten customers, would plan on fifteen so I wouldn't run out, but would be satisfied with at least six. Six paying that was, knowing Ted and Maddie and Mike would be eating free. I started on the flyers that evening after we closed up. I called it a *Blue Ribbon Night*, then listed the courses and the all inclusive price, $18.00. I had a flyer in the mail to the *Post-Dispatch* food editor by the next morning. After seven months of trying, I had yet to get a review, but that wasn't the sad thing, either. I was almost used to being ignored.

That afternoon, Friday, a cold front moved down over the Midwest, and the temperature was down in the fifties by the time Toby came by after school with his friend Peaches. This was the start of the sad thing. Peaches sat at the table closest to the door all by herself. She watched the floor and her running shoes, swung her legs occasionally. She played at being deaf and dumb. Rollie was leaving just as Toby dragged her in and deposited her there. We had no other customers, but even when I set a glass of Coke before her, she wouldn't look up. She left the Coke where I had placed it, sweating on the table and going flat.

Toby had gone right upstairs with Bev to practice with her leg again, something I disapproved of strongly and had told her so. People would get the wrong idea, I said. It seemed sort of creepy, even to me. But Bev said Toby's interest made her feel more normal, the leg not so mysterious and taboo. She said she wore her bathing suit the whole time, and if she were a swimming instructor, for instance, with two whole legs, she would have more children touching her suit, hugging her, and no one would call it creepy. No one, she told me, had strapped her leg on for her, not since she was a toddler. Even the therapists who taught her how, called it private and sanitary.

When Toby came down the back stairs, Peaches ran to his side and took a stool beside him. Bev followed soon after and gave each of them a slice of chocolate cream pie and a large glass of milk. "I know your aunt," she told Peaches. "And your grandfather is my lawyer."

Peaches looked down, giving no response.

"I guess that's not too exciting, come to think of it," Bev said.

"No, it's not," Peaches said. "I only came in here because Toby's on his way to my house. I don't care who knows anybody."

"Good for you," Bev said. "I don't really care myself."

Peaches finished her pie, then pushed her plate back. She turned to Toby, tugged on the short sleeve of his white school-uniform shirt. "Ready?"

"Almost," Toby said. He looked at Bev. "The lady I stay with still doesn't know I come by to see you. I never did tell her I know how to work your leg."

"She probably doesn't care about your coming by anymore," Bev said. "That was just because she was afraid for you at first. You're safe here."

"She probably does care if I put your leg on. Some folks get all bothered by that stuff."

"Don't tell her," I said, eavesdropping as I cleaned the stove.

"I really need some money," Toby said. "I really need some. I have to get me some spending money."

"What do you need?" Bev asked, but we both saw his game, and when she turned, I caught her eye and shook my head.

"I just need me some money," he said.

No, no, no, no, I whispered, but it did no good.

"Everyone needs spending money," she said. "But don't say need me. Say it right."

"I would like some extra money," he said, holding out his hand, his thick glasses glistening in the fluorescent lights. "I could use some extra money."

She opened the cash drawer and gave him two ones. "I know you don't have anything to buy that costs more than this."

Perhaps she hoped to win the game, at least call it a draw, by making the amount so small, but we both knew she had been blackmailed. To make it seem less like what it was, she also offered Peaches two dollars, but Peaches shook her head. "My parents don't let me take money from anyone not related to me, even if it's my birthday, which it is not."

Before they left I went out the back door, saying I needed to pick some basil, but really unable to watch the drama unfolding before me. I was sorry to have seen that sad thing.

The strength of loneliness continued to amaze me, take me by surprise. Was there a stronger force in the universe, I wondered, and as I did so, I looked down at what had been my herb garden, saw the destruction. Because the world seemed a hard place for humans that afternoon, I wasn't even surprised to see that someone had uprooted all my herbs, scattered the plants and dirt across the yard, trampled on most of the rosemary and basil, strewn the thyme across the parking pad. I picked up the few salvageable plants to take in and dry. I even found a few whose leaves could still be used fresh. I knew it would be winter soon enough anyway, and this vandalism was not as sad as blackmail and need.

That evening, Ted took me to Jefferson Barracks Park and we sat on the stone wall surrounding one of the buildings left from the Civil War. From there, we had a view of the St. Louis riverfront around the bend, of barges going up and down the Mississippi, of airplanes flying in above the Gateway Arch, and the traffic on one of the bridges connecting downtown to Illinois. As we sat, a freight train rumbled by on the tracks beneath us. I refused to consider my life, or anyone's, as a cycle, did not want to allow for downtime, so movement, progression, even if not real progress, was my comfort. I told Ted so. I said it made that stone wall we sat on necessary. I also told him about my herb garden and the meanness that continued to take me by surprise in this area of the city. He said it meant nothing. So there was one other mean person in town? There were lots more who were nice and kind. Consider how many lived around us, he said. I was bound to run across a few meanies. One or two.

I told him then about Toby's blackmail and, the saddest part, about Bev's giving in. I said I was surprised at the extent of Toby's selfishness and Bev's weakness, stunned in fact. Ted tried to put a good face on it by saying she was obviously acting out of love, and maybe we looked at things all wrong; maybe acting out of love was the real strength. I didn't buy it, of course, but I pretended to. I knew I could find peace by concentrating on all the people who lived in the homes and flats around me. I tried to believe most of them were good and kind, were people who, when they slept, dreamed of delights and ease, slept in deserved peace. And I did take some comfort in knowing people who acted out of love, willing to be hurt and used by it. But there was more comfort that evening in all those vehicles and bodies moving about us, going up and down and across the river, which was itself moving fast. When the mosquitoes started to bite, Ted wanted to go back to Bev's and my place above the café, but I convinced him to stay with me on our stone wall a little longer. I wanted to feel one more train shake the ground. I wanted to see at least five more barges pass down below.

BEV

*B*lackmail is such an ugly word." I looked into the mirror above
the bathroom sink for a moment, turned my head sharply
to the side, and delivered that line the way it had been done for
decades in *Perry Mason*, *Magnum P.I.*, *Columbo*, and other TV
dramas. Usually someone semi-respectable was confronted by
the detective, forced into the cliché admission. "I prefer to call it
a business deal," the villain would add. "We both get something
out of it." I did not amuse myself by such play, and it wasn't only
because mirrors and I seldom had fun together. Toby had blackmailed me, and the word wasn't ugly but the fact was. I believed,
however, I was still in control. Toby had won a minor skirmish.
True, I didn't want his foster mother, Lana, or Jeannie Lemp, or
any of the growing number of social workers, bureaucrats, and
court clerks to know he practiced buckling my leg on. Shelly said
it was creepy, and I, not as naïve or blind as Shelly believed, knew
it could seem so. That it was not creepy or perverted or odd or any
of those adjectives was impossible to say. It was as the woman who

sat on the wall beside me back in June had said about Toby's claim of innocence: the more you say something is not, the more it seems it is.

And so I was the blackmailee, the victim, the target, the one used and mistreated. So call me victim. So what? Maybe that attitude came from having lived with the words *handicapped, differently-abled, crippled, deformed, malformed, brave, amazing,* and the absolute worst, *special.* After the adoption was final, I would put an end to Toby's using me. Oh, I knew the dangers. I had shown him, by my actions, blackmail worked, and I had diminished myself by sinking into dishonesty. The goal, however, was worth the risks. As Toby's mother, I'd have years to set us both upright again.

Still, I was sorry Shelly witnessed my and Toby's shame.

Shelly called her dinner a blue-ribbon night, but I said there was little to win a blue ribbon for in a Newburg sauce. We used to have it in the dorm cafeteria, I told her, a creamy sauce to cover leftovers. She rolled her eyes at that and rushed headlong into planning the event. She not only bought white rayon and cotton blend tablecloths and napkins and four placemats for the counter, as well as white votive candles in clear glass holders, but she told me I had been misled in college. The Newburg sauce began with a butter in which the shells, crab shells in this case, had been simmered for hours, and no dorm ever went to that trouble. A white flour and margarine and powdered milk sauce with lots of salt, thick enough to hold all the beef chunks and pork pieces and carrots and peas and cabbage in one glutinous scoop, was no doubt what had been passed off to us college students as Newburg.

On Friday, October second, it rained from early morning to past midnight, the quality and amount of light never surpassing dusk. It was a steady, straight, hard rain with not even a hint of past warmth. We were much less busy than usual. Rollie and his crew had the day off, as did most of the work crews in the area. People stayed indoors, ate lunch from vending machines, maybe selected the four-day-old leftovers from the backs of their own refrigerators, or bought sacks of meat and fried potatoes from drive-throughs, but did not walk down a city street to a small café. Mike made it across the alley by late morning and had most of a pot of coffee all by himself. I spent the day leaning on the counter, watching Meramec Street turn into a fast-moving creek.

"There are two kinds of men," Shelly said to us just to make conversation, something I noticed she did more of when she cooked. "I've noticed it at Spurs 'n' Saddles. Men who can stand with their legs slightly apart and their feet planted flat on the floor, their arms crossed high across their chests, and those who can't. It's a center of balance thing, I guess."

"There are two kinds of women," I said, joining in out of boredom, becoming hypnotized by the rain. "Those who go through life aware of their looks and those who are surprised by their reflections."

Mike coughed, a series of loud and wet gags, wiped his mouth with a handful of napkins from the dispenser on the counter, and gave us his own division: "There are two kinds of people. Those who would fight death and those who wouldn't. No one ever gets taken when he says, 'Take me now. I'm ready.' Never."

While we talked, Shelly cracked the crab legs and removed their meat. Next she simmered the shells in butter, and sliced and oiled the zucchini for grilling later. The conversation wound down before she put the whipped butter into the rose-shaped molds, cleaned vegetables, and made the vinaigrette. I offered to help her numerous times, but was rebuffed with each offer. She worked better alone. She knew what needed to be done. She really was not busy. Watching her made me dizzy, which was why I mostly faced the window and the rain. My pie that day was lemon meringue because Shelly needed only yolks for her sauce, and hadn't wanted to waste the whites. Later, I'd make a few apple pies to be used as alternates to the blue ribbon night blueberry soup, but since the lemon meringue was sitting there, going to waste, I polished off two slices by noon.

Mike eventually swirled on his stool and faced the front window, too. He turned down the offer of pie, just leaned his head against the wall, sipped his coffee, and for long stretches of time, closed his eyes. At about one o'clock, Maddie waddled in, her mother's project and heir, Randolph James, taking up more and

more room inside her. She was about four weeks from her due
date, but she said Randy, what she called him to irritate her mother, was already trying to punch his way out. Though I reminded
myself there were many sides to a story, and Maddie's mother may
not be the 100 percent selfish and narrow-minded, controlling,
spoiled, rich bitch she seemed, not completely anyway, trying to be
rational and open-minded myself about poor unborn Randolph
James, I failed. All I felt for the future mover and shaker was pity.

Maddie sat at the table closest to the counter—she could no
longer climb up on a stool—and I gave her a large slice of pie and a
glass of whole milk.

"How are you holding up?" I asked, and her answer was a
shrug. Pregnancy had sapped not only her curiosity and interest
about the world around her, and not only her wit and humor I remembered so well from her school days, but also her conversation,
her speech. She seemed to be saving all her energy for the big job
ahead. More often than not, she shrugged.

She had come in the previous Saturday with Jason, the father
of her child, a skinny young man with large hands. His dark hair
hung in waves past his long face to his shoulders, a look more in
keeping with his father's or even his grandfather's youth. After she
introduced us, Maddie said she was yearning to join a convent.
Did I think a convent would take her if she was not a virgin?

"You're the one who told Maddie to sleep with me, right?"
Jason asked and winked at me.

"No," I said, as always trying to overcome the misunderstanding created by the Hilkers. "She didn't ask me. If she had, I would
have said 'don't,' just as I'm sure her and your own mother would
have."

Jason wrinkled his smooth child's brow. "Well, she wouldn't
have listened to you anyway," he said.

"Precisely," I answered.

"I want to go to one of those convents where no one can talk,"
Maddie said. She eased herself down onto the closest chair. She
wore a pale pink tent and her pink-covered navel popped up when
she sat.

"The world is too much with you?"

"Jason is too much with me. He's putting up a big fight about Mom raising our baby. He says he should have more to say about it. He says we should just get an apartment somewhere and the three of us live together. Like what would we live on? How would we go to college?"

"He's my kid," Jason said.

"I'll go into one of those that won't allow visitors. You have to talk through a screen, even when your parents die."

"Those are depraved," Jason said. "The priests and those really secret ones, the monks, they have tunnels and secret entries and all that. They just come in and rape the nuns, over and over. Usually they have three at a time, and the poor nun has to take them all on her straw mattress. Then they go back through the tunnels and whip themselves for being so bad."

Maddie rolled her eyes at me. "He's not Catholic," she said. "His mind is too small to figure out priests and nuns."

"I get it," Jason said. "The Catholics love sex, do it all the time, but they keep up this big front of not approving of it. They just sin and sin and then go to confession and get a clean slate."

I looked at Maddie. "I think he gets it. But I understand the pull of the cloister."

"What about the world ending in a few months?" Jason asked. "Think it will? Didn't Jesus or some other old-time guy say the year 2000 is all you get?"

"I hadn't heard that,' I said. "My guess is we'll all just go on."

"Jason's having his tongue pierced tomorrow," Maddie said. "He won't be able to eat much for a while. It's why we're here. He wants a barbecued pork sandwich for his last meal."

I nodded as though I understood the tongue piercing urge, though I didn't even have pierced ears. I enjoyed the hysteria and hype surrounding the new millennium, officially three months away, or one year and three months away according to purists. It had most TV people worked up. They used words like *prepare* and *disaster* and *protection*, looking calm and suave as if to reassure us as they talked about all the ways the world could crumble. I enjoyed it because it confirmed my belief that humans were the stupidest species on this planet. But, according to the letters to the editor in the *St. Louis Post-Dispatch*, most readers and viewers saw through the nice suits and hairdos to the nudge toward hysteria, and most resisted the bait. Still, someone was buying all the gas masks and camp stoves and large bottles of water. The fearful had cash in their dresser drawers next to their extra batteries.

"My mom already has twenty cases of tuna in the basement," Jason said. "And a toaster that runs on batteries. As if she's afraid we'll have to do without toast."

I laughed, then gave him his barbecued pork sandwich with a side of slaw, threw in a free root beer. I told him a battery-powered toaster was nothing. Goofy Jeannie Lemp, the social worker I was brown-nosing like crazy lately, had told us she bought the last battery-powered blender Target had in stock.

But on this afternoon of the gourmet night, Maddie was in without Jason, not talking about convents or batteries or much of anything as she picked at her wedge of pie.

Mike surprised me by opening his eyes and speaking to her. "I guess it'll be a big kid." He nodded at her stomach.

Maddie shrugged. "Whatever."

"My parents were like you and that boy you had in here before," he said. "Ignorant kids. I never thought of it like that until I saw you and him in here. They were so young, thirty years younger than I am now. Dumb as rocks. Dumber." He sighed and blew on the coffee I knew must already be cold. "I've wasted lots of time cursing them for being so inept, but they were just horny children. What did I expect? Competence?"

Maddie shrugged again. "I am so tired," she said.

"Then why are you here?" he asked. "Out in this rain?"

"Mom's having a baby shower later. I had to leave so she could decorate, said my attitude was not festive."

That was Shelly's criticism about my attitude toward her blue ribbon night, too, but in fact I was happy she had a project she could throw herself into. When I told her so, she said that so-called happiness did not make it to my face, and I hadn't once smiled about the exciting night to come. The thing was that even after Toby learned to work my leg harness, the overwhelming fatigue still attacked me, and my mind often seemed incapable of holding two thoughts in it at once. I could've still been recovering from the break-in, I told her, and besides, I said, she must've known I'd never been much of a smiler. On top of that, trying to get Toby was a continuing uphill battle.

"Excuses, excuses," she said. "You just cannot let yourself be happy."

Each time Shelly asked for comments on the votives—was three per table enough?—or if the tablecloths were well-enough starched, or if she should fold the napkins into fans or crowns, or if she needed a CD playing "dinner music" all evening, I did a Maddie-like shrug but followed it quickly with a smile. I did try to care, and mainly I agreed with what I thought she wanted, but my only natural response was a laugh when Mike said *Goober Peas* was dinner music and Shelly could have the cassette it was on, consider it his contribution to what he called Night of the Newburg.

Because the rain kept our business light, and we were empty by two o'clock, I closed up at three, then mixed up the dough for the pie crusts. Maddie left at three when I closed up, though I told her she was welcome to stay.

"Can't," she said. "The shindig starts at five. Mom'll want me to shower and put on my best sack."

I wrapped the dough in waxed paper, eight bundles of it, and placed them all in the refrigerator so they would roll out easier. I sent Mike home with some leftovers, and went upstairs to nap for a half-hour or so until time to cut up the apples. I sank down immediately into a dream of running uphill from someone I never could identify, and when the phone jolted me from my dream, I was winded and my feet, even the one I didn't have, were sore.

It was Howard. His ninety-six-year-old mother in Wappappello, Missouri was dying from blood poisoning. She had stabbed herself with a fork while trying to spear a fried clam strip, and the nursing home assistant had neglected to disinfect the wound. The infection had spread so fast and she was so old that antibiotics were useless, and she could go any day. So Howard had requested an extension of my case. The trial had been put off but not yet rescheduled, though he expected it before the new year.

"Relax," he said. "This just gives us more breathing room. Now the kid won't be so pregnant and pathetic when she takes the stand."

As I cut up the jonathans, Shelly browned thirty garlic pork sausage links, and then simmered them in sherry. Two of the dough packages were for her to roll out later, wrap about the cooled sausages, and bake. She called it pigs in a blanket, even though Ted had told her that to do it right, South-City style, she should use Vienna sausages and Hungry Jack biscuits.

"Regardless of their ingredients," she'd said, "I don't know what Aunt Peg was thinking when she used the broiler. You don't broil these piggies, you bake."

"Wedding jitters?" Ted guessed. Shelly had told him and me the story a few times since she'd come back from Mom's.

It was not new to me. I'd heard it first from Grandma, and Grandma'd put the accent on the frightening, dangerous flames, describing them as reaching to the ceiling. And I also remembered being upstairs at Grandma's, all four grandkids sprawled across her bed. It was Christmas Eve and Aunt Peg had been assigned the job of keeping us entertained until Santa showed up. She paced before the window, her black velvet skirt swirling about her knees as she told the eyebrow singe story, waving her hands in the air to imitate flames. We paid little attention, all of us having heard it before. Chuck and Chickie probably had heard it most often. Shelly was there, but now she claimed the story was new. It was a vaguely funny story of a vain and self-consciously flamboyant woman. I had always considered it thus, even though my cousins had different interpretations. When we were in high school, Chuck told me the lesson was "don't try to be so different." Chickie called it a great love story. "Dad loved her even without eyebrows," she said to explain her interpretation.

Shelly was right, though, to say it didn't explain the two children, Chuck and Chickie. I had never understood that connection either.

What did I think about Aunt Peg and the Senior Ms. America contest, Shelly had wanted to know. She'd asked my opinion about the pageant even before she told the eyebrow story, but before I could respond, she said I probably thought it a foolish waste of time.

"Not more than everything else," I said.

Now, as I tossed the apple slices with sugar and cinnamon in preparation for the blue ribbon night, Shelly turned off the stove and moved next to me, leaning on the work counter, staring.

"What?" I said. "I feel like a new kind of insect you've found on the back stoop and are deciding whether or not it can live."

"I'm just wondering if you have news for me. I've been wondering all day. Are you hiding something until after my dinner?"

"What news? Why should I?"

"The tests. The CAT scan, the EEG." She had thought Howard's phone call was Dr. Newburg with the results, which were not supposed to come until early the following week.

I was stunned by the drama she had created and must have been playing in her mind. Life and Death, starring Shelly. "I would have called you. Newburg wouldn't have told me. You think this is some sort of soap opera, and I have been told you're dying and have to break it to you gently? I hope you're not disappointed if the results show you have a healthy brain."

"I thought maybe I was supposed to call Newburg. That's all. I didn't think she had given you the results. I did think maybe they were in early. I am nervous. I admit that, but I also thought I was among friends, and it was safe for me to express my fears and not be ridiculed. When will I learn that it never works? I'm always misinterpreted." She left the kitchen then, before I could apologize. But would I have? Maybe. I did want her to feel safe among friends, but she should've been able to laugh at her own so out-of-proportion worries.

For our first blue-ribbon night, Shelly put on a long black skirt, so I put mine on, too, though I knew it would restrict my movements. Shelly wore black and gold ballerina slippers and a gold colored silk shell with her skirt. Because I needed extra cushioning on my fake foot to compensate for our uneven floor, I wore black hi-tops. I also wore the white silk shirt I'd topped my black skirt with the only other time I'd worn it, the night of the failed seduction. I had not tried to seduce Mike again, and he seemed to have forgotten the entire night. Oh, I still had urges, but none as powerful as my sense of shame.

Shelly and I were arranging and inspecting and lining up dishes of cut-up this and that, tossing the salad and mixing up hot mustard for the piggies when Mike entered from the alley. He wore his usual black jeans, topped for the occasion by a yellowed white short-sleeved shirt festooned by a nearly neon green and orange tie. I thought Shelly would be pleased he had made an effort, but she merely sighed when he appeared, went back to her chopping and mixing. As for me, I was touched.

At 7PM, we had no customers. Ted showed up at 7:15, but Shelly would not let him sit. She wanted our paying customers to have first choice of seating. Finally at 7:30, three tables filled up in rapid succession. Rollie came in with his mother. The chiropractor with an office a block away on Grand came in with a woman. The two thrift shop women showed up with their look-alike husbands. The women were both in their fifties, both stick thin, both with salt and pepper hair they held back with rubber bands, both favoring jeans and T-shirts with Disney characters on them. For the blue-ribbon night, though, they wore khakis and what looked like brand new white sweatshirts, one with Daisy Duck on it, the other with Pluto. But their husbands did not merely dress alike. They had the same jowly face, the same sorrowful brown eyes, the same reddish hair and reddish-gray mustache. Shelly had told me they were twins, but I hadn't known one of them was the head counselor at St. Hedwig's summer day camp I'd had words with. The character builder. I couldn't tell them apart, and all evening long, never did find out which was which. Both nodded at me across the room, smiled at me whenever I looked their way as if we shared a past.

By 7:55, all three tables had been served their pigs in blankets with hot mustard dip. Shelly was in the back, broiling the zucchini and stirring the Newburg sauce. Just as she was ready to set up eight plates, Sally Figg and her brother and sister-in-law, Peaches' parents, entered. I could tell they threw Shelly's routine off, so I seated them and put three more piggies in the oven. Four more customers entered ten or so minutes later, and then at least one other couple. I lost count, and soon Shelly and I were serving and clearing and refilling and ladling and mixing. We got into a rhythm that bordered on being too fast. Shelly's face was flushed, her smile was wide, and her eyes glittered. She created and flirted and accepted compliments as she hustled, and even talked Ted into refilling the iced-tea and water glasses. Mike offered to help, too, but she told him outright he was too shaky. I felt his disappointment, but knew she was right.

Once when I looked around and saw that everyone was eating, momentarily satisfied, I made up a plate for Mike who, as usual, sat on the stool at the end of the counter, turned half way so he could lean his head against the wall. As I set Mike's Newburg plate before him, Ted stood behind the counter, on the alert for glasses not all the way full.

Though we didn't have a liquor license—not worth the expense for the kind of place we normally were—people lingered over their meals, putting off dessert, and the place took on the party atmosphere Shelly had hoped for. But for me, it was like being underwater, Or else they all were underwater and I stood on the bank, poking them with my finger. I moved far back into the kitchen, turned my back to the diners, but could still hear voices: "That cat scratched her whole leg up...Hyacinths are more of surprise than surprise lilies...So I gave up...She made the honor roll after all...I bled for two days...She can lie all she wants...I thank my lucky stars...It means someone's talking about you." We had a spider behind the stove. I'd noticed his web earlier, and as I stood there, I saw him pause, just in the shadow of the oven handle, waiting for his chance to run across the kitchen. I thought a he, but guessed it was more likely a she. I had hoped she would not be burned, building behind the stove like that, so was relieved to see her alive. Yet at the same time, I wanted to catch her movement, stomp her as she took off for a cooler place.

When I rejoined the throng, Rollie insisted I sit with him and his mother, and as soon as I was seated, she leaned over and asked me who made my prosthesis. Dierkers Laboratory, distributed by Bi-State Prosthetics, I told her after the moment it took me to decide her question was not entirely rude, not as rude as it sounded. I didn't think she heard my answer.

"Notice who John's with?" Rollie asked, inclining his head toward the chiropractor at the table behind him.

"Who?"

"His ex," Rollie said.

"A very funny story," his mother said.

"No. It's sad, Mom. She's treating him tonight because he paid for her tubal ligation. She has a heart murmur and can't take the pill, but she doesn't want kids. Well, she had two with John, so I guess what she doesn't want is more."

"Isn't that funny?" Rollie's mother asked. Her round face was as unlined as her son's, her smile as wide. They could have been twins, too.

"It's not funny, Mom," he said again. "Know why they got divorced?"

I shook my head.

"He came home early one day, you know, the same old story. Caught her in bed with a guy."

"This is the funny part." His mother placed a hand on my arm.

"Mom thinks it's like a dirty joke she heard once, but she can't remember the punch line. Anyway, the guy she was screwing was John's brother. John's brother was and still is married. His wife is the director of the Make-A-Wish Foundation."

"Now, that's funny," Rollie's mother said.

"If it hadn't been his brother, John wouldn't have divorced her. Been some guy he didn't know, he coulda just forgotten it."

Rollie's mother laughed. "And now he's paying to tie up her tubes."

"Well, that's the sad part. He just can't say no to her."

"She's not good at saying no, either," Rollie's mother said, and laughed so hard, John turned and looked at us as if he knew he was the joke.

Later when I served dessert, Sally Figg grabbed my wrist and pulled me down into the empty chair at their table, so I got to meet Peaches' parents, the ones so famous for staying together. It occurred to me suddenly, though, that they could be called criminally negligent when it came to names: Peaches Figg was not a name for anything but preserves. As soon as I caught my breath, I told Sally and her brother Peter I was sorry about their grandmother.

"She's a good woman but she's had a good life," Peter said. "Especially since Grandpa died."

"He was a very angry man," Sally said. "It's partly why Dad became a lawyer."

Then Sally and Peter and Peter's wife Shirley ("a lady who gives me oatmeal," Toby had once said about her) took turns telling me about Grandpa. He was a frustrated, self-proclaimed inventor with suicidal leanings—it had taken him three tries before he got the right mix of poisons and took enough to kill himself. I found it sad that after all this time, he was still more interesting to his family than was the good woman dying right then, injured while going for a clam.

"He invented those orange cones used in road construction," Peter said.

"I didn't think anyone invented those," I said.

Peter snorted.

"Came up with then," Sally said. "He made a few dozen, old inner tubes cut and glued together, then painted orange, back in the 50s. He got paid for those. Some were used on the original Highway 70 exchanges, but he never got the credit."

"He should have patented it," Shirley said.

"Patented what?" I asked. "I'm sure they're not still cut-and-paste inner tubes."

Peter glared at me. "Those plastic rings holding six packs together?" he said. "His idea. He told someone, and the next thing he knew, they were all over the place."

"We all have ideas," I said.

Shirley sighed. Because I did not have their illogical view of good ole Granddad, I was seen as difficult, even hostile. They talked mainly for themselves, anyway, reminisced and dwelt in the past because it was their strongest connection.

They reminded themselves of his other ideas—the reusable Styrofoam cricket tube, a bookmark with a built-in magnifying glass, a triple stapler that could drive in three staples at once, spaced five inches apart. He actually made the cricket tube the same way he'd made the highway cones, by cutting and gluing. All of the missing credit made him angrier and angrier and so made Grandma's life sadder.

"Here's an idea of mine," I said. "Artificial nerves made out of some sort of electrical impulses that travel through wires and that could be inserted in the fake feet on a prosthesis and connected to a voluntary muscle. Since I don't know how the hell it would be done, I would hardly call myself the inventor. Did your grandfather think that getting the idea was enough? Did he think that the whole rest of the population sat around open-mouthed, didn't have ideas right and left all day long?" What was it about Sally, and now her kin, that made me angry? Their own irrationality, I told myself. Living in a gated community and calling it city living, passing off stories about a mean and deluded man as something worth telling, forcing me to crawl about in their stupid family tree. A better person than I would have held her tongue, smiled and rerun jokes in her head as the talk circled about her.

Sally shook her head at me. "It's just who he was," she said. "Don't get upset."

Later, I sat on the stool beside Mike and told him about Grandpa Figg and his idiotic grandchildren and the chiropractor's wife and Rollie's crazy mother, and asked him why all of it annoyed me so. Was it because they were utterly deluded, their stories so meaningless? "I want to care," I told Mike. "I mean, what else do we have if not our stories, our lives and the lives of those we care about? Why not care about even the ridiculous? Why remain superior? That way leads to loneliness."

"Look at that," Mike said. He pointed in the direction of the foursome that had arrived later than most, four people I hadn't seen in the café before. They were two black men, a black woman, and a white woman. One of the men had a shaved head, and it was that head Mike pointed at. "He has planes and angles that shine in the ceiling lights. His head's like a geodesic dome. He needs hair. No matter what he could say to me, tell me a story boring or interesting, I would watch his multifaceted head catch the light. Wouldn't hear a word. Wouldn't be able to help it. It's a problem, I think, for a preacher to be so easily distracted. What if someone wanted advice, and I was daydreaming about a body part instead?"

"Would you ever shave your head?" I asked. Mike's hair was thin and stringy, a greasy looking black with a few coarser gray strands. He tried to keep it brushed back, but a piece or two always hung near his eyes.

"My head's too susceptible to be exposed like that," he said. "I don't think my soft spot ever closed over."

By ten o'clock, all the checks had been paid and compliments given to the chef. The diners left in groups, some still telling stories, others seeming to listen. As Shelly stuffed the tablecloths and napkins in the laundry bag, I bagged up the trash and handed it to Mike. "Drop this in the dumpster on your way home, would you?" I asked, but he said he was not going home just yet. It was Friday and the night was young. He knew of places he'd be welcome.

"I'll do it," Ted said, and normally I would've accepted the offer, but the rain was just barely a mist by then, I was already at the door, and for some reason, I said, "It's okay, I've got it." I guess I was guided by fate, for standing beside the dumpster, looking toward our back door, was a slightly built Asian woman. And she was looking for me. When I saw a person, a figure move in the shadows, I moved immediately into the open under the streetlight, the bag of trash still clutched by my stubs. She moved closer to me. Her face was delicate with a button-like nose, a small mouth, and a narrow, barely rounded chin. Her glasses were thick and distorted her eyes, and her hands fluttered like dumbledores on a window screen as she spoke.

"I'm Toby's mother. You want my son, and I do, too, but I can't keep him. I can't even take care of myself. I never have been able to. I'm going to my people in Atlanta. Or I would be going there if I had the money. My time is up. I served it. I got probation and can leave the area if I call in, sign up with some counselor there. I got to get straightened out. I want you to have my son. I'll visit him sometime, maybe write him. I wrote your address down from this flyer I found. But I know what I can and can't do. Him. I can't do him. Never should have had him. I'll sign my rights to him away, can do it, just like that, so easy. My name's Angela Cheng. I can't give him to you, but I can get out of the way. I don't want that Lana to get him. Thinks the sun rises and sets on her ass. Got a man who makes money. That makes her the queen of Sheba. She goes to church, holy as all get out. Me, I don't believe. I have a temper. I've had a few men, maybe will have one more, a good one, but not as many as Lana says, telling all over how I take any kind of bum in who looks good. I don't. I'm coming from a place where I learned to take charge, but I don't know enough. I want you to have Toby. I'll sign my rights away. I haven't seen him since he was five. No, wait, seven. He came back when he was seven. Or eight. I think it was eight. I may have had a pass for his ninth birthday. But I need money."

Her hands were still fluttering, but jerking toward me. I reached for the one with the flyer, took it from her. "How did you know about me?"

"Not important. Doesn't matter. Lots of ways. What do you care? I need money to get to my people in Atlanta. Costs a lot."

"How much?" I'd been through this with her son already.

"Lots. It's not cheap. I have to fly. I can't drive that far. I get sick, dizzy. I want to rent a car when I get there. Jones can't come get me. He's down. Duane, too. Winnie can't drive. I may go somewhere else, but have to go someplace. Need food, clothes, pay the bills so I can get clear and get better. Lots of money. Need lots. I can do checks. They set me up for that. I'll sign my rights away. Just write my name. He's named for my best friend. His name means "God is good," even though I don't believe. I'll sign him away. But I need lots of money."

I turned and saw Shelly framed by the back screen. I was afraid she'd come out, or Ted would. The bag of trash was slipping from my hand.

"Wait here," I said, and her lips quivered as if in idle, waiting for a chance to start up again. I tossed the garbage into the dumpster, then said it again, "Wait here." I went in and right up the back stairs to my bedroom and my checkbook. I decided on a thousand, but didn't know why. I was sure it would be enough, at least at first. I also knew there would never be enough. I would end up paying more. I grabbed sixty from the kitchen cash drawer, too. Toby needed me. That much was clearer than ever. And it wasn't as if I were buying a son. I still had to get past Lana. Jeannie Lemp and all the rest would not approve of my generosity. That much I knew, too.

When I got back down, Ted was outside talking to Angela Cheng. "She's here to see me," I said to Ted. "It's okay." The three of us stood in silence as the rain picked up. Finally, he shook Angela's hand, said good night, and went back inside.

"I told him nothing. I said my name was Bertha. Mama's name. He was nosey. I said call the cops if you're so nosey, but then you came back. I told him nothing. Don't want trouble. I've had enough forever. Didn't say Toby's name. Mine means angel, but his means something about God. I don't believe in God, do you?" Her whole body was shaking.

When I handed her the check, her eyes lit up behind her glasses just as Toby's often did for money or pie or my deformities. I gave her the cash, too, and was tempted to hug her, wish her good luck. Keep in touch, I almost said, and laughed out loud at myself, making her jump. I knew she would keep in touch.

The flyer in my hand read "Blue Ribbon Night"

SHELLY

B ev may have given Toby more money, but not when I could see, so I was able to ignore the sense I had that they both had crossed some line. Maybe, I said to myself, she could get Toby and straighten him and herself out, and besides, I usually added, it was not so awful—life was full of actions and decisions and not many were 100 percent pure and good and righteous. Toby was a fairly rotten kid and Bev was a lonely woman and if they made each other happy, by whatever means, what was the harm? I knew this was a narrow view, but I was trying to see the good side. Broad views produced guilt, regret, and anxiety. People killing one another over a tiny piece of Middle-Eastern land that may or may not have divine history, but that if there was indeed a God, as I believed there was, It, the God, would not be place specific but universal. It would be as readily manifest in Siberia or Costa Rica or Lick Skillet, Arkansas, as in Jerusalem. But neither side would let that pile of rocks go. And the Serbs were fighting Croats with the same venom the Republicans fought the Democrats with in this country, or the Catholics had fought the Protestants in Ireland. Abortionists were attacked by the antis, and the pro-lifers cheered at executions, and hardwood forests were turned into toilet paper, and we were encouraged to own and then conceal handguns. What choice did I have but to take the narrow view? Hope was in the minutia; optimism survived only in isolated activity. I concentrated on my blue-ribbon nights and Aunt Peg's chances in the Senior Ms. America Pageant, worried on and off about my headaches.

As Halloween came and then went, Toby pulled another of his disappearing acts, this time staying away for more than two weeks, and Bev spent hours looking out of our windows, trying to catch a glimpse of his ugly face. The so-called holiday passed by that year with so little of the activity it used to mean for me, I almost liked it. The subdivision Richard and I had lived in brimmed over with children who, on October 31, traipsed endlessly up our drive and through our chrysanthemums for our candy and more. Richard delighted in dressing up our dogs, The Owl and The Pussycat, and I joined in what I considered only his fun, even rigging up the dogs' costumes myself, getting more elaborate each year. They were cowboys, bank robbers, dancing girls.

Bev and I had Mounds and Almond Joy and Three Musketeer miniatures. The café was closed and dark by the time the child beggars were set to arrive, but the porch light above the door to our apartment was on, and we had two jack-o-lanterns on the front stoop, candles flickering behind their evil, moronic smiles and crossed eyes. Ted had carved both of them on the back stoop that afternoon. We had one angel, two wrestlers, a witch, and a mermaid. At least three of the five, according to Bev, were too old to be making believe anyway. Later, Bev ate one Mounds bar after another as she sprawled across my orange couch and said she was disappointed. She had hoped for Toby, maybe with Peaches trailing behind and some of the other kids from St. Hedwig's summer day camp she knew by sight. But if not them, someone. She said it was too bad people were so afraid, too bad the parents stood back in the shadows and most took their children only to homes they knew or to church and school activities. She claimed surprise that

I wasn't upset by the dearth of children, seeing as how I strove for optimism.

"I'm not a kid person," I said. "Optimist or not," and I briefly considered the special equipment I had by virtue of my sex, the uterus, ovaries, tubes, breasts, all going to waste.

Bev switched to Almond Joys and asked why I hadn't made some fancy fudge concoction and tried to impress the neighborhood. I could even have put out flyers, she said, and I tried to look embarrassed. "Blue-ribbon fudge," she said. Yes, she'd found out about my attempts to advertise the first blue-ribbon night, but seemed to be mainly playing at being angry, the way I played at being sorry. I'd put out flyers for all the subsequent blue- ribbon nights, too.

"Nervous mothers," I said about the fancy treats I had not made.

Bev switched to Three Musketeers, and complained that all those years she'd hobbled from house to house dressed as a ghost or queen, often tripping over cracks in the sidewalks and falling hard and sudden, she'd looked forward to her turn at being the one standing still, the generous lady behind the door. When all the candy was gone, Bev went to bed.

Mike and Ted sat at the counter the next day, telling their own stories.

"Remember how safe you felt then?" Ted asked. His trick-or-treat days had been in Muncie, Indiana, where the terrain was flat, the clapboard houses wide spaced, and children walked either directly in the streets or in the drainage ditches.

"I got lost once," Mike said. "Had some kerchief or something covering an eye, and took the wrong turn in the dark, ended up on a street new to me."

I didn't know where this would have been, Mike and details never mixing well.

"I was a pirate, I guess. Maybe a bum. Some guy who was daddy for a spell burned the cork from a bottle of wine and blackened my face with it. That and the kerchief may have been the extent of my costume."

"I got two bags of stuff one year. One for me and one for my sick sister at home," Ted said. "Almost too heavy to carry."

"I ended up on a street of rich people. They had circle drive-ways and columns and concrete posts as tall as I was," Mike said.

Then it was Ted's turn. "I was a vampire. That good year, I was a vampire."

"They didn't have any better stuff," Mike said. "Those rich people just gave me a few pieces of gum, some hard candy."

I refilled both their coffee cups and went out to take the order from a young sleepy-eyed couple who'd just entered. It was almost noon, but they asked for biscuits and gravy, a side of scrambled eggs.

Ted's and Mike's stories were dull, yet I knew I'd have some of my own to tell, equally mundane, if not for the vise grip my head was in. And having hungry customers gobble up my sausage gravy would've made me smile, if not for the metal band tightening about my skull. The scans had revealed nothing. My head was normal on the inside, and Doc Newburg was pleased to be right. She still bet on some combination of *al-wel-gen*. In spite of her smugness and my dislike of her for killing her orchids with loud orgasms and bragging about it, I wanted to believe her. I just could not. My pains were powerful, and I had never in my thirty-six years suffered from any allergies, not even to poison ivy. Also, my thick, shiny hair seemed to be falling out faster, each strand losing its hold easier and more often, and I knew that was connected to my headaches and the blurred vision Doc Newburg assured me I did not have.

So as soon as Newburg's results were in, I made an appointment with Dr. Aiee, specialist in acupuncture and meditation, on Grand near Grandma's old house. Ed Aiee—"Just call me Ed," he said— explained the pattern of the magnetic field on the human scalp, and the two domains of magnetic flux. He preferred twirling and trembling needles (as opposed to thrusting), saying those methods created more friction and thus more electric stimulation. He used sixteen needles in my ear wells and earlobes, and a few others just behind my ears, all to stimulate the pathways to my brain, to balance my two domains. By Halloween, I'd had only two treatments, for Ed believed the first two should be spaced at least ten days apart. After that, they could be as frequent as thrice a week. Bev told me after the first one I was getting as crazy as Mom's Uncle Herbert's wife, Aunt So-And-So we called her, for neither of us could remember her name.

The story was she'd been barred from the offices of four doctors who pegged her as a hypochondriac. She'd resorted—Bev's word—finally to faith healing. The favorite family story was the faith healer who claimed to cure her nearsightedness, convinced Aunt So-And-So to throw away her glasses, and the poor woman walked about for weeks, bumping into things, running her Buick into the side of the garage, and placing the portable mixer alongside her head instead of the phone. "But Doc Newburg told me I can see, too," I told Bev. "She won't accept I have blurred vision, says ignore it. The faith she wants me to have is not in God, but in her, in medicine."

"Well," Bev said. "Aunt So-And-So finally died, so I guess she was sick all along."

I told her stale jokes were no help, and that I just wanted my pains to stop. She wanted to know if the needles weren't also a pain, and I explained what Ed had told me. "The needles create a sensation. A *deqi*, they call it. It is desirable. A sensation is desirable. It's not pain."

We were in the kitchen then. The back door was opened so the fall smells of dry leaves and leaf mold as well as windfall apples and pears and peaches from tiny fenced yards across the alley would overpower the harsh cleaners we used once a month on the oven. I closed my eyes and took a whiff but could still smell ammonia. I was relieved my headaches were not the result of a tumor or brain cancer, but there were nagging doubts. I could have something medical science had not yet detected or found a way to quantify and name. The pain was real. And my hair was falling out. And my vision was blurred. When I opened my eyes again, Bev was smiling at me. "Maybe you should think of your headaches as sensations. Not head aches but head feelings."

Funny, but I'd had almost the same thought when Ed Aiee told me about the desirability of the deqi.

I was loaded with goodies when I arrived at Aunt Peg's house, a rambling two-story monstrosity in Illinois—Uncle Ralph moved his family across the river thirty-two years earlier to save on taxes. Right after my third visit to Ed Aiee, the deqi still making my ears ring, I'd gone to the mall downtown and picked up the sheet music to "Bill Bailey," "Alabamy Bound," "Baby Face," and my choice, "In a Shanty in Old Shanty Town." I knew Aunt Peg would be able to ham it up nicely, make it tear-jerkingly funny. I also bought a lime green linen skort, a blue and green striped boat-neck shirt with long sleeves, and a linen vest that matched the skort. That was for the playwear segment. I bought another playwear combo in different shades of blue with mid-length Bermuda shorts. I'd also picked up a green ball gown with princess seams and spaghetti straps and a backless tangerine-colored sundress with a loose skirt just for fun. Those were only the beginning. If she became Senior Ms. St. Louis Metropolitan Area, Aunt Peg would go on to Senior Ms. Missouri, and then the national pageant, and she would need different outfits for each level. And in pageants, as in most else, you never saved your best for later. She had to go in swinging in playwear that emphasized her tight thighs and gave her hip line more curve.

As Aunt Peg tried on the clothes I'd bought, I asked her why she was going for the St. Louis and then Missouri title. Shouldn't she be competing in Illinois? Was it even legal for her to be competing in Missouri?

"I use your Mom's place as my mailing address for this," she called from her bedroom. "What they don't know, won't hurt them. And I think it's fair. After all, I have spent twenty-six years as a Missourian, my formative years, and this little piece of the Land of Lincoln is considered part of the St. Louis metro area. Besides, I may be gorgeous, but I don't want to take on that hot stuff from Chi-Town, those windy city babes who all have face lifts, get collagen injections as if they're flu shots."

"Right. You prefer nature untampered with."

"My bosom work was not cosmetic."

Well, not entirely, I thought, granting her that much. Gravity was hard on women with large breasts, and without their reduction surgery, Aunts Josie and Peg would have had back pains and that awful stretched out looking skin on top of what once was cleavage. But all the Stillwell sisters had had their necks done, too, had bits of collagen squirted in around their lips periodically.

In the green gown, Aunt Peg was a hothouse dahlia, brilliant gold on a strong and graceful stem. I could hear the judges sucking in their collective breath as their eyeballs dried up from their unwillingness to blink. "Competition be damned," I said as she modeled the outfits by parading before me across her great room. "You cannot lose."

She smiled but shook her head. "You know better than that. Come on, tell me what I'm doing wrong. Be brutal."

Because it was one of those glorious golden November days that made you believe the earth would not tilt any further, would come to its senses and stop leaning away from the sun—we moved out to the grand concourse of Aunt Peg's deck, and she tried on each outfit, practicing her walk. For two hours I watched and coached her, making sure she had a spring in her step, a fluid sway from one hip to the other, a nonchalance as if she walked down grocery store aisles with such grace daily. For Aunt Peg as for all us Stillwell beauties, that was nearly true. In fact, Ted had suggested I try a chiropractor for my headaches as if a misaligned spine was my problem. But my posture, my spine, was as perfect as Aunt Peg's was. Of that, I was sure. "Relax your face," I told her. "Let your jaw go slack. Pretend you have no cares at all."

Models and beauty queens had to look as if the runway, the can of soda pop, the designer SUV was all it took to give them total peace. It was why models were thought of as bimbos. Worry lines were not attractive.

Before I left, we decided on the skort outfit, decided she would get her dressmaker to whip up some wispy thing around the top of her gown to further soften her peaches and cream complexion. She said Chickie was sending one of those fringed jazzy numbers for the talent part, and in the meantime, she'd practice the shanty song just for me. "Chickie is just sick at heart not to be here helping with all this. But it's just that her career is taking off so right now."

I did not make a rude comment about Chickie's career and how valuable it was to sell detergent or to be Liza Doolittle in yet another mediocre dinner theatre rendition of a mediocre story. What a goal! What a life's work! And I knew my inward rudeness was jealousy, jealously it seemed that was as much geographical as anything. Chickie was not here. I'd stayed in town for Richard and his family business, had remained to recover from the sucker punch he'd delivered, and sure, I planned to be in Montreal soon. But I was lately afraid of my resolve. Ted could've held me. The café, too, while not even mine, had sucked me in. And there was Aunt Peg's contest and the puzzle of Mom and Dad to sort out.

I knew the old red of South St. Louis, cracked sidewalks and boarded-up windows and at least one shopping cart used as mobile home per square mile, could easily have been replaced by sand and sea and dunes. Bev and I should've been coated in salt. I told myself I'd open a beach place after I got my *grand diplôme*, and I wanted to believe it. But family had begun to seem an annoying glue that bound me, that made my life open and windy and free but protected. My family, the Stillwell girls and their hangers on, was like a city house with a leaky flat, black roof. Leaky or not, it was still a roof. Creaky or not, it was still a floor. I had taken to Richard's family more than to my own for a while, had welcomed the trade. His was less neurotic, I thought, for I understood mine too well—the tics, the pretenses, the damage done. But his had tics too. First there was a despotic kind of nepotism that forced all to be swallowed by the family business, all to express gratitude for its existence. There was an underlying current of superiority that was nearly invisible, hidden beneath the gratitude and religious faith and charity. And underneath it all was a thin strand of sadism, a delight at another's expense. Richard's uncle often told a story of driving his own blind grandmother crazy by sneaking up to the porch and suddenly scattering handfuls of gravel under her rockers, making her jump and curse her grandson. "How did that old blind Christian woman know all those words?" he'd ask with each telling.

My application to l'École de Cuisine, my best ticket to elsewhere, was due in two months, and I was on such a roll, my main problem would be deciding which of my creations to highlight. After the Newburg night, I did an eggplant stuffed with ground veal, then lamb kabobs, and last Friday, a lasagna made with proscuitto and roasted vegetables. In a few days, I would do a braised veal shank with saffron rice but would start with a cream of parsnip soup, in honor of Ted who still seemed parsnip-like and solid. That was an inside joke only I knew. Bev had agreed to make a marshmallow Black Bottom pie, though when I suggested it, I didn't tell her it had been Ted's favorite, the dessert he told me his mother made for him each year on his birthday.

This would be our fifth blue ribbon night, and we had attracted more customers with each one. Rollie and his mother and assorted members of the Figg family came to all of them. Mike still sat at the counter, giving us a seedy look even in what he said were his good clothes, but I had come to accept or at least ignore his presence. Aunt Josie and Uncle Al had been in for two of the four so far, and Aunt Peg and Mom had come with them once. Maddie and the father of her child, a skinny, long-haired kid named Jason, had been in two weeks ago, and the thrift shop women with their twin husbands had made it one more time. But we had new people, too, diners who were trying us for the first time, who liked us without knowing us.

Dad, I knew, would never show up because he ate only Mom's cooking and only at home. Holidays were exceptions, but even they required lots of pleading to get him out of the house. I wondered if I'd be able to talk him into coming for Thanksgiving—the traditional turkey and dressing, of course, but as I was planning it, even richer and more elaborate than usual. Maybe an oyster dressing. Maybe chestnuts and raisins. Cousin Chuck had already complained about having to go someplace without a TV, having to miss football, but in the true spirit of the Stillwell girls, I said screw him.

Thursday afternoon, the day after I'd made Aunt Peg practice her walk, was another gem. Our business was good, too: twenty-three paying customers all day, lots of barbecued beef sandwiches sold, and four servings of quiche. I decided to start on my soup early, do it a day ahead, partly to save time but mostly because cream soups were always better made ahead. I was proud of myself for knowing that even before I started classes. I felt gifted, like a real cook.

Ted sat beside Mike at the counter, as always lately, but Mike was too far gone for much of a conversation. Ever since Halloween, three days earlier, he'd been on a binge. On Tuesday, he'd been coherent, sitting there telling a Halloween story to Ted, but his mind and abilities grew soggier by the hour. All day Wednesday, he'd stayed in his garage playing angry sounding polkas the neighborhood could not shut out even with the storm windows in place.

We all prayed he'd pass out. Well, the police made him stop at midnight, but he'd started up again early Thursday morning, the real break not coming until around noon. The silence was so sudden, right in the middle of one of those torturous pieces, that neighbors stopped their activities, pulled their cars over, opened their doors, and looked confused briefly before they sighed in relief. A few hours later, he was back in the café, but lost in himself. We knew he wouldn't stay long, as his beer or whatever—no one wanted to get close enough to guess his drink of choice—was back across the alley. Nevertheless, Ted tried to talk to him. "Ever think you are destined for a whole new life?" Ted asked. "Ever think you're about to go on a journey?"

"I could shoot you," Mike said, swiveling on his stool and aiming a finger at Ted, putting it right at the end of Ted's nose.

"Sure you could," Ted said. "But that's not the point."

"It's all the point you need," Mike said. "Bang, bang. It's the point."

"I know what you mean," I said to Ted from back at the counter where I sliced parsnips. "My destiny's calling."

"Bang to you, too," Mike said, aiming his finger at me.

"Go home," I said.

It was after three, and we had no real customers, so Bev was sitting at a table in the window ignoring us, reading the recipe I'd given her for marshmallow Black Bottom pie, when Jeannie Lemp came in.

I had not seen Jeannie for a while, but as always, I had to hold back, almost bite the inside of my cheek to keep from giving her tips. Cut off that lank hair, suck in your gut, stand up straight, trade in those lumpy gathered skirts, a little foundation wouldn't hurt. She ordered my stuffed peppers, not on the menu on Thursdays, so

I talked her into a slice of bacon quiche. She had chosen the deuce along the wall, but after she ordered, moved to where Bev sat.

"I have news," Jeannie said.

"Have I passed a test, been forwarded to yet another desk?" Bev asked.

"This is only about you incidentally. But Toby's biological mother has relinquished her claim to him, even before a termination hearing was scheduled. He is now ready for adoption."

Bev smiled, but didn't seem as surprised as I was at the news. "Good. He's too old not to have a permanent home."

"We agree. Things may move fast now. Lana has to decide if she wants to adopt him."

"Which you prefer," Bev said. She had closed the cookbook and was looking across the table at Jeannie. Her statement sounded like a challenge, and I hoped her attitude would not get in her way.

"Permanence, routine, a smooth transition. These are our goals, what we prefer for Toby and all our children. But we try not to take sides."

"Good," Bev said. "But I think you should look closely at Lana. Even after all the trouble, Toby does not stay at her home every night. From what I can tell, he spends the night with the Figgs, maybe others, often. But you must know that."

Jeannie blushed. "How do you know? Is it just from what Toby tells you?"

Bev shook her head. "Not just Toby."

"Well," Jeannie said. "We will look into it. We can't know everything." I took her quiche to her, and she thanked me, looked down at the paper napkins she had spread across her lap, and coughed.

I left, knowing Bev and Jeannie were entitled to their privacy, and knowing, too, that as long as Ted and Mike were quiet, I could hear every word anyway.

"I have something to tell you," Jeannie said. "This is just a tiny part of any decision. But this is just so you know."

Bev leaned back in her chair, spread her arms out from her sides. "Hit me with it," she said. "Aim for my heart," as if she knew it would be not only bad news, but bad because it was some bureaucratic convolution and mumble-jumble.

Even from back by the parsnips, I could hear clearly and worried again that the chip on Bev's shoulder would ruin her chances. And the truth was her attitude annoyed me, too, as counter-productive as it was. Every idiot could guess you had to seem nice if you wanted to adopt a child. But before I could hear anymore, Mike came out of his trance.

"My mother never had pithy little sayings. Did yours?" he asked Ted.

"Nothing but," Ted said. "She was the cliché queen of Indiana. It was in her blood. Her ancestors did samplers."

"Never expect much from anything called a jamboree," Mike said.

I heard Bev say "Damn," saw Jeannie blush deeper.

"You've lost me, Mike old buddy," Ted said.

"Shhhh," I said, leaving my soup and coming out from behind the counter.

"It's most of her words of wisdom. What I remember. Well that and hate everyone not related to you, and don't expect anything from your kin."

"It's rough," Ted said.

"It's just a piece," Jeannie said. "It's one consideration." She stood to go, her quiche barely touched. As she opened her purse, Bev waved her off.

"You can escape faster if you let me pay. Go on."

"I thought you should know," Jeannie said before she left.

Mike continued. "No, see it is true about jamborees."

Bev lurched back to the kitchen and kicked the side of the stove, her favorite target. "Goddamn, goddamn, goddamn the DFS."

"What?" Ted asked. "What is it?"

"They cannot be serious," Bev said. "They cannot be so ignorant." She still seemed to be talking to the stove.

"Hold it down," Mike said.

"Why is there all this hassle? What kind of superficial bullshit is this? I want Toby, not a black boy, not because he's black. Not in spite of it." She kicked the stove once more, and as always, with her only foot. "They prefer same race adoptions," she said stretching out prefer. "I prefer they wise up."

"I'm going," Mike said. "If you're going to make so much noise."

"It's enough to make me hate people," she said.

I thought you already did, I did not say.

Shortly after Mike left, and without taking any leftovers for a change, Bev wound down enough so her tantrum became a series of loud sighs. She sighed all the way up the back stairs, calling down from the top, "I'll make those pies tomorrow."

Ted helped me clean up and suggested a walk to enjoy the fall weather. "It'll be good for you," he said as if he knew I was already trying to put a good face on DFS's procedures, reminding myself that the bi-racial part was just one minor consideration, that they had to consider all angles. Preference was not a legal term, anyway, at least I hoped not. And I decided to leave Bev alone, let her calm down until I was ready to tackle the job of convincing her DFS was not wholly stupid, which I would do as soon as I could believe it myself. That Bev's worries and disappointments had become mine in a real way, not just from sympathy, was not lost on me either.

The day, as I said, was bright and sunny enough that winter seemed far away. Even those little white daisy-like wild flowers, or weeds as some would think, that grew in the cracks between the sidewalks and the curb had been fooled into blooming. The broken bottles and fast-food Styrofoam and the throw-away journal newspapers people never retrieved could almost be ignored. Not entirely, though, and when I saw a Pizza Shack flyer caught in a still-blooming rose bush, I decided Bev had a point about my form of advertising. Well, my flyers had not added much to the mass of junk already swirling about, and enough of them stacked together could have kept a homeless person warm, I said to myself, joking, trying out excuses.

Ted and I walked a few blocks without talking, and I wondered what it said about me, walking under oaks and sugar maples and bark-shedding sycamores, but noticing litter. I tried to keep my gaze at eye level or higher, and the old neighborhood did look better that way, in short and precisely focused views. Good old narrow views. Once again I noted how essential they were for sanity.

Grandpa died nearly ten years ago in St. Francis Hospital. For his last two days he was maybe conscious, maybe not, but very restless as I understood bodies tended to be just before going. The day before he died, I walked into his hospital room and saw that he had thrown his covers off, was writhing about, and because he could've been in pain, I pressed his call button. I was spreading the sheets back over his restless body when a nurse came in, all sunshine and bustle. She was young and chubby with what still could have been baby fat, and she wore a smock decorated with teddy bears. She leaned down in his face, her forehead nearly touching his, and yelled. "Well, aren't you a wiggly worm today!"

The narrow view allowed me to keep going. She was only one person; Grandpa was probably safely unconscious; there were idiots everywhere. I used the narrow view later whenever I saw women with bears or balloons on their smocks.

"All those people who think the world will end at the millennium, " Ted said finally. "How will they get through January?"

"Feeling blessed?" I guessed. "On borrowed time."

"Or maybe cheated," he said. "Maybe too foolish to continue."

"Everyone continues," I said. "They'll re-count, say the numbers from some old delirious prophet's calculations were added wrong, and the end won't come for a few more years. Or they'll say it's a test of faith. Some will say it is an end, just a very slow one. The end itself can take decades."

"I wanted to be a monk once," he said. We were at Grand and Delor, waiting for the picture of a walking person to light up. "Just for order and sacrifice and a chance to think. I stayed for three weeks with the Trappists as an outsider, a way to see if I'd like it."

"You're full of surprises," I said, because he seemed to expect that response, though Ted as a monk would not have surprised me. Oh sure, according to a strict accounting, he was a sinner for being my co-fornicator. But he did have an aura of religion about him.

He was on a journey; he was gentle and helpful to me, and also to Bev and Mike. And like most in the religious life, he accepted free food as his due. That last was a throwback, I knew, to a joke Grandpa would've made. True, Ted's occupation should have been, but was not, against most religions—sneaking and spying and interfering and whispering. That he considered it merely a brief part of his journey made me keep my negative comments to myself, but detection seemed like nothing but an activity for eight-year-old girls: carrying tales home to get others in trouble.

"The monks were not a bit interested in predictions of doom," Ted said. "The apocalypse bored them. I liked that. It bores me, too."

"It lets people ignore their own troubles. That's its value. Here's a big problem coming up and you can't stop it. It's easier to look for it than to wonder why you're so mean, why your lover betrayed you. You can ignore all that hard stuff if the world's ending, if you're in line for a gas mask."

Ted squeezed my hand and we walked a few blocks in silence. I wondered if what he wanted from me was a pretty sounding board, a woman he could help and comfort for a while along his journey, and a woman who would talk to and listen to him. He could have been just as content walking hand in hand with any number of good-looking women who responded appropriately and made space for him in their lives, danced with and fucked him for fun. I hoped it was more than that. Or would become more than that. I hoped I would become more.

Richard had needed me. My psyche, my spirit, myself all joined to his psyche and spirit to create a new entity. Richard needed union. Even when we disagreed, we were like one mind fighting itself. Richard told me once we did not just want to be together, we were together, even at those times we did not want to be. Richard would have understood my unspoken Grandpa joke, would have known why I left it unspoken. But if all that was true, when Richard replaced me with Aurora, it was as if he got a replacement brain, an artificial heart. Within the chaos of my head, though, was the possibility that I was indulging a drama, remembering a joining that never existed. I shook my head to clear it, and the orange and red leaves blurred briefly, the colors running together in nauseating patterns.

"I'd like to come back as a goose," I said to Ted, then looked at his scrunched brow as he tried to guess where that had come from. Richard, I told myself, would have known. "They mate for life," I said.

"Ahhh," he said, squeezing my hand again. "But are they happy?"

True to her word, Bev made five marshmallow Black Bottom pies Friday morning, even as she waited on our eight breakfast customers and made a tray of high-rising biscuits. She had a sour look to her face all day, but she was polite to our customers and her movements were calm and precise. Once, late in the morning when we had no customers and I was rubbing a rosemary garlic paste into the veal, she leaned against the walk-in refrigerator and watched me. "How's your head?"

"Better," I said. "Twirling needles may work."

"I guess I made it worse with my explosion yesterday."

"It was bad already. You didn't change it."

"Why does stupidity rule the world?"

I shrugged. "Maybe it won't this time. Surely DFS is not crazy enough to keep a kid like Toby from a good home."

"Is it survival of the fittest? Stupidity always wins out, so the stupid must be better fit to live, to carry on."

"I'm sorry," I said, thinking again about the women who wore bears on their smocks. They survived, even seemed to multiply.

Mike stayed away all day, and his organ was quiet, too. Ted came in for a tuna salad sandwich at one, and loitered at the counter until we closed up. "What's the worst thing that ever happened to you?" he asked Bev, then took a bite of an Aunt Josie pickle. He claimed he dreamed about those pickles, so we always gave him extra. I knew the worst thing that ever happened to Bev was before her birth, before she was even an entity, and expected her to say so, but instead she said that was an easy question.

"Three years ago, we had a guest speaker for our first faculty meeting in August. It was a car dealer. Two of his daughters were in Agnus Dei and one had graduated. This guy had six brands of cars in four different locations in the metro area. He was and is a big shot. As near as I could tell, it was why he spoke to us. He told us to challenge our students, to give them encouragement but to make them work hard. Any of our incoming girls could have spit out the same pabulum. I was offended. It made as much sense as me telling his sales staff how to sell cars. I was ashamed of myself for not standing up and walking out. I'm more ashamed each day."

"What about you?" I asked Ted.

"It hasn't happened yet. It's about to."

"Mine was Richard's leaving," I said, though no one asked.

Ted bit into a pickle and nodded.

"I'm really worried about Toby," Bev said. "I called Shirley Figg and she said he'd been there for a few nights last week, but not since. Even though she's a frightened turtle, I called Jeannie, left a message for her to check up on him."

Ted nodded at that, too.

My fifth blue ribbon night was the biggest success of all. Rollie and his mother and Sally Figg, this time with a date, were there as always. Mom came in with Aunt Josie and Uncle Al. Roger from Auto World was there with another man he introduced to me as a fellow worker and two blondes about my age with very stiff hair. As I seated them, Roger said I was as beautiful as ever. Ted was there, as usual, but Mike, we guessed, was still sleeping it off, rolling about his bed and moaning. The other ten paying customers were strangers. One was the woman who had come in my first day in the café. She was with two other black women, all quite stylish in gabardine business suits and gold earrings and pins. Just as she had on her previous visit, she ordered a glass of wine. When I told her we still did not have a liquor license, she shook her head at me in what seemed pity, as if she knew we did have one and I simply hadn't looked hard enough.

What made that evening, November 4, 1999, so extraordinary, though, was the little round ball of a man the color of well-done pot roast who introduced himself to me even before I seated him and his female companion. "Food critic for the *Post-Dispatch*," he said, extending his hand. His fingers were short and thick like warm Vienna sausages. He had given me some name before that that sounded like Zippo, but it was his title I cared about.

"I thought you guys snuck around," I said. "Didn't announce yourselves."

"I haven't made you nervous, have I?" His words came out in puffs of expelled air.

No, I was not nervous. I assured him I was not, and it was true. This was what I'd waited eight months for. Ordinarily I would've been watching Mom pick at her food, sniff at a forkful or two, then shoot me a toothy smile when she saw me watching, but now I could concentrate on Zippo. I ground fresh nutmeg unto his cup of parsnip soup just as I did for Sally Figg and the others, but he was the one I watched eat it, and from three tables away, as I cleared the first course from Roger's table, I heard his spoon scrape the bottom of the cup. I decorated his veal plate with tiny bits of parsley just as I did for all the plates, and I thought I saw him make a note of it. I gave his table the same small bowl of grated parmesan to sprinkle on the greens in vinaigrette I gave to all the tables, and I gave Zippo and his woman no larger slice of marshmallow Black Bottom pie than I gave to Rollie or his mother.

He and his dinner partner smiled at each other, at the restaurant, at the food I thought, and I had to remind myself the smile signified nothing. He was not going to frown and so visibly tip his hand, no matter what he really thought.

While he picked up the last crumbs of his pie crust with the back of his fork, I placed a copy of our daily menu on his table, said please take it.

I spent that night alone, having told Ted I was exhausted. I had not told him or Bev who Zippo was, wanting to savor the possibilities by myself. My heart pounded and swelled inside my head, and instead of sleeping, I replayed the evening, detail after detail. The gossip, the noise, the laughter of the diners, their various praise of the dishes, comments about being well-fed or stuffed, all created the ambiance I looked for. And the food was, to use one of Ted's favorite words, *superb*, especially for a place with red bars on the windows and across from a pawn shop. I hoped Zippo would come back for lunch, taste my barbecue sauce.

I spent the weekend writing the review in my head and ran out of superlatives before midday Saturday. The veal was like the second coming. The saffron rice restored Zippos' faith in God. The soup was like a therapeutic massage for the taste buds. How do you describe perfection when it's already a cliché? "Blue Ribbon Night," was a headline I could have given Zippo. But I prepared myself for the bad, too, wanted to be ready in case Zippo had not liked the greens—hadn't they been a bit bitter?—or the rice—just a touch too sticky. Maybe he preferred his soup cooler. Maybe he was a no-taste jerk who got the job because he was the entertainment editor's worthless stepson. Then I thought maybe he'd lied, was not a food critic at all. I had seen no ID, no flash of critic credentials, and it may have been the fat man's ploy to get better service. Or free food. Was I supposed to have given him his meal on the house? Was it customary to treat the reviewer? I had assumed the *Post* paid but admitted I was operating in the dark.

Nevertheless, he had to have liked us. Predicting and expecting disaster was overrated as a defense, useless in fact. Positive hopeful outlooks worked better. Besides, good would result no matter what. Even a bad review was advertising, and if there were some negatives, they would only give me direction, tell me the areas to concentrate on. Lines, sentences, even whole paragraphs ran through my head for two days as I cooked and cleaned up and served and heard Ted and Bev and, by Sunday, even Mike say things I forgot immediately.

Well, I did remember Bev's whining about Toby, did know she called Shirley Figg, Peaches' mother, on Sunday. Also on Sunday, Ted tried to get me to go to Mass with him, but I declined. Bev called Jeannie Lemp again, too, left another message that she said would not be returned. She spent most of the weekend looking through the bars of our front window and down the block for Toby. Once, while watching leaves swirl down Meramec, she shivered. "I hope Toby's wearing his sweater," she said.

The review was in Monday's paper, the headline: Alibi Café, Schizophrenic but Good. The Schizophrenia part was "tuna sandwiches and biscuits and gravy are mixed with five course dinners. Chrome stools with red plastic seats but white placemats and tablecloths." That kind of thing. For a brief few moments, I thought Skip Zitich—Zippo's real name according to the byline—greatly lacking in imagination. Even a hack could have come up with the adjective *eclectic* to describe us. But I forgave all when I read that my cream of parsnip soup was better than any cream soup he'd ever had, that his veal nearly melted in his mouth and was just the right mix of brown and pink, that his companion wanted the recipe for the tomato, edamame, and corn sauté served alongside the veal and rice, and that the marshmallow Black Bottom pie was rich but fluffy. The entire five course dinner was—and here was Ted's word sounding even better from a new source—*superb*.

I bought ten more copies of the *Post*, planned to send a review in with my application and save some of the others to read on bad days. I hoped Richard would miss me a little when he read about me and Bev who were, according to Skip Zitich, local girls with flair. I read that word, *superb*, over and over. It meant so much coming from Skip Zitich. By ten that morning, we heard "Amazing Grace" waft lightly across the alley. I smiled as I cut out copies of the review and laid each one gently aside. I'd always said Mike shouldn't be at the counter when the reviewer showed up. My heart fluttered at how well synchronized the universe was. "Hey," I said to Bev. "We've got flair." I did a version of the "Brown Gravy Shuffle" behind the counter . "We have superb flair!"

But she had her jacket on, her hand on the backdoor knob. "It's all yours today," she said. "I'm off to find Toby."

BEV

Naturally, I was angry about Shelly's flyers. How could I not be? I had told her of my aversion to advertising of any kind. Yes, I knew she thought my views irrational, and perhaps they were, but they were mine. And it was my café. And her deciding her goal superceded my ideas, irrational or not, made me a party to what I was against. When Angela Cheng thrust the flyer at me that evening in the rain, the fact of it barely registered. I was too caught up in her need for money and my coming closer to motherhood. Later though, I understood Shelly had been going behind my back, and seeing it for the betrayal it was, I set her down and talked to her, a grown-up woman, as if she were one of my students. I explained that being forced to be a part of what I despised was essentially turning me into my enemy. Her response was to apologize—something that came so easily to her I doubted she heard her own words—and swear never to do it again. And her swearing, too, was facile enough that I distrusted her promise.

Yet I knew she'd seen me give Toby money, and my righteousness could appear to have no foundation, could seem so to myself as well as to her. Was it possible to take a selective high road? Shelly knew of only that one time I gave money to Toby, and when I lectured her as if she were a child, there had been only that one time. But by the third week of November, I'd given him money five more times. I kept score so I'd know how much I would have to undo and overcome once he was mine. I always gave in small amounts, though, knowing that made zero difference. Forty-two dollars so far.

Of course, I could not have lived with any awareness for thirty-six years and have believed in absolutes, and I knew that being compromised made me normal, and knowing that helped me keep my anger at Shelly in check. And though Shelly'd seen me succumb to my yearnings for Toby's presence, what she hadn't seen was worse: my paying off his mother so she would sign away her rights to him.

On the day before Thanksgiving, I received what I believed was the first of many letters from Angela Cheng. It was written in pencil on lined notebook paper, and the return address was not Atlanta, her admitted destination, but Peoria, Illinois: "I did the hearing, signed where they said. They said I should tell them the father, but I don't know who it was. I am ashamed to be so impure but happy not to believe in a god who would punish me. I did not tell them you gave me money. I hope I never do. T.J. is a friend. He will be by for more money I need. Whatever you have. I hope you are well and happy." Even though the termination of rights forms were already signed, copied, entered, and filed away, nothing was ever over, and this was even more serious extortion. So I knew I'd give T.J. a few hundred when he came in. Well, I rationalized, she was in need and it was only money, and I may have given it anyway. But I wasn't convinced by my own excuses. I wasn't a natural-born do-gooder. I didn't have a missionary's heart.

And I was being merely facetious when I told myself Angela's wishing me happiness was such a nice touch. I may as well have a tree planted in Forest Park for her, too, as I had planned on doing for Maddie's cub, Randolph James Hilker according to his fraudulent papers. He had come into the world two weeks late, November

6, and four days later Maddie had gone with some Agnus Dei girls to a football game at St. Francis of Assisi High, the boys' school for very rich Catholic boys. Jason, Randolph James' uncredited father, was a senior in another school just a few miles further south for slightly poorer boys.

But I never got around to the tree-planting business, at least not that day, because Toby showed up Thanksgiving morning, showed up about the same time the weak morning sun began to light up Meramec Street, and, as he had twice before, begged to hide out. My response was the same as always, but this time I had more questions. For one thing, he hadn't needed a daytime place before, and I believed he would be more missed over a holiday, more so than ordinarily (though as far as I could tell from Lana's nonreactions to his previous disappearances, that was not much). Besides, I was being considered—I hoped seriously—as his future mother, so I needed all the facts. Those were my words to him, too, after he rushed upstairs after leaning on the doorbell the entire fifty seconds it had taken Shelly to leap from her bed and run downstairs. "I want all the facts," I said. "No tricks. No lies."

He was panting, and his glasses, as usual, slid down his nose as he sat at our kitchen table, his head bobbing on his thin neck. For more than two weeks, from late October to early November, he'd been scarce, had returned one Tuesday afternoon for milk and pie without a hint of where he'd been, if anywhere, why he hadn't been by. Well, he didn't punch a time clock, I said to myself. He went to school during the day, and did his homework in the evenings, and maybe he had signed up for a soccer or volleyball team, or maybe he had been practicing for the school play or recital of some kind. I hoped so. I hoped he was learning how to be an accepted part of something. I knew I was kidding myself with such hopes. When he returned that Tuesday for his milk and pie as if he had not been gone, his responses to my questions were shrugs and grins. He'd been hanging around, he told me, doing nothing.

This time, I needed exact answers. Was it the burglary ring again, I asked, knowing if so, Shelly and I would have to prepare for another assault.

After two glasses of water, he was ready to talk. "They're selling stuff again. Poodle Baby says she'll cut off my balls and use 'em as earrings if I stay in her business."

Shelly laughed at that, but I hushed her with a wave of my hand.

"What does she mean stay in her business? How are you in it?"

"I watch. Can't keep me from watching. No law against that."

"How does she know you watch?"

"Might be one of her boys saw me. Told her."

"Might be?"

He sighed, looked at me as if he were the adult and I was the child deliberately not understanding. "Okay," he said. "Here's the real truth. I seen the stuff. Lots of computers and some big screens. A few boys bring it in, then take it out again. A red pickup takes some of it. I know her boys saw me watching because the ugliest one, a big ole white dude with hair on his hands, tole me to get lost. Another one, a nigger that the guy I stay with says could be my dad, says 'scat, shoo,' like I'm a cat."

"They could be the ones who were here," Shelly said. "They're mean, Toby. Stay clear of them."

"Nah," he said. "These are new, just been around for a little while."

I was interested in who they were specifically, but more interested in the other part, the guy I stay with. "Who do you mean, the one you stay with?"

"He's the one gonna get me. He'll kill me. He said he would just a few hours ago."

Death threats of a certain kind are familiar to children. "I'll kill you if you get in my flower bed," "If you track mud in on this floor, your life is worthless." Those are the garden variety kinds of threats that work not one bit because children take them as jokes. This was not one of those, and though I did not believe Lana's husband truly wanted to kill Toby, he did want to frighten him, and he had frightened me as well. He was a part of the ring, at least a silent partner. I was quiet for a moment or two, trying to get a feel for this, figuring out how serious this was, and Toby said nothing else, just watched me think. Shelly took all that silence as a call to action, jumped up and said she would fix us all a big Thanksgiving morning breakfast, and was soon rattling pans, chopping and stirring. Toby, meanwhile, must have grown tired of my thinking, for he finally said, "Okay. I'll tell you the really real truth."

According to Toby, Lana's husband was part of the burglary ring. Though he had been in the hospital the first time Toby'd been threatened, he now knew of Toby's fascination with the operation and the blackmail. He knew because Toby had attempted the blackmail yet again. I was disappointed to learn Toby wasn't smarter than the average hoodlum-in-training, foolhardy enough, in fact, to make the same mistake twice. His previous offer to keep quiet for money had been met with the scare tactic, but that was when Lana's husband was not around. Now that he was out of the hospital and a full member of the gang, he was determined to keep Toby quiet. And he told Toby he'd do more than just scare. He had already used beatings. Toby stood up and raised his sweatshirt to display two purple, crimson, and deep blue bruises on his back. "He thought this would keep me quiet. But getting whipped just makes me want to tell all the more. He said little unwanted bastards like me can disappear."

Wanted, wanted, I almost said to him. Not un. There was little to do with this information, little but hide him in our apartment until I figured out other options. As usual, I knew first what I would not do, and that was turn him back to Lana and her vicious husband. That meant no one in authority could know where Toby was, at least not until Howard Figg advised me, and if no one in authority could know, then no one at all could. Just Shelly and I. We had to be the only two in on it. Shelly because she was already in on it and because it wouldn't have been easy to hide a boy in our four rooms anyway. Because it was Thanksgiving, Toby wouldn't be expected back in school until Monday, and by then, if Howard called the authorities, Lana's husband could be behind bars.

Normally, this would have meant I had time to think. But the big family-love-unity-good-feeling holiday also meant people who only pretended to care would be looking for him, and it also meant

I had to either let the whole rest of my family in on the problem, or miss dinner at Aunt Marie's, or leave Toby home alone. I knew I couldn't miss dinner without Mom coming by, maybe with Dad and Grandma and whomever else she could talk into it, in shifts more than likely, all day long. And if Shelly missed, which I knew she wanted to, it would be almost as traumatic. Aunt Marie would believe it was a sulk, and would send Mom over to check on "baby Shelly." I also knew I couldn't let the rest of the family in on my secret. A secret shared by twelve people was not one. But more than any of those, I could not leave Toby alone and in danger.

So immediately after we ate, I told Toby to stay put and went across the alley to Mike's. I had never been in his flat, but I walked past the garage, closed and quiet for Thanksgiving morning, and up onto the wooden back porch. I knocked, pounded, and shouted, not afraid of disturbing anyone else since the barbershop downstairs would've been closed for Thanksgiving anyway if it had not gone out of business two months earlier. I stumbled off the porch and up the gangway to the front of his place and his front door, six concrete steps up from the walkway leading to the steps down to Gasconade. I rang the bell I doubted worked, banged and thumped on his front door until my hand hurt, then went back home.

Shelly said she would ask Ted to stay with Toby, but I decided to make that my last resort. For one thing, I knew she was looking forward to taking Ted to her mother's, introducing him to family members he had not yet met, mainly her father. And for another thing, something about Ted seemed sneaky. He was a pleasant, ordinary enough guy, even helpful and kind; nevertheless, I could picture him if left to his own devices going through my drawers, medicine cabinet, the mail, even our trash. Why I saw him that way, I didn't know. But for the moment at least, I wouldn't trust him with the secret of Toby.

Instead, I called Sally Figg, thinking Toby could stay with her or with Peaches' family for a few hours, but I changed my mind when she answered, said I just called to wish her a pleasant holiday. It suddenly dawned on me that Lana's husband would look for Toby at Peaches', and the Figgs may not be as committed to hiding him, may think it was only right to turn him over to his foster father. And if Howard Figg were there, he may see himself as an officer of the court, and before I had a chance to make my case with him, would feel compelled to call DFS or Jeannie and her ilk who had not proved themselves good for Toby so far.

As I wished Sally a happy Thanksgiving and hung up, I realized the only choice I had was to play sick and work hard at discouraging family concern. I would come down with something sudden so Mom wouldn't have time to run over on her way to Aunt Marie's, and something contagious enough to scare them off while not serious enough to make them worry. As I was making a list, adding and subtracting my symptoms—Fever? yes, but a small one—I heard "Now Thank We All Our God." As I thumped across the alley once again I did thank God for Mike, my savior.

"I was going to get dinner with all the trimmings down at the Salvation Army," Mike said after I explained what I needed.

"I'll bring you a plate from Aunt Marie's."

"That'll be pretty late for dinner," Mike said.

"Shelly and I'll whip up something before we go. She'll love to."

"And I'm not good with kids."

"You don't even have to talk to him. Just be there. Protect him."

"Well," he said. "I can do that. I have weapons."

Then I had an inspiration. "Your place. I'll bring him to your place with the food. He'll be safer."

He looked down at the keyboard and frowned, started to object, but I begged. "Please, please, please. They'll come looking for him at our place. They did once before."

"Your place is safe now. Alarms and such."

"But no one would think of yours. Please, please, please."

He gave in, and at 3:30, Shelly and I pushed one of the many shopping carts littering the alley from our back door to Mike's. It contained a fresh turkey breast still warm from the oven, a pan of corn bread stuffing, a plastic bucket of gravy, another of mashed yams, and a saucepan of cooked Brussels sprouts. Beneath it all was Toby, covered by a gold and pink embroidered tablecloth once belonging to Shelly's ex-mother-in-law.

The interminable two and a half hours I was in Aunt Marie's overheated and heavily perfumed flat, most of my mind was in Mike's place above the former barbershop. I didn't even know what Mike's place looked like, but I could see the two of them staring at each other, silent and frightened, ready to fight.

Aunt Marie and Mom and Aunt Peg and Cousin Chuck and Grandma—they'd all been invited to the café and a Thanksgiving dinner to beat all, prepared and served by Shelly. They all had accepted the invitation way back in August, but a week ago, Aunt Marie changed everyone's mind and plans. Her reason was Uncle Jack. He would not eat Thanksgiving dinner anywhere but in his own home, prepared by his own wife. That it was odd and insane went without saying, Aunt Marie said, but, she continued, we all knew Uncle Jack, knew he was the strangest of all, but was still family, one of us. She said to have thought we could change him or force him to be different was absurd all along, and Shelly must have been temporarily as insane as her father for thinking she could pry him out of his place. And Aunt Marie hated to say so, but it was mean spirited to try to change him at this late date, to force him to be normal, just so Shelly could show off her cooking, which she showed off at the café every day of the week, Aunt Marie herself having had three dinners there.

Shelly, who had been actively planning her extravaganza for weeks, making lists and trying out dressings and ordering the turkeys—the fresh breast we pushed across the alley was one of two in the café refrigerator—saw the last minute change of plans as yet another of her mother's hateful acts and sabotage, said she could've talked her father into coming to the café if given a chance, and had been waiting for the very last minute so he wouldn't brood about it ahead of time. When Aunt Marie complained about the thirteen people, ten crowded about her dining table and three upstairs in Uncle Jack's place, including Uncle Jack, Shelly said, "I, for one, won't be there. Ted either. We'll give her a break. Go to Acapulco for a week. Maybe Bermuda. Mom's turkey will be as dry as wallboard anyway," She said to me. "She'll have canned cranberry gelatin."

But not only did she want Ted to meet her family, he wanted to meet Uncle Jack and Cousin Chuck, said he looked forward to

talking with Mom and Dad some more. He told Shelly he liked
our family, missed his own in Indiana less when he was with ours.
"Okay," she said. "We'll go, and you'll see how neurotic my clan
is. You'll witness Mom's selfish vanity." And get a dose of her father, I thought when she said it. I had never decided which of her
parents was the bigger burden. But both of them knew, as all of us
did, that Shelly judged herself narrowly, picked one or two pieces
of herself and ignored all others. And we all knew that right now,
in her year after Richard, her culinary skills were where she saw
her success.

To take that from her and to do it as a last minute fiat was
cruel.

And Shelly had been right in her predictions. The turkey was
dry. The dressing was from a packaged mix, and the cranberry gel
came neatly in one piece from the can and sat quivering on lettuce
leaves. To even get to the food, though, we all had to put up with
Cousin Chuck's long-winded holiday piety.

Aunt Marie designated him as grace sayer, and in his grace,
Cousin Chuck did not merely address God, he invoked God's presence, addressed him or her or it as Giver Of All Good, Provider
and Protector, Mighty Host Who Prepared This Banquet, and so
on. He then asked this many-titled God to be present among us
who all needed guidance and who were thankful for—and here
came the list. I swear he named each sense individually, named the
four seasons with descriptions of each (in case God had forgotten which one we humans called spring or winter). Then he gave
attributes to each of us, maybe so God would remember us. I was
courageous; Shelly was determined; his boys were the future. That
kind of crap. He called his wife long-suffering to get a laugh, but
most of us sighed, seeing our captive selves in that description. By
the time he got around to being thankful for the food, I knew
it must be cold, the gravy surely congealed. Most of my mind,
though, was back at Mike's. I worried that he had no phone. One
of us should've been smart enough to have given him Shelly's cell
in case I wanted to check on Toby, or Mike passed out, or Toby
had to dial 911.

It was dark by the time the blessing wound down, and Dad
and Ted loaded their plates and carried them upstairs with Uncle

Jack. The three would eat in Uncle Jack's kitchen. Cousin Chuck stayed down with us so he could "share the spirit" with his sons. Shelly took one slice of turkey and one small spoon of corn casserole, and mainly pushed it about her plate during dinner. Of course none of the Stillwell sisters took much either—half-spoonfuls of potatoes, a teaspoon of gravy, one thin slice of turkey, passing on the packaged dressing—so Shelly's tiny plate was not seen as the protest she meant it to be. I was less than half there, but I did hear pieces of the talk around me. Aunt Peg said Chickie had a small part in a James Bond movie that would film in the south of France in February. Mom told of the daughter of a friend of hers who had risen to senior partner in a PR firm, and who said it took as much ass kissing as talent, but who also said the ass kissing was worth it, a necessary part of the process. "It's just who you are," Mom said. "If you're the kind of person who can do that, you'll get ahead,"

No one had a response to Mom's story. I heard an *Oh well*, and a *Well, well*.

"It's a good thing some of us can learn to put up with stuff," Mom said. "Or else we'd all be snarling at one another."

So many of Mom's stories were gently directed at me lately, me and my unreasonably self-destructive attitude at Agnus Dei. She wished I were better at kissing ass. I nodded and smiled across the table at her, and when she beamed, I had to admit she was cute. And I didn't merely mean Stillwell pretty, but she had an innocent belief that problems could be solved, solutions could be found, people could do it. We could. She saw herself as part of the solution. As a facilitator.

The Hilkers' lawsuit against me would be heard by judge and jury on December 23. I told Grandma that when she asked, and Aunt Peg said wasn't it amazing that her pageant was December 22, the day before. Two momentous events two days in a row. I laughed and said mine was probably not momentous, more like a waste of time, explained what I'd decided after the deposition: being sued was like being teased; if you ignored it, it could not hurt you. This was followed by a brief but uncomfortable silence as, I knew, they were worrying about my having been teased as a child. In fact, I'd hardly ever been. Patronized and gently excluded, but not teased.

Eventually, Cousin Chuck broke the silence and gave his expert opinion, said I should worry. The suit was stronger than my crazy lawyer had led me to believe. Both Mom and Aunt Peg reprimanded him for being negative: Mom said, "Bev knows more about it than you," and Aunt Peg said: "You're not a legal expert." But luckily for me and Cousin Chuck, the Stillwell girls and Grandma were more interested in the Senior Ms. America Pageant, and even Shelly perked up a bit as the discussion went that way. Chuck's wife was not ugly like me but had a full face with no discernible bone structure underneath, so she would never be called more than cute or nice-looking. Certainly not a beauty, her often being included in the list of Stillwell Beauties notwithstanding. After all, I was on that list, too. As a result of her merely honorary status, her comments about the pageant were ignored and her opinions not sought. I decided she *was* long-suffering.

By the time Aunt Marie served the pumpkin pie, I wondered if I could claim a slight stomach distress—let them think it was nerves over Chuck's comments about the lawsuit—and leave early. I was wondering, maybe too late, about what Mike meant by his weapons. What were they? Mike was unreliable and Toby was sneaky and apt to find trouble. When I added weapons to that mix, I was unable to reassure myself, but rather pictured one of them dead, then both of them dead, then one bleeding in the alley and the other missing. "I have to go," I said, standing so suddenly I made the cranberry gelatin wiggle and my chair tip over backwards.

"What? What is it?" Mom asked. They all looked at me with large and wide-opened eyes, mouths agape.

"Nothing. Just a stomach twinge. I'll feel better at home." I hoped God heard that, would take it as a prayer, and I wondered if the sirens I heard in the distance came from the café, just over a mile north.

"I'll drive you home," Shelly said, smiling broader than she had for days. "I'll come back for Ted later."

Before I had my jacket on, Cousin Chuck's wife said she knew it was just nerves. Then she asked me if I still wanted that little black boy.

By the time Aunt Marie walked me to the front door, my stomach pains and nerves were no longer the table topic. Instead I heard Aunt Peg advising all present to take extra cash out of their bank accounts before January 1, just in case. "The tellers screw up my transactions now," she said, "even before they have that computer dealie to worry about."

"Y2K," one of Cousin Chuck's sons said.

"Isn't he smart?" Aunt Peg asked the table.

"Notice Mom did not even ask me about my headaches? Not once," Shelly said on the drive home.

"I noticed," I said. I was bracing myself for trouble. Flashing lights, police tape. How could I have left Toby with Mike? Poor decisions made poor mothers. The papers were full of such stories. *I went out just for a hour...I thought his cousin could watch him...I told him to stay in his room.*

I prayed they were both alive and safe and I could be delivered from my stupidity, and when Shelly turned onto Meramec from Grand I knew part of my prayer had been answered. At least Mike was alive, was filling the neighborhood with "How Great Thou Art." I could only guess he would not be playing with such abandon if Toby had been snatched up or had run away.

"Thank You, God," I said for the second time that day, yet simultaneously cursing Mike's stupidity. "You're right about him," I told Shelly. "He is worthless."

"Who isn't?" Shelly sped down the alley toward the garage, sideswiped a utility pole as she made the turn, and knocked the side view mirror on the passenger side cleanly off. It made a loud clap. "Shit," she said without stopping. "Now I have a true city car." She sighed. "I told you my vision was blurry," she said as if I had challenged her.

As soon as she stopped, I jumped out and stumped into the garage, ranting about what kind of insane plan was it to bring Toby out in the open, what the hell kind of hiding did Mike think this was, were all his brains 100 percent fried, but Mike didn't hear me. He saw me, looked right at me but continued to play. Toby sat beside him on the bench, but kept his eyes on Mike's fingers and the keyboard.

"How de doo, how de doo," Mike said finally as the last chords bounced off the concrete garage floor.

"Why couldn't you just watch him in your place, safe and hidden as I asked? Tell me why?"

"Had to entertain the little snot," Mike said.

"Don't you remember you're hiding?" I asked Toby.

"Had to obey the big snot," he said.

"He's not safe here," I said to Mike. "What made you think he was safe here?"

"Intuition, instinct," Mike said. "*Je ne sais pas.* The Lord is my shepherd. We knew you were just being hysterical. Where's the food?"

"The food? The food?" I repeated myself, amazed he had the nerve to ask for it when he had endangered Toby, was endangering him.

"You promised us dinners," Toby said.

"We've been waiting," a voice from the corner of the garage said, and from the shadows stepped the blackest man I had ever seen. He was nearly as wide as the organ, and I jumped back at the sight, almost tipped myself over. "Just kidding," he said. "For myself, I mean. I've eaten."

"This is B.C.," Mike said. "He came looking for you."

"T.J.," he said, and reached a hand the size of a frying pan across to me. "Nice to meet you."

I shook his hand. "You want money," I said.

"I hate to beg," he said. "Whatever you have will be appreciated by you know who."

"What about the food?" Mike said.

"We brought lots over before we left. Besides, what we had was no good."

"Still," he said. "A promise is a promise."

"We didn't get any pie," Toby said.

I meant to take only Toby across the alley and home with me, but Mike said he would tag along in case we needed protection, making both him and Toby giggle. T.J. followed us out of the garage and stood by as Mike locked it up, and I was afraid he would want to follow me, too, so I told him to come by the café the next day, said I'd get money in the morning.

"Wow," Toby said, taking my finger as we crossed the alley. "You are for real the money lady."

When I told Mike I was serious and had not brought any food home, that there would be no more tonight, Mike left, said he guessed he knew what a promise from me was worth, and I almost reminded him he had not exactly hidden Toby, had failed to follow through on his part of the bargain. Instead, I said *sorry* and *thanks*. Toby, after all, was unharmed and safe.

"That guy just hears stuff in his head and it comes out through his fingers," Toby said after Mike left. "He doesn't even watch the keys."

"Yes," I said. "He is good."

"His real name is cockroach cause he's dirty and ugly but hard to kill. It's tattooed on his butt."

"He told you that?"

"Well, I didn't see it for myself," he said. "Yuck. I wouldn't want to look at his butt. And he's got no furniture. Nothing inside his place but blankets."

Toby also told me T.J. showed up while they were in the garage, asked Mike if he could hang out in the garage while he waited for me, and Mike said his music was free, anyone with eardrums was entitled to it. Toby said T.J. said he was only passing through and would be on his way north soon. I tried to get Toby to tell me more about his problems at the foster home, asking him if Lana knew about her husband's connection to the band of robbers, if Lana was in on it, too. Toby shrugged, said he guessed she knew nothing, said she was pretty nice most of the time. "She wants me to think of her as mom," he said. We were still talking when Shelly came in with Ted.

I had meant to tell Shelly I wanted Toby's whereabouts kept a secret from Ted, and if not for the concert in the alley and her run-in with the utility pole, I would have. Now it was too late. She had gone back to pick Ted up, he was there, and it seemed she had already filled him in, for he had advice. "Call the police. You'll make things worse if you don't."

I thanked him. I had no intention of calling the police. Not until I talked to Howard. Maybe never. The police would be no help until Toby got hurt.

Early Friday morning, Shelly went to Dr. Ed's for more trembling and twirling needles. Aunt Marie's dinner had made her headache worse than ever, something she hadn't thought possible, she said before she left. I told her I could handle the breakfast by myself, said if she felt bad, we could just close up, say it was for the holiday weekend. After all, I needed to talk to Howard anyway. "We'll see," she said. But when she returned before ten, she was smiling. Her headache was merely a dull pounding and could be lived with. And on the way home she had had a marvelous idea. She went immediately to the computer and typed up a sign: YOU'VE HAD YOUR RELATIVES' HOLIDAY DINNER, NOW HAVE SOME GOOD STUFF. She put it in the front window. "This is not really advertising," she said.

She had two fresh turkeys in the refrigerator as well as the one extra breast. She also had a bin of root vegetables and the ingredients for cornbread dressing with ham and yams in it. She knew many people had suffered through dinners like her mother made last night, no doubt even stuffing themselves on what they wouldn't give to their dogs most days of the year. "You go see Howard if you need to. I can do this. Just tell that kid to stay up there and out of my way. It's lucky we have all these ingredients, that I planned so well."

Pretending disappointments were blessings was so typical of Shelly, I wasn't surprised. "Isn't she amazing?" Ted asked me later when he showed up and she put him to work chopping rutabagas. I nodded. Amazing, yes. I could admit to that. But a strength? No. Watching her rush about, even hearing her hum as she worked, I understood that ignoring pain, covering it over, getting better too fast, led to loneliness. If you were sad, you should be sad, recover naturally, take as long as needed. I had that in mind when I told my students they didn't have to tell their parents all. Sure, I meant things that may frighten their parents—driving fast, experimenting with drugs and sex, flirting with disaster—but also their pains and sadnesses. For as soon as you tell someone, you are supposed to get over it, be cured. The person you tell won't hear of less, takes it upon herself to heal you, save you from sorrow.

Shelly did that for and to herself. As soon as she told herself she was sad, she told herself why and how not to be, told herself to get over it. Maybe it was a gift, as some of our family members thought, but I saw it that morning as a way of making the hole inside herself larger. By the time I left for Howard's office, she was rubbing a paste of olive oil, garlic, and rosemary in under the skin of both whole turkeys, telling Ted she wished she knew of a way to get Skip Zitich back down for this feast. It would be offered for two days or until the turkey was gone. Maybe it would catch on, she said, become a yearly event, a chance for people all over the area to recover from bad family food.

"I'll be back soon," I said. "Toby's watching TV. He knows to stay upstairs."

"Isn't she amazing?" Ted asked again.

Once I was in Howard's office, sitting in the petitioner's chair on the needy side of the gleaming mahogany slab, I decided not tell him about hiding Toby. This was not the environment of a rule-breaker, even a rule-bender, at least not small rules. Hidden assets may be another matter. I knew Howard would tell me what Ted had, to call the police, and I knew I would not, not until I knew more. As I looked at Howard's view—the Gateway Arch and the old courthouse in one frame—I realized I'd have to visit Lana myself, and do it as soon as possible, maybe later that night or maybe Saturday. I wanted a look at that bully she was married to. I decided I would drop in on Poodle Baby, too, claim to be in the market for a computer. Besides, Howard was not a bit supportive when I told him I wanted to adopt Toby. I needed a lawyer for the adoption, and now that Angela Cheng had given up all claim to Toby, I knew I could be called to a hearing soon. But when I asked Howard to go with me, he, like most people who learned of my desire for Toby, tried to talk sense. He shook his gray head, perfectly coiffed like a politician's, and got that sad look in his eyes, the kind of look the beautiful people get when they see someone like me, born with a few strikes against her. People like Howard wonder why we keep trying to make our lives miserable. He told me how difficult raising good children was, even ones you start with from scratch, and he even suggested that maybe I needed a pet, said he had a client whose outlook on life improved substantially when she got a kitten. Now she had four cats and was almost jolly.

But Howard, I did not say. I have already paid his mother off. Besides, I did not add, he helps me strap my leg on. I did tell him I would not be swayed, could always retain another lawyer. I also said this boy in question was a friend of his granddaughter Peaches, and that made him grimace.

"Her mother has no sense. Give a child a name like that and don't be surprised if she turns into an exotic dancer."

From Howard's, I went to the bank and withdrew five hundred more for T.J. to give to Sandy, knowing full well she would get little, if any, of it, not believing in honor among thieves or misfits. And it was while standing in line for the only teller that I made my decision to get farther away. Once I got Toby, I would sell the café, take him far from this neighborhood and its dangers, go to a suburb somewhere where the burglaries were not so visible or so closely spaced. Angela Cheng, T.J., Lana and her bully husband, Poodle Baby—none of them would be able to find us, and whatever school Toby went to would offer water polo and semesters in France. I knew I was planning a life for him much like Randolph James', much like that of the sheltered Agnus Dei girls I often despaired of, but my heart was suddenly light, the stale air in the bank lobby almost refreshing. *Safe* was a lovely word. The café was no fun, anyway, and though I did like making pies as I would do for the better-than-family dinner that evening, I was bored by watching people eat, by cleaning up their messes. Pitching mice to the inhabitants of the zoo's reptile house would have been as interesting.

When I got back to the café, Jeannie Lemp was sitting at the counter watching Shelly and Ted cook. "She wants you," Shelly said, motioning with her head at Jeannie.

"What?" I asked. "Want to quiz me about the black culture? Should I get into hip hop? Get a weave?"

"Bitterness won't help your case. I told you race is only one and probably a very small consideration."

"Okay. What's the buzz?"

"You've been worried about Toby's whereabouts in the past, so I thought it only fair to let you know the latest. He was missing all day yesterday. He hasn't come home yet this morning."

"Oh," I said, wishing I were a good enough actor to be worried or surprised.

Somewhere behind me, Ted coughed.

"I'm not worried," Jeannie said, proving I was right not to tell her what I knew. Nothing seemed to worry her. "I mean he does stay away every now and then. Still, we are checking with his friends and their families. Of course, we called the police, too, because you can't be too careful."

"No," I said.

"So if you see him, give me a call right away."

"Okay," I said. Another bit of the corrupting advice I gave my girls should have been this: you don't have to tell state officials the truth.

"If he doesn't turn up soon, the police will be by with a few questions," Jeannie said. "By the way, when will the better-than-Mom's dinner be ready?"

"Not until this evening," Shelly called, "but we have the usual tuna salad and egg salad for lunch."

"I'll save room for dinner," Jeannie said. "I'll be back. My Mom's turkey was tough as jerky."

T.J. entered as she was leaving, brushing past her on the side-walk. As soon as I saw him, I stumbled up to him as fast as I could, keeping him near the door so Shelly and Ted would not hear. I held onto his arm, and since tiptoe does not work for me, I yanked him down to my level. "Go around the back. I'll meet you where we were last night."

Moments later, we met before Mike's closed garage doors. "This is not a pattern," he said as he took the money without even counting it and stuffed it in his front jeans' pocket. "You won't see me again."

"I just hope Angela gets some of that money," I said.

He smiled down at me, shaking his head. "Who else would get it?"

On my way back to the café, I saw Shelly's mirror shining up from the cobblestones beside the dumpster, reflecting the pale blue November sky. I picked it up, carried it in, and set it down beside the cash register. "I guess you don't want this," I said.

She looked up at me and smiled, not worried about mirrors or blurred vision or much else now that she had a purpose and a plan. But Ted straightened up from his chopping board and walked over to the counter. Then he did a fine thing. He reached for my left hand, the totally fingerless one, and held it. He even squeezed it once, and held on as he spoke. "Life sucks," he said. "Don't trust anyone."

SHELLY

Post-Dispatch critic Skip Zitich's glowing review made absolutely no difference to our business. Nor did it have any effect on my family. Without consulting me, Mom took Thanksgiving dinner away from me, and no one seemed sorry to miss my good food. Even though I mailed each of them a copy of the review in case they had overlooked it in the newspaper, not one person said congratulations, or we knew you were good but not that good, or anything even semi-flattering. They all put on Mom's attitude that cooking was something I did to show off. Even Dad. "I guess it makes you feel important. No harm in that," he said when I told him the café was busier. A lie.

Well, I was used to the lack of a proper response from that group, but I was surprised that our business didn't pick up. Our Friday blue ribbon nights continued to draw close to our twenty-eight seat capacity, and the two-day "Better Than Your Family's Thanksgiving Dinner" was nearly as successful as the blue ribbon nights, but because I'd squeezed in another four seater, we could've served thirty-two at a time. I was even prepared to have two seatings if necessary, but, sadly, it was not. During the days we averaged another eighteen to twenty-two customers, but that was from seven in the morning to anywhere between three and four when we usually shut down. Sure, at times, we had to work hard, cooking and taking orders and delivering food and cleaning up, and small parts of the eight hours could pass in a blur, but I wanted to work harder, yearned for more of a blur.

Ted said the lack of response to the review I had been obsessed by and had schemed for for nine months was proof that what we want is seldom worth the wanting. When we get our desires, we realize they make no difference in our lives. Ted expounded upon that stale idea in many different words and used examples ranging from a child wanting ice cream to himself and a speedboat that, once his, did not produce the unmitigated pleasure he expected. He seemed to be on a roll with this topic, so much so that I day-dreamed during most of his treatise. We were sitting on the stone and concrete wall around St. Paul's until it was time to go in for noon Mass on the Sunday after Thanksgiving, and I was imagining Montreal. Because I knew it would be cold, I gave it a clean and crystalline purity, invented a kind of no-playing-around good-ness for the whole of Quebec. And even knowing I was wrong, knowing there was a mix of good and mean people everywhere and likely in the same proportions, and having read specifically about the strife that existed between the French and non-French Canadians, I persisted in imagining a place where car windows weren't smashed and doors were not kicked in. A place children did not have to be hidden. Why? The cold, crisp air made people need home and hearth and one another more. They were too busy trying to get in from the cold to be bad.

I laughed at my reasoning, telling myself that the cold would likely make people meaner, especially people like Bev who did noth-ing to combat their own cynicism, who seemed to feed it. When a Doberman Pinscher on a long leash interrupted my interior discus-sion by licking my argyle sock-covered ankle, I patted its head and heard Ted still talking about the insignificance of our wants.

"OK," I said. "It's not the Human Genome Project. I got your point long ago."

"You'll miss my insights when you're in Montreal," he said as if he had read my mind. He was still the only one who knew about my applying to l'École de Cuisine Internationale. Though Bev and I talked more about ourselves in the present lately, rather than merely rehashing old times as we had done at first—my reminding her how I'd clung to her buoyant leg in the deep end almost one whole summer—I hadn't yet found the courage to tell her about the cooking school in Montreal. I knew she would see it as an escape, abandonment. And I was constantly trying to get her to like the world, life, circumstances, to smile or laugh or relax, move through the world without the chips she lugged about on both shoulders.

The 10:30 Mass crowd poured through the center doors, large wooden structures with iron hinges, at exactly 11:50, then dispersed quickly. Ted and I left our place on the wall and entered the monument to past lives. Saint Paul's church was one hundred and twenty-something years old, built by money collected from descendents of French settlers and German immigrants who contributed out of duty, guilt, or in thanks for a relative surviving the flu epidemic or making a good marriage, thanksgiving for the rain holding off until the harvest was in. Its high vaulted ceiling and its plaster walls starting at about twenty feet up were painted with saints and angels, scenes from our mythology. The Ascension of Christ, the Coronation of Mary, the Agony in the Garden, the Betrayal by Judas, the Conversion of St. Paul all were there. That sunny but cool Sunday, two days away from December, the furnace was running, and all the low-hanging chandeliers and the track lighting were on, yet the size of the church, its odd shadows and dark wood and cold plaster and stained glass made it seem both cold and dark. Once seated in a pew, I shivered, and Ted hugged me, said Satan must be upset at my being there, was trying to break out of my soul.

I was in St. Paul's only because of Ted's repeated requests. I'd told him often he could go to Mass by himself, that my fallen-away and anti-religious self would add nothing to his experience, and if he were trying to re-convert me, he could forget about it. "But it won't hurt you to go with me," he'd said. "Afraid the church will be struck by lightening the moment you set foot inside?"

It was the first Sunday of Advent, and the readings and homily were about the anticipation of great joy. Even the songs were soothing and hopeful and full of forgiveness, and though the music was provided by a young man who strummed an acoustic guitar and sang so far off-key no one joined in, I was surprisingly happy to be there. I leaned over during the offertory and whispered to Ted, "If there is no hope for that musician in this life, there may be in the next." Yes, I was an optimist, with a real and firm belief that good things happened to those who made them happen, but even I was not brave enough on my own to anticipate great joy.

As we walked home from St. Paul's, Ted said there was one more place he planned to take me, and it turned out to be an ophthalmologist's office. Ted had made an appointment for me for Monday. He was more concerned about my blurred vision than anyone else, especially my doctors. My knocking my side-view mirror off convinced him someone had to do something. His theory that my eyes were causing my headaches was logical but wrong. Two doctors over the past eight months had given me vision tests, and I'd passed both. It was why Doc Newburg told me my vision wasn't blurry, or as she said, *bluwwy*. Ted knew her verdict but said I should be tested by an expert, by a real eye doctor. "Would you let your acupuncturist do heart surgery? Would you let your dentist do a pap smear?"

I admitted I would not do either of those foolish things. But even the folks at the DMV knew enough to test eyes. I said as much, but said, too, I would keep the appointment. I was warmed by his concern, his efforts at taking care of me.

My appointment was for 5PM, set late so I would have enough time to clean up after closing, but I ended up having to go to Mom's Monday afternoon before the eye doctor's and letting Bev clean up alone.

It happened like this. Shortly after the police left Sunday evening, Aunt Peg called and said she was supposed to have an information packet from the pageant committee—dressing room assignments, what was provided and what was allowed, that kind of thing. She knew they'd been mailed out because a woman in far west county, one she'd never met but who was the sister-in-law of a friend's friend, was a contestant and was reportedly upset at being limited to only two assistants. Aunt Peg needed the instructions, and as she was using Mom's address, the packet was at Mom's.

"Call Mom," I suggested, wondering if that was too logical to have been considered.

"I did. She has the instructions but can't drive at night and will be gone all afternoon tomorrow—some benefit party for the history museum. She said you should get them anyway, look them over. After all, you are my trainer."

I said I'd go over after the café closed on Monday, but because of the eye appointment, wouldn't be able to get them to her until much later.

"You and your doctors," she said. "All your health problems are because you let that nice husband of yours get away. And you know it."

"Let? Let?" I asked. "Had I a choice?"

"Not by the time you were aware of it."

Before Aunt Peg's call, though, two police officers, both men, one white and one black, the preferred coupling in the city, had been by. They appeared to be both in their early forties and in plain clothes, which meant dark suits and white shirts, one with a patterned and one with a striped tie. Both ties were mainly dark blue. They sat in our living room not like invited guests but more like financial planners, wanting us on their sides but clearly knowing more than we ever would. And they gave the impression they were merely following up on what was most likely a childish prank and not a disappearance. "Boys will be boys," either of them could have said, though neither did. I found myself waiting for it. I offered to make coffee, but they declined.

"You know this boy well?" Striped Tie asked Bev.

"He's been coming around the café after school," Bev said. "Since March maybe."

"Report is," Patterned Tie said, "you were broken into up here, this past summer."

Bev nodded.

"The ones doing it were looking for the boy. Up here. Why?"

"I guess they weren't too smart, were they?" Bev laughed.

They both laughed with her. "But you're the one who said it, that they must have wanted the boy," Striped Tie said.

"Really, I said it," I said. "I was home alone when the beasts came through the door. I was in shock afterwards. Didn't know what I was talking about."

"So the boy never stayed here?" Patterned Tie asked.

"No," Bev said. "Never."

"No," Striped Tie said. "Of course not. Why would two ladies like you let a kid like him stay without calling his home? And why would you lie about it?"

"Why would anyone think we would?" Bev said.

"Why would a kid want to stay here?" Striped Tie guy asked.

"Boys," Patterned Tie said. "Probably got punished and pretended to run. Did it myself once. Hid in my basement for a day."

"If you do see him, you'll let us know, right?" they both said.

"Of course," Bev said.

Then we all stood together, the detectives each shaking Bev by the wrist and me by the hand.

I was impressed by Bev's lying, by the ability. Mostly we were a family of rule followers. In my experience, we did not only what was legal, but what was preferred. We stayed within the ropes as we waited in bank lines. We saved our receipts. We took numbers in bakeries, and once we got our turns, we hurried so those behind us wouldn't get restless. We paid library fines, and if we were slower on the roadways, we stayed in the right lane. At least that was how I'd thought of us. Now there was Aunt Peg competing in a state and city that was no longer hers and so using a fake address, and Bev lying to the police as if she were Belle Starr or Baby Face Nelson's mother. She stood to the side of the front window, too, peeking through the mini-blinds until the police drove off, looking like a character in a mystery drama. Then she went to her room and opened her closet door, freeing Toby.

"Man, I almost sneezed in there," he said.

"This won't work for long. I have to do something before your face is on the news," Bev said.

What she chose to do was call Lana, not to admit she had Toby, but to arrange a visit. "It's not a good idea to drop in on people like Lana and her bully husband," she said as Lana's phone was ringing.

"I'm a friend of your foster son, Toby," she said when Lana answered. "You've no doubt heard I want to adopt him. I wonder if we can meet soon, just to get to know each other."

"He's missing! Where is he? Where is that boy? Do you have him?" Lana shouted so I could hear her side of the conversation from where I sat, across the kitchen table from Bev.

"I don't know where he is. I just finished telling the police that. But his disappearance is proof he needs a mother, and soon. Can't we at least meet?"

"It's not allowed. You have no right calling me. Toby's got a mother. Me. You're breaking the law talking to me. I'll call DFS. I'll call my lawyer." The line went dead, and as soon as Bev hung up, the phone rang.

It was Aunt Peg calling about the information packet, and not ten minutes after her call, Jeannie Lemp called and told me to tell Bev to stop harassing Lana. Jeannie gave me the message because Bev refused to take the phone. Jeannie said she knew Bev was concerned, as everyone was, and Bev may have thought the human approach, one-on-one, two would-be-mothers working together for Toby's welfare was a good idea, but it was not. "We have laws. We have procedures," Jeannie said. "Lawyers talk to lawyers, and lawyers talk to case workers, and case workers talk to case workers and to potential mothers. But potential mothers do not talk to potential mothers, not unsupervised. Conversations between them go up and down through the chains of responsibility, but not side to side."

When I started to repeat Jeannie's words, Bev stopped me. "I know the gist of it," she said. "I don't imagine her prose style is worth hearing."

"No," I said, though I had thought Jeannie's explanation about the right and wrong directions, vertical preferred over horizontal, deserved to be quoted.

Dad let me in Mom's Monday afternoon, but wouldn't stay down in her place without her. "I'm just going to grab something from her desk," I said. "Less than a minute."

"Well," he said. "I'll go on up anyway. I'd not like her to think I was snooping in her things."

"Snooping? I'm only going to take what she said would be right on the top," I said, but he'd already closed the door behind him. I could hear the stairs creak as he made his way home. The packet, a large manila envelope addressed to Peg Owens, was not out on top of Mom's desk as she'd said it would be, nor was it in the stack of recent mail or on the file cabinet or the side table or the desk chair. I walked through the other rooms thinking that, like me, she may absent-mindedly pick things up and lay them down elsewhere. But the envelope was nowhere. When the phone rang, I answered it, knowing it was Dad. "Finished yet?" he asked. "I really shouldn't let you go through her things."

"Just one more minute," I said. I hung up and opened her top desk drawer. Nothing but pens and paper clips, assorted coupons.

Next, I checked the side drawer that looked like two from the outside. It held numerous file folders, all labeled "letters," followed by a month and a year. They went from November '99 in the front all the way back to April '76, the month of her and Dad's split. That was what made me do it, but, not brave enough to snoop through the letters from that bad month, I selected a file from the middle of the pack, December '85. I expected love letters, or maybe some explanation of who she was and who her friends were and why she had divorced Dad and what she thought of me. Instead, I found testimonials, most written to get coupons and certificates. In a letter to Wilderness Outfitting, a catalog company specializing in tough-wearing casual clothes of corduroy and flannel and twill, she wrote: "Your extra heavy flannel shirt (page 42, Oct. catalog) held up so well that even though my husband was shot (accidentally!) while wearing it, the blood washed out and we buried him in it." The company's reply was a note of condolence and a twenty dollar gift certificate. To a mail order coffee company, she wrote, "My love affair with your coffee began the same time as my love affair with my postman, but lasted longer." The coffee people sent Mom a dollar off her next purchase. There were about a dozen more just for that month, and she'd received coupons or gift certificates from most, noted the amount of the coupon or certificate in the upper right hand corner of the company's reply, and stapled that to the copy of her original letter. Some, like a toothpaste company, apparently had not responded. "Your toothpaste," she'd written, "makes my mother's teeth so white, the yellows of her eyes are much more noticeable."

I read more, laughing as I sat there alone at her desk in her neat and quiet flat. The file from May '94 contained a letter to Better Foods, Inc.: "Your wheat germ gave me so much energy and made me feel good and vibrant and healthy. Now rather than sleep, I take my Jeep out hill-jumping." Better Foods sent her a two for one coupon for a loaf of their wheat bread, but Catch of The Sea was more generous: "I notice your extra crunchy fish patties contain more bread and cellulose than fish, and I congratulate you for sacrificing taste and standards in order to save the lives of sea creatures."

That got her a $5.00 off coupon for any Catch of The Sea product.

The phone rang again. "You're taking way too long. You have to leave now."

"I'm writing her a note," I lied like the best of the Stillwells. I closed the letter file drawer, and before Dad could come down, opened the bottom drawer. Luckily the Senior Ms. America pageant information packet was right on top, for just as I grabbed it, the phone rang again. "Hurry up, hurry up," Dad said on her answering machine.

An hour later, I passed my eye test as I knew I would. The blurred vision never manifested itself during the tests, and though the doctor dilated my pupils, took pictures of the way my nerves connected to my eyeballs, he said what I had known he would: All looked fine. I found his predictable response more funny than annoying for a change, maybe because my mother, that distant, manipulative, pretty-but-dried-up stick-of-a-woman, had a sense of humor after all. At least a hobby. Why did that make my heart lighter?

Ted agreed to stay at the apartment with Toby Tuesday evening because I was going with Bev to visit Lana. It was Bev's version of being a pest. "Pests get what they want," she said the night before when she asked me to tag along and Ted to baby-sit. "I can be one if I have to."

"What will you say to Lana?" I asked that morning as I stirred my gravy.

"I'll say, 'You have so many. Can't you spare one?' I'll say 'Race is an artificial division, and culture is shared among people.'" She removed a cookie sheet from the oven, twenty-four four-inch high biscuits, all golden brown. "I want to know if Lana knows her husband is a bully."

"Lana already said she won't talk to you," I said.

"But I'm a pest," she said.

Rollie and two other gas company workers came in then for biscuits and gravy, eggs over easy on the side. For the rest of the day, we weren't busy, but we had at least two customers in at any one time, about twelve at our usual late afternoon lunch, so Bev couldn't talk more about Toby or Lana. She did sneak upstairs often to check on Toby, though. The night before, she'd found an old American history book left over from an education course she'd taken years earlier, and had given it to Toby. His assignment for Tuesday was to read two chapters of it before dinner and be prepared to answer questions.

Dinner that evening was leftover egg salad sandwiches and Aunt Josie's homemade pickles and as the three of us ate, Bev quizzed Toby on the fate of the first American settlement at Jamestown, the reason people had come across the ocean in the first place, why they were so ill-prepared. When she told him she was going to see Lana, he asked if she could pick up his backpack, and she rolled her eyes, shook her head at him clownishly, and told him to think about how stupid that would be. "Aren't you in hiding?" she asked. "Do you think that's any way for a fugitive to act?"

"Well, don't talk to that old husband of hers," Toby said. "If you do, he'll tell lies."

Just then the doorbell sounded, and Bev sent Toby to his

usual place in her closet, while I went downstairs and let the two detectives in. I'd known we'd see them again, maybe many times. In the two days since they'd last been by, they seemed to have switched ties.

They trudged upstairs and took seats on the couch. They both sighed and said they had to be honest. It was looking bad, getting serious. Gone six days, no leads, no trace, they said. No one had seen him. And by the way, one of them asked, why hadn't Bev told them she wanted to adopt him. After all, that made her more than a woman who befriended him by giving him pie. Bev shrugged, told them it hadn't seemed relevant to finding Toby. They said they'd be the relevancy judges from now on. The thing was, they now believed it more likely Toby would have come to Bev for help, and while chances were slimmer and slimmer, miracles could happen and they both were certain she would call them as soon as she heard anything. They shook their heads and sighed at least twice more before they left, repeating that it was not looking good.

"I'm one of the certifiable bad guys now," Bev said after they left. "I'm one of the law breakers."

An hour later, Lana led us into her living room with its fake wood-paneled walls and bluish indoor/outdoor carpeting and lowered acoustic tiled ceiling. It was typical of the homes down there that even the stately old brick buildings without broken or boarded-up windows or without bars like Lana's were ugly inside. Many residents seemed determined to create the mobile home interior look. And my sense of claustrophobia was increased by great toppling piles of stuff. The chairs, end tables, in fact all flat surfaces were strewn with books, board and video games, backpacks, and jackets. Lana grabbed the clutter off two stuffed side chairs so we could sit, and deposited it in a larger heap at one end of the couch. "Five of us live here now," she said, "and none of us are neat. Including me."

We sat, and I waited for Bev to have her say, but instead Lana took the floor. "Forgive my earlier rudeness. We are too worried to do much that is normal anyway. Our lives are on hold. We keep saying this can't be happening, trusting in God to work a miracle.

Toby will turn up. That is what we say to one another daily. The other children can't sleep. It was good of you to come and share our anxiety and grief. I know you have a broken heart, too."

Bev and I nodded. Lana's living room was dusky, lit by two table lamps each with low wattage bulbs. It smelled of fried potatoes and old socks.

"What are regulations in times of sorrow?" Lana continued. "We need to be together." She had one of those faintly Southern accents with no harsh sounds, few true consonants, seldom a full stop. It was like warm puree, or maybe a custard. Though we heard she had raised a few children before taking on a new batch, she hardly seemed old enough. I guessed she was older than forty but not by much, and because she was chubby, her face was unlined and her skin was firm. She wore a loose, navy blue knitted dress, no waist, push-up sleeves, and she sat across from us with her knees apart, her feet planted firmly on the floor. I knew that thin didn't mean cold and mean and stingy, and fat didn't mean warm and jolly and generous, but I also decided while looking across at her, that women like her gave birth to those stereotypes. She was a mother, physically and emotionally.

She pressed her lips together to keep from crying, and just as Bev started to say something, beginning with "Look, Lana," a man at least half again as old as she shuffled into the room dragging a wheeled oxygen tank behind him. His short, crinkly hair was gray and his face was so many different shades of brown it looked sunburned or bruised. Plastic tubes hooked into each nostril joined at his neck and dangled back to the tank.

"Any news?" he asked.

Lana went to him, helped him to a seat on the couch. "My husband," she said. "These are the women from the café. That one wants to adopt Toby."

He sat, then peered over at us. "Yeah," he said. "The one that don't have fingers. She's the one wants him." He wheezed between his words.

"Me," Bev said. "I'm Bev."

He nodded. "Hear you've got a trick leg, too." Then he took out his handkerchief and coughed and gagged into it a ball of phlegm the size of one of Bev's biscuits.

Instead of saying what she told me she would, Bev said she was sorry and worried and anxious about Toby, just as everyone was. She said she was hopeful he was safe. Lana hugged her before we left. And because we knew Lana could've watched from behind her blinds, I pulled away from the house, drove around the block, and came to a stop in front of the house two doors down from Lana's, the one Toby told us Poodle Baby lived in. Bev was bold again, still trying out her pestiness, and she stumped right up on the porch and pressed the bell with her finger.

When an older white woman with hair like a new copper scouring pad answered, we both knew it was Poodle Baby, and Bev said she was looking for a computer. "Do you know where I can get one?"

It was a stupid beginning, and I fully expected the woman to give the rational answer, go to the mall, but she didn't. "I wouldn't have one of them things. They let the government spy on you. Perverts use them." She wore black stretch slacks pulled tight from her waist to her feet, a pair of skinny legs inside them somewhere. Her porch light was yellow.

"Nevertheless," Bev said. "I want one. I want to buy one. A big one. An expensive one."

"Sugar has one," Poodle Baby said. "She talks to people in Brazil with it. Who wants to do that, I ask her. She orders jewelry that way, but someone will take her card and run up charges like you wouldn't believe. I tell her that, too."

We were on the front porch, talking to a woman we didn't know about someone we didn't know or care about. Typical. I knew both of us would play by the city rules and not ask who Sugar was, just as Poodle Baby wouldn't ask our names.

"What about a television?" Bev asked. "Mine broke. I need to buy one of those, too."

"Honey," Poodle Baby said to Bev, "get your friend here to take you home. Are you on medication? This is a house, not a store."

"Someone told me I could buy things here," Bev said, and I was tempted to pull her off the porch.

"I had me a yard sale a few months ago. And the man over across from the confectionery had one the day Alice got home. Don't know what he sold."

"We have to go," I said, and did pull on Bev's arm. "Some finesse," I whispered to her as we both stumbled down the steps. "Is this what you call investigating?"

"I can't believe the people who buy her stolen goods are subtle. Don't you imagine they just ask for what they want?"

"You're the one who watches the cop dramas, for Christ's sake," I said. "You should have learned something by now. Remember, the cops put her out of business once already. Do you think she'd talk to strange women on her porch about her garage full of stuff?"

"Maybe I at least made her nervous," Bev said, and was quiet until we got home. When I pulled up to the curb in front of the café, she said "Well, I accomplished one thing I intended to. I saw the husband." She planted her feet on the street beside the curb and pushed up and out of the car. "Some bully, huh?"

That evening Bev wrote a letter to Lana, and she delivered it along with a lemon meringue pie the next morning, Wednesday, early. Bev said she merely set the pie and the letter down on the porch, rang the bell, and stumped back to her car as fast as possible. Of course, she said, there was nothing fast about it, and she was sure whoever came to the door saw her waddling down the walkway like a wounded goose. But surprise had not been her intent anyway. It was just that she hadn't wanted to talk to anyone, answer questions about her letter. As soon as she returned from the pie delivery, she called the police, spoke to one of the detectives. "I may be making a mistake, but I trust you to investigate this thoroughly, including the burglary ring," she said.

"Toby must be protected. I may have been wrong to try it myself." She used the phone in the café, on the desk under the back stairs, as if afraid she would not go through with it if alone, so I heard that side of her conversation. Bev admitting out loud she was wrong, or as she put it, "may have been," gave me a slight feeling of vertigo. She'd done it in the letter to Lana, too, but even so, hearing her say it was like hearing Grandpa's old dog talk or Mom laugh. A shock.

Her letter to Lana read:

"I have been hiding Toby, protecting him. I believe the burglary ring is real, even though Toby may have lied about other things. He does appear frightened. I have called the police who, in spite of my suggestion, may return him to you. As one mother to another, I trust you will help keep him safe. I still want to adopt him, and so will be trying to prove myself worthy. No easy task, as I seem to have been wrong about so much. My main hope is your bowing out. You already had children, and you have others now. Please let me have this one." She signed it, and added a postscript about enjoying the pie.

Before that Wednesday morning letter or the call to the police, though, on Tuesday night while Toby was still with us, she talked to him.

"Lana's husband looks funny with his tubes, doesn't he?" she asked him.

"You think just cause he got that stuff coming from his nose, he didn't hurt me?"

"Can he run? Does he have enough breath to raise his arm?"

"He stood there," Toby said. "He told the other guy to beat me. Don't take much breath for that."

"You know the police will guarantee your safety," Bev said, and I felt a moment of panic. I wasn't surprised that Toby had lied, but the police were not bodyguards. "I'm going to insist they put you in a home with protection," Bev told him. "Not back at Lana's just yet. I still don't know what or whom to believe."

Toby shrugged. "I can go back. Ain't nobody after me."

"But you won't go back. I hope you won't, not until all the facts are in."

"I could use a few dollars," he said.

"Not this time," she said. "No more of that."

Later, when she showed me the letter to Lana, she said, "I may be in jail by tomorrow."

But because it was Toby's last night with us, we had a party. Before her talk with Toby, Bev had bade Ted a pointed good-bye, and when he did not get the hint, said, "Why don't you give us a break for a while? You don't live here." I stood behind her and shrugged at Ted, said I'd see him later for dancing. So for a while, it was just the three of us. We had root beers and chips with French onion dip and packaged cupcakes. For about two hours we played first hearts and then scrabble. Toby's glasses reflected the fluorescent ceiling light in our kitchen, but his smile was wide, his greenish teeth exposed. He laughed with his mouth open at the words he made up and Bev let him get away with: *wayby* and *beddy* and *zumming*. As I watched her watch him, I pictured her on one side of a gorge, Toby on the other. Her sadness lay in not being connected. She was fine with him for now, but peripheral, and she knew it. She was not a consideration except as someone he could use or play around with. He wouldn't miss her much if he never saw her again. No matter that she gave him what she could, worried about him, hid him, plotted and planned for him, tried to believe him, if Bev weren't around, he would find someone else. I knew she knew and accepted her position, maybe by this time in her life resigned to not being necessary.

Later, after Toby was asleep on the couch and Bev was sitting up beside him, watching his chest rise and fall, Ted came back. He was taking me to Spurs 'n' Saddles for one of the many Tuesday night contests they held, this one for a Texas dance called Four Corners. It would be the first one we entered. The contest was scheduled for after midnight so the regulars could still do all the other dances, but even so late, I was sorry to leave Bev alone. We whispered goodbye to her from the top of the front stairs, and when she didn't respond, I went back and patted her shoulder. I wasn't sure she felt my touch, for she merely gave a slight nod and kept staring at Toby.

Ted and I won the Four Corners competition, the first thing I'd won without wanting or trying to. We had not even practiced. Oh, I knew one reason we were the judges' favorite was our look. We both wore dark and tight jeans and long sleeved shirts so white they shone in the dark. We had mother-of-pearl buttons that caught the light, and we could see our faces shining back at us from our boot tops. I wore my hair in a high-riding ponytail that bobbed along in time with my pivots and half-steps. Our prize was merely a free admission for two to Spurs 'n' Saddles, but after the contest was over a few drunks came up to us and said we were so good we should give lessons, gushed that we were good enough to go on tour, win big money.

At Spurs 'n' Saddles, the last dance of the evening was always a slow one made for clinging tight and swaying, and as Ted and I held each other on the dance floor, I told him my application for l'École de Cuisine Internationale was ready to go. "I'm using the cumin-encrusted cutlets on Asian vegetables," I said. "I like the way so many tastes and expectations are mixed up, thrown together in it. I'll have my application in the morning mail."

"Montreal is so far away," he said. Then he told me about a case he was working on. "I have some damaging information on a person but don't want to use it."

"Why?" I asked, not caring at all. His heart was still beating fast from our workout. I could feel its syncopation with mine. Montreal suddenly seemed just what he'd said, far away.

"It could hurt someone. But if I don't use it, I will have taken money under false pretenses. Justice will not be served."

"Don't tell," I said. "Your job is stupid."

He laughed.

"Go for what won't hurt. Justice doesn't exist."

"You mean it's elusive?"

"I mean it's too abstract. It's like fun or good sex or success. It doesn't have a definition."

He held me closer. "All good things are beyond definition."

Like love, I thought, and I let myself think it.

It was 2:30 by the time we tiptoed up the back stairs, careful of the creaking boards under the kitchen linoleum. The front drapes had been pulled tight, and we could sense the sleeping Toby on the couch rather than see him. As I opened my bedroom door, Ted whispered that he'd be in in a minute after he visited the bathroom. But no sooner had I closed my door and turned on the overhead light, than he was back in the room with me. "This place is getting more crowded all the time."

"Toby'll be gone tomorrow," I said.

"More than Toby," he said. "I just ran into Mike. He was wearing an Agnus Dei Angels T-shirt and coming out of Bev's bedroom. He beat me into the bathroom. He told me December has always been his luckiest month."

Lucky in love, unlucky in almost everything else: one of my relatives, ancient already way back when I was a child and no doubt dead by now, used to say that. Could have been Mom's uncle Herbert. No matter. If right, it was okay by me. So Mike felt lucky. I was feeling lucky in love, too, and though it went without saying Bev could have done better than Mike, he was someone, something. And something, anything, was always better than nothing. We were a lucky household that evening. I was happy for us all.

BEV

I may have screamed. No one has said. I wasn't listening to myself. I was looking down on it all, the blaze in my bed, amazed. How had it happened, and why now when all else was chaos, and I was about to turn myself in as a lawbreaker, and Toby was in my home for what I hoped was not the last time? Why did I hear "The Battle Hymn of the Republic" so jubilantly pounded out at one in the morning and start to cry? I had a reason for tears, of course, and he was asleep on Shelly's orange couch. But what was it about Mike's playing that turned on the weep, weep machine? It wasn't the hour, though I knew Mike had seldom played that late, or rather early, and I imagined some other soul in the hood was already calling the police, and I couldn't blame whoever it was. Sleep was precious, and once interrupted, could ruin the following day and thus a job or a friendship or at least a diet.

I was a criminal and Mike was, too, for disturbing the peace, so I wished he would stop playing, black out or whatever he was no doubt on the verge of doing that passed for sleep, and do it fast. I had been lying in my bed for almost an hour, trying to sleep with my leg still attached as I'd done each of the nights I guarded Toby, so I angled myself out of bed, put on my flannel robe, and went down the back stairs. I looked out across our parking pad and alley to the corner where two alleys made a T, and saw Mike's garage lit up, the door that slid sideways more than half closed. When the last chorus ended and John Brown's truth went marching on and on, echoing into the night, I said his name sharply—"Mike"—not calling but projecting it to him as a warning. A further pause made me continue. "Mike. Stop it."

The night was still. A light rain began to fall as I stood there. I closed and locked the back door, reset the alarm, and went back upstairs, noting the neighborhood remained silent. Not even any squealing tires or heavy bass thuds from passing cars. No sirens. Before getting back in bed, I checked on Toby, and while I was tucking yet another blanket around him, I heard knocking on our front door. Ever since the break-in, I'd kept the front porch light on continuously, so all I had to do was peer out through the drapes and blinds to see who was there. At first, I saw only legs, one pair belonging to a man, and the sight made my chest go cold, my palms sweaty. I was home alone, the sole protector of a boy. Lowlifes had stormed through once before. I wished I had a gun. Why hadn't I bought one, been trained to use it? If I survive this, I told God, I'll buy a big powerful gun. I'll not be like an unprepared and foolish virgin ever again. I heard three more knocks, then the man stepped back from the door, shaded his eyes with a hand, and looked up toward me, trying to see through the light. It was Mike.

"Didn't want to use the bell and wake the little snot," he said after I let him in. "Just came by to see what you wanted." He walked right on up the stairs, and I followed.

"I was warning you," I said to his back, the Lee Jeans tag just at eye level. "Didn't want you arrested."

He passed the living room where Toby slept without my having to remind him to be quiet, went straight back to the kitchen, but turned sharply to the right and into my bedroom. I was right behind him, and he turned, closed the door, and pulled me to him in the dark. He kissed me, and though his nose and cheeks were cold, his tongue was warm.

At first, I kept my leg on, even when I was stretched out on the bed, my robe on the floor, because he said he wanted to unbuckle it himself. "If the little snot can do it, I can," he'd said. But the job was too much for him. His fingers seemed unable to receive messages from his brain, and I finally removed it myself.

He was drunk, yes, but not so much he didn't know my name or what he was doing. He was good, I guess. At least it worked. I felt electrical connections travel across hot wires that went throughout me, radiating from my vagina to my eyelids, the roof of my mouth, my one baby toe. Had I all my fingers, I knew I would have felt the wires burn my tips, too. With his body pressed heavily on top of mine, I inhaled his sourness and looked closely at the lines crisscrossing the square inch of his neck my face was against. I had to nearly cross my eyes to bring them into focus, but they were beautiful. I traced his Y-shaped shoulder scar with my finger. Also, I was not entirely there. I was above me, circling my bed. My orgasm was first, and his soon followed, sudden and wonderfully sticky.

When I slept, I had the running dream again, that I was running on two whole legs and feet, but this time Mike was beside me. We were both naked, but had bodies that were works of art, so much prettier than either of us had in reality. It was as if our heads were on bodies from a different species. We were at a race track of some kind, a wide asphalt one probably for car races, and we laughed and tripped as we ran. Once, I skinned the knee on my left leg, the missing one, but kept going.

We made love, a phrase I'd always appreciated, once more early in the morning, and when I got up and dressed to deliver my pie and letter, he turned over onto his face, and snored into my pillow. Nothing I'd ever done had made me feel better.

The next morning, I had the courage to do what I'd already planned—call the police and turn myself in. Sure, I would've done it anyway, but now it was easy, the decision simple and clear-cut. I had real hope that Lana would recognize my love for Toby and stand aside. I knew I could make the cops and DFS and the courts see that Toby needed protection, at least for now. I was strong enough to insist on it.

I almost kissed the detectives when they came for Toby an hour after my call, and I did kiss Toby, reassured him things usually worked out for the best. That wasn't some fake Shelly-like optimism, either. I meant it. When Jeannie Lemp pointed an accusatory and officious finger at me later, shook it in my face, I felt like grabbing her in a bear hug, the poor stupid but well-meaning government flunky, tickling her until she was human again.

Mike came back Wednesday, Thursday, and Friday nights and every night for the following week. Meanwhile, Howard Figg convinced all parties that my hiding Toby and lying to the police had resulted from a justified fear for Toby's safety, and that my efforts to protect the boy were noble. *Noble*, at least, was his word, what he told me he'd convinced them of. I was charged with nothing. And Howard assured me Toby was safe. He was not with Lana, but that was all I was allowed to know. Howard shook his well-coifed gray head at me once again, and said with my civil suit coming up by the end of the month, I could do us all a favor by not even asking where Toby was, forgetting about him for a few weeks.

Jeannie and Lana were still against me, noble or not. Jeannie told me so when she stopped in on a Saturday, a week and half after the detectives took Toby. "We both thought you were intelligent and mature, straightforward. Now, we have lost all trust in you. It's all gone. Every drop."

I smiled, refilled her cup of free coffee as she sat at our counter and bitched. I was sorry I'd lost her trust because it would make my bid for Toby harder to make, but her boss, I'd learned from the detectives, was on my side now, thought Jeannie should have protected Toby better. And the detectives were disappointed to learn not only that Poodle Baby's burglary ring was still operating—that much of Toby's story was proved true—but that Lana had let him hang around where he could get hurt by it. The detectives said she should have been more careful, and I had a feeling they were on my side, too. But that was not why I smiled at Jeannie. I smiled because I could not keep from it.

People who frown are people who don't get enough sex. The old jokes were true. Jeannie Lemp may have been even more socially backwards than I. It hit me suddenly as she was slurping her coffee and scowling. She'd never had an orgasm, at least not one involving another being.

I laughed to myself. Good thing I wasn't teaching high school girls any longer. I knew the advice I'd give now would create enough righteous indignation to power four or five Christian radio stations.

"I'd like to advertise our next blue ribbon night," Shelly said as I was contemplating Jeannie's unblemished state. She stood behind me with a flyer in her hand.

I turned and smiled.

"I won't do it if you are still against it. It's just that we can bring in so many more customers. We can take reservations, have a 6:30 and a 9:00 seating."

"I don't care," I said. I was still smiling. I could feel the stretch in my muscles.

"It'll be an early Christmas feast. I'll do prime rib and Yorkshire pudding. Your pies can be mincemeat. Okay?"

I nodded at her, and nodded again later when the two thrift shop women came in with their twin husbands for barbecue beef sandwiches. One of the twins gave me a brochure with a registration form for something called the Courage Games, athletic events for the physically handicapped.

"You could have fun with this," he said.

I did not ask him to define *courage*, did not have to choke back the standard rude remarks, including thanking him for patronizing me so. Little of the normal bile was there. Instead, I said, "How kind of you," then crumpled the brochure and threw it in the wastebasket next to the register, making sure he saw. When he frowned at me, I beamed at him, told him I thought he was courageous, too.

SHELLY

I had gone along with Aunt Peg and the Senior Ms. America Pageant out of a sense of familial duty, and of course because I thought it would be an interesting diversion, and, perhaps mostly, because I knew I was needed. My beauty smarts mixed with my discipline and organization would make the difference between Aunt Peg being a winner or first runner-up. I had listened to Bev claim this one and all beauty pageants were exercises in vanity, pure wastes of time. "You don't think this is real life do you?" she asked. I admitted contests were not as important as creating something that nourished and satisfied others, admitted it mainly to keep her bitchiness in check. She was crabbier if she had opposition. But I did say this was real life, though, because it was happening and we were all alive. What else could it be? She told me not to get carried away with the idea of creating stuff. "Food is not a cure for stupidity," she told me as if I were one of her wayward students. "But," she continued, "at least it's not useless as decorating yourself and parading around is. Which you've done often enough."

"Right," I said, in search of peace.

But had I been in the St. Louis County Community Center, I could not have said it. For the two days of rehearsals and then the actual pageant, my blood skipped through my veins. I relived the Miss Convention Center pageant of 1982, the year I won. That had been my first pageant, my previous crowns having been homecoming queen at Cleveland High and the Little Miss Pevely Dairy title I won just from Mom sending in my photo. The Miss Convention Center competition was a full-blown, four-round contest, and all during it I felt as if each of my cells was perked up, was multiplying and connecting and doing what my DNA directed with peak efficiency. My eyes sparkled brighter, my step was lighter, my curls bounced as if spring-loaded. I knew all that just by watching the others, all of us at our best, giving off such energy we could nearly glow in the dark. Aunt Peg's contest had the same feel. The hope backstage was thick as steam.

The community center was a large concrete bowl with bad acoustics but roomy enough for both a runway and a judges' table with computers. Felt banners of wreaths and candles and Santas had been hung on the walls to soften the echoes, and huge blower fans on forty-foot poles kept the hot air circulating. Crock pots bubbled backstage and at strategic spots in the auditorium giving off Yule smells of oranges and peppermint and cloves and pine, yet once all the trunks and garment bags were brought in, the ubiquitous smell of seldom-worn or new clothing—mothballs, fabric softener, sizing, and naphtha—blended in as well.

Thirty women, fifty-five and older, from St. Louis city and county were vying in the first round for the title of Senior Ms. St. Louis Metropolitan Area, and at least twenty of them had a chance. Those who clearly had no chance were grandmother types with cushiony bosoms, liver spotted hands, and facial wrinkles they were probably ready to describe as character lines. They looked soft and kind in loose-fitting corduroy jumpers and turtlenecks that hid their wattles. Some of them had not even covered the gray in their hair, seemed almost proud of it. I imagined they'd read about the contest on the back of a bag of Mamie's Potato Chips—the oddest possible sponsor—and thought finally here was something for mature women who were not concerned solely with looks, most of theirs having gone by then, preserved only in shoeboxes of snapshots. Some women were willing to believe anything, the most outlandish that they'd ever reach an age when their looks wouldn't matter. Two of the women competing looked more or less like Barbara Bush, and one was almost a dead ringer for Golda Meir, mole and all. Besides those, there were a few who had no chance because they just didn't know what beauty was. They were heavily made-up and as skinny as starving Appalachian teenagers, overdressed even for the practices in glittery outfits, but unaware of the ravages wrought by ultraviolet light. They were tanners, and their hides looked well cured.

The rest were contenders, though. I had seldom seen so many high cheekbones, white and straight teeth, long lashes, comma-like dimples, full lips, lifted and separated breasts, satiny smooth shoulders with blades like sheathed knives, long and lean thighs, gently but surely curving calves, and delicate insteps in one room. These were women who knew how to care for what God had given them, conservationists of sorts.

Aunt Peg shared a dressing area with two other contestants, one a tall black woman whose skin was so creamy and smooth I wanted to examine it with a magnifying glass, and the other, a short and bouncy sixty-seven year old, cute but no pageant winner. Her name was Brigid and she had the pink and white mottled skin you'd expect on a Brigid. Worse than that, though, in her youth she'd been a smoker, so she had lots of tiny but deep lines cut into her lips and the skin surrounding them.

On Sunday and Monday, we rehearsed and were given some general instructions, like only two electrical appliances per contestant could be on at any one time, and the Christmas tree could not be turned on. The pageant was Tuesday, the twenty-second.

Bev had not yet seen or heard from or about Toby, could only trust, as I knew she was trying to, that he was safe and she'd see him soon. She had a California Cruisin' Moon bicycle, a banana yellow one that had been in the window of the bike shop on Grand, stored under the café's back stairs, making the so-called office nearly inaccessible. She knew it'd be a late Christmas gift, maybe weeks late. She had a gift for Mike, too, wrapped with his name on it and out under the tree Ted had bought and that he and I had decorated. "A tree?" she'd said. "You really want one of those up here, just for us?" She hadn't objected to the small one downstairs that we had placed right in the window, rearranging a few tables to make room for, and she'd accepted the holly sprigs in the bud vases and the wreath on the café door with more equanimity than I'd expected. Well, she had not exactly objected to the tree upstairs, either, just made us feel foolish and too much in lockstep with the consumer culture for thinking of one—"You have to be like everyone else. I forgot. It's required." But for all her posturing, she wrapped a box in gold paper and tied it with a red ribbon, then placed it under the tree for Mike almost as soon as Ted spread out the sequined tree skirt. I hoped the box contained clothes of some kind, his ratty T-shirts and dirty jeans smelling moldier by the day. I knew that once a woman slept with a man, she had the right to dress him.

Because of the Monday practice, Bev had the café to herself and said she didn't mind. I had said why not just close up. We had already decided to close on Tuesday, the day of the pageant, even though it didn't start until 7PM, and, of course, on Wednesday for her trial, and we'd done so well on Friday night that we could easily have taken an even longer break. But Bev asked what would she do if she were off, and I didn't push it, guessing the café kept her from worrying too much about all she had to worry about. Toby's safety may have been moved down to number two on her list, but I knew Toby's future and whether he would spend it with her was number one. Number three would have been that stupid jury trial and suit brought by the Hilkers and still not resolved, having been put off until the day after the pageant. Bev claimed not to be worrying about that at all, but I believed any time a group of people had to make a judgment about you, you were in trouble. Most of the incomprehensible and ludicrous decisions I knew of had been made by groups. And somewhere on her list, maybe just under the trial, should have been Mike the Cockroach, written in large red letters and underlined. A warning. Or maybe he wouldn't make her list any more than the trial would. Maybe he was only an item on my worry list. Seeing Bev with him was like seeing her fall for a prisoner through one of those pen pal programs in which lonely and gullible women with money write to hardened criminals who claim to have found Jesus and want to go straight. Or like seeing her fall for a priest. I knew Mike would hurt her, and had to rationalize vigorously with myself, reminding myself I wasn't a judge and wasn't so smart about love or sex or any combination thereof anyway. I told myself they weren't really a couple, just two people having sex, and sex with Mike could be as good as sex with anyone—it was all the same in the dark. And if it was love, if Bev thought it was love, there was nothing inherently harmful in such thinking. Love was a magic word like hope, and sex may have been a magic word, too. And even more to the point, it was none of my business and worrying about what I could not affect was useless, and each time I caught myself doing it, I told myself to stop.

Another item high up on my worry list was Angela Cheng. I'd listened to a message she'd left on the answering machine recently. A simple one. "It's Angela Cheng. I'll call back some other time."

"Who's that?" I'd asked Bev, not trying to trick her, but truly having forgotten.

"The wrong number," Bev said.

About an hour later it hit me. Toby's mother calling Bev could lead only to trouble, and I said as much to Bev, who told me some things had to be followed through, no matter where they led. Then she borrowed a line from me, but coming from her it was the remark of a simpleton. "Let's hope for the best."

I'd advertised most of my Friday blue ribbon nights, distributed flyers behind Bev's back, but for the Christmas feast, she'd said I could advertise, so I was able to do it up front and take reservations, set up two seatings, one for 6:30, and one for 9:00. I served an English Christmas dinner to forty-four customers that Friday, the most ever. I did a garlic-and-cracked-pepper-encrusted beef tenderloin, Yorkshire pudding, sprouts, beets with orange slices, and potatoes in cream. I started with a fish chowder, served mixed greens before the cheddar and stilton course, and ended with mincemeat pies almost no one wanted and individual custards with fresh raspberries. I was already planning my new millennium dinner and knew I'd advertise it as a "Surprise, we're all still here!" celebration or something like that as a joke on all those who were preparing for disaster or rapture, depending upon their religious leanings.

One of the pageant organizers, a young blond man who worked for Bayer, another sponsor, said this competition could be it, not the beginning of the line but all there was if the computer systems failed. He smiled when he said it, but said it so often I decided he was not entirely joking. "I've got my money in a sock at home," he said once, also supposedly a joke.

"He's a bright bulb," I said to Ted, who helped out with practice by carrying Aunt Peg's garment bags, rolling the piano about.

"He's flirting with you," he said. "All these new millennium worries make good pickup lines." Ted had given me my Christmas gift early, but it wasn't something he could put under the tree. He'd taken my car in the week before and had a new side view mirror put on. Funny how he worried so about that missing mirror when I hardly missed it at all, could see all I needed to see by turning my head. Besides, I'd felt safer in our neighborhood driving an already damaged car. Nevertheless, I thanked him, considered it a birthday present, too. My birthday was Christmas Eve, a fact I'd kept from Ted partly because I'd done nothing for his in July, back when I still thought he was a critic and I was not yet sleeping with him. But beyond that, and despite the happy face put on it at the pageant, age had the power to frighten me.

The pageant started at seven o'clock on December 22, and the master of ceremonies was a former Hall of Fame shortstop for the St. Louis Cardinals. He gave a brief welcome, thankfully passing up the corny and seasonal references to the beautiful contestants as stocking stuffers, though he did say there wasn't one he wouldn't share his gas mask or bottled water with. He introduced the judges—a sports commentator and self-styled film critic, an owner of a local chain of appliance stores, a women's studies professor at the University of Missouri, the curator for special collections for the St. Louis Art Museum, the manager of one of the most expensive downtown hotels, and a former Miss America. The lights dimmed, the orchestra started in on "There is Nothing Like a Dame," and the thirty women in evening gowns paraded about the stage and runway in a carefully choreographed walk. Even the Barbara Bush ones looked pretty in satin and silk and taffeta, and almost all were graceful in their seldom worn heels.

After the song had been repeated twice, time enough for the judges to follow the progress of a favorite or two gliding across the stage, or for a nervous contestant to trip, falter a bit—which no one did—the former shortstop called each one up in alphabetical order to introduce herself, tell her age, her occupation, her familial status.

"Hi," Aunt Peg said to the judges, the only one who had done so so far, and the shortstop was already at the O's. She paused and smiled widely, looking golden and radiant, like fun and money incarnate. "I'm Margaret Mary Philomena Rose Stillwell Owen. The Philomena was my first confirmation name, but I had to change it to Rose when St. Philomena was discredited."

The shortstop acted as amused as he had said he would during rehearsal. "That's quite a handle," he said.

"You," Aunt Peg said, looking at the whole auditorium at once, and clearly meaning every one, "can call me plain old Peg."

She got applause for that, just as I'd predicted. Mom was against the words *plain* and *old*, but I told her that was the joke. Who would look at Peg and think she was plain or old?

When it was her turn to stroll down the runway by herself, she managed to catch the eyes of a few spectators and at least two judges, winking at them as if to say "what a kick," even—and this was a talent I had not known she had—blushing as she paused when back on the stage, as if embarrassed to be having so much fun.

Bev worked as my assistant backstage, ostensibly helping with costume changes and makeup touch-ups, giving advice, but really just hanging around because I hoped she'd enjoy it as much as I did, and because if not her, I'd have been forced to take Mom on as the assistant. And Bev did pay attention to Aunt Peg, but when the other contestants got their turns, her attention faltered. She talked instead to me and a few other trainers and assistants about lying. "How do you stop someone from lying to you?"

Most of us, me included, gave the obvious answers: Don't listen. Ignore the lies. Don't pay attention. Don't reinforce the behavior.

"But ignoring could put him in danger. What then?"

We all admitted that was tougher.

"I mean, I know the standard child psych answers," she said. "If it's not ignore him, it's put him on one of the popular designer drugs. But can you risk a child's life? You know, the boy who cried wolf finally died."

She was confusing herself and all of us, and I wished she would save the analysis and conclusion, if one existed, for later. I missed some of the contestants, and it was not that I wanted to watch them closely to size up the competition, but because that was what the pageant was for. The effort, the care, the glamor, the women exposing themselves, having the nerve to say I think I am beautiful or good enough to show my stuff to you—all that was exciting. And I didn't pray for slips or trips or any mistakes. No one wanted to win that way. I wanted each to be smoother and taller and prouder than ever. I didn't want to miss something that would not be re-done because I'd been listening to a person talk in circles about a dilemma that would be there hours or even years after the pageant was over.

Still, Bev kept going. "I know I'm reinforcing him somehow, but why me? Does he lie to everyone? Or is it my disdain for authority he's picked up on? Sure, he got away with blackmail, and that didn't help, but does he see me as an easy target because of my need? I keep trying to put myself in his position to figure out what he has to gain by his lies. But I'm stumped. A few nights on my couch. Making me worry. A bit of a diversion. Maybe it was fun. I can't think of anything else."

"If he's doing it for fun," another trainer, the daughter of the tall black woman in Aunt Peg's dressing area, said, "you have to ignore him for sure. Fun's a bad reason for anything."

"I have to figure it out before I get him," Bev said, and the other assistant picked up on that.

"Get him? You want to adopt him, a real child who already lies and has other habits? Uh, uh, girl. My sister's getting artificial insemination. It's better that way. Have your own. It's cheaper, too. Even with your bad leg, you can give birth."

"My leg," Bev said, "is not bad. It's a good leg, and it better be for the ten thousand it cost."

After the evening-wear segment, the contestants changed into playwear. Women their age had weak stomach muscles, so no matter their workout regimes, they wouldn't look good in swimsuits. *Playwear* was a general enough term to cover bicycle suits, jogging suits, sundresses with full skirts, caftans for those with numerous flaws to hide, or short shorts for those like Aunt Peg who had parts to show off. Aunt Peg's playwear outfit was one Chickie had sent from Hollywood along with the beaded dress. It was a white silk sleeveless shell tucked into Christmas red satin tap shorts. Her strutting and bouncing about the stage in it to an endlessly repeated, deafening, and defiant version of "I Enjoy Being a Girl" made it clear her muscles were tight, not a hint of wiggle, not even her upper arms. And she wore two thin gold chains with tiny gold stars hanging from them, one around her neck and one around an ankle. Matching gold stars were stuck in her earlobes. Mom had wanted her to wear a cross on a chain, but the rest of us vetoed that. "Too hokey," I said. "Crosses," Grandma said, "are not playful."

There was an intermission after the playwear segment and before the talent portion, and because Mom and Aunt Josie came back to give Peg advice about her song, I went out front to visit Ted who was with Uncle Al, Grandma, Cousin Chuck and his wife and sons. Dad, naturally, wasn't there, but sitting off to the side, near but not with my family, was Maddie and child. "Psst," she said. "Hey, pssst." I waved.

I'd given away tickets to others, too, in an attempt to pad the audience and applause for Aunt Peg, and I saw Rollie and his mother and John the chiropractor with a woman I'd never met sitting behind Maddie. Sally and Shirley Figg were in the bleachers with Peaches, and I thought I'd seen the two thrift shop women earlier. None of them knew Aunt Peg, but I'd made it clear when I passed the tickets out whom they should cheer for. I'd given a couple of tickets to Jeannie Lemp, too, but her "extreme disappointment" in Bev would keep her away.

"Hey, hey," Maddie said again, waving wildly with her free hand as I approached her. It was my first look at Randolph James, the creature who, unaware, had caused some trouble for Bev just by being. He was wrapped in some sort of yellow fleece thing that zipped up the front. Maddie held him up to her shoulder, his back to me, and he dangled down past her waist, much longer than I expected a six-week-old to be. She shifted him so I could see that he had a wild tangle of black hair in the center of his rather pointed head, spit bubbles around his partially opened mouth.

"Want to hold him?" she asked, leaning closer to me.

I looked around for Bev, but didn't see her, so I turned back to Maddie and said sure, why not, wondering if the question was automatic by now, if so many others had wanted to hold him. She placed him in my arms, and I was startled by how light he was, so much lighter than he looked, barely a presence yet in the world.

"What gets me about him is how much he needs," she said. "He needs something all the time."

I handed him back to her, his lightness making me uncomfortable.

"Does he eat enough?" I asked, picturing him evaporating, maybe blowing away.

She didn't answer that, but began talking about him the way people do their dogs, giving him rationality. "He doesn't like orchestras," she said. "Cried when that stupid dame song started. So much for Mom thinking he'll be musical. But he smiled at the ones with long legs showing. Already a leg man. And he may have some sense of color, too. He spit up at that doughy one in the dirt colored running suit."

He looked up at her, smiling at her voice, so I said the obvious. "He seems to like his mom."

She shook her head. "Not much. He cries more with me than with Mom. She's the one who gets up and gives him his bottles at night. She calls him R. James, and gets upset when I call him Randy."

I saw Mom return to her seat, and knew I should go back and check on Aunt Peg, so I said good or that's nice, knowing Maddie was not interested in my response anyway. "Jason's sister gave me a year at New Bodies Health Club for Christmas," she said as I turned to go. "My stomach's still flabby."

"Uh huh."

"You judge me as empty headed and selfish, but you could be wrong."

I wasn't judging her at all, and said as much, remembering how much smarter she had seemed to me before she gave birth. She'd been able to see through Toby's lies, for instance, once called him a blackmailer to his face.

The judges had made a first cut during the intermission, so that all thirty women wouldn't have to perform their talents and we could get out before midnight. This was what they called the semi-finals, and Aunt Peg, of course, was one of the remaining fifteen. She was to go on in the number eleven spot, though, and all that waiting would have made many contestants nervous. Not Aunt Peg. As I watched the other numbers, she used her cell phone and spoke to Chickie who claimed to be on the beach at Malibu, even though the sun had already set even in California. Chickie told jokes to keep her loose, mainly about bimbos and blondes, and Aunt Peg laughed so hard she cried at a few of them. Meanwhile, Bev had given up her job as assistant, so I had Mom whispering into my ear. She said she had come back to help me, and when I said I did not need help, she said that sentence was always a lie.

What she whispered in my ear as I watched the other talent was about Ted. "He's not what he appears to be. I have a bad feeling about him. Don't be fooled into thinking he'll stay around for long."

I was the one who wouldn't stay around but did not tell Mom. Rather, I imagined myself in a small but cozy room, the kind I'd rent while I was in Montreal. I would be able to be anyone I wanted to be there, maybe a person with no family, a mysterious beauty who watched the snow pile up, not caring if it ever melted. "Look at contestant number seven," I said. "Who would have thought she could do the splits?"

"He's the reason for your headaches," she said. "You're worried about him leaving, and too proud to say it."

"My head does not ache at all right now." It was the surprising truth. Competition may have been a better cure than twirling needles.

"Don't change the subject," Mom said.

"The subject for now is talent," I said. "Let's stick with it." Then I had a thought. I pointed to the dancer on stage. "If her teeth were any whiter, the yellows of her eyeballs would be more noticeable. Don't you think?" I turned around to look at Mom, who was frowning.

"I don't get it," she said. "Is that supposed to be a joke? Maybe you do have a tumor."

I had to admit Chickie had done well with both costumes, but especially with the short beaded dress Aunt Peg wore for her ragtime piano number. It was supposedly white, but each tiny bead was iridescent and the dress not only shimmered, but under the spotlight, became all colors. In spite of my weak attempts at stacking the audience, attempts I knew all trainers had also made, the audience had been trying for fairness, applauding each act politely and evenly. Up to Aunt Peg's act, that was. Her rendition of "In a Shanty in Old Shanty Town" brought prolonged applause, even some foot stamping, for being so hammy and sentimental. Every one of the judges was smiling as Aunt Peg took her bow.

The second intermission was designed to give the judges time to narrow the field further to five finalists. Though I wasn't worried about Aunt Peg making the cut, while backstage I had to pretend to be as part of a solidarity with other contestants and trainers. One of the women who looked like Barbara Bush said to me, "Surely maturity and dignity are more important in a contest like this than well-preserved bodies and bleached hair." I nodded, tempted to ask what planet she was from.

Ted stood at the entrance to the dressing rooms, as close as men were allowed, and motioned to me, but when I got close, he said he was just waving, wishing me luck. "You're wishing me what I already have," I said, partly meaning him.

"Have you ever lost a competition?" he asked.

"Never. And I don't recall ever worrying about not winning. Naïve on my part, I guess." Then I told him about Chickie coming in as only first runner-up in the Miss Convention Center pageant the year after I won it. She lost because she stumbled a bit over the poise-segment question. She said happiness was more important than health but changed her mind and said she didn't think you could be happy if you were in poor health. A mistake. Surely some of the judges had arthritis, diabetes, at least spastic colons. I wasn't sure why I told Ted that story about Chickie, and then suddenly I was sure. Envy. She was on Malibu Beach and I was here, making a success out of a café the owner didn't care about, adapting to circumstances, yes, but not taking a real direction as she had when she left young and never looked back.

So what if she only got commercials and small walk-ons, maybe a few lines and silly ones at that—"Yes, Mr. Bond," was one of her three lines in the new movie. She had stuck it out, hadn't wasted years on selling siding. Reporting on her failure was an act of envy, what Grandpa had meant when he spoke of original sin and how we all had the ability to overcome it. "I'm sorry," I said to Ted. "That's a silly story." When I got to my room in Montreal, I'd work on overcoming envy.

When Bev came back to see how Aunt Peg and I were doing, sent by Grandma, I said we were nervous because others were listening, but then I pulled her into a corner of the hallway, and said I had a confession. I hadn't known I would do it. Maybe it was the realization I was lucky, or it could have been my facing up to my envy and pettiness, or it could have been my own belief that she had finally done the right thing about Toby and was happier anyway now that she was having sex with Mike. Whatever the reason, I decided she should know. "I've applied to l'École de Cuisine Internationale, a cooking school in Montreal. If accepted, I'll go there and study for eighteen months, the full program. It's what I want to do."

She looked at me hard for a long moment, during which time the lights flickered to send all audience members back to their seats. Her mouth was opened, and her tiny eyes were beadier than ever. Finally she sneered, then sighed. "No big deal. Everyone leaves. I should have expected it."

"I'll be back," I said, not sure I had decided to come back.

"Sure," she said. "Sure you will. But it doesn't matter. I started this café by myself. I've done most things by myself."

The house lights went out and stayed out as the spotlight shone on the shortstop and the final portion of the pageant began. All thirty contestants were once again lined up on stage in evening gowns, and they swayed and walked about the stage to another song, "The Most Beautiful Girl in the World." The shortstop then read the five names the judges had given him, in alphabetical order. Peg Owens was number four. The five finalists moved forward while the losers left the stage to polite applause. This was the poise segment, time for the questions, but these women were too old to be asked how they would help the world, make it better. We had discussed it, all the Stillwell girls, and had decided the questions would be about looking back, dispensing wisdom gained from a well-lived life, maybe sharing your fondest memory. Nostalgia was always a winner. And we'd coached Aunt Peg on possible answers. We all knew that though the pageant title contained the designation *Ms.*, the unmarried, the free lover, or the hard-edged feminist who would not see herself in the context of family had no chance. We told Aunt Peg to use the word *family* at least twice in her answer, no matter the question.

The woman before her was the black woman whom she shared her dressing space with, strikingly beautiful in a silver halter top gown and a diamond choker. Her question was one we'd predicted: Assuming you have gained a substantial amount of wisdom by now, what would you do differently? Here was her mistake. She said she had learned that life deserved to be celebrated, that all events—birthdays, promotions, even small awards and successes—should be acknowledged. No holiday should pass by without being celebrated as much as possible. Restraint was not a virtue. She said all that, and I could tell the judges were going for it. It was upbeat; it was simple; it reminded all of us of regrets and failures but stressed celebrations and holidays at the same time. But she faltered at the end. She continued talking about holidays that were gone, opportunities missed, unrecoverable fun. She said, "Like here. It's the Christmas season and the hall is decorated, but the tree's not lit. What good is a tree that is not lit? I say, 'Let there be light.'" She pointed at her trainer who took the cue and plugged the extension cord into an outlet. The audience *ooohed* and *aaaa-hed* as the twenty-foot tree on the side of the stage became blue and red, but the shortstop motioned to a stage hand, and the tree went dark immediately.

I was surprised neither the contestant nor her trainer had known about the tree. We were all told that the second day of practice. Apparently the Fire Marshall had done an inspection on Sunday, late but better than not doing it at all, and he'd found cracks in the wires on the longest strand of lights wound about the tree, and the county was not prepared to take a chance on fire on government property. The light strand could have been replaced, but, the shortstop explained, county workers, many of whom were already on Christmas vacation, would have to be paid double time to work that week and the pageant committee decided just to shine a spotlight on the tree. The shortstop had told us he thought all the holly and greenery and banners made the place cheery enough, and we had all agreed in order to get on his good side. That this contestant hadn't listened closely enough that second day did not please the judges.

Her trainer stood beside me in tears. "Why did they have the extension cord still attached if we weren't supposed to plug it in?"

I had no answer except to suggest that they may have had to pay double time to get someone to remove the extension cord. It was partly a joke, though it didn't make her smile.

With the black woman out of the way, Aunt Peg had an even better chance. The shortstop joked with her before her question. "Is there anything in the auditorium you want to rearrange or set on fire before we begin?"

Aunt Peg merely smiled, too smart to answer and seem to be rubbing the embarrassment in.

"What role has beauty played in your life?" he asked. It was not a question we had anticipated, though we should have. I held my breath.

"I want to say first of all, I agree with the wonderful senti-ment expressed up here moments ago. Celebrate the day. All of us contestants should, win or lose. These are three days of fun that won't come again." She earned a round of applause for that theft. "Now about beauty," she said. "God has blessed me and my family with physical beauty, and all of us have worked to care for and be worthy of this blessing. We did nothing to deserve it, so we won't exploit it. But we do not see beauty as merely physical. One of my nieces was born without a leg and without most of her fingers, but we all think she is beautiful."

It was a good answer, a winning one, but I felt as if I were still holding my breath, afraid to look at Bev who I knew was backstage somewhere. But why should she be angry? She knew what she had been born without. And Aunt Peg had said a nice thing. But my rationalizations weren't working. Bev had been used, her missing pieces used for someone else's glory, used to wring the hearts of the judges. Aunt Peg's smile was beatific. Bev's deformities had been reduced to sentimental sludge, made equal to that shanty in old shanty town.

By the time Aunt Peg was named Senior Ms. St. Louis Metropolitan Area just moments later, Bev was already pulling her car out of the parking lot. It was Maddie who saw her go. "Wasn't that a sweet thing for your aunt to say?" she asked after she told me Bev was gone. "Randy misses Bev," she said to explain his wails.

"Why would Bev be so sensitive after all these years?" I asked Ted, all of us huddled together near the runway for Aunt Peg's triumphal walk. Ted didn't know. "Doesn't she know all the answers are bullshit anyway? She's the one who bitches about the garbage on TV, so why can't she recognize garbage in a place like this, too?"

Ted shrugged again. Randy continued to wail, and Grandma wiped away her tears as Aunt Peg accepted her crown and the dozen long-stemmed American beauties. I went outside, joining a few of the losers standing about the door, still in evening wear, some smoking and all talking about the money they'd spent to lose. One of them said she had been sponsored by a Honda dealer, and another said she had taken up a collection at the bookstore she worked in.

"Yours did great," they said to me. "She deserved to win."

I thanked them, and I said what I did not believe. We were all at the mercy of chance and circumstance. One loser said she was heading to the Landing to celebrate as my winner had said they all should, and a few laughed at that, not mean or fake laughs either.

It was a cold night, but so clear, I could see not only both dippers and Orion, but also the Andromeda Nebula. Ted came out and put his arms around me from behind. "We're already twenty-four hours past the Winter solstice," he said. "The days are getting longer."

Then I remembered what the next day was and why Bev may have rushed home. Her trial was tomorrow. Maybe she had not been offended after all. I leaned back against Ted's warmth and asked if he was going to the courthouse with us. I thought I felt him nod.

BEV

I considered it one foundation of insanity: never being sure whom or what to trust. In my position, I did not trust social services, nor did I trust the police. And I did not trust Toby, either. Even though I knew he was in real danger, I didn't know what the danger was. And the report Ted Younger later read at my trial made it seem I was a danger, had been a danger to minors like Madison Hilker and Toby. I was not to be trusted, and I suppose that is true enough in certain circumstances, but I was not the immediate and physical danger that Toby feared. Add to all that more proof that trust was a fool's game: Shelly had trusted Ted who was not what he seemed, or at least was more than he seemed.

Getting up on the morning of the trial, sliding over to the side of my bed and reaching for my leg and strapping it on, testing it out, flexing the knee once or twice before stumbling into the bathroom and looking at myself in the blackened mirror above the sink was harder than ever. I had to make myself look pretty, well not pretty of course, but presentable, or as I thought of it, normal and ordinary. My limp hair flew about my comb like radio waves, nearly too fine to be seen but crackling in all directions. My eyes were smaller and beadier because my lids were puffy from lack of sleep combined with the dry heat blown about the flat all night long from the vents I'd installed when I bought the place so the radiators could be removed. A mistake, I had come to realize. Shelly'd told me my hair was too fine to be shampooed often, so rather than wash it, I moussed and sprayed it, pushed and yanked and twirled it into some kind of shape, finally making it look like a bed of straw a small dog had made a lopsided nest in. Then I splashed cold water on my beady eyes to make the skin around them shrink back in pain. Ugly never won a jury's heart, Howard had said but in less offensive words. "Look nice," was how he'd put it. "As if your missing parts are inconveniences but what people notice only on second glance." Shelly said breathtakingly beautiful probably never won a jury either, but we both knew I need not worry about that.

Shelly thought I was angry at Aunt Peg's mention of me in her winning pageant answer, and after Shelly got home from the crowning, she asked me at least four times if I were angry. My answer of *no* didn't satisfy her, and I knew I'd eventually have to say *yes* so she could explain that she'd had no part in it, and then comfort me by explaining all the Stillwell girls' thoughtlessness and lack of sensitivity, which I was already well aware of. In fact, the reason I wasn't angry was that I'd grown used to the deliberate mention of me as a beauty, something done in my hearing to flatter me. I knew they loved me and all that stuff and felt sorry for me, too, but I also knew the Stillwell beauties drew a distinct but unspoken line between inner and outer beauty and in their own minds would never mix the two. I hadn't left the contest suddenly because I felt used by Aunt Peg, nor was I worried they'd all look at me with pride at how good they were to include me, but rather I knew all of them, even Dad and Chuck's wife, would try hard not to look at me. I left to avoid that awkwardness.

Besides, I had initially felt a bit used by Shelly, as I had been by all my other roommates. Shelly was proving to be as temporary as the rest, family or not, was taking my hospitality and turning it into a time-out, a place to catch her breath before her flight, her launch pad. Of course, the truth was, I was temporary, too. The Alibi Café was temporary. I decided to sell it as soon as I had Toby, so more than feeling used—which I got over immediately—I felt ashamed of feeling used.

In the beginning, Shelly had been largely an annoyance, a nuisance, my poor cousin who needed help. I had given in to family pressure. "She's not good at making decisions," Mom said about her. "She sees life as if it's a competition of some kind with a finish line, a tallying of points," Dad said. "She never notices what goes on around her," her mother said. So I took her in. And though all those judgments about her were true, she proved tougher than any of them thought; she did not need a mother or a caretaker or a protector or a guide, and she did not need me. Though she was still an annoyance, and still and forever family, I had begun to consider her a friend. And now she, as all friends did, was leaving.

The trial was scheduled for ten o'clock, but Shelly and I met Howard at the county courthouse at nine. He found a small meeting room on the third floor, outside the courtroom, and we met there for absolutely no reason. We had no strategy. We had little to plan. We were going to listen to the charges and essentially laugh them off, but in a nice way. They were ridiculous. That was Howard's stance. I was to be surprised and dismayed at being so unkindly attacked. In fact, I was not surprised, never had been. I had expected no more from the Hilkers or their kind.

Well, the judge was delayed on some official business, and when we were told the case had been pushed back to eleven, Howard told us he'd use the time to run across to his office and make a few unrelated calls. Shelly and I, with no business to take care of, went to the basement snack bar for muffins and coffee, and while down there we saw Jeannie Lemp. She was standing before a row of vending machines across from the snack bar, and she nodded to us with a stone face, then looked down at her palm, counting her change. I had known she would be in my courtroom on official business, recording all the dirt the Hilkers had come up with or had made up and planned to spread out at the trial. I doubted then she'd pick up anything beyond the obvious lunacy of their suit, which she already knew about. "Hi, Jeannie," I said, but she pretended not to hear. Served me right for being such a hypocrite; she was not someone I would ever go out of my way to say *Hi* to, and we both knew it.

We went back up and met Howard in a different but identical meeting room at 10:45, and at exactly 11:00, we assembled in the courtroom, the jury in its row of seats to my right, Hilkers at a table like ours to my left. Donna Wicher, their lawyer, and Howard moved away from us peons and talked low and gestured toward us and the judge's bench and even the ceiling. Shelly guessed they were discussing the case, and I agreed it was possible, but I knew they could also be talking about their golf games. After all, this was a small case, a boring case.

Maddie waved to me from their table, and then she picked up Randolph James from his baby seat and moved his hand in imitation of a wave, too. Shelly and I waved back at Maddie but both of us grimaced when she did that trick with the baby's hand, using him as if he were a puppet. Though I didn't wish Maddie any harm, I hoped the jury were watching so they would see what kind of silly girl she had turned into. Shelly was right when she said Maddie lost most of her intelligence when the gave birth. "Let's hope it's just misplaced," Shelly said when I agreed with her. "Not truly lost." Finally, Maddie put the baby back in his seat, lowered it to the floor, and slid it under their table.

By the time Howard came back and sat beside us, it was 11:20. Eventually, the bailiff came by and whispered to Howard loud enough for me to hear. The judge's car had been rear-ended just a few blocks away, and was the cause for this delay. Because it was approaching noon, Howard and Donna Wicher agreed that the trial could be postponed until 1PM. Even the bailiff agreed that it would go fast once started, and the jurors were signed up for the whole day anyway. We'd all be home for dinner, no matter what. The bailiff called the judge's cell phone, and after she pushed some afternoon thing back, it was all arranged.

Maddie crossed the ten feet or so to our table and said her mother said it was okay if we joined them for lunch. Her parents' treat. We both said no at the same time, admitting later we couldn't think of anything worse than listening to Mrs. Hilker talk and watching Maddie play with her baby. We went back to the snack bar, and once in our same booth with chili dogs and root beers before us, I said this was the most boring trial I'd ever been to. I said it was a trial all right, the whole experience aptly named. But Shelly wasn't listening to my silliness. She stared over my head, then she stood partway up in the booth to wave, and shouted "over here."

"I could have sworn that was Ted," she said when she sat back down. "I expect him to be around for moral support, but I guess that was just some guy with a similar jacket. I'm sure he'll be smart enough to look for us down here when he's told the trial has been postponed." She played with her hot dog, not eating the bun, taking only a few bites of the chili. "Greasy," she said. "Some think that's a good thing. Not me. The root beer alone is a few hundred calories."

As it turned out, Ted was there for the trial, but not for moral support. When I realized his role in the proceedings, I wanted to do what the Stillwell girls had planned on my doing when they foisted Shelly on me, protect her. Before he showed up, though, the trial was even more boring than the waiting had been, and a few of the jurors seemed to be pinching themselves to stay awake. As Donna Wicher talked to the jury, explaining the charge and saying how serious it was to influence a minor negatively, that one mistake could ruin a life, I looked around. This was not a TV or movie courtroom. Sure, the judge sat on a chair behind a raised desk; she wore a robe; there was a chair near her for the witness to sit in; the jury sat in a straight row. But there was a Christmas tree decorated with candy canes and quilted ginghamy santas and angels in full view, right behind the witness chair. The floor was a great disappointment, covered with cheap but long wearing carpet rather than the terrazzo or tile that would make a nice sound as a witness approached the chair. There were no carvings, no thick heavy wooden railings, and no statue of justice. All the tables and chairs and benches were blond wood, heavily polyurethaned and shiny and nearly plastic. We all played our parts under harsh fluorescent lights, and people waiting for other trials or the merely curious and time killers kept wandering in, sitting for a while, then leaving. Some of the jurors were understandably more interested in the door's openings and closings than in my case.

When Howard put me on the stand, he read my deposition out for the jury, and I said it was correct. That was all. Then Donna Wicher got to ask me questions.

"Did you ever have nicknames for the girls in your home-room?"

"Yes," I said. Howard had told me to answer the questions in the shortest way possible and not to volunteer anything.

"Did you have a nickname for Madison Hilker?"

"I called her Maddie as everyone did," I said. "With a name like Madison, there aren't too many choices for nicknames." Howard frowned at me.

"Didn't you call her Dumbo?"

"Well, yes," I said. "But I was fair about it. I called all the girls Dumbo when they did something dumb, something groaningly obvious or stupid. She was not my only Dumbo."

"Didn't it occur to you that you were taking unfair advantage of your position of power, calling them names?"

I waited for Howard to object. I knew from TV that these questions were leading and irrelevant. When it became clear Howard would say nothing, I looked at the judge, but she seemed occupied with some kind of paperwork, maybe, I thought, related to her rear-ending. So I answered. "They called me Ms. Burp. To my face. It was a joke. They'd pretend I'd misunderstood or that their tongues had gotten tied up." I didn't mind talking about this with Donna Wicher, but it was a waste of time.

"Did you call Maddie Dumbo for getting pregnant?"

"No," I said. "It was too late then."

She went on about nicknames and power for a while until I saw Howard look at me, seeming to be nodding. After a brief period of confusion, I realized he was moving his head from my prosthesis to my face, and I remembered what he had said I should say. "They called my prosthesis a name," I said. "All my girls did."

"Your Honor," Donna Wicher said. "Tell the witness to answer the question, not volunteer information."

But the judge was looking at me. "What name did they call your prosthesis?" she asked.

"All my girls called it Hortense." Howard had wanted me to choke a bit when I said that, but I could not. It was enough that I didn't laugh. "It was Maddie who named it." I saw her smirk at me from her table. Her hair was blond for the trial, and for a change, the kind of blond that is found in nature, like the petals of a sunflower. And she was not wearing her eyebrow piercing. We both knew we were acting.

Donna Wicher then said I could step down.

When Maddie took the stand she said only good things about me, except to complain that I read poems out loud too often and lost her interest. Then Mrs. Hilker had a turn and she said I had given Maddie the idea she could tell her mother lies, that it was enough to pretend to be good. Howard cross-examined Mrs. Hilker and made her admit she was at least fifty percent responsible for what Maddie was, how she'd turned out. "You can't say 'turned out' when talking about a seventeen year old," I whispered to Shelly. "Why not sixty percent? Or forty-two?" Shelly whispered back. Mr. Hilker took the stand, too, but the only new thing that came from his testimony was that he was a podiatrist, not a heart specialist as Maddie had claimed.

Howard then read from my deposition again, explaining that I had not denied making the disputed remarks to the girls, but even taken out of context and isolated they did not sound harmful. Didn't the jury agree? I looked over and saw a few nodding, even a few women who Howard said would be a tougher sell. They were ready to vote my way and go home before the roads got clogged up. I could almost hear their thoughts. What can I put under the tree for my son's new trampy girlfriend who will probably give me a pair of cheap earrings? I have to find something Grandma won't just throw away. Let that poor deformed woman go home. She is innocent. That foot doctor has lots of nerve. That was when Donna Wicher called her witness, Ted Younger, and made me want to shield Shelly.

Of course, none of us can protect one another. Mostly parents cannot help their children, lovers are useless, friends are no good. Shelly was sitting beside me, and I heard her single intake of breath when Ted promised to tell the truth. I didn't have to look at her to know she sustained a blow with each sentence that crossed his lips. Me, too. I knew Jeannie Lemp was taking notes, and none of what she was hearing would help me adopt Toby. It looked bad and some of it was.

After Ted did his worst, looking hangdog as he revealed my nasty and irresponsible side, the jury went off to deliberate. Howard winked at me before he left the two of us standing in the hallway, neither having the heart to go to the snack bar yet again. Besides, Howard said it would be fast. Sure enough, we were called back into the courtroom after a mere fifteen minutes of standing about in shock. The news was good. The jury had found for me, against the Hilkers. They had believed Howard's argument that a few words, well-meant or mean-spirited did not matter, could have had little effect on a lovestruck, hormone ruled sixteen-year-old girl, especially one like Maddie who had been raised with no idea that her actions had consequences. I thought the last part unfair and uncalled for, but had been too concerned with Shelly and Ted and even with what Jeannie was hearing to complain to Howard. Because we had filed not only a demurrer but also a cross-complaint, the Hilkers were ordered to pay us $100,000 as compensation, *relief* was the term used, as well as Howard's fees. Howard would get a large portion of the relief, of course, and he said it would take a while as the Hilkers would no doubt appeal. It was even likely that the relief would be reduced significantly or taken away. I shrugged at all that.

Shelly was quiet most of the way home, except to tell me she thought we should just go ahead and close up the next day, December 24, too. Few people would come anyway, she guessed, sounding weak and old as she said it. Besides, she continued, she didn't think she could overcome her urge to pour Drano in the gravy, to mix Raid into the barbecue sauce. She faked a laugh when she said it, but I knew she was not being entirely facetious. I wanted to pour poison down a throat, too, but my fantasy involved a chemical burn on a specific private detective's gullet.

Mom called soon after we got back home, and I tried to

sound chipper, happy that the case had gone my way. "Well," she said, "truth will out." She wanted all the details, so I gave her what I had—the carpeted floor, the judge getting rear-ended, the Christmas tree, the bit about the nicknames, the relief that could never come. I did not mention Ted or his back-stabbing comments which the jury had discounted but which we could not and Jeannie would not either.

Just as we were sinking down into our gloom, slumped about in the darkened living room (Shelly said she would die before turning the tree on), Cousin Chuck and his wife came by, something they had never done. Mom had called everyone to spread the good news, and Chuck said the newly crowned Senior Ms. St. Louis Metropolitan Area was babysitting, and they were heading to the jazz and blues clubs down in an old area off South Broadway, a few miles east of us. They wanted both of us to come along, celebrate my victory.

It surprised me to hear them say *victory*, for though I had used that word with Mom only hours earlier, I did not feel victorious. That surprise may have been reflected on my face, because Chuck assured me the excursion hadn't been planned around my trial. "We do this every year," he said. "We met thirteen years ago at Steaks and Jazz on Ninth, so it's always our first stop."

"Fourteen years ago," Chuck's wife said to all of us, and then to me specifically, "You don't have to dance. Don't worry about that. You just listen to the music and talk real fast during the breaks." Shelly sighed so that I knew she'd go if I did, and I was tempted, suddenly wanting something completely different. The flat seemed small and stuffy and confining, had the ambiance of a place people like us made suicide pacts in. She wouldn't be good alone, she said with that sigh, so she may as well escape with me and the other relatives. Before we piled into Chuck's car, a Ford of some kind that, thank God, was a four door, I played on their mistaken sense that the trial had been a worry and that I deserved my way, to make them wait until I rounded up Mike to go with us. I hadn't seen him since Sunday, but his place was dark and he didn't respond to my poundings on the front or back doors. I thought he'd probably want to know how the trial went, but I also knew it was more than possible he'd forgotten all about it, maybe had forgotten even his name and my own over the past three days.

The music was good, I guess. At least Chuck and his wife said so. "Aren't they good?" they asked after the Backyard Blues Band was finished, and "Good, huh?" they said to us when The Blind Disciples finished their first number. I had to admit they were loud, and every singer provided a full, all-out wail. Most were wailing over lost loves and I amused myself by thinking I could understand why their lovers had split after hanging around such crybabies.

We went to three clubs, each one small and dark and smoky, and Shelly finally started talking as we hurried up Allen Street from Seventh to Ninth. "People alive today are deliberately crazy," she said. "We are meant to be kept off guard, not knowing what to believe. Like with tuna. There's all that Japanese dolphin business. Are they killing dolphins along with tuna? They say not anymore, and we are able to eat tuna guilt free now. But why don't we feel as sorry for the tuna as for the dolphin? Dolphins are smarter, but stupid people get protected, why not stupid fish? See, none of it makes sense."

She sounded less intelligent than most of my Agnus Dei girls had, but I didn't comment on her stupidity, just kept walking with my head down and my hands in my pockets.

"On purpose," she continued. "We eat cows but not horses. We draw a line, but it is imaginary and arbitrary. Someone does it for us. And each politician has learned to use the popular words like *family* and *character* and *honor* and *children* and *future* and *equality*, tell us what we want to hear, and that makes us want to hear none of it. We can say it along with any of them, so why listen, and so we don't pay attention, and then we end up really screwed." She paused before we entered the Great Grizzly Bear. "We are meant to be off-balance so that when someone lies he can claim it was a misunderstanding, a mistake, or at worst, misinformation."

She'd been practically shouting all of it in my ear as we scurried up the two blocks, but the wind that whipped around the corners like a raucous band of ghosts knocked against my ears and blew her words backwards. Backwards words, I thought. She was still saying the obvious, telling me what we'd both figured out years ago. I considered it beating our lives and times down with an old stick. But maybe she was entitled; maybe we all were allowed times of stale rants. If not for them, the world would be much quieter. "You already knew all that," I said, though I had meant to let her jejune remarks pass.

When we were seated once again, an old black man pounding out the blues on an upright in the corner, she looked at me as if I fit into that group of people whose words meant nothing and who talked just to lie. As if she had always suspected me. She narrowed her eyes and shook her head at me mournfully. Her voice was low and hesitant, weepy. "Why would he complain about Montreal being so far? What difference does it make where it is?"

"It's in Canada," Chuck said, looking proud of himself. "It's up there." He pointed toward the piano. When the waitress asked, he ordered a bottle of champagne. "We're celebrating," he said. "Stupidity lost today."

"Hah," I said.

We spent Christmas day at Aunt Marie's, the usual family meeting place so Uncle Jack wouldn't have to leave his nest. We'd drawn names for the gift exchange. Shelly had Dad, and he got two gifts: a cashmere muffler in a green and gray plaid, and a black cowboy hat, one of those normally given a designation in gallons of how much it could hold if turned upside down. I asked Shelly about it, and she shrugged, not interested enough in the hat to discuss its type or size. I gave Grandma mink earmuffs, and Chickie, who had stayed in L.A. for Christmas, sent me a pair of asbestos-lined oven mitts decorated with little coffee pots and cups with steam rising from them in two lines. "It's to help with your business," Aunt Peg said, and Shelly snorted. I smiled and looked at Shelly who rolled her eyes. She had yet to smile, not even when Aunt Peg's gift to her was a beaded dress almost identical to the one she'd worn in the talent competition. "Keep it for when you get old enough to be Senior Ms. America. Only nineteen more years," Aunt Peg said.

"Thank you. It's just what I wanted," Shelly said, her voice flat and low.

When I held up Chickie's mitts, I expected a laugh, even a bitter one would have been better than the snort. Instead Shelly said, "I hope they fit," which made Aunt Peg defensive.

"You don't need fingers to wear those," she said, and I nodded, hoping Shelly had at least been trying to make a joke.

Throughout dinner and even after, all anyone wanted to talk about was my trial, though Aunt Peg's new crown was inherently more exciting. My trial held the most interest because none of them had been witnessed to it, and had to rely on my account— and of course Shelly's, but she wasn't talking—and so were never satisfied. Mom wanted to know about the Christmas tree. How had they gotten away with that, she wondered. What about separation of church and state.

"A tree is purely secular," Dad said.

"Even so," she said. "It seems wrong. And what if it's a murder case. What role does the tree play if someone is given the death penalty, then has to look at those quilted angels?"

Grandma shared my disappointment with the carpeted floor.

I described the color of Maddie's hair, said her baby had a pointed head, and even told them that the Hilkers had invited us to lunch. I didn't tell them Ted had shown up, had stabbed us in the backs. I was never impressed by the romancing of innocence and thus the tragedy of its end, of the simple and naïve being lauded as Wordsworth and his gang would have had it, so I didn't want to say, even to myself, the cliché of what is this world coming to, or add that people were getting so mean and treacherous. But I did think we'd seldom lived in times of such fake complexity. I mean, I knew Ted considered his decision difficult. He had a job to do and he had to do it no matter whom he hurt. He wouldn't have been the man of integrity he wanted to see himself as if he'd done a half-assed job, not checked up on me, not taken notes. But his choice was really the same old one—love or money. The reason he would've given for wanting to do a good job was money. He'd been paid, would be paid more. He didn't want to take money under false pretenses. Blah blah. If he'd not been paid, there would've been no problem. So he chose money over love as weaklings had been doing since the creation of the first monetary system. He could pretend to be caught on the horns of a dilemma, pretend it had to do with honor or some of the other words Shelly credited the politicians with pushing, but I knew better. Maybe he did, too. And I was not blameless. Why was I on trial? What did the Hilkers want? Money. Why did I fight back? Money. I did not want to give them any. I was not fighting for my good name, long gone in their circles and surely not restored now that I'd won. We all knew Mrs. Hilker was not calling up her bridge group and saying, "Well, I was wrong about Bev. I want to set the record straight. She is blameless. I know because the jury said so."

When we got back to our flat later that night, there was a letter on the floor of the front hallway, pushed through the mail slot. It was from Ted, of course, and Shelly knew it was full of *I'm sorries* and *you should understands* and *I had to do its*. She didn't even read it, just tore it up while still in the envelope and tossed it in the kitchen trash. "You see," she said. "It's designed to make me like him again, but it's really nothing but excuses. Nothing about me, all him. I don't have to read it to know its point is poor, poor me. It's why your dad got the hat."

"You don't have to apologize to me. I've always known how sorry you are." I said. "Remember that?"

"Oh God," she said. "Grandpa's back among us, and he brought one of his song titles."

Here is what Ted said that hurt Shelly: I had told my students that "life sucks"; my own family thought I was stubborn and irresponsible; the principal of Agnus Dei said all homeroom periods were more orderly without me; I had told Toby to lie to his foster mother; I lied to the police and the state social services about Toby's whereabouts; I left Toby under the care of an alcoholic bum, for some reason deciding the bum was more capable of protecting him than the trained social workers would have been; I'd let that same bum spend the night with me, make love to me in my bedroom while Toby slept in the living room; I'd shown Toby, "an impressionable ten-year-old boy," how to strap my leg on and then how to take it off, even though the straps were normally under my clothing, and paid him to keep quiet about it.

What was wrong with that list? First of all, my family would never have said I was stubborn and irresponsible, not even joking, though they may indeed have thought it. Second, it was needlessly cruel to refer to Mike as a bum, and not true. He had a place to live, after all, and I didn't think he mooched off anyone but me. Third I had trusted and still did trust Mike more than all the trained state worker drones I'd met, believe that a point in my favor. Fourth, I'd worn my bathing suit when Toby worked my buckles. And fifth, none of anything that had to do with Toby was relevant to the Hilkers' case, Maddie's ruination.

He was right about my telling Toby to lie to Lana, something I shouldn't have done, and right about Toby's petty blackmail, too. But what he said about Mike in my bedroom, making love to me, that was the only part of his spiel I approved of. I wished Ted had stressed that part.

After he was finished, I turned to Howard. "I don't think any of that is relevant," I said, and Howard did stand up and object after the damage had been done. I didn't mean with the jurors, but with Jeannie who would use this against me, would find reason upon reason in what Ted had said why I should be denied Toby and a chance at motherhood. But most of the damage I believed in had been done to Shelly. I did not have to look at her to know she was stupefied. Even she could not put a good face on such betrayal.

After a great shock or sorrow, people do not give you the reaction you expect. You look for the weeping and gnashing of teeth, wailing like that done in the blues clubs, but instead you get a false and forced calm. That, at least, was what Shelly showed me. She moved slower, moved carefully about the flat the way people with new eyeglass prescriptions descend stairs, trying to seem normal. And in the giant scheme of things, as Mom used to say, Ted's betrayal was not a tragedy, no matter how shocking. He was just some guy, one more who walked away. I knew that was what she told herself, too, was why she kept her spine straight and her chin up.

She stopped cooking for a week, though, saying it had been a long time since she'd had a vacation, and thought she was entitled. Well, I started to say, you haven't even been here a year, and we are closed every Sunday, and never opened at night except for your blue ribbon nights, but saying that would have been merely an argument reflex. I did understand—even on her days off she cleaned up and practiced new dishes and typed menus and shopped—and more than understand, I didn't care. She could take time off. If I'd been as tired and disillusioned as her empty stare told me she was, I would've gone ahead and closed the café. I kept it open that week, the one between Christmas and New Year's, only on the off chance Toby could get away from his safe house and come by. Of course I hoped his safe house was more secure than that, but I couldn't stop my fantasy of seeing him walk in and hop up on a stool.

So I worked alone during the holiday week, and most of my customers listlessly pushed their food about their plates, stared out the window, yawned open-mouthed, and didn't even eat Mom's homemade pickles. I had the heat cranked up, but the twentieth century was ending cold, and the wind chill was in the minuses. Some of my customers kept their jackets on inside. The winds, though fierce, did not seem able to get rid of the clouds. As soon as some were blown east, replacements came in from the northwest. Low, thick clouds had been scuttling over the area for days, and were sapping our energy, our joy. Most of the diners, me included, wanted to curl up in a pile of quilts and come out in spring. Maybe the forced good cheer of Christmas itself had been enervating, the last straw, more than most of us could handle.

Rollie said his mother had spent Christmas in the basement of her house, angry at him for a slight he still wasn't sure of. He called it "Mom's meltdown," saying "She was due. She had not gone off the deep end for a while. I knew something was coming."

The thrift shop women said the thrift shop had been broken into on Christmas Eve, and this was the second time in as many years. Their insurance company representative was urging them to move, telling them how much lower their rates would be in other areas. That made them sad, of course, but by the way they looked at their plates, I thought my tuna salad made them that much sadder. John the chiropractor, who had always come in mainly for Shelly's smiles and teasings, said the problem was that our food was too summery. We needed more hot stuff. Without her stuffed peppers, without even her barbecue sauce or the pots of chili or creamed soups she would have whipped up, we had nothing that people looked forward to on minus degree days. Rollie said the grilled cheese was maybe the only exception, but seemed to agree mostly with John.

"Notice," Rollie said, "the city workers filling in the potholes outside don't come in here. And they're right outside. They all go to McDonald's."

I put up with that atmosphere for three days, but by the third day didn't even make my egg salad because no one wanted it. I made only pies that could be served warm like apple and peach, even though the peaches needed lots of help to have any flavor at all, and I let my customers depress me. I gazed out the front window along with them, hoping to see a small black boy in large, broken glasses coming my way. But I never did. Finally I asked Shelly for help. She didn't have to come down, but couldn't she suggest something easy that I could do that would liven up the place, bring the pothole fillers in?

"Prosperity sandwiches," she said. "They're made from holiday leftovers and so just right for this time of year. Dad used to insist we have them at least once in between Christmas and New Year's."

So I bought a few turkey breasts and roasted them the evening before. I bought a honey-cured ham from one of the expensive outlets out in west county near Mom and Dad's, and rye and white and egg bread from a Lithuanian bakery in our section of the city. The only thing I needed exact directions for was the cheese sauce, which Shelly gave me, adding that a few threads of saffron would keep it from being so bland. A prosperity was a simple layering of turkey breast and ham on top of a slice of bread, the whole thing covered by a dipper or two of cheddar cheese sauce. I crisscrossed the tops of mine, per Shelly's suggestion, with green pepper and onion strips, then slid them in under the broiler until the cheese blistered and the bread was toasted. Shelly told me to print out a sign for the front window announcing the prosperity sandwiches, or else even the regulars would be going to McDonald's. I did and it worked. Even the two detectives whom I'd hidden Toby from came in, as did Sally Figg and her sister-in-law Shirley.

"As I passed by, I saw your sign," Sally said as they sat at the table beside the tree. "I haven't had a prosperity sandwich since I've been old enough to care about my figure. And congratulations on winning your case."

So for the last two days of that week, I was sort of busy, as much of a success as I could be without Shelly. I appreciated as always the regulars, but found myself pleased by the number of diners I did not know, had never seen. Shelly had rubbed off on me that much.

On New Year's Eve, as the millennium turned, the citizens of the world decided to celebrate as if the rapture or the computer failure that would disrupt the money and water and energy supplies would make another year moot anyway. And I made prosperity sandwiches for the three of us—Shelly, Mike, and me. For lack of anything better to do, or more precisely the desire to do any of the many things we could have done, we sat in front of the TV and watched the world carry on. By eight in the evening when he showed up, Mike was just barely able to maneuver across the alley to our place. He was earlier than I'd expected. I'd heard his playing the evening before and had gone over. In between "Away In a Manger" and "Do You Hear What I Hear," I'd invited him for New Year's Eve. He thanked me, then said he'd been in a two-day poker game. When I said I'd been trying to get him for more than a week, he shrugged, said the game may have been longer than he thought. I laughed. I knew it was possible that he had no idea where he'd been. And I was relieved to hear him playing again: a part of the neighborhood was missing without his recitals. In one technical sense he was my lover, and I could call him that without telling a lie. But in the real meaning of that word, he was not my lover and never would be. Though he was a man I loved, he'd lived too much of his life separate from me and too poorly to be able to love me, for me to be any abiding concern of his.

When he showed up at eight on New Year's Eve, he was angry, but about what we were not entirely sure. He said we all were assholes and may as well admit it. He included himself in that group, said *we*, meaning humans I guessed, had screwed up everything we had touched or dreamed of. Could we believe it, he asked. We even screwed up our own dreams! We were the very definition of assholes.

"Well," Shelly said. "Not the definition."

As my New Year's Eve party began, the three of us sat on the couch and watched footage of the century that had already turned in Europe. Every time one of us said something to the other—we knew better than to talk to Mike—he interrupted and told us what we were.

"I resent that," Shelly said once.

"You resemble it," he said. "You asshole."

I laughed at that, as if the evening could become more festive or at least more normal if we all believed what was happening was funny, what we were hearing was a joke. I worried I was turning into Shelly.

Soon we stopped talking and turned the TV up, so, though he continued to call us names, we couldn't hear him clearly. After what was truly a whole hour of that but seemed like many, he suddenly stopped. We looked at him and held our breaths. When his eyelids remained closed for five minutes and his facial muscles grew limp, we tiptoed out to the kitchen and ate our prosperities in peace. I expected Shelly to remind me whose fault it was he was there, but she did not seem in the mood.

"He is more than his disease," I said. "It's like one dot on the whole area that is him."

She nodded.

Even if he can't love me, I thought and was tempted to say, he wouldn't have chosen money over me, over us.

When we returned to the living room, we saw that he'd managed to throw his head back and down across the arm of the couch while the rest of him was still imitating a sitting person. He was not so much snoring as gurgling, and I worried that he could choke to death in his sleep. So I picked up his head and lined it up with the rest of his body. Immediately his snores became nasally, and, I thought, safer.

Though sitting there and watching TV with my depressed cousin and a drunken lover should have been a sad start on the millennium, I found myself a little impressed by the show mankind could put on. I disagreed with Mike. We were not assholes, at least not all the time. Sure there were lots of fireworks, and the Eiffel Tower and The Spanish Steps were lit up and other glitzy crap like that, but some groups danced and played games and read poetry and even prayed. And those who prayed did not do those "help me" kind of prayers, but rather prayed in thanksgiving and appreciation for what was and had been, prayed to a deity or deities who were not wishful fantasies but could be found in ourselves. Perhaps we had progressed in the few million years since Homo Erectus took his first unsteady steps, and I wondered what we were on our way to being. Maybe something.

By midnight when the St. Louis residents displayed their firepower and shot their assault rifles from their second floor windows into the night sky, Shelly and Mike were both snoring. And they both slept through the phone call that I, thinking it was Mom calling to wish me a happy millennium, did not answer. Not that I didn't want to talk to Mom, but I was peaceful between the two snorers, warm and lazy and close to drifting off myself. Instead of Mom's voice, though, I heard one I barely recognized say "Happy New Year, Bev. Maybe it will be." Even before she finished, I knew it was Angela Cheng, and I guessed she wanted more money. A problem that spanned millennia.

The second of January, 2000, was a Saturday, and Saturday was the day the *Post-Dispatch* printed a few restaurant reviews in a special dining-out section. Shelly usually read it carefully, even after the review by Skip Zitich that had made no difference to our business, but this Saturday, she was not interested. "What do you expect me to learn from that?" she asked as I set the restaurant section I had not read on her bed at 6:30AM before going down to start my biscuits. I'd been skipping the gravy since her vacation, and not because I couldn't do it as well. The truth was her gravy was often lumpy or gummy, and besides, I didn't like gravy even when done right. I preferred bacon and sunny-side-up eggs with my biscuits. And it was my café. I was just whisking my fork about in the bowl to mix the wet ingredients with the dry when I heard her scream. She was all the way upstairs, and I knew I'd closed the door above the back stairs. Nevertheless, I heard her scream. "Oh," she said. "Oh, My, God."

I dropped the bowl of flour and milk and stumped upstairs as fast as I could. She stood in the kitchen, waving a page of the *Post-Dispatch* above her head. "Here," she said. "Here, here, here."

I took the page from her and read the review, the follow-up visit to the Alibi Café, by Skip Zitich. In the first sentence, he claimed he always did follow-ups. Then he said he had been in for a very good Friday night, and so had decided to visit us on a normal weekday, see how we were with ordinary food. His judgment was that we were outstanding. He said we "turned the ordinary into the extraordinary." He said our prosperity sandwich, an off-menu item, was better than any he'd had, and he wondered if he'd detected just a hint of saffron in the sauce. "Even the presentation," he said, "consisting of blackened vegetables on top of the sandwich, was classy." He said the owner, Bev Burke, had worked all alone the day he was in, cooking and serving and cleaning, an even more amazing feat when one realized Ms. Burke had an artificial leg. He suggested that a visit to the Alibi Café for an after-Christmas prosperity sandwich become a yearly tradition for southsiders. He concluded by calling me *differently-abled* and *special* and then marveling at my working against such odds.

"Superb," Shelly said. "Don't you remember? He did not call my blue ribbon night *very good*, as he says here. What he wrote the first time was *superb.*"

SHELLY

Damn it, I said to myself each morning for two weeks. Shape up. Yes, Ted was a back-biting, lying, no-good son-of-a-bitch, and not nearly as good a dancer as he thought he was, but I already had this pain with Richard and had survived that. And Ted was not my husband, so I need never see or speak to him again, could consider him merely an annoyance, a cloud of gnats, dog poop on a sidewalk, a car commercial. I worked on it. Get up, damn it. Get busy. Be beautiful. The heart, I said to myself as I went back to the kitchen and the café, is a muscular pump. The brain is a tangle of neurons. Emotions may be in the frontal lobe, but wherever they are, this is my heart, my brain, my lobe. I will not be jerked about. Ted, I reminded myself, had been just some money-grubbing asshole, a snitchy little private investigator. Even in grade school, I'd known enough to avoid snitches.

But even if I had succeeded in getting over Ted, my loneliness would prove hard to get over, partly because others went missing by mid-February, and when I looked back to the way it all began,

I realized even before Ted showed his true colors, I missed Toby, too. He was the first to be absent, taken away back in December and not seen since. Then Ted, whom I worked at making easy to miss, or more precisely not to miss, and most days I managed to call him enough names to succeed. Well, I guessed I couldn't listen to "Brown Gravy Boogie" or a few such without tearing up a bit, but those tunes had not been my favorites before Ted, and were seldom heard away from Spurs 'n' Saddles anyway.

More inhabitants of our world would be missing as the new century crawled on.

But I went back to work.

In the nearly one year I'd been at the Alibi Café, I'd been of-fered deals on food—cabbages and tomatoes and peaches, squir-rel and deer and fish, mainly fish. A gas company worker who'd been in once or twice with Rollie offered me a whole cooler full of spoonies, fresh from the Mississippi, seventy-five pounds of cat for a mere forty dollars, and he'd throw in the cooler. Another guy, one I'd seen in the Alibi only once before, offered all the carp I wanted, also from the Mississippi. I declined both. I knew the "Father of Waters" was not clean enough to eat from, especially not fatty fish like those. I was offered better fish, too, like four largemouth bass, shiny and sweet smelling, and a dozen fair-sized trout. I bought the four bass, which made seven orders when I pan fried them with hush puppies, but I passed on the trout because their shiny sides didn't spring back when pressed, weren't as fresh as I wanted them. One of the twin husbands of the thrift shop women offered to get all the soft-shelled turtles I wanted. "Good, strong, and sweet meat," he said. "And turtles have no cholesterol." I turned him down, too, because I didn't know how to prepare turtle, not even what parts to eat.

But in January, the butcher Dad had recommended and whom I trusted had a deal on venison. A hunter in the neighborhood had sold it to him, and though deer season had been over for close to two months, the venison had been well and quickly frozen, so I bought it to use in my ragu. One of the secrets of a good ragu is a base of strong red meat. I had once bought rabbit from a hunter in the neighborhood and used it in my ragu, but it proved too mild, tasted like chicken.

The venison was fine. I sautéed it with thyme, garlic, a carrot, and a little beef chuck for balance, then ground it all up before simmering it with tomatoes for a few hours each day. Another secret of a good ragu is time. The flavors had to blend, so I ground the venison mix on a Wednesday for one of my blue ribbon Fridays. A cold one. One of a whole string of cold Fridays.

To keep their spirits up, our customers talked about the thaw, waited for what the local weather predictors told us came every year. As January became February, they talked more about the February thaw, and I liked the sound of that word, *thaw*, decided after hearing it daily that even if I didn't know its meaning, I would believe it denoted gentleness, a calm. "It would be a good first name," I said. "For a woman."

Rollie was in when I said it, and he laughed. "My name means glory combined with wolf. Combined how? It's really R-O-L-P-H. I'm named for an uncle, my mother's dead brother. The kid was only eight, but he died when he put on a jacket that had been hanging out above the wood pile, and so upset a black widow who'd been setting up housekeeping in the sleeve. He was just a skinny little kid and one bite did him in. Hadn't been for that spider, who knows what my name would be."

One of the thrift shop women said she knew the thaw would come by Valentine's day. It always had. It kept her sane. "I need light," she said. "I'd be whimpering like a kicked dog without my light board."

"She sits in front of it for two hours a day," the other one said. "Even then, she just shuffles and mopes about."

Ted no longer hung out in the café; Toby was hidden away somewhere and not allowed to come by; and Jeannie Lemp had declared she would never show her face in Bev's place again. But by February, many of those I thought of as regulars showed up even more often, looking as miserable as the weather. John the chiropractor was in three mornings a week for my biscuits and gravy, and at least two afternoons a week for lunch. Rollie seemed to be always there, as did the thrift shop women. Sally Figg came by for lunch during the week, too, often with her sister-in-law Shirley, and once on a Saturday with her niece, Peaches. And the city workers filling in the winter potholes had been spending lunch time with us since Bev's prosperity sandwiches. The regulars usually talked to Bev or me, or, naturally, to whoever was across the table from them—one thrift-shop woman to another, Sally to Shirley Figg. Or they dined in silence. But sometimes Rollie or John the chiropractor would say something, like about the thaw, and the rest would join in, keeping their seats and not always turning toward whoever spoke last, but answering in a voice clearly meant for the group. The day the thrift-shop woman, the thinner one, said the thaw would come before Valentine's Day, for example, John the chiropractor said he'd had jonquils half up by Valentine's Day the year before last, and Sally Figg said last year a number of her tulips had budded early enough to be killed, and one of the pothole fillers said he recalled a February when his forsythias bloomed twice, but a few others said that was nothing. Forsythias always bloomed and froze. It was their pattern. They were a stupid plant.

As I made my barbecue sauce and listened, nodding and smiling when appropriate, I was aware of time passing. I could see the shadows on the wall move, hear the air molecules tumble lazily about my ears, feel my cells die off. It wasn't that time moved fast, but rather without Ted or any desire to replace him, it moved at a slow crawl, slow enough to be noticed, seen. Gradually the minutes accumulated. I expected my acceptance from l'École de Cuisine Internationale in February, and as I waited for the mail, I used the mailman's appearance as a time marker.

I waited for my acceptance from l'École de Cuisine Internationale, even though Bev was the cook people talked about now, my blue ribbon nights having been downgraded by critic Zitich from superb to very good. Two other newspapers—one an entertainment rag and the other a weekly journal for South City—had written up both the Alibi Café and Bev. She had been asked to speak to a church youth group about overcoming her handicap, and an organization that tried to find employment for special needs workers called to ask if she would train a few, maybe hire some. The attention did make us busier, always a plus, but made Bev crabbier. She needed me, so I willingly took on the role of protector by telling those who wanted her as a spokesperson to drop dead, but in a nice way, much nicer than she would have.

Even with the downgraded review, or maybe because of it, I retained my interest in creating dishes capable of transporting people to places beyond their normal lives, yet occasionally asked myself what I would do with *le grand diplôme* once I had it. Perhaps I'd come back and cook for the Alibi Café as I told Bev I would. Well, I already knew how to do that without the eighteen months of study. Or maybe I'd open my own place, swankier and not in St. Louis, but I didn't need a degree to do that, either. Slowly I came to understand the truth: I was not looking for a job, not looking for a career. What I wanted was a path that would lead to a vista, a way to begin to follow something to somewhere. Sometimes I thought cooking school was that path, and sometimes cooking school seemed a clear waste of eighteen months. Such doubts, though rare, frightened me, made me question my resolve.

Still, my desire to create never wavered, would, in fact, flare up at unexpected moments, like when I saw the thrift-shop women in their Rams sweatshirts and imagined the lives they lived with their twin husbands, watching old TV comedies sent through cables to their homes at night, maybe a bio of a former child movie star or the current Prince of Wales instead. Or I pictured one hanging her face over a light board, her turtle-catching husband holding her stringy hair back at her neck. I would feel the void in their world as a mirror of the void in mine, and would once again yearn to uncover culinary secrets.

So as we plodded through the first part of the twenty-first century, I trained myself not to feel Ted's absence, or Toby's, and then there was Mike. All three were missing, but the word missing truly did apply to Mike, his disappearance another reason the season was lonely.

We'd seen him a few times in the first week of the year, sitting on his usual stool, looking and smelling as if the dumpster were his true home. And mostly he'd been sober. He was still planning on divinity school, said St. Paul started his preaching in mid-life, changed his direction and life suddenly for Jesus. "Course St. Paul said some hard words, wanted all those Ephesians and their like to behave. I won't tell my congregation anything except Jesus loves them. God is on their side like a powerful buddy, a patron," he said. "See, if people feel good, they act better naturally. That's my theory." And on at least two evenings that first week of the millennium, I heard his concert late, "Now Thank We All Our God" wafting across the alley after midnight. But for more than three weeks we'd heard nothing. No concerts. No Mike. No sign of him.

Bev finally reached the end of her patience, her limit of hope, and called the police. Fifteen minutes later, when she saw the patrol car in the alley behind his place, she said "Let's go. We have to tell what we know."

"About what?" I asked. "We know nothing. Besides, he's been gone before." Still, I went with her.

Bev told the police—a young man and a young woman—that Mike had talked about starting divinity school in January, and I said the same, but neither of us had understood clearly what school, or if he'd even narrowed it down. The real ones in town, we were sure, would not have him, nor could he have afforded, we guessed, so much as a three hour course. The name he'd given most often was Circle of Life, but he'd also mentioned one called Covenant. Bev thought those were the same place. Anyway, Mike had not told us where it was or, my big question, why in the world they would take him. Bev was certain it was a correspondence school, and would have nothing to do with his absence, anyway. "I don't know why I brought it up," she said. Her breath, all of our breaths, came out in puffs of vapor.

"You two aren't sure of much," the policeman said, too obvious a statement for either of us to comment on. Each of them banged hard with their sticks on the front and back doors with no response. We'd gone more than two weeks before without seeing him, but this was the longest, and Bev said she had a bad feeling about this disappearance. I thought being without Toby or without the distractions of her trial may have made her worry about Mike more, and I was sure this coming and going had been a pattern of Mike's long before we knew him. There could've been dozens of people in various parts of the country who stopped their work, maybe turned toward one another at the sight or sound of an organ, and said, "Remember Mike? What ever happened to him?" On the other hand, it was horribly cold. The cold that had arrived before Christmas hadn't lifted. As Rollie said, we may as well have been living in North Dakota for all the relief we'd been granted. That was why the fabled February thaw was so antici-pated. "Check the Salvation Army," I said, knowing people went there for warmth.

"Sure thing," the policewoman said, writing it down in her small spiral notebook.

But I knew as soon as I said it the Salvation Army was a useless lead. Mike already had a warm place.

Later that evening, the police got the property management company that represented Mike's Texas landlord to give them the key to Mike's place. No luck at the Salvation Army, they said, though some down there knew Mike. We were on hand when the police went up to Mike's place, but were told to wait outside until they checked it out. After a while, they called down and said we could look, too.

"There's little to go on up here," the policewoman said.

Little was right. Mike's apartment, as Toby had said after spend-ing Thanksgiving there, was nearly empty. A full-sized mattress, six polyester-filled pillows with no covers, a narrow refrigerator with no freezer compartment, the box the refrigerator must have come in covered by a sheet and with a set of salt and pepper shak-ers shaped like dogs in its center, a radio, a CD player, 3 CDs of gospel music, and two aluminum and plastic tubing fold-up lawn chairs: that was it. A rope clothesline stretched from the top hinge on the kitchen pantry door through the kitchen and into the liv-ing room to a curtain rod above one of the front windows. A pair of black jeans and two pairs of briefs were hanging on it. The win-dow shades or blinds had probably come with the place, as had, we guessed, the gas stove. There was a brown furry rug covering most of the bedroom floor. A few extra pairs of jeans and some T-shirts were stacked in two corners in the bedroom, and a navy blue nylon jacket with plaid flannel lining was hanging on the closet doorknob. The closet was empty. Most of a loaf of Bunny bread and an unopened jar of horseradish sauce were in the refrigerator. A three-year-old *Road and Track* and a fairly recent *London Guardian* were in the bathroom, and a well-thumbed copy of *Notes From The Underground* was beside his mattress. His pantry contained only cleansers and sponges. Two of our café plates sat in the plastic dish drainer beside his sink. He had no lamps, but all three large rooms had overhead fixtures.

His place did not look like one someone had left on purpose, but it was possible he had better stuff, had left the junk behind. Still, if he had better stuff, we'd never seen it. We all had the feeling this was it, his life defined by these possessions. He hadn't cancelled his lease the property manager said, and he hadn't told us goodbye. "Well, he is impulsive," Bev said to me, but as a comfort to herself. And I added that little he had ever done was deliberate. She picked up on that. "Yes. With Mike, one way leads to another, then another and another."

We convinced the police to break into the garage—the property manager had not given them the key for it—knowing the organ would be the biggest clue. Sure enough, it was there, sitting sad and still. "No," I said. "He didn't leave on purpose." But none of us knew if that was a good or bad thing. In less than a year, Bev and I had been involved with the St. Louis police force three times—this and Toby's hiding out and our break-in—and we'd had different policemen or women each time. If there'd been a regular one or two assigned to our neighborhood, we'd have almost been friends already. They may at least have become customers. These two fresh ones were such kids they made me miss the detectives we'd lied to about Toby. They said they would turn in a missing person's report, though they had only our description of Mike to go on. "Photos," the woman said, "are always better."

Her partner rolled his eyes. "Better for what?" he asked her. "We mainly locate these kinds when they turn up dead, usually so long dead they're unrecognizable."

They dusted Mike's garage and his flat for fingerprints, and I asked what good that would do. It wouldn't tell us where he was, and not even who he was unless his prints were already on file.

"We already know who he is," Bev said.

"Maybe there will be a second set," the woman said. "Foul play."

"Or only one set," the man said. "But that may tell us more about the one you call Mike."

"All angles," the woman said. "We cover all angles." She looked like a high school cheerleader, and her voice was so high pitched and perky I could not imagine her saying "Stop or I'll shoot" or other cop lines and getting any response.

So here we were in the first week of February, all of us waiting for the thaw and growing lonelier. Toby, Ted, Mike: all gone. It was possible, just barely, that Mike would come back, that "Jesus Wants Me For a Sunbeam" would fill the neighborhood. It was also, we both believed, likely that Toby would be back sitting on his stool, maybe calling Bev Mom. Ted, though, was gone forever. He had left three messages on our machine upstairs, and a few down in the café as well. He had sent me two more letters I'd torn up before reading. I knew he knew where to find me. I knew he was a coward as well as a traitor.

"What happened to the bum?" Rollie asked once, and for a moment I thought he meant Ted.

"I don't know who you mean," Bev answered.

"Sure you do," he said. "Used to be propped up here, looking nearly dead."

"Doesn't ring a bell," Bev said.

The needles Dr. Aiee set spinning in my ear wells each week still caused *dequi*, but otherwise stopped working in late January, and my headaches came thumping angrily back without the double vision, but with a new corollary, dry mouth. Dr. Aiee said my *chi*, my life force, had turned stubborn. I had a clog he couldn't move with stimulation. He was stumped, so I called Doc Newburg and said I was ready to surrender to her allergy theory, but still couldn't do the whole eight week test. I said I didn't have the will for anything that prolonged. Besides, I reminded her, knowing that even the doctors with the best bedside manners forgot you as soon as your twenty minutes were up, I was a gourmet cook, tasted all my creations. I asked for a shortcut, a hint.

"No such thing," she said. "But you sound tense. Maybe it's psychological after all. Are you *wuwied*?"

"Worried you're not going to tell me much over the phone." I wondered why doctors hadn't progressed in their business practices to the level of lawyers, didn't charge for minutes of phone time. They only got paid when you came in.

"I'm *twansfuwing* you to Janet. Come in as soon as she has an opening."

"My life force won't flow," I said, but I was already on hold, so I hung up.

Though my blue ribbon nights had not earned the respect, attention, and acclaim I had hoped for, I continued to come up with crowd pleasers. Besides my venison ragu, I did a scallops au gratin with root vegetable fettuccine, a roast pork loin with pumpkin seed sauce served with garlic mashed potatoes and roasted eggplant, and stuffed chicken thighs with honey and dried fruit served with sweet rice and braised lentils. My customers were happy; therefore, I told myself, I was a success. Cooking was a service, not what you did for glory.

I told that to the writer from the Everyday Section of the *Post-Dispatch* who came by with a photographer to do a write-up about us, mainly about Bev and how she'd surmounted her disabilities. During the interview, Aunt Josie gave him a few good lines he clearly did not know what to do with. He asked if even as a child Bev had seemed determined to do what normal children did, determined to overcome her differences. He sat with Uncle Al and Aunt Josie and Bev and me at the table in front of the window one Tuesday evening after we'd closed. I'd wiped up with a new spray cleaner scented with lemon, and I decided the smell was too strong, a clean smell but not taste-tempting like garlic and grease. The writer wanted background for the photos already taken—a close-up of Bev's hands as she made change, and one of her carrying plates to John the chiropractor and his date at the deuce in the far corner. *Differences* was the word he used, hesitating before he said it, clearly not wanting to say handicapped or disabled or deformed.

"What differences?" Aunt Josie asked. She was wearing a cream-colored cashmere cowl-necked sweater over a short red wool skirt and knee high black boots with two-inch heels. Her hair was the color of honey and it curled in around her face, softening all angles.

"Well," the writer said. "She has an artificial leg, not many fingers."

"Both her legs work just fine," Aunt Josie said. "How is artificial relevant?"

"And I haven't much of a chin, either," Bev volunteered, then laughed.

"The leg is what you mean by differences? The fingers?" Aunt Josie asked, looking to Uncle Al for help, so convincing even I could almost believe in her confusion.

"If you want to call those differences," Uncle Al said, coming to his wife's rescue, "I guess she did like all of us do. She made do. She did fine. She always had what she needed."

"But her leg is missing," the writer said.

"Was," Aunt Josie said. "You can buy a leg. She's bought many by now. She knows how to use them, and that looks hard to me. I guess that's what you mean."

"He means," Bev said, "did you always know I was special? He wants you to say yes."

"She makes the best pies, don't you think?" Uncle Al asked the writer. "Have you tasted her lemon meringue?"

"You can buy chins, too," I said then to make Bev laugh, which she did. The writer shifted uncomfortably in his seat, ready to look shocked at my crassness if Bev did.

His photographer had taken a few shots of me, too. In my favorite one, I had been stirring my barbecue sauce, wearing the dark indigo stretch jeans I'd bought for line dancing and a maroon long-sleeved T-shirt. My hair was tied up in a sort of loose ponytail with a matching maroon ribbon. The photographer asked me if I'd ever modeled, and rather than tell him about my time at Sue Spritz, I pretended to be flattered, turned aside, and blushed. Like Aunt Peg, I could blush voluntarily.

Three days later, the article ran with three pictures—two of Bev and one of me—and the next day, Saturday, we were full. For the first time, all our tables and chairs were taken. Many of the new customers were more of the people who wanted Bev to speak or endorse or support, who wanted to use her in studies. She was disgusted by the attention, she said, and hid upstairs all day that Saturday, letting me work alone, so I was sweaty and nearly out of breath before noon. She hid out for most of the following week, too. "Say I'm dead. Say I'm insane. Say it's all a hoax, done with mirrors. Say I've grown a leg. Tell them to find a paraplegic and leave me alone."

Of course I did not tell them any of that. I said merely that she was unavailable.

By Thursday of that week, the clamor for her had died down considerably—one representative from the March of Dimes and one phone call from a graduate student at Saint Louis University who wanted to use Bev in a study of stamina—and also on that day, Thursday, the thirteenth of February, we finally got interesting mail, three good pieces and two bad. The first good piece was a letter to Bev from Toby. The envelope was addressed to Miss Bev at the Alibi Café, and the salutation was "Dear Miss Bev."

> I am writing this letter to practise. My tutor said I should write to three friends. I wrote to Peeches and to Lana and now to you. My tutors name is Herman. He is nice and not because he is paid to be. He says there is not that much money. Big joke. He plays on a softball team and promised to take me to his games when they start in a few months. Where I am is okay. Don't worry about me. I know I have caused some trouble for you, and I am sorry. I miss the pie you gave me. Yum, yum.
>> By for now,
>> Toby Cheng

Bev read it out loud to me twice, and to herself probably hundreds of times. After carrying it around in her pocket for two days, she eventually taped it to our bathroom mirror. It was written on white paper lined in red and in true palmer method cursive, rounded loops and all lower case letters reaching just to an imaginary line half as high as the upper case letters. If Bev was upset at being in third place after Lana, she did not mention it. Of course, the envelope had no return address.

One of the other pieces of good news was from the Missouri Department of Family Services. The hearing on Bev's official petition to adopt was scheduled for February 28, one o'clock. She was advised to bring her lawyer and, if she chose, a friend or family member who would vouch for her character and ability, the seriousness of her request. Copies of the letter had been sent to Howard Figg and to Toby's case worker, Jeannie Lemp. Bev was nervous, she said, knowing that Jeannie Lemp had heard all that negative stuff Ted spewed out at the trial, but she was also eager. "They're still considering my request, allowing me to make a formal petition. It means they were not irreparably distressed by what they heard from your boyfriend." And she said she was pleased to be getting it over with, one way or the other. "Toby is in desperate need of guidance. Way beyond in fact. He may be too old. We can't waste more time."

"Toby needs love, too," I said, wounded by the "your boyfriend" crack.

She gave me a Bev sneer, lip tented all the way up to her nose. "Oh yes. Love. I must remember how valuable that is. His mother probably said she loved him the day he was born. Probably says it now as she cries in her beer. No doubt Lana loved him. Whoever he's with now loves him."

"All the more reason," I said, "for you to say it, too. At the hearing, I mean. You do love him. And no matter how overused the word is, you have to say it often, have to start thinking it now. Let yourself get a little soppy and soft for the next few weeks."

One of the pieces of mail I put in the bad category wasn't really bad but more annoying like junk mail. It was another from Ted, and I tore it up. "Poor Ted," I said to Bev. "He so wants to be forgiven for being an asshole. He just can't live with himself. Boo hoo hoo."

"I never liked him," Bev said. "You should trust my intuition sometime."

The next letter was one I'd been anxious about from the moment I'd read the return address, l'École de Cuisine Internationale. Though I'd convinced myself of the certainty of my acceptance and had nearly fallen for my own positive line—not *if* but *when*— now that the response was in my hand, that hand was shaking. The decision had been made, irrevocably. L'École de Cuisine Internationale seemed my destiny, and I believed my entire future was at stake. I forced myself to understand it was not my whole future, and I would never know my destiny anyway. I took a deep breath, bracing myself for failure by reminding myself that getting turned down would make me work harder, and I could only be knocked down if I let myself be. I added some other positive pep talk even I knew was crap, and then I opened the letter and read of my acceptance and more. I was among a select few approved for six months of study in Paris as part of the eighteen-month program. The Paris part would be at the end, and classes were forming in Montreal in April and in May. My acceptance was good for either start date. I showed the letter to Bev, and she did reach out and hug me, tell me congratulations, but her voice was flat and her hug lacked pressure. I blamed it on her mind being on the upcoming hearing.

It was close to seven o'clock on a cold February evening, twelve degrees Fahrenheit. We had not had the thaw we expected and deserved. The moon was almost visible above the rooftops, and when it would be, we would see it as only a sliver. A lonely time in a sad season. Yet I had received good news; we both had, and I thought we should celebrate. I suggested Marcel's, an expensive French restaurant. It was downtown, so wouldn't be busy on a Thursday evening, and it'd be fun to dress up. I laughed at my wanting to dress up, made it a joke, and explained that Ted's idea of a night out had usually involved jeans and a cowboy hat. "Our lives are changing. On the verge of a change. You will get Toby. I'll go to France."

"Toby's future is undecided," she said. "Besides, Mike's missing. It's cold, and I don't look good dressed up."

"But," I said, restating my case. "Certain moments in life need marking, memorializing. And these two letters on the same day, not to mention Toby's cute letter, point us toward our futures. But mainly, I want to go out. I'm not ashamed to want to dress up and have fun."

"Take your mother. I hate going to restaurants, not when we have to be back at work in ours at 6:30 tomorrow morning."

Who screened all those calls from people and groups wanting to use your missing leg? I could have asked that. Who worked all alone during our busiest days, busy because of you and your missing leg and fingers, while you hid out, offended that what you did not have was more interesting than what you did? Instead of asking either of those, I did what we'd always done, did as I'd been taught. I agreed with her that it was silly to go out to a restaurant when we had to get up for ours in the morning, and she was right about dressing up being a silly idea of mine, and it was not truly good news about Toby, not yet.

There was one more piece of mail, though, and we almost pitched it. It came from the City of St. Louis, and we both assumed it was either a notice about recycling or a legislative summary provided by our alderman, a list of how much good he'd done by sponsoring legislation that would make it illegal to put political signs in our yards, or legislation that increased the penalty for planting bushes close to sidewalks. We'd had such from him before, and never once had he addressed the gunshots we often heard, day and night, or the many broken car windows. The last announcement we'd had from him told of the new centralized police station, a "super station" he called it, further from the people but with more technology. Catching criminals clearly was more important to the city than stopping crime.

This letter, though, was not what we expected. It came from the city inspector who told Bev she had one month to have the tiles replaced on the façade of her building. Failure to replace the tiles would result in a $200 fine, added to whatever the city would charge her to send a crew over to beautify the façade for her. She said she was outraged, and it was not about the money. True, she said, the tiles were missing, others were cracked. Had been when she bought the place.

"So what?" she said. "I had to install bars and alarms. My car window's been smashed. The place next to the pawn shop across Meramec has had its windows boarded up since before I got here. The gas company's been digging the same street for nearly a year. Cones and barricades and torn-up sidewalks are part of the landscape. And then the city comes along and fills the holes in so they can be dug again. But my tiles are a blight!"

They were, we both knew. The broken and missing tiles were ugly. Still the tone of the inspector's letter was ugly, too: unfair, big-brotherish, and challenging. The citation squashed any hope that Bev would reconsider dinner out, but I wanted to go then, more than ever. Nonsensical and unfair demands were like insults and sorrow. They needed antidotes, and the sooner the better. I would never give a city inspector the power to keep me from going out and having fun. Besides, I was going to Paris, and even Montreal where I would go first was something, was better than here, and I wanted my excitement acknowledged and my efforts rewarded. The letter made the Paris part especially sound like a coup. Shouldn't someone say *Good job*, and mean it? Well, I had friends other than Bev, but the café being as demanding as it was, and Ted having taken up so much of my free time, there were none I'd seen in a while, and none so unattached they could go to dinner with me at a moment's notice, so I called Aunt Peg. Would she go if I picked her up, I asked, and only after she said yes did I call Mom, even then hoping to get her answering machine.

"Oh," Mom said when I asked. "If you really want me, I guess I could go. I was really looking forward to a hot bath and an early evening."

I never could figure out what made her so tired. She did little with her days. "You should stay home then," I said. "We'll go out some other time."

"Nonsense. When my daughter calls, I must respond. I'll do it."

So we went.

I wore an ivy-green, jewel-necked, silk shirt over black velvet slacks. Mom was in a purplish gabardine suit with a silver-gray shell underneath, and Aunt Peg wore a gold lamé top, sleeveless and with a draped neckline, over a white wool, short skirt. As he seated us, the waiter told me how lovely the color green was on me, pointed out that it matched the centerpieces—green weedy stalks in a round glass. He had a large face with balloon cheeks and jowls, a muddy complexion. Mom touched his hand when he set her first martini down and said she hoped the drink would not make her silly. The way she giggled, I was afraid she was going to ask him to guess her age, force him to say we all looked like sisters. Luckily he escaped before she could engage him in conversation.

I waited until our stuffed portabella appetizers and the champagne I'd ordered arrived, before I gave them my news about l'École de Cuisine Internationale. They both said "how nice," and "good for you" in genteel lady ways. They were not a bit interested. They wanted instead to talk about Ted, and even before we ordered our entrees, both tried to help me get over him. Neither knew about his backstabbing, and it was clear they assumed he had dumped me. They were afraid I'd sink down as far as I had when Richard left. "You don't sleep with your lights on, do you?" Mom asked.

The truth was, I did, but had done so every night I spent alone ever since our break-in, even before Ted. Only on nights when Ted had stayed over, had I let it go dark. So his absence had increased my use of my lamp. Mom was right, but I said, "Of course not."

Aunt Peg was concerned about my headaches. Were they getting worse, she wanted to know. Because if they were, I should know another man would come along soon. Well, she was right, too. My head was pounding even as she spoke, but I refused to admit a connection. "My head is better," I said.

"Life is a cycle," Aunt Peg said. "Up and down, up and down. When you are down, you will go up."

I nodded. Of course, I did not subscribe to that cycle model of life at all.

"And who needs a man anyway?" Mom asked. "My days are full enough without one."

Doing what, I almost asked. Writing letters?

But my celebration had been taken away. Just like that, they were pitying me about Ted, so as soon as I could, I brought the subject back to l'École de Cuisine Internationale. No one had yet been excited about my news. "I'm going in April. I'll go to Paris for the last six months of my program."

"Chickie's going to somewhere in the South of France in a few weeks," Aunt Peg said. "To film that Bond movie. I'll see if she'll go up to Paris and look around while she's there, tell you what to expect."

"We all know what Paris is like," Mom said. "We've seen pictures, movies. I don't think Chickie's scouting about will give us much more."

"But she is so good at finding the best places, bistros and shops and clubs. She has a knack."

I should've called Dad, I decided, though I knew even he wouldn't have been happy for me, would've wondered out loud at my selfishness, so clearly demonstrated by my ability to get over not just Richard but also Ted this fast. "Must be nice not to care so deeply," he'd say, and I could almost see the furrows in his forehead as he said it. So I changed the subject again, despairing of getting it back to me and my acceptance, and told instead about Bev's citation from the city. It turned out they knew the inspector, Hruzcka. "Hungarian," Mom said. "He and your father used to bowl together."

"They owned the Golden Eagle," Aunt Peg said. "His family, I mean. Way back. Ralph's parents used to eat there. A nice little bohemian café. Wasn't it on Chippewa?"

"Yes," Mom said. "A neighborhood place." She laughed. "He told Jack they called it the Golden Eagle because his grandfather, an immigrant, knew those two words were popular in America. His grandmother wanted to call it Happy Eagle or Lucky Eagle. But they were all surprised to learn there really was a bird called the Golden Eagle." She shook her head. "And the food was terrible, Peg. Remember when Ralph took us all there and we had meat so tough, once we got it in our mouths it was like chewing gum?"

Aunt Peg giggled, and Mom did, too, and they each ordered another martini even before our main course arrived. Our waiter winked at me when he brought their second round. "We should visit Clem," Mom said. She turned to me. "That's his first name.

Clem Hruzcka."

"Let's," Aunt Peg said. "He used to have a crush on me."

"On me, too," Mom said. "Who didn't?"

"Next Wednesday," Aunt Peg said. "We'll pay the inspector a visit." She laughed louder. "I say Wednesday because it's the day you are most likely to find a city worker in. Ralph used to say that."

"Wear your crown," Mom said, and they both giggled more. But eventually, as giggles do, theirs died down, and they both began giving me looks of pity. I knew they would soon be back on Ted's dumping of me, so I brought up another new topic and told them about Bev's hearing. It worked. They talked then about her desire to adopt, tsking and clucking in confusion. They knew she was making a mistake. They guessed her worry over the petition was why she had not joined us for dinner. Mom thought maybe she was already having second thoughts, and Aunt Peg said now would be a good time for second thoughts. "He's already a mess," Aunt Peg said.

"All kids are," Mom said. "Name me one who isn't."

Aunt Peg sighed. "Even Chuck's are video game fanatics. Those things warp your mind."

I ate my veal Oscar—the crab meat so strong it almost overwhelmed the sweetness of the veal—and imagined how they'd react if they knew about Mike, not his disappearance but his place in Bev's life. They'd both seen him sitting at the counter, had no doubt sniffed delicately and then dismissed him as part of the neighborhood, a piece of local color. The property manager said he had rented his place two years ago. After the fingerprint check—only one set found in the flat or on the organ—the police had given us the news immediately. He was already on file. His name was Walter Michael Von Reid, not Mike Gibson. They said he'd used Gibson before. Bev told me she wasn't surprised at that news, but it disturbed her by being yet one more indication of how little we knew about one another, how gullible we were, how easily we created ourselves. "It's just a name," I said. "If he were trying to create himself as you put it, wouldn't he have done a better job, made of himself something more than an alley rat and derelict organist?"

The three of us split an order of bread pudding with hard sauce, though the waiter told us we needn't worry about our figures and should splurge on dessert. As we passed the dish around, taking bites, Aunt Peg said the next title on the way to the Senior Ms. America was Senior Ms. Missouri. The competition would be March 20th in Jefferson City, and she wanted to change her talent portion, and also wear a more pastel-colored gown in honor of the equinox. Mom agreed about the gown, and though we did not set a date, we all promised to go shopping together soon. I said I thought Peg's talent was perfect and advised against changing it. She argued, saying some of the judges would be the same and she did not want to repeat herself. Besides, she wanted more emotion in her talent, real emotion and not melodrama. She wanted to accompany herself on a deep and true love song, and was thinking of "Fly Me to the Moon." Mom groaned, but we ended up agreeing to consider it. Peg had the final decision, we said, and we would try to keep an open mind.

Our waiter's name was Georges, and before we left, he said next time we came in we should ask for him. We all smiled, and Mom touched his arm again. When we paid him, I asked if he knew where Marcel's bought its butter molds that turned out fleurs-de-lis. I already had rose-shaped molds for my blue ribbon nights, but fleurs-de-lis were such an appropriate touch now that I was on my way to Paris. Georges let the corners of his mouth sag down as if he felt great sorrow and admitted he did not know.

Mom and I dropped Aunt Peg off in Illinois, but came to a standstill on the bridge almost all the way back into Missouri. A truck carrying pigs had overturned on a curve at the base of the Poplar Street Bridge, and the police and highway workers were chasing pigs about, while others were working to raise the trailer up ahead. No one was seriously injured. That was the report we were given by the woman in front of us who had been told by someone else up ahead. Doing her part, Mom got out of my car and passed the information on to the driver behind us who asked if she wanted to get in the car with him. "No, honey," she said. "Just close your eyes and relax. It'll be a while."

Sitting there for nearly an hour forced me and Mom to talk, and was how she ended up telling me about Uncle Ralph, whom I barely remembered, and Aunt Peg. "They used to hug and kiss at the dinner table when we were all at Mom's on Sundays," she said. "He seldom took his eyes off her, no matter what else was going on. His big, green eyes would follow her every move. Even when he was talking to one of us, he looked at her. It was love, yes, but a little creepy, too." Then she took a breath and blew it out noisily. "And I was jealous. Well, of course I was jealous!" She paused for a second or two, then plunged ahead. "I shouldn't tell you this, but Ralph was mine first. Peg took him from me. She didn't mean to, of course. He just couldn't look at anyone else once he saw her. Dad was sorry for me, but Mom was practical, fair but strict. She said no one could control love, but she insisted they wait to get married until I found someone else and was at least engaged. You know, to make it easier on me."

I looked at her, the headlights of eastbound cars hitting her face, and even though she sounded sincere, I thought of her letters and her ability with lies. I did not want to suspect her, and her story did explain a lot, but she was Mom, a woman not given to self-revelations, a woman who would lie for a half-off coupon on a loaf of bread.

"You can imagine the pressure that put on me. I found Jack as fast as I could, but still feel guilty about having loved Ralph better. Always."

I had no response except the obvious.

"That's sad," I told her. By the time we started moving, I knew that was my only response. "It's sad for all of us."

"It was better for Ralph," Mom said. "Peg was fun. I never could enjoy life like she could, still can't."

"Does Dad know?" I asked after I stopped in front of the building containing their separate flats. His windows upstairs glowed.

"How would I know what he knows?" she said. "I don't think

about him and what goes on in his mind as much as he thinks I do. He's a very strange man, you know."

Two days later, Saturday, Sally Figg was in with her sister-in-law, Shirley, telling all of us about Howard's father, her grandfather. She'd mentioned him before. He was a frustrated inventor. "He came up with an idea for inflatable shoes," she said. "He drew the shoe, had it figured out. The soles were old inner tubes, cut into foot shape and glued on to the uppers."

Shirley chimed in. "He did a lot with old inner tubes. One of his favorite materials."

Sally clicked her tongue. "Well, there was a lot of it around. A good inventor uses what he has. Anyway, he had the idea that a bicycle pump could be used to inflate the shoes to the desired pressure, different pressure for different kinds of walking."

"Why were old inner tubes around?" Rollie asked. "Did he live in a dump?"

We all laughed, not so much at Rollie's joke, but because sunlight filled the front window. The thaw had arrived the day before and was predicted to last at least a week; sixty-four degrees was the high and that came with a wind from the southwest that smelled like warm dirt. I'd made a springtime lamb stew for the blue ribbon dinner the night before, and had sold so much we had only a pint left over.

"This was way before those Nike pump things," Sally said.

"What happened?" one of the city pothole fillers asked.

Sally and Shirley both shrugged. "He had ideas," Sally said. "But they just never went anywhere. Didn't know the next step, I guess."

We all laughed again. "Poor old guy," someone said.

"It made him crabby all his life," Sally said. "Miserable to be around."

We all laughed at that, too. I was still laughing when I answered the phone beside the cash register. "It's Peg," Mom said as soon as I said "Alibi Café."

"She's dead."

When I hung up, I gave the news as if it were a normal sentence, not one I'd have reason to say only once or, even better, not ever in my whole life. "Aunt Peg died," I told Bev. Another one gone missing in the new millennium.

Just then a fat man in a chef's hat and white smock entered the café and immediately started singing. "Hey good lookin', what you got cookin'?" His voice was high pitched, almost falsetto. Horrible. He clowned up his act, shaking his belly and bouncing about, skipping between the tables, and ended up kneeling on the floor and looking up at me from the other side of the counter, almost under a stool. "You have received a message of love from Ted Younger," he said, panting heavily, hand over his heart. "Ted hopes you will forgive him." His bloated red face, wet with sweat, looked like some kind of internal organ.

I turned back to Bev, put my arm around her. "She died in Lord & Taylor, fell face first into a rack of gowns. The clerk knew CPR but couldn't revive her. The paramedics couldn't either."

Rollie walked over to the still-kneeling, fat chef and grabbed one of his elbows, used it as a handle to lift him up, then turn him around. He stuffed a dollar in the fat chef's smock pocket, then pushed him toward the door. "OK, Bub. That was real cute. Ha ha. Now go home."

"What about an answer?" the fat chef asked at the door. "Is he forgiven?"

"And forgotten," I called.

Bev was not yet crying, nor was I. "Mom said she went fast," I told her. "Standing up one minute, fingering a lavender chiffon."

"We better close up," Bev said. "I'm sure we should be somewhere."

"Standing up one minute," Mom had said. "Then BAM. Down. Gone."

"The Senior Ms. St. Louis Metropolitan Area?" Sally Figg asked. "That was her, wasn't it?"

"Chuck's, I guess," Bev said. "We'll go to Chuck's and take lots of sandwiches."

"She died happy," Mom had said. "Surrounded by designer dresses. It's a blessing to die happy."

BEV

Shelly said loneliness was rising, more of us were going, were gone. She went through the list, hers beginning way back with Richard and ending with Aunt Peg. I thought mine would go back several more years to Grandpa, but knew she was right about the increase. Four who were part of our lives for most of a year were gone. Aunt Peg for good, forever. As in all families, some bonds were tighter than others, and I had two different kinds of aunts. One was Dad's sister I saw once every year or two. She lived in Arizona with her husband and had four children and three grand-children who lived nearby. I had never seen the grandchildren and could barely remember when I'd last seen those cousins, but I liked that aunt who had a cackling sort of laugh, raised ostriches, and had worn baggy, shapeless dresses that displayed lots of her splotchy bare legs last time she was in town. Aunt Peg, though, was a shadow of Mom, one of the Stillwell girls. She was one of Mom's other sides, nearly an appendage. Marie-Josie-Peg could have been one entity with a four pronged growth—Shelly-Bev-

Chickie-Chuck. And no, I did not miss Aunt Peg when she died, not even by the time of her wake or funeral, but the knowledge of how I would miss her, how empty Mom would seem with only half her shadow, was the source of my sorrow.

Also, fifty-eight was too young. Aunt Peg would have been Senior Ms. America, a title I admit I'd thought silly, but one she would have carried with style and humor. She would never get to see Chickie's James Bond movie, come to know whomever Chuck's boys dated, or see her first great grandchild who I predicted would be Hilton's love child, the first of many. As I used to tell my students, unfair was a 100 percent meaningless word, but then Aunt Peg's heart giving out suddenly and completely was meaningless, too. She had never smoked. She did not use drugs and starve herself as many beauty queens did, and she seldom had eaten fat. She had exercised and had seemed as stress free as a conscious person could be. But her heart stopped anyway. And yes, things do. All is finite. There will always be an end. Knowing that was no comfort. Each end is unique; each death creates its own sorrow.

At the wake and funeral and in the days leading up to both, all of us Stillwells, even if we were Burkes and Owenses and Sturgises, and (in Shelly's case) Belchers, cried when we comforted one another, contemplating without saying it out loud the future without Aunt Peg, but we didn't weep or sob uncontrollably, shout our distress to a God who had done this. As Grandpa would have said, did say when his own mother died, it was because we were mostly English, too much so to be good criers. We needed a drop or two more Irish blood to keen properly.

Shelly took over the funeral food, saying something about all of us contributing according to our talents and abilities.

"Don't make anything too spicy," I said. "Some of Aunt Peg's friends are lots older than she was." I meant those old dowagers she had served with on the symphony board and the Cahokia Mounds Society. Many of those women were well into their seventh decades, a few their eighth, had held their offices for twenty or more years. Aunt Peg had held no office in either group. She had joined both organizations, she often said, for the chance to wear designer clothes and prance about for a cause and not solely for vanity. Both groups sponsored balls and parties, and most of the women wore pearls and Jones of New York ensembles even for the meetings.

The wake was a Tuesday from two to nine at a colonial-themed mortuary near her home. The mortuary director had been Aunt Peg's escort for a few of the symphony balls, and he kept dabbing at his eyes as he talked to us all—Shelly and I had gone with Chickie and Chuck as they selected the casket and provided the newspaper obit information. Watching his eyes well up, I decided his was a real sadness, not just the damp dabbing he may have done for all clients. He said he had been in the audience for the Senior Ms. St. Louis Metropolitan Area pageant, and he believed she should be buried with her crown.

"It really messes up her hair," Chickie said. "We can place it on a table beside the casket, but she can't wear it."

He shrugged. The family was always right. Later that evening, I went with Chickie when she took the dress and jewelry she'd decided her mother would wear, and at the sight of the thin gold chain with a sapphire heart dangling from it, a gift from Ralph for one of their early anniversaries, the mortuary director's eyes watered again. "Yes. That is just so her," he said.

"She wore it more than any other piece." Chickie had chosen a white wool coat-dress with gold buttons and elbow-length sleeves. She'd added a white and gold scarf for the neckline, to be arranged under the necklace.

"Mom's neck is not bad," she said. "But I don't think she'd like people just standing above and staring down at it, seeing it from such an angle. And I chose the coat-dress because it should be easier to get on her."

"You shouldn't have worried about that," the mortuary director said. "We can get anything on. Absolutely anything."

Chickie then gave him a packet of press-on nails, two inches long and gold to match the buttons on her dress.

"A cinch," he said.

Chickie laughed sharply. "Well, I didn't think they would pose a problem."

The wake was well attended. Grade school and high school friends of the Stillwell sisters, some former classmates of mine—

Chickie and I had been in the same grade—and a few of Chuck's grade school friends I hadn't seen for years showed up. Of course, Ralph's siblings and in-laws and cousins and parents were there, as were the committee women, Aunt Peg's neighbors, Chuck's coworkers, most of our café regulars who'd been at the pageant, five of the other contestants, including the runner-up who was now scheduled to compete for the title of Senior Ms. Missouri. Chickie's Hollywood agent sent a floral piece made of sunflowers and twigs with a card that read "Sharing your grief." Another floral arrangement like the first but larger was also for Chickie and read "Because I cannot be there with you. Love, Carruthers Falls."

"Sounds like a small town," Mom said, but Chickie sighed at our provincialism.

Carruthers, she explained, was a former Hollywood hairdresser and now an independent producer, and Chickie's latest lover. "He may be a keeper," she said, and even in her grief, closed her eyes and smiled.

Perhaps because like attracts like, most of Aunt Peg's friends were good-looking women in expensive clothes. They were what Rollie once called Mom and her sisters, well-preserved. They were also huggers. Their fur collars rubbing against my neck and chin and their cloying perfumes called Compulsion or Cravings made my nose itch and my throat feel raw. Most of them kissed as well as hugged, and left great smears of red or purple on my cheeks. They told us, Shelly and me, that we must be the nieces. They said they'd heard about us, claimed Aunt Peg often bragged about what we did.

"What did we do?" Shelly asked, and most smiled sadly and patted our arms.

"Courage," one said. "Not so much what you do, but what you have. Courage."

"She means that leg and fingers stuff," Shelly said. "She means you, not me. I'm courageous by association."

"Amazo the wonder girl," I said. "Look on me in awe."

"Did she have breast reduction surgery?" a woman asked me as she gazed down at Aunt Peg, her own breasts taking up most of the space from her shoulders to her waist. "She said she was contemplating it, and seeing her from this angle, I know she must have done so."

I just smiled.

"Did you hear about her wedding reception?" a woman with long witchy-looking gray hair asked.

I nodded.

"Of course you know the eyebrow story," another said. This one was short and dressed in green linen, her own eyebrows thick and dark and straight.

"I guess you've heard she catered her own wedding reception?" a pair of unnatural redheads asked, almost in unison.

We told them all we knew that story, though Shelly, who was usually beside me, said we should say *no* once in a while and let them tell it. So many looked disappointed at our knowing.

The funeral Mass the following morning was at St. John the Evangelist in Collinsville, Illinois, a parish Aunt Peg had belonged to, off and on, for more than thirty years, but one she'd recently, officially quit. She had left the whole Catholic Church, she'd said in a long and angry letter to her priest with copies to the archbishop and even the pope. The letter had been sent sometime during the previous summer, Chickie said. Chickie was the one who knew what was in it, as her mother had read it to her over the phone. Aunt Peg had been angry about a notice in her bulletin urging parishioners to write their congressmen in support of a bill to make human cloning illegal. She wrote that this preoccupation with the right and wrong ways to reproduce humans or whether to allow science to use the unborn to make new cells was a ridiculous non-issue. In fact, what cloning did was grow cells, and that was the same thing that happened in the womb. Different method was all. You could not clone personality or soul or spirit, so there was no fear of making lots of quarterbacks or movie stars or popes for that matter. Everyone knew people were more than a conglomeration of cells. The church, she said in her letter, must be in the clutches of hysterical clucking old wives, the same spirit that had condemned most science in the name of preserving God's ways, and she could not be part of such a stupid group. Why not write to your congressman and ask for an increase in the minimum wage, or no tax on food? Anyway, she said goodbye to the Catholic Church forever.

"Mom said 'please do not send me any more envelopes for my donation either'," Chickie said. "She said she would send her money directly to cloning research from then on."

I was standing in the back of the mortuary room with Shelly and Chuck as Chickie explained it all. Aunt Peg was stretched out in the front of the room. Soon we would have a short prayer, one last look, and the lid would close over her beautiful face. "Odd," Chickie said, "St. John's burying her, the congregation praying for her soul, even after she quit."

"It's what the church is for," Chuck said. "That's what the priest said." The pastor of St. John's had told Chickie and Chuck that the church was for spiritual, not political, help. It had to take care of you when you needed it. It was like a family in that way, he had explained. Even a family you may argue with or even hate.

"Like Frost," I said, but none were familiar with the reference. "'Death of a Hired Man'," I said. "'Home is the place where when you have to go there, they have to take you in.'"

"'In the beginning was the Word, and the Word was with God and the Word was God'," Shelly said. "I don't know much about the Bible, but I know St. John's gospel."

"What made you say it now, Sister Mary Shelly?" Chuck asked.

"It's poetry," she said. "Bev recited some, and so can I."

"I don't think that guy Mom dated did her hair so well," Chickie said. "He made it too poofy on the sides."

The church was as crowded as the mortuary had been the night before. Chickie's son, Hilton, was a pallbearer, as were Dad and Uncle Jack and Ralph's two brothers, and a much older man who had lived next door to Aunt Peg for a few decades. His stooped shoulders and dark thinning hair reminded me of Mike, and as we were asking the angels to welcome Peg into heaven, I thought about Mike. Mom told us yesterday that she knew Peg was sashaying about heaven already, making friends with most of the angels and saints and making Grandpa laugh. I doubted there was a heaven, but if so, Mom may have been right, and I caught myself hoping Mike was not among those she made friends with. I wanted him to be one of us, the living, to walk in the back door of the café soon, looking for leftovers, to climb the back stairs behind me once again, unstrap my leg before he undressed. I recalled the salt taste of his tongue and how large his eyes would open at the moment of his orgasm. Mainly, I thought about the heat that raced across my body—toes to hair follicles and back down—and the feeling I had with him that I could burn from the inside out until I was nothing but a carbon shell.

I was surprised when it was already time for communion, and tried to force myself to pray harder than ever for Aunt Peg's soul. My thinking she did not need it, or that there was no one to pray to anyway, was no excuse.

Shelly and I left the graveside ceremony ten or so minutes before everyone else and hurried back to Aunt Peg's house where Chickie and Hilton were staying for four more days until they would leave for France for the James Bond movie. We put four eye of round roasts in the oven, put out the dips and the seven kinds of cold salad Shelly had made, and made the coffee. Shelly had had twenty pounds of shrimp delivered that morning, and she put a pot of water on to boil for them as well.

My mind was still as much on Mike as on the food or Aunt Peg or anything funereal. And the part of Mike my mind was on was sex, his equipment, his desire, what it meant. Did all sexual activity from kissing to petting to orgasm make men feel loved as it did for women? Did men separate someone desiring their bodies from someone loving them in the way women, I mean me, could not. Did a man feel more valued and with a bigger excuse to live after a good fuck as a woman did? Orgasm seemed to me the epitome of being alive, and I had had just a taste of life. I had fucked a mere nine times in my thirty-six years, all near the end of the last millennium, all with Mike.

Were there scenarios that explained his absence? Maybe in his way of letting things happen rather than making plans, he had stumbled upon someone who needed an organist, and maybe that was for a church that already had an organ, and suppose he was going to come back for his one of these days, what we referred to as days of course being in his chronometry a few weeks. Or maybe he'd checked himself into the VA hospital after having been found sleeping in an alley, and was getting well enough to come back for his organ and me. But the police, I knew, must have checked the VA. Maybe he'd bought a bus ticket to Florida on a drunken impulse to get warm and hadn't come up with enough money yet to return. Or maybe the hospital he was in was in Florida and the police wouldn't check there. He wasn't wanted for anything, after all, was merely a missing person. Wherever he was or had been, it was likely he was making his way back to me and his organ. Even as I became better at lying to myself, though, I knew where I was headed, could see my self-delusion for what it was, hope. And I was not the rose-colored glasses idiot Shelly often pretended to be. I knew he could also be dead somewhere hard to find.

Shelly asked me to check on the beef, and just as I was searching through Aunt Peg's gadget drawer for her meat thermometer, Mom and Dad and Chickie showed up, followed soon by the rest of the mourners.

"How is it," one of the mourners asked me even before I'd sliced the beef, "your aunt competed in the St. Louis pageant if she lived here?" She was an elegant woman, about five-ten with short steel-gray hair and large pale blue eyes lined in black.

"I don't know," I said.

"Don't pay any attention to Annie here." This was said by a man who stood beside the woman, Annie I guessed. He was bald and red-faced, and his suit pants were belted across the widest part of his stomach, giving him a humpty-dumpty look. "She's had a hard life." He placed a hand on Annie's arm, and they both laughed.

"I just wondered how she got away with it," Annie said. "I mean, I knew where she lived but didn't make the connection until today."

"She fell in love with a priest," the man said, inclining his head toward Annie. "Got him to leave the priesthood, she did."

"I wasn't trying to cause trouble about your aunt," Annie said. "It just occurred to me."

"The answer is one she took to her grave," I said, but they looked shocked, and it hadn't sounded like the joke I'd meant it, even to me. I turned away from them and started slicing the roast beef for sandwiches.

"I was just his excuse for leaving," Annie said. "The ex-priest, I mean, who will remain nameless."

"Bob," the man said. "Father Bob, then just Bob." He put his arm around Annie. "He left the priesthood, then he left our Annie."

"I lost my faith over that," she said.

"Said she wasn't sexy enough, didn't he?"

She nodded. "Desirable was his word. I wasn't desirable. Peg knew all about it. She left the church with me in sympathy. Wrote a nasty letter to the bishop all about it."

"I'm sorry," I said.

"She was good like that," the man said. "Peg was. Very sympathetic. How'd you learn to slice without any fingers?"

"I have a finger," I said, and held it up for them to see. "It just gets in my way."

The funeral party moved along with lots of talk about Peg and more laughter than I'd expected. Her friends would miss her as we would, but as with all of us, the missing would dawn gradually, would grow. Now there was only the knowledge of the pain to come. And for the moment at least, reminiscences of her yen for the spotlight gave them as much joy as pain. Her piano playing, her sense of style, her desire to be different but not laughable, her staunch loyalty, her constant fight with the church fathers, and the near legendary love between her and Ralph were the main stories. I heard the eyebrow story five or six more times, having taken Shelly's tip and letting them tell it again. In imagining my own funeral, I knew it would not be nearly so much fun, not for a crab like me.

Throughout the afternoon, Chuck's boys were asked the typical boring adult questions: How's the fourth grade? What are you learning in third grade? Their answers were "fine," and "I don't know." At just a year ahead of them, Toby was considerably more articulate. I was pleased to discover it. Chickie talked to some of the mourners about her life in Hollywood, and Shelly told them what her course of study would be like at l'École de Cuisine Internationale. All the mourners agreed that the Senior Ms. Missouri and the Senior Ms. America pageants had lost their glow and interest when they'd lost Aunt Peg.

People started to leave in the late afternoon, and by dark, it was just family. Ralph's family were all gone by seven o'clock, and then it was just Stillwell descendents scattered about Aunt Peg's great room in our dark dresses and suits, slumped on her leather sofas like so many throw pillows. Stacks of plates, cups, and glasses covered the baby grand at the far end of the room. Someone wondered out loud if the dead finally knew the answers, and someone else quipped maybe they at least knew which questions were pertinent. My family and their kind were like that about death. They became simpletons, talking about the dead as if they had turned a corner and taken an escalator up to heaven, were still themselves but just somewhere in the clouds. Then Chuck said one problem with humans was we did not turn to ourselves, to each other, for answers. We went to so-called experts like priests and psychologists and philosophers, all the while maybe living and working with someone who could solve a mystery or give us insights. If only we would ask. The next thing I knew there was a game of sorts arranged. Each of us could ask a question of the group. Nothing personal.

Grandma would not play, was incapable of it, she said. Her child was dead, and that was unnatural. Parents should not bury their children. And it was her baby at that. "I'll never survive this," she said. "I'll be someone quite different from now on. And to think, she never scrubbed a floor, never got down on her hands and knees, yet is already gone." We all said "there, there," to Grandma, and I thought of Toby and how I would feel if I were still alive when he died, already thinking of him as my own in spirit and in fact if not yet in law. Then Mom started the game. "Who cares more about female beauty?" she asked. "Men or women?"

Aunt Marie and Uncle Jack and Chuck and his wife all agreed on the answer—women.

Chickie was not so sure, claiming she had to display her beauty to the mostly male directors and producers over and over, for every role. But the rest of us finally sided with the first answer. "Use all those women at the wake yesterday as an example," Dad said. "Each one commented on Peg's outfit, her makeup, her looks as they stood over her. I didn't hear one man do it."

Chuck said the next question should be harder.

Shelly was next. "How do we find our purpose in life?" she asked. "If we've all been put here for some reason, how do we find it?"

The room was silent for a moment, then Dad said, "Your talent is your purpose. You do what you are good at. It's why you're here."

I bit my tongue. Biology is why you're here, I wanted to tell them all. Cells reproducing without consciousness.

Chickie said she agreed with Dad, but the rest seemed bored by the question.

Chuck wanted to know what was so interesting to the American TV viewers about perky or chipper news readers. Chickie's answer was that they were nonthreatening so would not make any of the viewers feel stupid.

Chickie wanted to know why people had children, or—she looked at me—adopted children, or even had pets. All this while Hilton was sitting in and listening.

"What is the point of complicating our lives?" she asked.

I answered that one. I said without some trouble and worry, you may as well be dead. They all stared at me as if I had just admitted I had an incurable mental illness, so I explained more. "Not that we seek out trouble. We don't have to. But little of it makes for a bland life. People in comas have no worries."

"Neither do monks," Uncle Jack said, but I disagreed.

"They worry about one another and their families and friends on the outside. We all worry about those we love or even like a little." I thought Uncle Jack, who lived one story above his ex and insisted on seeing her everyday, would understand that much.

And when I thought of it, I knew the oddity of Uncle Jack leaving his second floor nest for this burial party was a profound example of his care for and worry about Aunt Marie. I decided not to point that out.

The questions flew faster. "What do people see in musicals?" Escape was the best answer. "Why do dogs roll about on decaying matter?" That one was from Chuck's wife. "To celebrate that they, at least, are not dead yet," someone said. "Why are wars such a unifying force in nations and humanitarian concerns are not?" That was Dad's. "People are naturally bored," Aunt Marie said in reply. "Wars break up the monotony." Someone asked why people belong to religions. Was it mainly for social life, a sense of belonging to something, or did faith need the help of a group to stay alive? And another question was why didn't we all join in as cheerleaders for the wealthy and powerful as their methods clearly worked; they were the winners. "Who are these people questioned in the polls anyway?" Uncle Jack asked, and no one knew, but one guess was they were fictional people, the answers made-up. Hilton asked why high school teachers were so fond of the five-paragraph essay, and even I did not know the answer to that.

Finally the game wore down, and we sighed, some of us looking at Chuck and wondering why he had ever believed we could provide answers for one another. Mainly though, we thought about Aunt Peg, missing her finally in an activity she would have been part of.

"Only four Stillwell beauties left," Grandma said, but Mom and Aunt Marie and Chickie corrected her at once.

"No. Six," they said almost in unison.

"There were seven," Mom said. "Now there are six."

Grandma turned her head to the window and sighed.

Chuck's youngest boy said, "My grandma may know the answers to all those questions you asked by now."

Aunt Marie snorted and said she doubted it. "Heaven," she said, "is a place without these questions. A place where none of what we live people concern ourselves with is important. Or else it wouldn't be heaven."

"Do you realize," Chuck asked Chickie as if it had just dawned on him, "we're orphans now?"

She nodded. "Makes us seem younger. Are we regressing?"

I laughed at that, only later deciding if Chickie was not, I was, had regressed, was once again the grade school and high school girl who believed she could fit in with the group, could be someone's best friend, if she tried harder, told herself something would happen simply because she deserved it. This time all those lies I told myself were about Toby.

Howard tried to break through my delusions. I felt him doing it and held on tighter. I was the perfect mother for Toby; therefore I would soon be so designated.

"What came out at your trial is damaging to your adoption petition," he said.

This was two days after we buried Aunt Peg, a week before my hearing. I listened as he spoke with as much of my mind as I used when listening to conversations in the café. He'd been saying the same since my trial. "You're setting yourself up for pain," he said. "Do you mean to do that?"

Are you crazy? he meant. As crazy as you look? He wore yellow slacks and a Pacific blue knit shirt. It was a Friday afternoon, and his appointment after me was a 2:30 tee time. Shelly had the café by herself for the afternoon, but we had agreed she could handle it. She was not doing one of her Friday blue ribbon dinners that evening so soon after Aunt Peg's death. "Just a week ago she was alive, planning on going shopping," Shelly'd said that morning. I nodded. A week could be short. One more week, and I'd have Toby.

"There's the leg business, letting him strap it on and all, that seems unsavory to so many. Then there is hiding him." He was listing the strikes against me. "And race," he said.

Well, that one I could answer. I was writing a speech about it in my head, would have it perfected by the hearing. How many races were there would be my starting point. If three—Caucasian, Negro, and Mongol—then Toby looked like one, but by his mother's last name was also another, so he may as well partake of all three and be raised by me. I would also say race was arbitrary.

Where were the boundaries? Was it hair type and eyelids and skin tone and straightness of the nose? I knew my arguments were adolescent, deliberately simple, but I believed social workers and judges who listened to them fell for the simple.

"You let a disreputable character watch him," Howard said. "You chose that character over the law or anyone official."

"I did, and I'm not sorry," I said.

He sighed. He leaned back in his swivel chair and put his hands behind his head, elbows out like a breast-side-up trussed turkey. "I'll say you were well-meaning. I'll say you were afraid. I'll use what worked before, and say you were noble." Even when he narrowed his eyes in consternation, he looked successful. If I did not get Toby, his look said, Howard would not be the loser. He never lost. I wished I had a look that said as much.

Back to my race speech. I would say race existed in the minds of the big talkers. It was a thing only because it was shouted about so much. I would say we were all part of the human race. And I would end my speech with a joke of sorts. I'd say that I'd never called out *Amen*, during sermons. "Even I admit to some differences," I'd say.

"Whatever happens," Howard said to end our fruitless meeting, "remember the golden rule of legal behavior. Answer the questions, but don't elaborate. The more you say, the more trouble you'll have."

"And wear something motherly?" I joked. "Isn't that part of your advice?"

He laughed, and I realized he thought all my outfits were motherly. Anything that covered my lumpy body had to be. I thought of Mike's discussion about the way people looked. All alike, he'd said. Once he got to a certain age, he'd said, people started to look like ones he knew or had known; they all resembled one another. He decided there were maybe ten faces and an equal number of body types that could be mixed and matched. Soon though, he changed his mind about that. Everyone looked exactly the same to him. He did not distinguish between sizes or shapes or colors or, sometimes, even sex. "It's a sign I'm nearly dead," he said. "All are alike." As he spoke, I realized it was why he took me, and at that time, I was not insulted. Rather, I liked knowing I was as good as anyone else to him, my body was as good as all bodies.

Howard's talk and stern, fatherly frowns had not frightened me, and even in the elevator on the way down from his luxurious office, I once again dismissed the mistakes I'd made. If DFS considered any of them serious, I wouldn't have come this far with my petition. The hearing was a formality. Howard was being lawyerly, racking up the hours of advice and thus padding his bill.

A week later, I was in the St. Louis city courthouse, and rather than in a courtroom, my hearing was scheduled for the judge's chambers. The courthouse was old and so was full of the mahogany and oak trim, terrazzo floors and vaulted ceilings, I'd missed at my trial in the county. The judge's chambers were stately and elaborate, consisting of a large office with casement windows and crown molding around the high ceiling, a dressing room, and an equally impressive conference room where we were to meet, we being me and Howard and Shelly and Jeannie Lemp and another functionary from DFS, someone higher up, a supervisor of some sort, and, of course, the judge, The Honorable Herman Landermeier. I was relieved to see he was a white man, and so not as likely to care about race issues as what I had dreaded most, a black woman judge. I knew my becoming hopeful at having a white male judge contradicted all my claims of innocence about race and how little it mattered, but no one could read my thoughts, and if I had to, I could make myself stop thinking anything offensive, at least until the hearing was over.

Before I got to the hearing room, though, Jeannie Lemp laid a hand on my arm, and told me a few things. She said she knew some of it as Toby's case worker, and had investigated the rest on her own. The gang of thieves, including Poodle Baby, had been taken care of. Three men and Poodle Baby had been arrested, were out on bail for the time being, but would go to trial in March. Toby would be safe then, and probably was already as there was no reason to get him since the gang's activity had already been found out. They need not fear a snitch. Besides, there were quite a few other snitches, many neighbors who were already scheduled to testify. She said she visited Toby often, and he was adjusting well.

She said Lana had not filed a petition to adopt Toby because she feared he was too troubled for her to manage, told too many lies, and was already attracted to the criminal element. I thanked her for the information, knowing she did not have to tell me any of it, and so must have decided I was acceptable for Toby, or at least was better than nothing now that Lana had pulled out. I took it as a gesture of approval, if not friendship.

The Honorable Herman Landermeier was about my age with a delicate face and thin fingers, the index one on his right hand often resting alongside his nose. He sat at the end of the table, and I sat to his right, Howard beside me and Shelly beside him. Jeannie and the other DFS worker sat across from us. Judge Landermeier glanced at his watch, then tapped the stack of papers before him, and looked directly at me. He said he had read Toby's complete file. Because the stack was at least four inches thick, and Toby was just barely eleven, I joked with myself that it must have included what his first word was, how often he'd sneezed, what his favorite candy was. But my jokes were sad. I knew no one had taken that much interest in him and his development. I was sure of it. Angela would not have known if he'd had pneumonia. Landermeier said that the courts tried to bend over backwards with hard-to-adopt children like Toby, tried to overlook much in order to give them homes.

He said he was not persuaded the racial difference was worth worrying about, and my age was not a problem as Toby himself was a mere seven years from adulthood. My disabilities were no drawbacks, and single women had long been considered acceptable candidates for motherhood, though he personally did not approve of it. He said my finances were in order, and he was pleased I had established a friendly relationship with Toby already. I nodded and smiled, said *yes*, and *thanks*, not even a little sorry not to give my race speech. He said the Department of Family Services had been asked to be heard, a quite common practice, and would comment on my moral character. Before he turned the floor over to Jeannie, he admonished her not to waste his time by rehashing what he knew about the civil case or my having been in trouble for telling my students to lie. He said that was all nonsense, a nuisance lawsuit as my lawyer, and he nodded at Howard as he spoke, had so clearly explained to him already.

Howard interrupted to ask why Jeannie was allowed to present information we had not seen and so had not prepared an answer to, but Landermeier waved him off, saying nothing new was being revealed. This was merely the DFS's response or recommendation.

Jeannie pushed her chair out, causing a leg to squeak across the hardwood floor, and stood. Before she was completely upright, Landermeier told her she did not have to stand, but she did stand all the way up anyway, and then she read from a page she clamped between doughy fingers, looking down at it and not up at any of us as she did so. Her long, limp hair hung down and blocked her face as effectively as a veil would have. "Speaking for the Department of Family Services, we cannot recommend Ms. Beverly Burke as the adoptive parent for Tobias Cheng because, though it would be hard to prove and so prosecute her for, we believe her guilty of trying to buy Toby, paying his birth mother to terminate her rights." She stopped. That was it, the only complaint. I was almost happy about it. She looked across the table at me. "She knew it was illegal, or she would have told me or someone in DFS about her contact with Angela Cheng." She sat.

"It is new," Howard said, and that surprised me for a moment. Then I remembered Ted had not included my contact with Angela in his report at my trial, and I wondered why not. Surely, if he knew later, he'd known then. And a more important question was why now. Why had he told Jeannie what he knew now? Landermeier said I could consult with Howard before explaining, but I shook my head. Though it surprised me by coming out now, it was not hard to explain.

I admitted giving Angela Cheng the money. I said she had asked for it, and I'd known she was in need. I said it was not a sacrifice, as I didn't care much about money, maybe because I had more than enough from the Foxborough settlement. I explained that I hadn't sought Angela out, but rather had been found by her because of a flyer my café partner had distributed about the neighborhood. I said I guessed she knew about me and the café from Jeannie or someone in DFS who talked to her about Toby. I said I did not ask her to terminate her parental rights, and in fact, when she did, I still thought Lana was planning to adopt Toby and I was not guaranteed him anyway. I said all that, and because it was true, I came close to believing in my own innocence. But I also knew more, knew better. I had hoped I was getting closer to having Toby by paying Angela, and I had known it was a mistake. Jeannie was right. I had been afraid to tell DFS, and I had paid the extra to T.J. for Angela so she wouldn't turn me in. Knowing all that made me try to look even more innocent. "I did a good deed," I told Landermeier. "I gave someone who needed it money to go away and start a better life."

"It was an act of generosity befitting a good parent," Howard said, but he sounded tired.

"Have you heard from Ms. Angela Cheng again?" Landermeier asked.

"No," I lied.

He made us take a break while he decided Toby's fate, and as we sat on an oak bench alongside a wide and empty hall, Shelly said she thought it would go in my favor, no matter how Jeannie tried to sabotage me. "The judge smiled at us as we left," she said. "And he said all that other stuff was nonsense. It's a good sign. He wants Toby to have a home."

I knew Shelly was being her usual sunny-side up self, but I wanted to be persuaded, so I encouraged her by saying "I hope so."

"Of course," she continued. "Even Jeannie said they cannot prove any of that was criminal, was really buying a child. And the seller is usually more at fault, isn't she? More to blame?"

I leaned across her and looked at Howard until he turned to me. "I'm not a judge," he said. "Anything is possible."

Landermeier's speech was even a bit flattering, calling me generous and loving and desperately needed, but he said my disregard for the law and truth was not an auspicious beginning to a parent-child relationship, especially one in which the child had demonstrated some tendencies toward the same. He said the judge almost always took the DFS recommendation seriously, and he saw no reason not to in my case. "Anything that even smacks of child buying cannot be tolerated. Petition denied." Rather than bang a gavel, he placed both palms face down on the table and pushed his chair back. I had lost. That quickly, Toby would not be mine. There was no appeal. Landermeier said he was saddened by the outcome and by my actions that caused it, sorry mainly for Toby who was running out of time. He shook his head at me, and I thought he did look sad.

"Jerkwad," Shelly said, but he did not seem to hear her.

Afterwards, Jeannie waylaid me once again on my way down the hall. "It's not personal. I hope you know that"

But what else was it? What else could it be but personal?

"Toby did give his consent, said he wanted to be adopted by you," she said, "And none of us in DFS will try to keep you from seeing him, from being his friend." She touched my shoulder and gave it almost a squeeze. Her hand and her breath were hot and damp. "I mean it. I am sorry."

"Ignore her," Shelly said, taking my arm to guide me away.

"Thanks," I said to Jeannie, hearing it come out as a whisper. I hadn't enough breath left in me to cry, nor enough to shake Jeannie's arm off. I'd been reduced to nothing but politeness. Without them touching me, I could have blown away.

SHELLY

I missed Bev's bitching. March came in like a lamb, the February thaw lasting a solid three weeks, and Bev was lamb-like, too. But I wanted the complaints. One day the previous summer, I'd felt so weighed down by her negativity, I'd made a list, discovered that by noon she had bitched to me about six different things: the gas company pork-barrel project Rollie was part of; the city dwellers who lived behind gates and homeschooled their offspring; the arrogance of the Hilkers and their ilk; the way our customers chewed with their mouths open; commercials on FM radio; and the stuffed peppers I'd created using mushrooms and rice—she'd said the thought of stuffed peppers on a hot summer's day nearly made her puke. And that was well before she'd become the handicapped poster girl of the day or been targeted by the city inspectors for her broken and missing tiles. The only time all year, the brief time, she took a break from chronicling the incompetence and stupidity and general slovenliness of humans, often me included, was that few week period Mike came by at night, and her orgasms made her happy. But even if he'd stayed around, her happiness wouldn't have lasted. She'd have grown as used to orgasm as she was to running water or sunshine. For a while, I'd considered that her unrelenting complaining, now that I lived with her and listened to her endless string day in and day out, contributed to my headaches.

But when she stopped struggling so against the world she was forced to inhabit and took up her position in the mainstream, zombie-like, it was as if she'd gone away, too, disappeared along with Aunt Peg and Mike and Toby, leaving me behind. I missed her.

In the second week of March, she continued her uncharacteristic behavior. First, she stopped watching television, 100 percent, cold-turkey stopped. She announced it one evening after one of her cop dramas ended, and she clicked the power button. The television would stay off, she said, unless I turned it on, which I was free to do. The next day, she hired a work crew to replace the front tiles, then called inspector Hruzcka's office to report it, getting in just under the wire.

"People still piss in the alley." I ached for a reaction. "You'll spend all this money, knuckle under to city pressure, and the neighborhood will still be filled with scum and derelicts, will be as ugly as ever."

She merely nodded in agreement, her stare blank. And she began smiling in a vacant almost ghostly way at our customers, told them when they left what she used to sneer at me for—"Hurry back." I missed the sneers.

I noticed her walk growing even more awkward as she dragged her prosthesis about behind her, letting her fake foot scrape across the floor. Well, she'd always had a lurch to her step, a hesitation caused by shifting between the real and artificial, but this dragging came from not using her mechanical knee, keeping it locked and her prosthesis stiff, something I'd thought would require even more effort.

I considered ways to make her angry and thus bring some fire back into her tiny eyes, make her face not quite so pale. I could talk about how our business was growing, tell her my plans for moving, discuss plans for an extensive advertising campaign, print and radio, call it one last effort before I left. But needlessly upsetting her seemed cruel, and instead, whenever she looked at me, I smiled at her. "I'm worried about you," I told her at least once a day.

"Don't be," she usually said. Or "no reason to be."

One Wednesday afternoon we closed before three o'clock so I could take her with me and introduce her to our butcher. I assumed she would keep the Alibi Café running once I was gone because, though she had said nothing about the future, she had had the tiles repaired, such rule-following a hint she would stay. Besides, I was merely a café add-on, had not been part of her original plan. I'd been using Reuben Meats, a wholesale shop run by Mark Reuben, a butcher Dad had worked with years ago at the IGA on Broadway. Like most people I dealt with, he claimed he gave me better deals than he actually did. Sure, his prices were lower than many, and he did accommodate me with any cut and size I asked for, but to hear him tell it, he gave me bargains never before encountered in modern times; what he gave me was the next step up from charity. "I'll take care of your partner, too. Same or better. Not that I can do better," he said. His face and balding head were as red as the uncured pork butt on the table behind him, and he nearly glowed as he talked. "I like to see young businesses grow strong down here in the old neighborhood. It's good for us all." It was his usual line, and he said it with such sincerity each time, I expected strains of "The Star Spangled Banner" to swell up from the background when he finished. I would not have been surprised to see his bloody gloved hand covering his heart. Before I left, he told me his divorced son was moving back from Dayton. "Smart guy with lots of business sense," he said. "Maybe he'll call you."

"But I'm leaving town," I said.

"Stay," he said. "Good things find you if you stay put."

Reuben Meats was a mere two miles away from the café, but spring pothole filling had begun in our neighborhood, and three streets I normally took were virtually impassable, especially at rush hour on our way home, so I had to zig and zag through streets I seldom traveled. That was how I saw the shingle—"L.L. Fredericks,

MD" written across the top, and underneath, instead of a phone number, "No appt. necessary. Walk-ins welcome." It was odd enough to snag my attention. Not that I expected a cure or even relief from my headaches anymore, but I knew I was compelled to keep searching, the effort in some superstitious way having become as important as the result. Maybe Fredericks couldn't cure my headaches, but I doubted he or she could harm me. And even though I'd always believed my efforts could override it, I accepted fate grudgingly, thought it could've been fate that blocked those other streets. So when the next day, Thursday, was slow enough that we didn't even have much clean up, and by 2:30 we had only Rollie and a fellow gas company guy eating banana cream pie at the counter and talking lazily about the Cardinals' spring training, I took off and walked to Dr. Fredericks'.

Dr. Fredericks turned out to be a man, and one patient of his I spoke to called him Lloyd, though I never did discover what the other L stood for or which L was for Lloyd. His practice was set up in the downstairs of a semi-detached two story brick home, one of those at least ninety years old and in need of tuck-pointing, its gutters half off and the front one cutting a diagonal across the upper story, its porch sagging, and the concrete steps from the sidewalk to the porch listing sharply to the right. I guessed the upstairs was condemned, for a strip of yellow police tape roped off the stairway. Dr. Fredericks had no receptionist and no nurse.

When I entered the house and faced the roped-off staircase, I saw a pair of closed pocket doors to my right, and a large waiting room with orange molded plastic chairs lining each wall to my left. A hand-lettered sign taped to the wall instructed me to sign in, and followed up that instruction with an arrow pointing down to a pad of paper on a low table. I signed in. There seemed to be three ahead of me, and a young man with a blood-soaked bandage covering most of an upper arm said Lloyd Fredericks was the only doctor he trusted. "Too bad the lawyers and corporate quacks are out to get him," he said.

When my turn came about an hour later, Lloyd Fredericks was direct and fast. He stroked his white moustache rapidly as I told him I'd been given nasal sprays, antihistamines, eye drops and eye examinations, EEGs and a brain scan, twirling needles and an allergy diet I had not followed. All for a headache that waxed and waned but seldom disappeared.

He snapped his fingers when I finished. "An infection," he said. "What else? Couldn't be anything but. In the sinuses most likely, but maybe somewhere else. Who knows exactly? Nasal spray and those other things are no good for infections, and infections cause headaches. Take some of these." With that, he rolled his office chair back from his desk to a metal cabinet, opened one side door of it, and scooped out a handful of pill containers. "Samples," he said. "Some good antibiotics here. Won't hurt you, just kill any infections you may have."

"I thought doctors tried to avoid antibiotics except in extreme cases so that patients did not develop immunities."

He shrugged. "Up to you. But looking into the future can cause headaches, too. What you may or may not develop later is poor reason for a decision now. Take me. I'm doing good, making people feel better, curing the few odd here and there, doing my job, but I could be in jail tomorrow. Already I'm banned from all hospitals." He laughed a young-boy laugh like I'd last heard from Toby, more giggle than laugh, and continued. "If that scares you, you better not listen to me. But no matter how bad you feel now, you'll feel lots worse before you get out of this life. You'll have headaches, or maybe stomach pains, maybe joints and muscle cramps and shortness of breath, whatever. But don't look into the future, predict what could happen. I don't know about you, but all that makes my own head nearly explode."

I reached for the small containers of pills and raked them across his desk into my purse. "How often do I take these?"

"Oh, two, three times, once or twice a day. "I'm not sure. See how it goes." But he giggled again. "There are instructions on the containers. You can read them. And I like you, so that'll be ten dollars." He held out his hand. "I charge whatever I want. Not paying off any machinery or lab bills. No medical plan'll have me."

As I walked back to the café, I had to turn my jacket collar up because the wind blew hard from the north, bringing in cold. The air that had carried a touch of spring for weeks now smelled like snow. My cheeks were stinging, but I hummed one of Mike's old hymns as I walked. And not because yet another doc in a long line had given me more hackneyed advice, but for some reason I knew as if it were profound that I was not seventeen and not yet sixty. My eyes watered, my legs moved, a blister was forming on my right heel, my back was straight, and I breathed through my mouth. I was Shelly at thirty-seven in the middle of the country in mid-March, about an hour before dusk. My vision was clear. I smelled diesel exhaust and frying pork chops and cigarette smoke. I crossed Cherokee Street at a stoplight, making a driver who wanted to turn right stop with a squeal and extend her pointer finger up to the sky. I laughed, did the same with my pointer, then slowed to an amble as I crossed Cherokee Street. This was now.

In the weeks since Aunt Peg's death, Mom spoke to me more than she normally had, even calling me just to talk some evenings, and one time, surprising me by asking my advice. "How long do I bake this old chicken called a roaster? You're supposed to be the expert."

I wanted to know more about Aunt Peg stealing Ralph, about Ralph being Mom's first. I wondered if I would ever have heard that confession if not for the overturned pig truck and our sitting on the bridge for hours. Well, that, I guessed, and the martinis. Instead, Mom concentrated on l'École de Cuisine Internationale and any future Teds I may have, dispensing this advice: "You're too old to be starting new things. You probably won't find a new man, so stop hoping and looking. You are already grown up, nearly middle-aged. Whatever you are, it's you now. All this striving and searching, starting school and moving and trying to remake yourself will lead nowhere. Accept what is." Naturally, I resented that kind of nonsupport, no matter how used to it I had become, but as I walked home from Fredericks' I thought how close her advice was to his. The present counted. This was me now. Of course, she was wrong. I would have *le grand diplôme* from l'École de Cuisine Internationale and would be better for having it. And I would have another and a better lover. But now was fine. For now.

That evening, Bev and I ate tuna salad on nearly stale rye bread along with her mother's pickles, and I told her what I'd discovered and also what I'd learned years earlier when my parents split, or half split, or whatever it was they did. "It's easy to be sad," I said.

She looked at me for a moment as if trying to remember who I was, then went back to crunching her pickle.

"I know you're sad about Toby, and I'm sad, too. For you and for him. But here's the thing about sorrow. You don't have to ignore it, but you can get over it. Fast. Now I'm sad, now I'm not. How? Because you remember you're alive. You are breathing. You are seeing and thinking and even if what you are thinking is sad, you are still thinking. That knowledge takes the sadness away."

She sighed at her sandwich and nodded. "Yeah," she said. "You may be right."

I knew I was and said so, but her agreeing so easily tightened the steel band that existed just under my skin and was wrapped about my skull. How long would it be, I wondered, before the antibiotics worked.

I wanted my March blue ribbon nights to be worth remembering, both for me and for our customers. It would warm me in Montreal to know the group back in the Alibi Café reminisced about a specific dish, maybe looked forward to my preparing it once again. So I planned a few spectaculars. For the Ides, I chose riblets of veal that I would braise first in vermouth, then cook up in a stew of pearl onions and baby carrots and an egg-cream-horseradish sauce, and serve over rice. I would accompany it with a medley of stir-fried squashes. The first course would be a pureed beet and sour cream soup, served cold. I planned a salad of spinach and watercress and pine nuts for between the veal and cheese courses. Bev agreed to make seven strawberry-rhubarb pies, and she did not complain of one thing during my planning and preparation, not even when I insisted on going to three markets to get enough seedless black grapes to go with the mainly white cheeses when we both knew few of our customers ever ate the grapes. I had looked forward to at least an eye roll, but got nothing.

That afternoon, I asked her to stay beside me as I salted the veal riblets so I could give her a lesson in selecting good cuts. I was sure she wouldn't continue my blue ribbon nights without me, so would not likely use veal riblets again, but the lesson applied to most meat. Fat, of course, meant flavor and tenderness, but the fat had to be evenly distributed. I explained that, and told her a piece of meat with a large white spot of fat, for instance, would end up tough unless slow cooked with moisture. And the most tender meat was closest to the bone.

"If you salt it ahead of time, then keep it at room temperature for about an hour, the salt will work as a tenderizer," I said, as I salted the riblets. "And you can dry cook only tender meat."

"Uh huh," she said. She was doing as I had asked, standing behind me and watching and listening, but her *uh huh* was so meek, it was nearly a cry. It pulled me around. I turned and hugged her, my fingers sticky with veal. "I won't go," I said into her neck. "I'll stay right here. I can't leave you. I don't want to."

I cried then, and she surprised me by returning my hug, crying along with me.

John the chiropractor came in while we were leaning against the refrigerator, crying and hugging, one wet ball of cousin, and I heard him cough a few times to get our attention. After what was probably a few minutes, I heard the door close behind him. The phone rang, and we continued to hug and cry as we listened to Aunt Josie's message: she was bringing Grandma in for dinner that evening. The postman came in and dropped our bills and catalogs beside the cash register, getting no response to his comment on the sudden shift in the jet stream that was bringing the cold down on us. We sobbed and wailed and hiccupped, our tears wetting each other's cheeks and chins and necks. Nothing short of a much longed-for organ concert could have broken us up. Nothing except time. After about twenty minutes, our muscles were stiff, our necks ached from being held at their odd angles, and our tear ducts were empty. We were suddenly quiet. Bev patted my shoulder and stepped back. I looked at her and smiled, then stood on tiptoe and kissed her forehead. She turned around then, heading toward the largest work area beside the stove. "Gotta get my crusts going," she said and soon was banging bowls and sifters and rolling pins.

As I cleaned the squash, a peace settled about me. I was not going. This was me, and the café was my destiny, my place. Bev needed me. We became who we were meant to be by being needed. It was that simple. Maybe I'd petition to adopt Toby myself, let him be raised by his Auntie Bev.

BEV

It was barely spring in Montreal, chilly even in May. That news was from Shelly in one of her daily e-mails. She was working with what she called dark seasonings, those that add background rather than heat, like oregano and tarragon, and on warm sauces and marinades. Her teachers, both of them, were arrogant older men, "not as virile as they think, not even with their smocks un-buttoned so their gray chest hairs show," she'd written. Both flirt-ed with her, but that was nothing she couldn't handle, certainly nothing she was unused to as a Stillwell beauty. She used to say that phrase, *Stillwell beauty,* as if it had quotes around it, and she did add the quotes in her e-mail. That made me smile. She told me before she left she did not consider me one of the beauties, never had, her saying that a gift of sorts, a long-hoped-for honesty from at least one of the group.

She had left for l'École de Cuisine Internationale five weeks earlier because I insisted on it. Crying may be cathartic, and the kind that is not just self-pity, not just the woe is me that our mothers taught us to make fun of when we saw it in ourselves, but is instead an empathic crying for someone else's sorrow, as Shelly's crying for me was and as my crying for Toby was, may have been more than cathartic. It may have been a connection, a bridge, a bond. Nevertheless, it was not the end, not where we were headed, and not sustainable. Shelly had to do something.

"Go to Montreal," I said. "Do not stay here with me. I don't want you." I meant it. L'École de Cuisine Internationale had been a dream of hers almost since her first batch of pork gravy was stirred up in my kitchen, maybe even before her subconscious revealed it to her consciousness. She had no call to give up on it for sentiment.

She may not have been too old to start something new as Aunt Marie told her, but she was, as I was, too old to go about quitting things she wanted. Quitting, I told her and knew it was true for me mostly, was the way that seemed easy but ended up the hardest.

After The Honorable Landermeier said I was not deemed a fit parent for Toby, and DFS and Howard both told me there could be no appeal since it had not been a trial anyway, that the decision was final and over, my quest for Toby ended, I moved inside myself. I retreated in order to curse the world and my position in it as a half-formed freak who would not win and should have known it because the world was run by incompetents and nitwits. Instead, I came up hard against my part in my own sorrow.

I had quit teaching in a fit of pique at being misunderstood and, as I told it to myself, bullied, even though I liked teaching and had been good at it. Maybe Mom had been right, her claim that quitting ruined my life only a slight exaggeration. I had quit other things, too. All those failed friendships I used to toughen myself with, used as reminders that I was on my own, were in fact what I had given up on. The high school pals, for instance, who started dating and so preferred to be with their boyfriends all the time rather than with me and so were no longer friends of mine became interchangeable characters in stories I told myself about my own cursed luck. The truth was they did not want to be with the boys all the time, only most of the time. I could have been with any of them some of the time. It was I who quit calling, jealous because I had no boyfriend and likely would not ever have, mad because the friendships were no longer the exact same as they had been.

That went for my more adult friendships, too, with room-mates who moved out and in with their lovers and with whom I could have kept in touch. I could have accepted the new balance, but instead I quit. When I looked at my life, I saw quitting as my modus operandi. I told Shelly all that, said she had to go. So she did.

She went to Montreal, and she almost took Ted with her. It happened like this: Shelly wanted a going away party in the café, wanted the regulars to have one free meal, one of her elaborate creations. I told her they were not her friends, just customers who chose us because we were convenient, safe, cheap, possibly good, but not because they liked us. She was letting sentimentalism clog up her system.

"Invite them," she said. "They'll come."

"Well, of course they'll come," I said. "It's free."

"They like me," Shelly said. "You'll see."

So we had Rollie and his mother, the thrift shop women and their twins, the Figg family, John the chiropractor, Maddie and Jason (who were no longer speaking to each other), Roger from Auto World, and the St. Paul's crossing guard. Shelly made paella. It was near the end of the dinner when Ted showed up, and Shelly, basking so in love and appreciation, dropped her guard and agreed to talk to him. They stood out by the alley for nearly two hours, came back in long after the party was over and I had the kitchen sparkling.

"Ted's going with me," was all she said then. I couldn't look at them.

The next day, she explained more. Ted was sorry for what he'd told Jeannie about my giving money to Angela. He said he thought he did it accidentally, but it may have been out of anger at her not talking to him, not giving him a chance to explain. He had run into Jeannie at Sav-A-Sum about a week before the adoption hearing, and my name came up. He had told Shelly that he would not claim innocence, nor would he pretend to understand his own actions or their motivations.

"How easy for him," I said.

"Yes," she said. "I agree. But knowing he is not perfect may make it easier for me. I won't be disappointed. Maybe." She shrugged. "Think about it. How can a person change? Do we ever? And can't we love each other as we are?"

I shook my head at her rationalizations. "You're finally tired of being alone," I said, and saying so made it clear. "Me, too. I do understand. But don't expect me to like him."

She said she understood my feelings, and mentioned him only one more time, the night before her plane left for Montreal, and she said she'd made yet another reversal. "I told him Montreal is not his destiny. I'm going alone," she said. "He stabbed us in the backs. Sometimes you have to be brave enough to see what is right in front of you. I don't like what he is."

As I had with Shelly, I also cautioned Toby against quitting, but that caution fell on deaf ears.

He had changed in the few months he'd been kept away in safety. He had added a few inches to his legs as boys can do suddenly, and his pants were short on him. He slouched a lot, had a newly developing case of acne to go with the permanent grayish rash on his face, and he seldom smiled at me. I missed what had been a disarming and nearly permanent smile the same way I missed Mike's yeasty taste. I knew Toby did not know what or whom to resent, whom to blame for the life he'd led so far, but I guessed he'd finally decided or been told his lot was more rotten than most.

One day in late April, he showed up, back on his old stool at the counter. "What's up?" he asked, then ducked his head. He was back in class at St. Hedwig's, and had been asked by the physical education teacher to join the softball team. It was on his mind that first day he stopped by.

"Guy asked me specially," he said, then shrugged to show it meant nothing to him. I tried to hide my pleasure in his being sought out, knowing the request grew out of an effort by most of his teachers and social workers to give him some positive experiences, especially as he had just come out of hiding. I knew he knew it as consolation and control, too, and I worried that if I acted too happy at the idea of him on a team, he would quit. He was smart enough to know people with his best interests at heart, ulterior motives to his way of thinking, wanted him to latch on to sports as an alternative to burglary rings and blackmail. "Don't care for softball," he said. "What's so special about hitting a ball with a stick? Like trained monkeys or something."

I let that go, partly from trying not to push it, and partly because I agreed with his assessment. "Want some pie? It's raisin today." Raisin had been one of Shelly's suggestions last winter after she read about it in a cooking magazine. It was now one of my favorites.

He shrugged, so I gave him a piece.

"What position do you play?"

He ignored that. I was grateful he wanted to come by after school for pie, and I was trying to gain his confidence, regain it. He knew I had wanted him, then knew the adoption had not gone through. I was not sure how much he knew about why it hadn't worked out, how my contempt for regulations I could've guessed at even if I didn't know them had ruined our chances.

"Shelly's gone, " I said. "She's in Montreal studying to be a better cook."

He nodded, quite used to people in his life coming and going, missing for a while and then showing up again as I guessed Angela had done. So I kept quiet about who else wasn't there. It was enough that we were.

"Still have your tutor?" I asked.

He smiled at that, the same old Toby smile that made his eyes glisten through the thick lenses. "Yeah. He's cool. He'll probably adopt me."

"Good," I said, knowing it was good. If only someone would.

"Never had a dad before. He comes by at night, helps me with my homework."

Toby lived in what the DFS called a group home, a temporary solution just until he could be sent to live with another foster family. Jeannie Lemp had told me about it. It was on Jefferson, just over a mile from the café but close to St. Hedwig's. A crew of social workers and aides took turns staying there on a day-and-night rotating basis, and six children stayed in the home, all about Toby's age or older and so not likely to be adopted. Two nights a week, they had group time during which all the children and their counselors met in the common living area and played games, each getting his turn to choose the game, which could be anything from charades to a board game to a knowledge or trivia game. The chooser also got to be the judge or referee. Jeannie had told me about that practice, acting as if it were an innovation.

"Good for their self-esteem," she'd said, calling it a "way for them to express themselves, a way to learn problem-solving." She carried on about theories of play and the benefits on developing personalities, and I almost sneered, told her she was saying something that was first of all obvious—*oh my, play is beneficial! What won't they think of next*—and at the same time blown all out of proportion—*If only I'd played more Parcheesi, I wouldn't have robbed that gas station*! But I held my tongue and kept my lips straight. I hadn't exactly come out on top following my own judgments, and so I was trying to suspend my criticism.

But those group nights were exactly what Toby wanted to quit. I was at first pleased when he said it, recognizing once again that spark of intelligent life in him, that ability to see through and beyond, but I also knew too much quitting led to loneliness.

"Remember that night we played scrabble?" It was the night before I'd called the police and revealed his hiding place, back when Ted was still considered a good guy, and I had hope Toby would be mine.

He nodded.

"It was fun, wasn't it? Why don't you suggest scrabble when it's your turn?"

"See," he said. "It's all that turn stuff. And we have to get 'into' it. Those counselors take notes on how we act, what games we want. If one of the kids cries or curses, they write it down. They want us to smile. It's not the same as playing with you."

I knew little about child psychology, little except for some phrases other teachers had used that I'd always made fun of, but

I knew I would not treat Toby the way I'd been treated most of my life. I'd been raised to accept this paradox: There was nothing at all wrong with me or my life, and whatever was wrong was best ignored. For example, no one in my family asked me what had happened with my petition to adopt Toby, and that was because they'd asked Shelly and so were busy trying to ignore the bad news, pretend it was all for the best. I decided I'd have to treat Toby, for as long as he would allow me to know him, as I wanted to be treated. "Here's the deal," I said. "Those games and group time are some sort of therapy, and not just for fun. And that whole idea may be as dippy as can be.

"The counselors probably think they have to keep track of your emotions, and they may be wrong about what your frowns or outbursts mean. But every now and then, they may also be right. And you should not quit things that could have even the slightest, most remote chance of helping you. The games won't hurt. Well, maybe they'll bore you, but that's also a part of everything you'll eventually get used to. I won't tell you they're good for you, or should be fun, or any of that. But I do advise you to go along, play along. Quitting can become a habit."

The next time he came by, he told me he'd quit the group nights. "First they said I couldn't, but then they gave in and said I could just stay in my room. They are so stupid. If they know how everyone should be, why aren't they better off? None of them has any money at all. The dorkiest one is Jared, and he gets there on a bus. Doesn't even have a car, and he's trying to tell us what will make our lives better. He starts every sentence with 'It seems to me.'"

"What's wrong with that?" I asked.

"Lots," he said, then kicked the counter as he explained it. "If it didn't seem to him, he wouldn't say it." He sighed dramatically and stepped down from his stool. "And it's the kind of thing he says so we think he's not telling us what to do. It's a sneaky way of making us act right. Like you and all the rest do." He walked to the door, and turned back around. "I wish people would leave me alone."

He may have become taller, but was still so skinny I could see some of his vertebrae through his thin T-shirt as he walked away. "Oh, Toby," I said to myself, "they will leave you alone."

I called Jeannie Lemp that evening. I still thought of her as a white mouse, a prissy automaton with so little personality she worked on the cases of others to avoid facing her own emptiness. She had ruined my and Toby's life, I said, knowing it was not true. I had done that. She had merely uncovered my mistakes, non-entity that she was. I talked to her now and then only for Toby's sake, and she responded, seeming at times almost friendly, and after we finished talking about Toby she would confide in me that her mother was driving her crazy, or she would describe the one-act play she was writing in her spare time. She had told me earlier that Toby's tutor, an African-American man in his early twenties, working on a doctorate in electrical engineering and supplementing his stipend by working for DFS, had expressed absolutely no interest in adopting Toby.

After Toby walked out that afternoon, I called her with an of-fer. I had money with or without the "relief" being appealed by the Hilkers. I would pay for Toby's education. I wanted to put aside $200,000 in a fund so he could go to a good high school, a good college, and if there was any left, even graduate school if he wanted to. I'd been mulling this over for a while, had even considered and rejected Baxter Academy, an expensive high school the civic lead-ers of the metropolitan area sent their offspring to as a prelude to Yale. I had thought enough about it that I'd decided Toby could get in even without proper preparation—private grammar and junior high—because he would fill a color slot, but I'd eventually rejected Baxter as a good choice. It would be like throwing Toby to the wolves. Baxter was populated by smart and rich and high-achieving children who were told they were the best of the best. Baxter children not only believed that, they counted on it. No, I'd think of someplace else for Toby, or he would think of a place for himself, but wherever he went, the money would be there. I'd not set out to impress Jeannie, but she said she was anyway, claimed to be excited about telling her supervisor my plan. She said DFS would handle the fund. Over the phone, I said that would be fine, though I knew I'd have Howard do it. DFS handle an education fund? I was amazed it could pay its own phone bills, much less handle someone else's money. I had only let Jeannie in on my plan in case there was some law against what I proposed. And I knew there were some functionaries who had to sign off on it, maybe a whole hierarchy of functionaries.

The next day, Toby returned, ate a piece of strawberry chiffon pie, and mumbled *fine* when I asked how he was. I was relieved to see him, would not push him for more of a response. Each time he left, I was half afraid he would never return.

With Shelly gone, the café was all mine, and so it went back to being plain and boring with just the kinds of food I knew how to make. I stopped the blue ribbon nights, needless to say, and even stopped the fancy breakfast and lunch offerings like stuffed peppers, omelets, and quiches. And I got rid of the barbecue sandwiches, too, not interested enough in barbecue to create or even to buy a sauce. For breakfast, I did bacon and sausage and eggs, all served with biscuits. For lunch I did tuna and egg and ham salad sandwiches, sliced roast beef, corned beef, or pastrami sandwiches, all on white or rye or sourdough, and served with cole slaw or macaroni salad, chips, and Mom's pickles.

Still, the café now was a vastly different place than when I'd opened it a year and four months ago before Mom and the other Stillwell girls talked me into taking Shelly in. For one thing, I now had bars on the windows, steel doors, and an alarm system. But on the plus side, I had Toby in every now and then, and I had other regulars. I was seldom all by myself. For the few weeks I'd struggled to get my breath back after the Honorable Landermeier had knocked it out, I'd smiled more at the crew who hung around the café for Shelly. Now that she was gone, they seemed to remember my smiles and they hung around me, talked to me, sat a while even after their plates were empty. I didn't mind the company. I had once considered selling out and moving to a safer neighborhood, but my sudden aversion to quitting and my wanting to see Toby whenever he'd let me made me stay. I'd even had my tile façade repaired without contesting what I continued to call officially sanctioned extortion. My front was now brilliant and black and shiny, a fact that made no difference as the pawn shop was still across the street and the beauty shop next door to it remained boarded up.

I made one kind of pie each day, recognizing pie baking as one of my most useful talents, and with no one to give the leftovers to, and no one to share my meals with, I ate three and sometimes four slices by myself in the evenings. In just five weeks, I gained three pounds. But I did not eat alone all the time. Skip Zitich, the food critic, took me to dinner about once a week, and I became the companion mentioned in his reviews—"my companion raved about her stuffed flounder," or "my companion had to wait five minutes for her water glass to be refilled." And though neither of us considered the dinners as dates, I looked forward to spending an evening with someone besides myself, and he seemed to have gotten over his amazement at my deformities. He did say, though, that he would never forget the prosperity sandwiches, made me promise to serve them after next Christmas.

I still kept the outside lights on all night long, front and back, and still wedged a café chair under the back doorknob before coming up for the night. I slept lightly and jumped at most 'hood noises, and I kept my old leg, now a spare, just under the bed and within reach in case I needed a weapon. I considered all that the legacy of our break-in.

Sometime in early May, Mike's landlord's property manager came by the café. He had a new tenant for Mike's place. "Got to vanish that organ," he said. Though he would have been within his rights to sell it for back rent, he explained, the landlord had convinced him to be big about it, give it to anyone who wanted it. The closest to kin or a friend that Mike had had, as far as anyone knew, was me. "Course I haven't dug deep into it," he said. "Won't either. You're welcome to the organ." So I took it.

I had the two deuces on the west wall moved to the basement for storage and had the organ put in their place. Most of the regulars had heard it—they would have to have been deaf not to—but few had ventured back to Mike's garage to have a look. Now they *ooh'd* and *aah'd*, touched it as they would a relic, said it certainly looked like an expensive instrument. One of the thrift-shop women said she knew for a fact it was worth "real money." The third day it was there, Mom and Dad and Aunt Marie and, the biggest surprise of all, Uncle Jack came in for lunch. I thought of how pleased Shelly would have been if he'd ever come down during her time in the café. Why wait until now?

The answer was a doctor's visit. Uncle Jack had complained lately of a suspicious pain in his side, and on the way back from tests arranged by his doctor, Aunt Marie had talked him into visiting the café.

"Well," she said. "Half the battle was won. He was already out." She'd called Mom and Dad from the hospital to make it more of a plan he couldn't get out of.

All four of them claimed fascination with the organ, too, and, not wanting to discuss Mike with them, I merely told them it was something I'd picked up in the neighborhood. Then I told Aunt Marie I had had an e-mail from Shelly just that morning, and she had taken to calling herself Michelle instead of Shelly, feeling more French and thinking she fit in better that way. Aunt Marie nodded, said, "All those ailments were just in her head, you know. Never did know anyone unhappier." I started to answer, defend Shelly's optimism, but Aunt Marie's interest had moved to the organ. "It's one of those pump things, isn't it?"

I said it was. In the e-mail, Shelly had also said her headaches were milder but not entirely gone, and she had resigned herself to carrying them with her forever. "As much a part of me as my dark hair," she'd written. "Maybe more a part. A few more very bad strands of my hair have already turned gray."

Aunt Marie started playing around with the organ, experimenting with the key board and the pedal, and then, without anyone noticing it right away, she started doing Aunt Peg's song, "In a Shanty in Old Shanty-town." By the time she did it through once, we were all listening, and she started up again, this time adding words, hamming it up very much as Aunt Peg had. The organ was no piano, though, and what had sounded jazzy in Aunt Peg's rendition, now was too full of echoes, and the result was eerie, as if the organ itself were sobbing at the song. Not a good sound, but oddly interesting. When Aunt Marie finished, we all applauded.

Uncle Jack was sitting on a stool beside Rollie, and when Aunt Marie's performance was over, he started talking as if Rollie were an old pal and they were sitting in a bar on a rainy afternoon, had already killed a few beers apiece. "Isn't she something? Isn't she remarkable?"

Rollie nodded.

"None like her," Uncle Jack said. "Lots of people claim to be one of a kind, but no one is like my Marie. Never could be."

"That was the other one's song, wasn't it? The Senior Ms. whatever," Rollie asked. "I was at the pageant."

"Yeah," Uncle Jack said.

"That one, the winner, was the one I wanted first. Peg," he said. "I was with Peg first."

I wondered if I should cough or something to let him know I was listening. Instead I stood as still as possible.

"Peg threw me over for Ralph," Uncle Jack said. "Just like that. 'You're a nice boy,' she said, but then flung her arms wide, as only she could do, the grand gesture, you know. 'But there's Ralph,' she said."

"Bad luck," Rollie said.

"No, that's the thing. Good luck. Marie turned out to be the best of the bunch. But she always felt like second place. I think that's why she divorced me. She never could stop feeling inferior."

In one of her recent e-mails, Shelly, or Michelle as I tried to think of her, had said she felt a great freedom and lightness to no longer be caught up in the Stillwell web, her parents' mess.

Mom sat at a table near the counter, and when I took iced teas to her and Dad, she told me the organ was a wonderful addition. "You always know just what to do," she said.

"That organ takes up some of the customer space, though," Aunt Marie said, and sat beside Mom. She was right. Without the two deuces, I could now serve only twenty-eight, the original number of seats I'd started with. And one of those would be on the far stool, squeezed in beside the end of the organ, so it was only twenty-seven comfortably. Shelly, I knew, would not like that arrangement. Well, when she came back, we could rearrange. If she came back, I corrected myself. Before she left, she swore she

would return, and said the same thing in her e-mails. But I knew
how paths led to other paths, how the road could fork and then
fork again, and I was not counting on it. Besides, by the time her
eighteen months was up, Mike may have come back to collect his
organ. I was merely holding it, protecting it for him.

Oh, I knew with each day, each hour, his return became less
and less likely, but still I imagined it. The back screen door would
slam, and his "*how-de-doo*" would ring through the kitchen. He
would rake his lank hair back from his forehead as he looked
around, the tiny horseshoe scar on his chin white against his red-
dened face. Sometimes, I could believe in that scene, and I added
Toby to it, the three of us standing and smiling as for a photo, a
family of sorts. When my imagination took hold like that, I could
feel Mike's breath on the back of my neck. On those days, I made
lemon meringue pie, one he and Toby both liked.

acknowledgements

Thanks to the entire four campus system of the University of Missouri and to the University of Missouri-St. Louis campus for the time off, so valuable to my writing this novel.

Thanks, too, to the friendly and helpful therapists at St. Louis Shriner's Hospital for Crippled Children.

And most thanks of all to Ben Furnish, the smartest editor I know and to Susan Schurman for her sense of design.

about the author

M ary Troy is author of three previous books of short stories, *Joe Baker Is Dead*, *The Alibi Café*, and *Cookie Lily*. Her honors include the Nelson Algren Award for fiction from the *Chicago Tribune* and the Devil's Kitchen Reading Award for her book *Cookie Lily*. She teaches at the University of Missouri-St. Louis, where she directs the MFA Program. She is also editor of *Natural Bridge*. She has lived in Arkansas and Hawai`i, as well as Missouri.